BEAUTIFUL SOUP

Reviews of the Author's
Previous Books

His characters are haunting . . . I have rarely enjoyed finding a writer as much as I have enjoyed my own discovery of Jacobs.

—ROBERT CROMIE
CHICAGO TRIBUNE (NET BOOK WEEK)

Quietly amused, wry approach that gives distinction to Mr. Jacobs' work . . . his dry humor would be hard to improve on.

—ELIZABETH EASTON
THE SATURDAY REVIEW

The characters who climb Jacobs' ladder are in search of a friend or a lover, but the ladder is shaped like a corkscrew, most of the rungs are missing, and there's no room at the top . . . Give us more Jacobs.

—PLAYBOY

Hypnotized, the reader is compelled to listen.

---

*Here is an author who sees life clearly and with humor
everything there is to know.*
—PUBLISHERS WEEKLY

---

*Move over Philip Roth, Mel Brooks, Heironymus Bosch.
At last we've got another original . . . an already master.*
—ANN ROSENBERG
PHILADELPHIA INQUIRER

---

*Every page—every half page—yields some sudden jolt of
comic or lyric observation . . . He likewise manages to
satirize our all-too-human foibles and failures without
becoming too blackly unforgiving.*
—THOMAS M. DISCH
WASHINGTON POST

Beautiful Soup

HARVEY JACOBS

Ringpull

First published in the United States of America
by Celadon Press in 1990
This edition published in the United Kingdom
by Ringpull Press in 1994

Ringpull Press Limited
Queensway House
London Road South
Poynton
Cheshire
SK12 1NJ

ISBN 1 898051 12 7

A CIP catalogue record for this book is available from the
British Library.

Typeset by Datix International Ltd, Bungay, Suffolk
Printed and bound in Great Britain by Clays Ltd, St Ives plc

*For Mel Jacobs, and for Gail Rubin who was
killed by terrorists while she photographed flowers*

But oh, beamish nephew, beware of the day,
If your Snark be a Boojum! For then
You will softly and suddenly vanish away,
And never be met with again!

. . . .

Soup of the evening, beautiful soup!
—LEWIS CARROLL

. . . also it causes all, both small and great, both
rich and poor, both free and slave, to be marked
on the right hand or the forehead so that no one
can buy or sell unless he has the mark, that is, the
name of the Beast . . .

Book of Revelations
Chapter 13 Verses 17–18

I

POWER is the perfume. It mingles with the other perfumes, the food smells, it seeps between the sounds of dishes and utensils and whispers. We reek of power. The air is more nourishing than the meal. This pure sense of belonging brings water to my eyes. I would not be surprised if other eyes are wet. There is fusion here. We are one.

Of course it is not the same for the children. Amos is bored. He is thinking of TV shows he is missing. Amanda is happier, content just to be here. She reaches for a fork and begins to play with it. Trina lifts it out of her hand. Amanda doesn't mind. She adores her mother. I reach for Trina's lovely hand. I give it a squeeze. Her hand is unresponsive. Understandable. She must be feeling the pride and purpose of the moment. She does not want to complicate that splendid emotion. She does look gorgeous. Her profile could be on money.

Even her father is still. That is unusual for Homer Brogg. He is perpetual motion. My mother-in-law, Lauren, looks over at him. His tranquility prompts her to check to see if he is alive. Homer nods solemnly, as if this was a church not a hotel.

Music begins. Lights fade. A screen is lowered behind the dais. We are about to see a video.

The scene is a hospital delivery room. The walls are painted in gay pastels. The nurses wear rainbow gowns. The obstetrician is in blue pastel, the anesthesiologist wears pink. The soon-to-be mother is radiant in a lime green nightie. She is a long-haired blonde of about twenty with huge eyes and bow lips. The excited father, masked and standing to her left, wears a white suit, tie and shoes. There is one red dot on his tie. They seem poised to sing but in fact everyone is highly concentrated.

The mother suddenly leans her head backward. There is an incredible smile on her face, a lovely blush to her cheeks. She moans but not in pain. Her moan is tremulous. The father bites his lip. He makes a funny face. A nurse looks over at him and titters. She has seen this kind of thing before.

The child is born. The doctor's back obscures the actual gush of life (and that is just as well considering the family audience). The nurses bustle about sponging the infant. It is a squirming, healthy male who is already howling for attention.

"A boy," the doctor says. "A wonderful, strapping fellow."

"How did you do that?" the father says. The jubilant mother touches him gently on his nose.

"You had something to do with it," she says.

The head nurse takes the baby. The music changes to a driving, suspenseful chord. She carries the newborn to the *Hoffenstein IV*. The machine is as new as the baby, the latest model, pristine titanium and chrome. The nurse switches it on and lights dance. She presses information into the keyboard. A glass slab slides forward and the baby is placed there.

There are quick, full frame portraits of the others in the room: father, mother, doctor, nurses, anesthesiologist. Their faces have lost the triumphant smile. The baby's face seems older.

The *Hoffenstein IV* withdraws the slab and takes the tyke into itself. A canopy closes over the baby like a camera lens focusing. A metal arm darts from the canopy and stamps the baby's head. The mother gasps. She sits forward. The father restrains her. The baby wails, more startled than hurt. The slab ejects him.

The head nurse lifts, comforts and carries the child back to the doctor who has put on a pair of glasses. He examines the Bar Code stamped on the tiny forehead.

"Mrs. Martin, I am very pleased to tell you that your son is . . . Code A. Yes, we are talking Major Administrative Potential here."

The father steps forward to see for himself. He bends over the A-Coded male. "But Ellen is Code K and I'm Code G," he says. "I'm a plumber. A damn good plumber but a plumber."

The doctor lovingly embraces him. His voice is all compassion. "There is the miracle," he says, "in your proverbial nutshell." Music rises as the father himself presents their son to its mother. Under her nightie, two splendid breasts rise like volcanoes. We know the baby will be well fed and on his way.

The music crests. The screen goes to black and is withdrawn on cables that lift it out of sight. A mellow voice announces, "Ladies and Gentlemen . . . the man. The myth. The beloved. Let us welcome Dr. Lawrence Hoffenstein!"

If somebody had said to me, "James Wander, you will someday be in the same room with Dr. Hoffenstein," I would not have believed it. And if they told me what I would feel when the man appeared, all one hundred pounds of him, a skeletal elf with a tuft of white hair crowning his huge head, pencil legs carrying him toward the podium, one arm waving in a greeting, if they told me the depth and resonance of my response, I would have said bullshit.

Dr. Lawrence Hoffenstein moves, frame-by-frame, across the stage, leaning into the thick, still air like a paper boat fighting invisible current. The air becomes time. Time is the current he fights and we watch the incredible battle. Hoffenstein propels himself forward. We stand and cheer. Such explosive admiration demands outlet. My belly is an old stove. Coals are shoveled into it, I boil and broil. Steam shoots from every orifice. I glow, sweat drenches my shirt, I nearly lose consciousness.

I grab for Trina's arm. It isn't there. The rush of blood subsides. I am still vertical. That alone strikes me as miraculous. My father-in-law once told an interviewer that he depended on an *inner gyroscope* for his own stability and I know what he meant. Hoffenstein creeps along as the cheers peak. They are his tailwind. Pride is his sail. He takes the microphone and waits for quiet, he holds up his arms in the universal gesture for enough-is-enough. But it isn't enough, God knows. It isn't nearly enough. His arms cork our frenzy. The screen lowers behind him. Video amplifies his image ten times.

There is his Bar Code, the first. It wriggles with the wrinkled skin of his ancient forehead. But there it is and we cheer again. Hoffenstein lets his head bow, he can't fight the outpouring of affection. Then there is total silence.

It happens without any cue. We quit our noise the way country bugs abdicate their insect song at exactly the same instant and leave you to drop through the soundless hole. Hoffenstein raises his head as best he can, sips water from a crystal glass, and speaks.

I expect him to creak like an old building, I expect him to gargle rust. I am wrong and a fool. This is the voice that changed the world. It snaps out at us, it flails at us, it thunders from a mouth no wider than a drain. On the video screen his magnified tongue thrashes between fragile teeth. Each tooth marks a victory, the man is a hundred years old.

"Here I am," Dr. Lawrence Hoffenstein says, "much to my surprise. A handful of lust and dust. Your wonderful applause, your generous cheers come to me like echoes through snow and I remind myself that all is vanity and a striving after wind. Please, friends, be seated. We are family. This is a family affair."

It feels wrong but we sit. Not all at once. In clumps and clusters. It is hard to sit in his presence. "At this time in my life I not only hear my own echoes, I see them. They are fleshed out and palpable as milky young girls. What do I see? I see a time when this planet was in the clutch of spiders. Our world was woven into a malevolent cocoon of disharmony and hatred. Earth writhed in space. We made stars vomit. We cracked the skin of creation. Our children dreamed of a fiery final mushroom cloud. The sweet air turned rancid. Our moon was startled. Our trees were turning to bonsai with tangled limbs. They shed their leaves. Their roots sucked acid. Where was hope and where was God? The spiders waited. They injected our brains with arrogance, greed, poisons so virulent as to unravel our very DNA. Disease ravaged every neighborhood. We encased ourselves inside leaky condoms of self-interest."

Dr. Hoffenstein begins to cough. He coughs violently, in separate hacks. His hand grabs for more water. He floods his throat with a long drink that dribbles down his chin. The video makes it look like a waterfall. We gasp in unison but his gyroscope works and he recovers himself.

"Then it became my privilege and my honor to develop and perfect the *Hoffenstein I,* the Human Bar Code."

Of course we leap to our feet cheering again. We vent for a full five minutes. Then we settle back into our seats. Hoffenstein listens and sees more of his echoes. He keeps us waiting.

"Does the man have a sense of timing?" Homer Brogg whispers

to me. That is Homer's supreme compliment, since he has none himself.

"Now, with virtually total acceptance, 99.8 percent of the inhabitants of blessed Planet Earth are coded at birth. Name, social security number, sex, birthdate and most important . . . degree of potential. The Hoffenstein Gradation does not say to any individual 'This is what you are' but 'This is what you can be!' Within each Code designation there is ample room for personal achievement. For minimum and maximum Actuality Realization. What a person does with his or her Code is entirely up to that person. Codes are determined democratically by the Prime Mother Computer whose only purpose is the welfare of the Earth and the citizens who dwell upon her generous bosom."

We applaud as a picture of Earth appears on the video screen. She is beautiful, perfectly formed, deliciously placed in a universe of such harmony as to turn numbers into music. "Only I know the location of the Prime Mother Computer who we jokingly call Surrogate Madonna. And let us never forget those true heroes and heroines who built her, then willingly died to protect her secrets. They are with us tonight and I do homage to their glorious ghosts. Let us remember them now."

The screen is covered with unknown faces. We bow our heads. How many of us would agree to give our lives to the future without even the fanfare of war? They did their job in record time knowing that when it was done they would be executed and their executioners executed in mass suicide. Even their burial place is unknown except to Hoffenstein. They pledged their spirits to eternal silence. So many of the faces are young. I look at my own children and shudder.

"Friends, family of mine, let me say that I shall never forget your tribute to me tonight. I shall remember every face in this room. My very atoms hold your images like guarded treasure. When I recycle into flowers or birds or beasts or as part of another human life, my most minute fragment will still remember you, will remember this evening. And believe me when I say that from the pinnacle of my obscene age echoes come to me not only from the past but from the future! I hear and see a choir of millions united in a synchronous hymn of joyous praise. A cathedral spire that shines brighter than gold. Are these only the dreams of a doddering scientist? That is for you to decide. Only you. Make my vision live! Be Proud of Your Code!" He reaches up a spindly arm, a blue hand touches his own Code, tapping his skull.

A waiter drops a tray and dumps dregs of mousse on a mogul. Who cares? They both scream, "Be Proud of Your Code!" We all scream out as Dr. Lawrence Hoffenstein walks backward until he is swallowed by the billowing curtain. I kiss my wife and my mother-in-law. I shake hands with my son and embrace my daughter. Homer slaps me on the shoulder. Our flag and the Earth flag are on-screen now in colors so bright I wince.

I see Trina putting the tassled menu into her purse. She wants a souvenir. I grin at her. She wrinkles her Bar Code in response.

It is hard for me not to believe in Luck.

Sitting in Homer's office alone I think to myself, "What chance has a bee against a rose?" I look at family pictures behind Homer's tremendous desk, a whole shelf of photos in lucite frames. One shows my Trina as a schoolgirl sitting on top of a spotted grey horse. She is so royal, so in command. Her bud breasts are thrust forward like weapons of war. Her eyes catch circles of sun.

Other pictures show Homer with Lauren, with Amos and Amanda, with me on a hunting trip in Western Canada. There are many glossies of Homer with the great ones: artists, scientists, politicians, heroes. He stands alone with Dr. Hoffenstein on the prow of his yacht, *Fulfillment*. That picture is larger than the others and framed in gold leaf.

The office is splendid with panoramic views. New York's rivers converge, streams of silver flow to the harbor. I see far beyond the Statue of Liberty (Homer calls her Libby) to the Atlantic. The city is a garden from up there with bridges arching like inchworms. Today that city is drenched in light. *Thine alabaster cities gleam undimmed by human tears. America, America . . .*

Wooden walls hold the carved logos of Homer's corporations. Brogg Atomics, Brogg Genetics, Brogg Communications, Brogg

Mines and Minerals, Brogg Entertainment Enterprises, Brogg Realty, Brogg Marine, Brogg Frontiers. His head produced wonders, his dick produced Trina.

I press the button on his VCR. What comes up on the projection screen? My Amos and Amanda rolling in diamonds. The time we took them to Vail. Homer circles them on a snowmobile. They toss snowballs at him. He pretends to be mortally wounded or at least mortal. He tumbles onto a drift. He lays flailing his arms mimicking agony. The kids bury him in gobs of pure white snow. That is the tape he keeps on his machine. The man is special. He knows his priorities. Family, family, family.

Homer comes into the office carrying a bulging briefcase. He throws it on the desk. "Jim, I am sorry to be late. You want something to drink? Coffee? A soda?"

"Nothing, no, thanks. I'm fine."

"Wasn't last night a pisser? Do you know what? I cried. I turned to butter. Talk about inspiration. Was there a cynic in that room? Was there? There are no atheists in potholes, eh?"

"It was a wonderful evening, Dad. Don't apologize for your tears. I think we all wet our faces. Trina couldn't stop talking about it. The offspring were actually moved. Amos was all questions on the way home. I heard Amanda telling her doll about the birth scene."

"Did that work or did that work? You know we produced the video. We went a hundred thousand over their budget but it was no time to skimp. Hell, my father found that scene stealer rattling around some toilet lab up at Columbia University. If it wasn't for Ulysses Brogg a certain Dr. Lawrence Hoffenstein would probably still be banging his hippo head against a stone wall. If there was a wall left."

"I know that, yes. If it wasn't for your father's faith and vision . . ."

"It wasn't faith or vision. And my father didn't listen to echoes. Was that perfect? *Echoes from the future, echoes from the past.* What a speaker. No, my father listened to facts. He saw consequences. They were bricks to him. Building blocks. And he had a bodacious set of balls."

"I'm sorry he passed away before I met him. I only wish he could have lived to . . ."

"You're so right, Jim. I should have had him stuffed and mounted and hung in the hall outside for the idiots to ponder. I remember when they coded me. I was in the first wave, three years old. I put up a hell of a fight. They held me down. And it hurt. It wasn't like now. I kept trying to scratch the damn Code off my skin. My mother kept feeding me Mallomars to calm me down. I loved my Mallomars. Chocolate tits. Did you know that Mallomars have seasons? You can only buy them Fall to Spring. So what happens to Mallomars in the Summer?"

"Wasn't there a danger back then? Suppose your Code came up, say, F, Limited Potential. Wasn't it Russian Roulette? I'm surprised your parents didn't take the exemption. You were qualified for Uncoded if you were more than a year old."

"Yes, I was in the transitional group. But my father owned Hoffenstein, remember? That accident wasn't about to happen."

"But the coding was random."

"I worry about you, James. You know that the chances of getting an A Code at random are a few million to one. You can consider yourself a very fortunate young man. It happened, you won the lottery. I got some help. That's the way it was back then. There had to be some promises kept. I mean, there was strong opposition. You can't imagine. They almost had my father killed. More than once. If you couldn't guarantee their own children A Codes, how far do you think it would have gone?"

"I never thought much about the beginning. For me it was all just there, in place."

"Well it was a bloody road to get there. Someday we'll sit and talk. I'll play some tapes for you. We'll spend an afternoon down in the vaults and you'll learn some history."

"I look forward to it, Dad. You should write a book."

"I should but I won't. Why give ammo to the crazies? There are still crazies. There are still jails. No book. Not for another century at least. I'm no movie star hanging her pussy out the window. I want a coffee. You?"

Homer buzzes his secretary while he pulls papers from his briefcase. He flops into his chair. It lets out a puff, a leather fart. He has something in mind. I wasn't called to talk about last night or how it was in Mallomar days.

"We're poised for a jump at the jugular. I am about to pay $56 a share for Star Insemination. I should have control by tonight."

"Congratulations. It strikes me as a positive move."

"We'll see how positive. It's a demented operation. A bunch of fuckups. The company needs a new Executive Director. Total re-thinking and reorganization. It's got to be done and you will do it."

"Homer . . . Dad . . . what can I say?"

"Say thanks. This is your toy, James. You touted me onto this deal. Now you make sure that Homer Brogg is not elected asshole of the month. You know I've been planning to broaden your power base. If you can effect a turnaround at Star it would be no small thing. The board would have to show gratitude. Face it, they're suspicious of nepotism and they should be. They like you, son, but let's make them love you. I'm not keeping this seat warm for some dingus or cunt that doesn't have Brogg stamped on his or her equal opportunity backside. I have no sons but you. I want all this to stay in the family. I want that more than I want anything. You and then Amos or Amanda. Trina is a lost cause for business. We both know that."

"It's just not her talent."

"Don't put Trina down. Never dump on your own wife."

"I was only saying what you already know."

The coffee comes on a cart. There are the cookies Homer likes, imported from England. Homer's secretary spreads a napkin and pours. She's an icy bitch, a classic D Code who loves her job. She sweeps up Homer's crumbs and body dander and takes them home with her to cuddle. The woman has no life outside the office. She's been with Homer forever. She would kill for him. She comes from watching him chew on Brit cookies. Homer waves her away.

"Let me ask you frankly, Jim. Are you and Trina getting along? I had one eye on her last night. She seemed distracted."

"We're more than getting along. We're fine. Really. I think it was the occasion. The emotion. We're solid."

"Good. Thank God. Lauren and I have been married thirty-seven years come April. I'm not saying it was easy. Fortunately, there's an inertia to marriage. A weight. It lays like a rock on your chest, a tombstone. It's got its own gravity. That kept me in place more than once. Thank God. There are always rough spots. Fric-tions. But they can be overcome."

"You want the absolute truth? When I feel turbulence I look over at Trina and remind myself that I might just be the luckiest guy in the universe. And I don't believe in luck."

"Why don't you believe in luck?"

"I believe in making my own luck."

"Believe in luck."

"Fate, maybe. Even destiny."

"Luck. Plain bare-assed luck. Believe. Maybe you're too young.
Maybe that's your problem, James. When a man tells me he doesn't
believe in luck I draw an X across his face. Unless he's a plebe. Like
you."

"The point is, I believe in Trina, the kids, my job, myself. I
admit that maybe four o'clock on a rotten morning I might wake up
and ask a few questions but who doesn't?"

"You've got to be forgiving in this life. Face it. Women make
lousy mothers. Men make lousy fathers. Kids make lousy children
and pets crap on the rug. Accept it and relax. There was a 20th
Century saying, my father had it hung on his wall, *Kill 'em all. Let
God sort 'em out.* You follow me? Listen, getting back to reality. Star
Insemination is a launch pad or a dead end. It could be an important
profit center. Their concept is on-target. The better the sperm the
better the chance for a higher Code. That's close to the truth.
They're just not getting their message across to the market. Why?
How? That's for you to figure out."

"I had a thought. A name change. *Fabergee Sperm.*"

"Elitist. How many people know about Fabergé eggs?"

"The people who can afford Fabergee Sperm."

"There's where we collide. I want to broaden the consumer
base. Reach out. Not concentrate on the A, B and C Codes. I want
to go all the way to Z. Hell, that's the demographic segment that
wants upgrading. They're our thrust. Forget Fabergee. Give me a
name like Little Squirt. Remember, we can't guarantee how the
machine will code their babies. We can only tip the odds fractionally
in a positive direction. That's our edge. To the uppers it's a small
edge. To the lowers it's the light at the end of the tunnel."

"I'm on it. I'll institute a research scan of . . ."

"Fine. Research all you want. But I'm buying your intuition,
Jim. I'm buying the sudden flash. The bulb over your head. And take
good care of my Trina. Amos. Amanda. My treasures. What the hell
else have I got in this world?"

Homer finds Trina on her horse. He kisses the picture. His

secretary will wipe away the spit before she goes home if she ever goes home.

We shake hands, we pat Codes. I leave richer, more secure, entrenched. Is it *luck*? Is that it? Something else. I worked for all this glory.

Lance Bedlock is lucky. The recipient of random gifts, a harmonic convergence. His face was carved by clean mountain water running down a slab of rock. His eyes are flat blue jewels. His body is perfectly muscled and proportioned. All six feet four inches of him coordinate. Even his blond hair is choreographed. He is a superb athlete. His voice rolls like a truck on a highway. Everything about him works. He is coded A+ like me but my Code comes as a surprise. His is assumed.

When we finish our game of squash at the club I am a puddle of sweat. Lance is a little moist. There are stains on his BE PROUD OF YOUR CODE T-shirt but no more than from a light drizzle. My own shirt hangs limp and soggy like the skin of a rhino. Lance won five of our six games. He wants the loss back. No matter how many games we will play in the future he will never get it back but he wants it and will plot.

We leave the court. I wonder if he slept with Trina. They went together before my time. When I came to the Brogg empire they were considered a couple. Why Trina switched her affection I will never understand. Maybe there was too much perfection between them. She can measure herself against me but with Lance it was white-on-white. Of course he slept with Trina, white-on-white. Still, there is a vague chance that he insisted they wait for the consecration of marriage. He's that kind of guy.

"I heard the old man has marked you for Pope," he says, stripping down in the shower room. His tool is twice as long as mine and more sculptural. He has a marble cock, a Brancussi. Mine is more of a club fighter, more acquisitive. But that could be wishful thinking.

"The talk might be premature."

"Come on, Jimsy, he gave you Jew Juice, didn't he?"

"We talked about Star Insemination, yes."

"So where did I go wrong? First Trina, now this?"

"Old story, Lancelot. The best man won."

"But seriously, my heartfelt congratulations. Besides, you're his son-in-law and we know God works in predictable ways."

"I want you to come over with me as Executive VP Marketing. I need help."

"Thank you, Jimbo. Count on me. Did you really come up with Fabergee Sperm?"

"Who told you that?"

"Homer himself. He was pissing pearls in the adjoining stall. We had to talk about something. I told him not to worry. Everybody has lapses."

We turn on the showers. Steam fogs the tiled cubicle. Lance turns to smoke. "This could be a real challenge. It's an interesting playground. The old man is really optimistic." Lance's voice comes booming through the droplets. He sounds enthusiastic. I bend to pick up the soap that slithered out of my hand. I get a slap on the ass. It is like a handshake. He is on my team.

There is a single silky hair on the toilet seat. It is eloquent calligraphy, curled like a wave in a Japanese print. From that single clue I construct the ocean of my wife.

Hoffenstein spoke of seeing echoes from the future. I know immediately what he meant. When I first saw Trina, still a school-girl, I felt myself inside her. I pumped honey into her from across the Brogg Enterprises conference room. My Fabergee Sperm paraded like an army across the polished table, leapt into her delicious lap, penetrated her designer jeans. I knew we would make babies. I saw the babies floating like summer clouds. I never believed any of it would come to pass. Trina was impossible. Beyond having. The sail on the horizon.

Beautiful, slim, blonde, blue-eyed Trina grew in an Iowa corn-field, detached from her stalk and began leading cheers with dew drops still on her pink nipples. What had such a girl to do with sullen, obsessive, motivated, cynical James Wander? Nothing. Why did she marry me? I don't know. I am the recipient of miracles. We have been married for fifteen years. Was there a time before that? Yes. None of that matters anymore. I hope I am remembered fondly by the others. But it is of no consequence.

I leave the curled hair undisturbed, a precious artifact. Amos and Amanda are sleeping. I have not seen them today. I know how time accelerates and that I should spend more time with the kids during these choice years. But tonight I am full of myself. I want things my way. The maid has gone home. Trina is in the media room watching television. I sneak through my space. I want to watch my wife watching. Some people watch birds. I watch this elusive woman for my education. I watch her dress, undress, eat, comb, pluck eyebrows, walk, talk, smile, frown. I watch like a spy. I open doors by accident to catch her on the can or patting cream onto her thighs.

If I could I would peel back her Code and peek into her head. I want to know everything about her. I know she is mine but still I mass troops on the river that separates us and order my engineers to build quick bridges. As fast as they are built they are exploded by hidden artillery. Sometimes they rust and crumble. The river can never be crossed. When I fuck with her my penis is an antenna probing for signals. Trina is hard to read. She moans and yells but when she takes me in her sweet mouth she won't swallow. She spits me out into a towel. I hate and fear that. I would swallow all of her. I love her sweat. I am her cannibal.

There is this perfect wife draped on a sofa. Her large eyes are focused on the wall screen. There is an aerial shot of a huge barge piled with garbage. An umbrella of gulls follows the clot of drifting refuse. An anchorwoman from a helicopter says:

". . . and believe it or not this barge, the *Kotchka*, has been drifting the waters of the world since late in the last century. At first she was the pariah nobody wanted, the Flying Dutchman of urban trash. There were endless legal battles waged to determine responsibility for the horrendous mess. The problem was never resolved. When we began disposing waste into outer space the *Kotchka* became a floating antique, a landmark . . . should I say seamark . . . and today she is protected by the Planetary Trust, precious to scholars and historians not only as a reminder of the Pre-Hoffenstein Confusion but also as a time capsule loaded to the gunnels with every kind of 20th Century souvenir from pop bottles to training bras. Archeologists beg to disembowel her but the Trust is adamant . . . the floating fossil floats on. From somewhere off Tahiti this is Cheryl Dickstein for Channel 13. Be Proud of Your Code."

The PBS logo appears as an announcer with a voice like a growl says:

"*Eternal Garbage: Voyage to Forever* was funded in part by the Zenoil Corporation and by your viewer dollars. Stay tuned for *Favorite Newscasts*, repeat performances of . . ."

I find the remote on a table and kill the picture. Trina jumps. I am always catching her by surprise. "Nothing but garbage on TV," I say.

"I was waiting for the eleven o'clock news. The weather."

"Weather doesn't matter in the city. And I have something to tell you. After which we will rejoice together and make love. Homer called me in today."

"I know. Congratulations, darling. It's wonderful for you."

"He told you?"

"Of course he told me. He's my father. I wasn't exactly shocked to pieces, Jim. You deserve it."

"Lance had his eye on the job."

"You targeted the company."

"Lance agreed to come aboard as Executive VP Marketing."

"Jim, we have to talk. I want you to come into Amos' room."

"Forget that we have children. Tonight let us pretend that we are children left to play house. We meet, play with toys, I feel a strange uncontrollable buzz in my scrotum. You blush at your reflection in my hot eyes. You are troubled yourself by a pantheon of tingles and unexpected dilations. We . . ."

"Come with me now. This is important."

I follow Trina to our son's room. Going in there is a clash and affirmation. Books and sports equipment are on the floor with his clothes. The walls are covered with pictures of ball players. Even his media bank is in a mess with disks and tapes in piles. The computer screen is left on picking up information about mermaids. Why mermaids? Does he have a paper due? Amos is snoring. I look down at him. It is strange to acknowledge snores coming out of a baby. But he is no baby anymore. He is thirteen. How did that happen?

Trina opens the door so more light illuminates the subject. The subject is Amos' forehead. I bend for a closer inspection. He is wearing a Bar Code decal pasted over his own and it is filthy. It says he is a licensed cuntlicker.

"Scan it."

"I did scan it. So what?"

"It's vile."

"All boys do that. I did that. I didn't know they're still selling those things. We used to get ours from a candy store run by a Code Y who slobbered all over the ice cream. His name was something like Omar. We would go in there and make a sign shoving a finger through a circle of fingers and Omar would lift a box of those things from under the counter. They were a buck. I wonder what Amos paid for this."

"I can't believe I'm hearing this. Jim, do you want him put into a remedial group? Is that what you want?"

"Why should he be put in a remedial? I'm sure he doesn't run around wearing it. He's not a retard."

"And suppose one of his friends says something?"

"Why would anyone say anything? They probably all wear them. It's a stage. An inevitable part of growing up. A rite of passage. Forget it, Trina. Don't even say anything to him. I mean, if that's the worst he's in good shape. You didn't find a bag of drugs taped to his armpit."

"Tampering with a Code is a serious crime."

"Oh, please. Are you going to call the cops and report him? Are you going to rat on the kid for wearing a porno Code to bed? For godsakes, it's no worse than a baseball card."

"Act like a father for once in your life."

"I will. First thing tomorrow I'll beat him to a pulp. He'll be sorry he ever heard of Dirty Codes. I'll kill the little pervert, maybe castrate him. We'll ship his remains to a military school. Now let's just you and I fuck around like in the olden days. You know how I get after squash. And Lance decimated me. He carries a torch for my job, my wife, my condo, my life. It eats him that we both have the same Code and he was born rich on top of it. I had to marry rich, bugger my way up the ladder. So he takes it out on me at the court."

"Take that thing off."

"I'll wake him. He's probably dreaming of a hot car with a chrome ass. It's dangerous to wake an adolescent. I read that if . . ."

Trina reaches down and peels the Code off Amos. He grunts and turns over. She crinkles the plastic into a ball.

"There. You've saved the child. Now let's dance naked on the terrace."

"Now we go down to Shopping Delight. There's no food in the house."

"You want to go shopping now? Food in the house brings rats and mice. Bugs. Mold."

"I didn't do any shopping today. I don't like a house with no food."

"We'll shop tomorrow. I'll call in sick. We can make a day of it. Just the two of us. We'll go from market to market."

"I need orange juice. Detergent. Bread. Salad greens. Bottled water."

"I like it when you talk dirty. Is this loveplay? Do you really mean you want to get dressed and go out for groceries?"

"That's the price of admission."

"I don't believe you said that. In front of your comatose werewolf cub. Spawn of the devil."

"I didn't mean it like it sounded. It just slipped out."

"It just slipped out? What am I hearing? You are your father's daughter."

"What if I am?"

"Then we have a fair deal. Sex for supplies. Basic. Done. Tap Codes on it."

Amos gurgles and sighs. We back out of his room and I shut the door. "You want to check on Amanda? Christ knows what she's up to. Nine is a vicious age. She might even be into sugarless gum."

"Amanda is fine. Don't forget the coupons from the *Sunday Times*. And the deposit bottles."

"I'll try to remember. And remind me to get a box of Mallomars."

"Mallomars. What are Mallomars?"

"Chocolate jugs. Your daddy loves them. He told me so. Why are you playing dumb? You must know that Homer Brogg is addicted to Mallomars."

"I haven't the slightest idea what you're talking about."

"He never mentioned Mallomars. That's Homer. He knew you could use them against him."

Trina has changed into her shopping outfit. She wears tight denim pants, my sweatshirt, sneakers with racing stripes. She is as trim as Homer's yacht. A breeze shapes her hair so it falls in curves around her Code, arching back and dropping to frame her face. The woman has incredible cheekbones. They hold her skin like struts in a model plane streamlined and efficient. My wife is beautiful. It always surprises me to remember that I have a beautiful wife.

"Listen, about Amos. I will talk with him. It doesn't thrill me that he buys ersatz Codes. I mean, boys will be boys and all that but after seeing Hoffenstein the other night he should have acknowledged at least the emotion of respect. Kids are so damn unfeeling."

"I blame a lot of it on the school, Jim. They don't emphasize history. The children think they're the first ones ever to inhabit the planet."

"Yes, you could say that. It's the one area where I question the Hoffenstein Dictum. I mean, Future Focus."

"I don't question the Dictum. I never said that. I mean *history*, not the past."

"Come again, honey?"

"The stuff going on just before coding. What they call the Events Cluster. The mess. Not the rest of it."

"But how can a student be expected to understand the Events Cluster if they don't know or care what went before?"

"Minds should be cleared, not clogged. The Dictum says there's nothing if there's not Efficient Input/Output. No mother wants her son constipated with information."

"No problem with Amos. He doesn't know what happened before interactive holograms."

"He needs to know about order and chaos. Not everything."

"We could give him a crash course. It isn't easy to convince a likely lad that there really was a time before Globalism. It's hard enough for us so-called grownups to keep competition alive. Of course that was the core of Hoffenstein's genius. The idea that within the bounds of your Code you can move from bottom spectrum to top. At least we have Motivational Dimension."

"You question the Dictum and now the Competitive Guidelines? I'm worried about you. You sound like a Slime."

"Not quite, Trina. I'm very much Inside The Circle and happy to be there. You must know that. You don't have to be a Slime to recognize that things can be made better. Or that there are problems. The Slimes don't have a monopoly on honesty."

"Honesty? It sounds like dissent to me."

"This world was made for me. You think I would rock the boat. I have my work, the children, you. Even the respect of Homer Brogg. And I got rhythm. Who could ask for anything more."

"Well don't send Amos mixed signals. Just tell him never to buy those things. Tell him he will be punished."

"That should do it, Trina."

"You're being sarcastic. But it's the quick way to a desired result. Tell him if he is ever caught wearing one of those disgusting ersatz Codes he will be sent to remedial. And say it like you mean it."

"If I say that I'll sound like my father. Why does Amos keep forcing me to sound like my father?"

"Maybe there's no other way to sound if . . ."

"The question was rhetorical. You don't have to answer every question."

"Why not? What are questions for?"

"Good question."

"Now you're being snide."

"Do we have to go shopping? Can't we go home and have intercourse? Look at that moon, a perfect crescent. And there are stars. This is a night for unabashed bliss."

"After the market. Remember?"

"Then stop your hair from slapping at my fly. Talk about mixed signals."

"I didn't know I was sending signals."

"Because you are a natural transmitter. The worst kind. Did I tell you I love you?"

"I love you, James."

"Good. That's settled."

We revolve into the Food Forest. After ten they lower the lights and change their tapes to the sound of night birds. The ceiling glows purple and a soft wind rustles the plastic trees. I follow Trina who pushes a cart that looks like a reed basket. She matches products to her coupons saving us money. The same woman who has twenty pairs of shoes lined like birds on a closet rack is glossy with the pleasure of knocking a dime off the price of dishwasher detergent. *Sic transit.*

The Forest is bountiful. We wander aisles and navigate tunnels. We pass waterfalls and climb styrofoam hills covered with grassy carpeting. Trina's basket is brimful of survival items like bread and milk, sardines and bottled water. She piles in a romaine lettuce and greenhouse tomatoes. She finds Caesar dressing and a can of coffee. She goes back to Produce for alfalfa sprouts and a honeydew.

She detours to Cereals and selects a box of bran flakes, then cuts around to Pasta. I watch another shopper, an older woman who stands deciding on spaghetti sauce. There is a fat child, Code L, in her basket holding a toy gun and firing bursts at the animals that appear and disappear on the market walls. I remember the battles with Amos who was not permitted to pick up a gun at the door and hunt animals. It was hard to explain to him that A's have a special responsibility. Amos' clear A and Amanda's B+ had always seemed a splendid gift to us. Now I wonder, after Homer's little speech about convenient manipulation. Even Homer can't have that kind of clout, not anymore, not bloody likely.

The L child leans over to fire at a cave man holding a spear. The image of the Neanderthal turns colors and disintegrates.

"Excuse me," I say to the mother who is holding her spaghetti sauce. "Your son is shooting at people. That's a clear violation as you must know. Animals are one thing."

The woman, a Code P, scans me. Her face floods with blood. She puts the sauce into her basket, then smacks her kid in the face. It lets out a tremendous wail as she grabs the Hunter Gun from its plump fingers.

"I am sorry," she says to me. "It won't happen again."

Trina is embarrassed. She hurries down that aisle and turns down Soups and Juices. The night birds drown the child's emissions which have turned to breathy whimpers.

"Why did you interfere?"

"Because the child was firing at a human form."

"It's not our business. Did you read their Codes?"

"Yes, Trina, I read their Codes. So what?"

"Why would you pressure them then? The kid's behavior was self-evident."

"That's a rather haughty attitude."

"We're rather haughty. What did you expect to accomplish?"

"What I accomplished. Positive reinforcement."

"I doubt it. You frightened the mother is all."

We roll past shelves of soup. Trina is sulking. She sucks at her lower lip. I stop the cart.

"What are you doing, Jim? We're finished except for the specials up front."

"I want some soup."

"Canned soup?"

"Why not. I haven't had canned soup in years. I want some."

"I have no soup coupons."

"I am prepared to pay the full price, Trina."

She chews at the lip as if it were candy. It is not in my best interest to antagonize her but I can't stop myself. I begin loading cans of soup into the cart.

"Did I ever tell you I thought King Oscar was the ruler of all fishes? That he had a flounder queen? I did. I fantasized about them. Oscar was a role model."

"There's a lot I don't know about you," she says. "Can we go now?"

"Yes. We can go now."

I push the cart slowly along. Trina trails after me fuming. I can smell her steam. She is not too angry to forget the specials. She selects a roll of marked-down paper towels. She reaches for a new brand of toilet paper. It is her revenge. She knows I am orthodox when it comes to toilet paper. I am entirely loyal to Cloud Cover. I came to our marriage with several rolls.

My memory of subsequent events is dim. It never came back, not after all the therapy.

There is a clerk mopping up shards of glass and spilled cooking oil. He works near the checkout register. I remember that the oil glitters with stars reflected from the ceiling. I remember the complaint of a mourning dove. The girl at the checkout smiles at me and says, "Good evening. Did you enjoy your romp in the Forest?" I say, "Yes, very much, thank you."

Then I remember sliding. I remember my foot hitting the slick. I remember losing balance. My hands and arms cradle cans from the cart as I fall forward. I remember flipping over the counter. I think I remember the taste of the rubber belt against my mouth. Sometimes I almost remember the cool of the glass on the scanner that reads each UPC. Do I imagine the sound of the glass cracking apart or do I remember that too? (Trina says she screamed a warning. I have no memory of that.) Some noise comes out of me along with the gush of blood but I can't tell what noise it is. There is a security guard looking down at me. Trina wipes at my face with one of her paper towels. Then the paramedics load me onto a gurney. Mostly I remember the ceiling glitters with every kind of color. I remember marveling at the wisdom and beauty and integral harmony of the lovely dots of light. It does not seem to me a manufactured heaven. It seems like the genuine item, the real thing. I remember gagging on my salty blood, then dying.

I am some kind of bug. No, a sea creature. My shell is ivory white. Tubes extend from my body tunneling liquids in and flushing sludge out. I float just beneath the waves and I can hear talk from the tip of the beach.

"So this old guy goes up to the whore and he dodders out in this oatmeal voice, 'I got to have a woman.' So the whore looks at this antique and says to him, 'Mister, screw off. You've had it.' So the old guy says, 'I have? How much do I owe you?'"

How do I know their language? Probably I have been in this puddle for a thousand years. I look up through brown water.

"Trina, I still can't understand why you do your own grocery shopping. Isn't your maid Code Q?"

"Don't ask me again, Mother."

"She likes to shop. It keeps her in touch. I can relate to that," Homer says. "The important thing is, he got off easy. He damn near lost an eyeball."

Amos says, "Can we sue them?"

"Absolutely," Lauren says. "It's a clear case of negligence. Your father will do very nicely. Very nicely."

"His hand is moving," Amanda says.

I float closer to the surface. It is tempting to reveal myself. But what will the sun do to me? It could fry me to a black crisp. I might be edible, as desired as an oyster.

"She's right," Homer says. "The klutz is waking up."

"That isn't funny," Trina says. "When can we get a private room?"

"I'm working on it."

The ozone leak has been plugged, Homer's chemical company found the proper scab, I should be reasonably safe in their atmosphere. I could join in their society. If they will forgive my carapace and tentacles. I could walk among them telling stories from the sea. I could tell Amos vital tales.

"When the disease called AIDS got out of hand victims banded together into what they called Biting Battalions. They attacked the uninfected snapping and biting at random. Before the vaccine there was mandatory tattooing and then the camps. Infected babies were put to death. That is how it was. You see, Amos, there was a Before You. Before Me. Before Mom. Before Us. Before . . ."

Amos should know these things.

"What is he burbling about?"

"Get the children out of here," Lauren says.

"Yes. Amos, Amanda, go to the waiting area. Read magazines."

"But he's waking up," Amanda says. "I want to see his eyes pop open."

"I already know about the Biters. Big news."

"Amos, take your sister to the waiting area."

"If you didn't give them what they wanted they bit," Amos says. "Sometimes they just bit. People had to wear clothes like toothpaste tubes. You couldn't knife them or shoot them because of the blood splash. So there were nets."

"Shut your mouth," Homer says. "Your little sister has ears."

I leave the sea. There is no going back.

"Trina?"

"Jim?"

"Welcome to the land of the living," Homer says.

"Thank God," Lauren says.

Homer goes to get a nurse while Trina explains my accident to me. Yes, the supermarket. Yes, the crap on the floor. Yes, the splat. Is everyone OK? Yes, we are fine and the kids are just outside.

"Break it to him gently that he lost his balls," Homer says following a large nurse into the room.

"It was an honest mistake," the nurse says. "Happens all the time. How do you feel, Mr. Wander?"

"Confused. How long have I . . . ?"

"Twelve years if it's a day," Homer says.

"You've been unconscious for thirty hours," the nurse says. "I hope your dreams were sweet."

"Tepid. Nothing special."

"Sorry about that."

The nurse props my pillow. She wears a BE PROUD OF YOUR CODE button. I scan her. D+, not bad, but at the bottom of her Potential Scale.

"The doctor will be in to see you soon."

"Were there any internal . . ."

"None. Only the cut. And our best tailor sewed you back together. You are a lucky fellow."

"I am that. Luck is my middle name."

"You might feel itchy. Don't mess with the bandage, though. And try not to move around too much. We don't want you to exert yourself. I'll send in two gorgeous children to say a big hello to their Daddy, then everyone must leave. We want our patient to rest."

Amos and Amanda are summoned. They stand like soldiers. They have never seen me immobilized. They are frightened. I assure them that there is no permanent damage.

"Of course you realize we couldn't hold your job open. You're finished with the company. We don't employ defective executives," Homer says.

I nod and try a smile. A slash of pain splits my skull. I touch the cap of the bandage that covers my pate and forehead. It comes down over my left eye and across my nose.

"Let's all sign his head," Homer says.

"I don't think so," the nurse says. "Time to go."

"What's your name?" Amanda says to the nurse.

"Nurse Eames. What's yours?"

"Amanda Wander. I'm going to be a nurse."

"That's nice," Nurse Eames says.

"But impossible," Lauren says. "Scan her Code."

Amanda begins to weep. Trina throws her mother an evil look.

"I'll be back later tonight," Trina says.

"No, please. Just go home and relax. I know how you hate these places. Thanks for being here, all of you. I mean that sincerely."

"I wouldn't have missed it," Homer says. "Do you know you rang up $1.49 on the tape? Plus tax."

As they are about to leave, Lance comes carrying a bouquet of sterilized flowers.

"I heard he was dead," Lance says. "But I brought the flowers just in case. They suck up oxygen."

"Visiting hour is over," Nurse Eames says. "All of you go play. Mr. Wander needs his sponge bath."

"His sponge bath?" Lance says. "Move over. So tell me, Homer, do I get his title?"

"No problem," Homer says.

"Trina and the kids, too? The whole package?" Lance says.

They leave. Nurse Eames gives me a wash and changes my gown. The old one is full of blood. It looks like a captured flag. She pulls back the bed curtain. I see my roommate. As I am about to say something, Lance comes back, holds a finger over his mouth, presses a pack of condoms into my hand and leaves again. I put the rubbers into a night table drawer. The man has wit.

My roommate is a swollen face, a blue balloon stuck to a spindly neck. I try to scan him but I can't make him out for the puffing. He reads a baseball magazine. Three tubes connect him to bottles and hanging bars. Stuff drips into him and flows from him in a pinkish ooze. He reminds me of the neon signs advertising specials at Food Forest. Seeing his tubes I check myself. I am tubeless.

He lowers his magazine and turns like an owl. His eyes wince, his face spasms. Nurse Eames must have told him my Code. His reaction tells me he is low centile. His mind is already working for position. Being A+ this is nothing new. It happens ten times a day. His face relaxes, not a pretty sight. He is a pumpkin a month after

Halloween. But he has found some foundation for comfortable communication. A+ or not, his tubes make him feel superior. Every universe has its rules for dominance and in a hospital tubers reign.

"You got flowers. They took my plant."

"I just got the flowers. Not five minutes ago."

"They'll probably leave them there."

"I don't think so. When the nurse sees them she'll put them out in the hall. My flowers won't be treated any better than . . ."

"Your wife is a real blouseful. I saw her come in."

"Thanks very much."

"I got one cousin in Vermont sent the plant. They want I should give it to the children's ward. Over my dead body."

"What are you in for?"

"Fight. Asshole tells me Joe Dimaggio hit safe in forty lousy games. Total schmuck. I hear you fell in a supermarket. Jesus, how did you do that?"

"I'm not sure. Some oily shit on the floor."

"So you took a flying flop. Jesus. So what's your wife's Code if you don't mind my asking?"

"My wife? Is that relevant?"

"Is it a secret?"

"My wife is a B+ cusp A− if it makes any difference."

"Jesus. She must be some tumble. I heard plenty about those."

"Do you mind? You're talking about my wife."

"You're right. Excuse me. By the way, my name is Robert Tipski. I drive a cab. My own. Code Y and proud of it."

"You should be proud of it. James Wander is my name. I'm in business."

"Business is right. Wasn't that Homer Brogg in here?"

"It was. He's my father-in-law."

"Holy floating turds. You're related? Plug me with a warm salami. A celebrity."

Nurse Eames comes in and says, "I see you two have met."

"He's my long lost brother," my roommate says.

"You want me to leave the flowers?" she says.

"Take them to the kids' ward."

"I will. Thanks, James."

"Not my plant. I want it here in the morning. You hear me?"

Nurse Eames gives me a pill to swallow and takes Robert

Tipski's temperature. She checks his IV, then clicks off the light.

"The sun goes up the sun goes down. Another day another dollar," Robert says. A poet.

From the street we hear a car alarm.

"That could be my cab."

"Forget it."

"They never turn off. We got to listen to that the whole night?"

Out there in the dark street a Slime is robbing a radio. The wounded car lets out a howl. The car alarm stops, then starts again. It is a sound I usually despise but tonight I follow it like a line. Robert farts and groans, affirming life.

I sit gift wrapped, in a metal chair. Nurse Eames is my archeologist. She finds the end of the bandage and removes a clip.

"This is like coping with a roll of Scotch Tape," she says. "I can never get them started with any kind of grace."

Dr. Hyman Zipper, my age, jovial, Code B+, a Maximum Achiever, stands watching. He is humming some tune as he aims a spotlight on my forehead.

"James, you won't be able to focus at first. When the eye is uncovered you might feel dizzy. There's a lag while the brain adjusts. No sweat. This too shall pass."

"Will there be a bad scar?"

"You had a nasty gash. But nothing we can't remedy. A hundred stitches will leave some residue. Even if it's the Grand Canyon we have plastic surgeons who can do you nipples to toes. The eye itself was not affected. So you should be able to play the violin."

"Here we go loop the loop," says Nurse Eames.

"I wouldn't mind a dignified scar."

"The moment of truth," says Dr. Zipper. I feel a rush of light and tip forward. The nurse steadies me.

"This isn't at all bad," the doctor says. "There is some scarification but minimal. All in all . . ."

Nurse Eames vomits into my lap. She makes a gurgling sound

and turns away.

"There is no excuse for that kind of behavior," Dr. Zipper says sharply. "You are a professional. Control yourself."

"I am sorry. I couldn't help it."

"Clean him up and cover him up."

She wipes her mouth with her sleeve and begins to wrap me again.

"Would somebody mind telling me what's happening here? Why am I being bandaged? Why did the nurse throw up?"

"Nothing is happening here. She saw nothing. She will say nothing. Everything is fine. You're healing nicely. Take him back to his room. And please remember, Nurse Eames, you are not the only one with a stomach. What did you eat last night? Noodles?"

"Eggplant with noodles, yes."

"Bathe him. Change him. Take the rest of the day off. Go to a movie."

I am back in bed and worried. It is hard to imagine a scar terrible enough to evoke such a reaction from a medical woman. I wish they had let me see myself. With no point of reference I turn myself into a horror movie. My roommate is thumbing a *National Geographic* probably browsing for breasts. He looks over to me with some trepidation. He knows I am troubled.

"There's an article here about a garbage barge been stinking up the ocean since . . ."

"Since the eighth decade of the last century. I know about the garbage barge."

"Excuse me, A+. You know about everything. Pardon my shit. I was just making conversation."

"Just leave me alone, Robert. I'm thinking."

"I'll bet. That's terrific. I lose my tubes today."

"Congratulations."

"To me it's important."

"It is important. I'm glad for you."

A Chaplain enters the room. He is built like Lance, with a large head and a rosy face. He carries a bible in a jeweled metallic cover.

"Good day and God bless you both," he says.

"Gezuntheidt to you, too," Robert says.

"You must be James Wander then?"

"Him. Not me."

"Ah, James. May I have a moment to speak with you, son?"

"I'm very preoccupied. Full of myself. I don't mean to be disrespectful. But at this particular moment . . ."

"Dr. Zipper asked me to visit." The Chaplain comes closer to my bed and pulls the curtain. Robert waves and goes back to his *Geographic*.

"I assume that Dr. Zipper realized that I am concerned and even apprehensive. He could have come himself."

"Mr. Wander, the doctor saw something when your bandages were removed."

"Since the nurse regurgitated I suspected that much. He didn't understand that I am very well prepared for adversity. He should have simply told me what . . ."

"Do you believe in God's eternal wisdom?"

"Why shouldn't I? I am a very lucky man. I owe some pain. So whatever they saw, believe me, I am ready to handle it. What did they see?"

"Young, vibrant, brilliant, privileged, everything ahead of you."

"And some good things behind me. A hound would be happy tracking my spoor. Accepting all that, Chaplain, what did Dr. Zipper . . ."

"Unforeseen complications. The accident resulted in . . ."

"So be it. I will need extensive cosmetic surgery. Maybe glasses or a patch. Is that it?"

"James, it might have been a freak combination of trauma and the laser they use to read the UPC labels."

"What labels?"

"On the boxes, bottles and cáns."

"The product codes?"

"Yes, exactly. The ones we mail in for contests and premiums. My wife is an ardent saver of Tropicana orange juice codes. Our house is full of orange towels, orange wristwatches, even a set of miniature orange trains."

"Is that relevant?"

"Dr. Zipper feels that might explain the alteration in your Code."

"My Code? Are you telling me my Code has been bruised or obliterated? I have to go through recoding?"

"Not exactly, no."

"What then?"

"I used the word *alteration*. Not obliteration."

"What's the difference? It comes down to corrective . . ."

"James, you know it is absolutely forbidden to tamper with a Human Bar Code. That's the first Hoffenstein Principle. If Codes could be . . . manipulated . . . it would destroy social order. We'd take a giant step toward oblivion. You wouldn't want that kind of world for your wife, your children, yourself. Of course not. Now pray with me."

The Chaplain kneels down at my bedside and opens his metallic bible.

"The cover is reflecting light in my good eye."

"I am sorry. It's tooled in the Holy Land. The jewels are common stones but the work is magnificent. Some people tell me it's pretentious but I tell them . . ."

"Stand up, please. Talk to me. My *alteration* is the result of an accident. An act of God. God in a frisky mood, but still God. Surely in such circumstances even the Hoffenstein Principles . . ."

"Please, Mr. Wander. Do not blame this on God. You slipped on a supermarket floor, hardly a celestial event. Use God to accommodate, not to accuse."

"I wasn't suggesting God spilled oil on the floor of the Food Forest. I was using *act of God* in the legalistic sense. Tell me, what am I? B? D? What?"

"Courage, Jim. Fortitude."

"E? F? G? H? What?"

"It isn't that simple. It rarely is. Your metamorphosis is a bit more exotic, if that's the right word."

"In basic English, what does my Bar Code read?"

"The Lord works in mysterious ways. That may be a cliche but cliches are nothing more than a summation of the quotidian. Your Code is no longer strictly human. There must have been turmoil at the checkout. Who knows how it happened. You are coded as pea soup. You are pea soup now."

I hear a wet pop, then a scream. It is a blast of laughter and agony. The Chaplain pulls back the curtain. It is my roommate. He is pitched forward half-on and half-off his bed. His tubes dangle dribbling fluids. His mouth is open still shaping a howl. The Chaplain rushes to examine him.

"This man is dead," he says.

"Look at his plant," I say. "Bush green as if nothing changed. Indifferent. And they say plants are sensitive to the slightest change in the mood or health of their owners. If you ask me, that is false and idiotic. Certainly not that plant. Look at it. Completely uninvolved. If you gave it water right now it would drink. There is no sign of leaf agitation or any wilting of the stalk. Nothing. Nothing."

"Just don't move, Mr. Wander. I'll get help."

The Chaplain rushes outside. I hear him calling for a nurse. I get out of bed and grab the smug plant by its glossy foliage and rip it out of the clay pot. The roots come up in a knot shocked by the glare.

"There you go, Robert," I say. "The son of a bitch won't make it to the kiddie ward. Not while you still have me for a friend."

When they fly in with the electrodes and begin blasting at my roommate's deflated chest I say, "When he heard about my reclassification it was too much for him. His Code couldn't handle it. He died for me. Do you understand that kind of sacrifice?"

A strange nurse takes a wilting stalk out of my fist. I am given a shot by an intern.

I sleep like lead.

"I am your wife, Jim. Suppose you came back from the dentist wearing dentures. You'd have to take them out sometimes. I'd have to see your bare gums. Or suppose it was me. If I lost a part that was visible would you want me to go around in a bedsheet?"

"Possibly. I'm not sure, Trina."

"We share things."

"I don't mind sharing things as long as they're not my terrible things. You despise ugly. You won't cut into a lobster."

"You're not a lobster, Jim. What happened to your sense of humor? The worst that could happen is that we have a good laugh."

Trina snaps the sweatband that has covered my forehead since they sent me home from the hospital. She climbs on top of me and presses her sex against my belly. I chuckle a clucking sound.

"Is my Apache laying an egg?"

"Your Apache just remembered an old phobia. You know those steel brushes they use to clean the streets? I dreamt about them all through my childhood. I thought they were moustaches of damned souls come to brush me to death. I was dreaming too high. I never realized they were sex dreams until now."

"That's very flattering." She flattens out. Her fingers massage my temples.

"Love, it is so good to be home. Everything seems incandescent. Trivia blazes. When I was inside you it felt like my missile fired multiple warheads."

"Your missile? Jesus. Maybe there was brain damage."

"I was looking for the right image. Blunt instrument didn't do it. Did you ever see pictures of an undersea volcano? Flame in the water? Fish turn orange. Seaweed turns purple. Shells are opalescent. Bubbles are pearls. That's what I felt like when I came." I roll Trina over. "I'm going down there for another look. I wish I had a camera."

"We just finished doing that."

"I know. Let's not talk for a while. Let me do incredible things to you. Feel free to show gratitude."

"Stop it, darling. You have got to take off that stupid headband." Trina does a flip and leaves me kissing a damp sheet. I sit up.

"You know I actually look forward to getting back to the office? When did you ever hear me say that? I can't explain it but I am living in a land with nothing but horizons."

"You're evading the inevitable." Trina is crying. Tears drip down her cheeks and curve to her lips. She licks at them. I taste her salt.

"Alright. You win. But please, please be totally honest about your feelings. We have to live with this."

"I'll be honest. The truth is, I don't expect to feel much of anything. We're not talking grotesque or terminal. We're talking minor inconvenience."

"We're talking cosmic joke. Go ahead, do it."

I close my eyes. Trina pats my face. I open. She smiles a sunrise. I grin back. She lifts away my headband with two fingers. I watch her face. Absolutely no sign of revulsion. Her face is blank. Now I feel tears on my face. I reach out to embrace my wife.

"No, thanks, I'm not hungry. But it looks delicious," she says.

"What?"

Trina goes pale, the color of the eggshell wall. She trembles. A puff of air escapes from her bottom like a soul leaving a recent corpse.

"No thanks, I'm not hungry? But it looks delicious? Is that compassion?"

"James, forgive me." She is twitching. Her eyebrows arch into knots. I see a pulse leap in her neck. Her voice is changed to splintering glass. "It was spontaneous. What did you expect? I scan and react like a normal person. A reflex. Is it my fault you're not yourself?"

"How can I not be myself?"

"I am trying to tell you my reaction was perfectly innocent. You can't punish me for that. Stop glaring. I love you. I'm here for you. In time I'll adjust. We'll send the kids to a nice boarding school. They'll come to understand. And I didn't lie to you. It does look delicious even if I am not a fan of pea soup. When did I last order pea soup? I can't tell you. I love cream of asparagus or broccoli, even shrimp bisque. You know that. You must know that."

"Trina, please, calm down. Here, let me put the band back on. I know it isn't easy for you. Do you want a pill? Trina, there's a glaze over you. You'll make yourself sick."

I WILL surprise Homer Brogg. I will make him a gift of myself. Patting cologne over my ruined A+, I hum an old song. I am a slug in the morning but today I glide through the essentials like an oiled dancer. I realize that I am feeling optimism and hope.

Trina is unconscious from the pills she took last night. All things considered, she held up nicely. I expected much worse. And she said "I love you. I am here for you." Amos and Amanda are off from school for Status Day. How the year is flying!

Homer's mandate was "take all the time you need." The benevolent dispenser of all the time I need will be startled when I walk into his office today armed with a bundle of notes on the Insemination restructure. He will protest but admire. Homer believes in the work ethic as the only ethic.

I put on a blue suit and shirt, a red patterned tie and the alligator boots Lauren Brogg gave me for Christmas. The day is grey. I wear my Burberry and a canvas hat. I look myself over. Trina is right. Dressed we are less crazy. I must have been insane. I hid my head from my own family for the better part of a month. The headband lays on the bathroom sink. Let it be. I want Trina to find it. I want her to know that we are moving forward again.

I pull my hat down over my Code, as low as the law permits. To hell with that. I tilt the brim up and find my attaché case.

The hall is empty, the elevator is empty. Riding down I realize it is a splendid elevator with wooden walls and a natty carpet. The brass doors are a marvel. The push buttons are polished to perfection. I feel actual affection for the elevator.

And the lobby. It has its original marble walls restored by the co-op Board of Directors. The lights are hidden in baroque sconces shaped like arms and hands. There are bentwood chairs and deep sofas. The concierge sits behind a great walnut desk that could be a bar. It is a fabulous lobby and I am proud of it. Even the uniforms of the concierge and the doorman are ideal, crisp, military but softened by the arrangement of metal snaps and oversized collars. Peaked caps top all that magnificence. I live in an impressive building.

Milton, the concierge, says, "Good morning, sir. Glad to see you up and about." I return his greeting with a flick of my free hand. His voice is exactly right. Its modulations are a small miracle. I believe the man's sincerity. He is warmed to see me recovered and vertical. I will remember this at Christmas. He will be rewarded for his excellent services.

"Mr. Wander," Henry the doorman says. He presumes to shake my hand. "Shall I call you a taxi?" I tell Henry I will walk a few blocks. "It's drizzling. Would you like to borrow an umbrella?" I tell him no. I want to feel the drops. The walk will do me good. I tell him I have missed exercise. It is much more than I ever told him before. He seems surprised but remains in control. I wonder if he scanned me. Probably not, since the day is full of shadows and I am as familiar to him as the door handle.

I voyage out into my city. People rush past with their umbrellas unfurled against the tepid rain. They are moving mushrooms. The whole town is my garden.

After a few blocks I decide on the subway downtown. I have not been in the subway since we showed it to Amos on his birthday. But today I want to feel close to strangers. I want to smell wet newspapers and sniff dank clothes. I want nourishment for my five buck fare. I get it.

The train comes quickly. It is spacious and clean. Music plays over the PA system and I recognize the tune I woke humming. That seems a good omen. I read the Motivational Messages that line the cars. I hear Homer reminiscing about the days before the Clearance when subways were roach trails, corridors for murder. In those days the cars and seats were covered with splashes of rage. Those cars were displayed in the Museum of Popular Culture when I was a child but my parents forbade me to venture to that floor. They have been removed and scrapped of course but I have seen pictures of the *graffiti*. It is hard to imagine the deadly artists pissing spray paint venom. It is incredible that they weren't Processed sooner. What is it that Hoffenstein wrote about "the oatmeal souls of the so-called liberals"?

My train is quiet as a ship. The people seem interested in their Mandatories. Everyone must carry some Focal Point, a paper, book, pamphlet, even a letter. I am amazed at the variety of items the passengers hold. I peek out over the top of my *Wall Street Journal* to watch a young girl browse her mystery novel. She has a sweet, round face outlined in a blue hood. She is Code F and I envy her that. The way she sucks in the words. I read with suspicion. So many automatic defenses. The cute little F gulps down phrases and paragraphs as if they were gospel. Her face shines with simple joy. I return my eyes to columns of numbers. Brogg is up a point. Homer will be in a receptive mood. His stock is his temperature. He thrives on fever. His heat gave me Trina, the children, the elevator, lobby, Milton, Henry. This morning I am content to be his planet.

The Landmarks Unit of the Planetary Trust has preserved the maze under the World Trade Center. On my way to the World Financial Center and Brogg Tower I stop at the video wall and watch advertisements jigsaw and form across two hundred flat-faced TV screens. I dive into the converging crowds. Three subways meet here forming a delta of flesh and commerce. I sop up morning energy like the F girl sopped up words from her paperback. I pass stores selling coffee and donuts, greeting cards, clothes, pharmaceuticals, candy, gadgets, coins, mutual funds, toys. I follow a concrete tunnel, walking on a rubberized floor that bounces me along. An escalator rolls me up to the next level. I am revolved through a door following electric arrows.

Why did I get into the habit of cabs and limos? This is the real world, the heart of the hive. The crowd shoves me along. I veer toward a lucite tube that leads to Brogg Tower. I can see the Hudson and the Jersey shore. The tube is lit by a pure, round sun that turns it into a welder's arc. But it is cool, expertly air conditioned.

The tube divides into tributaries. The final passage to Homer's tower is marked by a blazing logo that hangs from invisible wires. BROGG ENTERPRISES. And the slogan IMPROVE ON THE EGG that Homer found in some novel. Beyond the sign is a spinning door, the last. I am halfway to that door when I sense threat. I see the outline of a man move toward me. I know instantly that I will be accosted by a Beggar Slime. I flex but keep my rhythm. I can smell him from his silhouette, the special street stink they exude like fog.

I give money to licensed Beggar Slimes but not often. I know it is ridiculous to encourage them, even specious, superstitious. When something good happens to me I want to give back. There are ample Regeneration Programs and no reason for humans to live like beasts. Of course, Beggar Slimes can be amusing. I was once approached by one with no arms. When I held out a coin there was no place to put it, only stumps. That Beggar Slime looked me in the face and said, "For an A+ you are a schmuck. Put it in the shirt pocket." I lived off that story.

The Beggar Slime moving toward me has all his parts. He seems drunk or drugged. His arms beat against his trunk, his legs fight for balance. I am in an expansive frame of mind so I dip into my coat and probe for loose change. At the same time, I look for the guards. There is no excuse for the Brogg access to be unpatrolled.

I am tempted to ask this Slime how he got to the tube. They are adept at survival. That quality is what allows them our indulgence. Still, the passageways are off-limits. My Slime is classic. He wears a T-shirt three sizes too big for his buckled chest. It has a picture of a palm tree and some faded message. His pants are stained with a green patch that spills like fungus from the crotch. Oddly, his shoes are new and polished to a gloss. He has no socks. Stems of hairy skin rise from the fancy root shoes. His head is a mass of matted hair held down by a hat that must have belonged to a woman. It is tied under his chin with a bow. We make eye contact. His eyes are pus brown, his nose swollen. I scan him but his Code is lost under scabs and sores. My hand lifts from my pocket clutching a fistful of money. There is enough to keep this Slime happy. I am a bonanza.

I reach out. It is traditional for Beggar Slimes to hold a cupped hand low so that the coins can be dropped without contact. This Slime makes no such gesture. He stares at me blocking my progress. He makes no move to receive my gift. His mouth dribbles liquid the color of his eyes. He is oozing spit. Groans come from his throat but they are aggressive not appreciative. There will be trouble. If he moves I will smack him with my attaché case. That should be enough. He can hardly stand up.

His own hands dart suddenly into his pants. He pulls out a spoon in one and a remarkably sophisticated Sanyo can opener in the other. I know the can opener because Amos gave us one for our anniversary. God knows where this Slime found a battery operated can opener. He clicks it on. It buzzes like a bug. He wipes the spoon over his lips. It clicks against hidden teeth. His tongue darts out and waves at me. He howls. I realize he is confronting a bucket of pea soup. He likes pea soup. He rushes at me brushing my nose with the buzzing can opener. There is no way to explain my condition to an incoherent Slime. I throw the change at him. He will not stop to pick it up. It would buy him a gallon of soup but we are past logic. I slam his head with my leather case and dodge around him.

He is actually running after me. His stem legs bend and thrust in impossible directions. He will certainly not dare to take on the revolving door. The door takes me. I am halfway through when it jams. The Slime has wedged himself into a quadrant with one leg stuck outside. He pounds with his spoon at thick glass. His can opener is on the floor buzzing and rolling around. It is minutes before security comes to free me and drag the Slime away. I fix my coat and pull my hat down front.

An officer says, "Mr. Wander, I can't imagine how he got down here. The damn subway exit guards don't give a crap who gets through. Are you alright?"

I wave him off. Other guards are dragging the Slime back through the tube. They have him by the hair and ass. His can opener is still buzzing on the floor but he has his spoon. It catches sun and flashes like a sparkler.

"Why didn't you wear a bag over your head? What did you expect?" Homer says.

"You're the one who lectured me on the criminality of Code obstruction and the wisdom of the law."

"And I stand by what I said. You should have stayed home."

"I feel like I was attacked by a shark or a giant clam. The

damnedest thing is, I think the man was D Code. I can't be certain.
His face was a puddle. He could have been a lawyer or a producer."

"The Codes can only set maximums. Some people insist on
fucking themselves. It's human nature."

"He tried to open me, Homer. He would have stuck that thing
up my nose and lifted the top of my skull."

"Don't personalize everything. It was Code Reaction, no more,
no less."

"That's what Trina said."

"You told her? You shouldn't have involved Trina. You should
have swallowed it, Jim, hug the rail for a while. Tuck in. Take things
easy until you're yourself."

"That's the question. Who am I? Besides, I was going webby
sitting around. And I had a major inspiration about Star Insemination. Maybe, just maybe, we should not come on like a snowplow.
Maybe we should be a little subtle, tantalizing."

"Subtle and tantalizing sells shit."

"Hear me out. Close your eyes and listen. *Ultimate Fusion
Presents . . . Megababy.* At first it sounds a bit negative like a nuclear
explosion. But it clings, it is zippy. Our advertising would involve the
fathers without compromising their egos or casting aspersions on their
virility. My concept is that the lab comes up with some way to actually
integrate some of daddy's traits . . . like the family mole, pattern
baldness, the little things every father wants to inflict on his offspring.
So the kiddies aren't total strangers even if they end up with Code
Advantage. You see what I'm struggling toward?"

"Tradition. You're talking old-fashioned tradition and that's
powerful. You're definitely on to something, Jim. What we lose in
potency we gain in tradition. Even if your little bastard outcodes you
at least he's got the ancestral wart on his beautiful ass. Nice, Jim.
Excellent. I'll bring Lance in on this."

"Not yet, Homer. Let me think it out. It's premature to expect
Lance to come up with a marketing plan before we have a product.
My feeling is . . ."

"Jim, you are on hold. Face facts. I can't risk a major division
of Brogg to a soup can. It sounds brutal but don't take this the wrong
way."

"I am James P. Wander, Executive Vice President. I gave you
grandchildren."

"That's easy for you to say. This is a public company. We have thousands of nervous stockholders. Jim, our best people are working to get you dispensation. The second we have a go you're in surgery and this unpleasantness is history. Your Code is back in place and we're back in business. But it takes time."

"I don't even like pea soup."

"Especially *Vigor Salt Free*. You should have picked a better brand. You taste like diluted frog sweat."

Homer roars and slaps me on the back. I try a chuckle. I choke on it. Homer holds my head in both of his hands.

"I don't like what I'm sensing here," he says. "You don't have the option to cave in. The sun will come up tomorrow. Bet your bottom dollar. Are you listening, James?"

"I am, yes. Thanks, Dad."

"So, did you hear the one where Adam says to Eve, 'Watch out, honey, I don't know how big this thing gets?'"

"Of course I heard that. I heard it in kindergarten."

"What goes around comes around," Homer says. "Son, there's a Crunch game tonight. Use the company box. Take Trina and the kids."

"They could use some relaxation."

"Then it's settled. And Jim, cover up. Get one of those Zealot caps. Pull the peak down. There's no sense looking for trouble."

While I wait for the company limo to take me home I call down to Brogg Sports Adventures. They send up four caps and sweatshirts.

The Zealots are Homer's only losing investment. But the man loves the team. He puts up his own money to keep the franchise black on the books. He collects cards, uniforms, programs, autographs. The game is where Homer borders on humanity. How could I turn him down?

Driving out to Pride Park in New Jersey with my family capsuled in Homer's own limo, I am in an expansive mood. It's been a while. Crunch is instant nostalgia. I feel like a kid.

I look down the highway to where the glow from the stadium balloons a flower of light. I wear my Zealots' cap and shirt as do we all. Trina convinced me to use a medical wrap on my head along with a Code Concealment permit. The doctor was agreeable about renewing the Concealment and there was no point in upsetting the children with long explanations they couldn't handle past shock.

We enter Pride Park through a private gate, then take the elevator to the special boxes. Homer's is easily the largest and best located, hanging directly over the Zealot Home. It is a while before we realize it is Unique Night.

"That's why Dad isn't here," Trina says. "I wondered about that."

"He said he had to prepare for the Monetary Conference."

"That wouldn't stop him from going to a Crunch game. It's that he can't handle the deformity."

"You're probably right. Homer is big on bilateral symmetry."

The crowd stands to cheer as the Uniques are brought in. They parade in handicap groups though all are classified Code Defective. It is a touching sight watching them struggle with tenuous balance or to keep their wheelchairs in a wobbly line.

"I don't know if I'd have brought Amos and Amanda," Trina says.

"Why? What the Uniques have isn't catching."

"No, it isn't catching. But it is there."

Amos is mimicking the twitching of the palsied. Amanda giggles until Trina comes down on both of them.

When the Uniques are seated the stadium darkens. The sudden withdrawal of candle power makes me shiver. I reach for my children. A single spotlight hits the field as music begins. There, in an ornate wheelchair decorated with gold filigree is Jelly Elbow holding the year's Poster Child in his lap. In the center of the field, Jelly Elbow jumps up from the mobile throne and lifts the semi-paralyzed little boy like a trophy.

"Jelly Elbow!" Amanda yells. She has seen him on TV forever. Amos makes the clucking sound that is the comedian's trademark. One of his best loved characters is a chicken. The clucking echoes from thousands of voices in the dark.

Jelly Elbow clucks back and prances with stiff legs. Then the music segues into Be Proud of Your Code and we all sing together.

"Ladies, Gents and Kids," Jelly Elbow says, "this, wonderful evening for my little Unique family has been made possible by you and the Brogg products you bought over the year. So let's say a special thank you to our dear friends at Brogg who made it all happen." Then he chants, "Brogg, Brogg, Brogg" as the crowd picks up volume and this time a spotlight hits our box.

"Oh, Jesus," Trina says. "Who knew?"

We stand and wave to the darkness. Jelly Elbow thrusts the Poster Child toward our box and helps the boy approximate a greeting. The video cameras have picked us up and we are projected onto the giant Galavision screens. I think thank God for the bandage. My face burns like cooking coals. Amos is loving this. Amanda is delighted to see herself ten stories tall. Trina does her best to smile and look better than the moon.

All lights fade. When they come on again, the United Nations Crunch League logo glows on the screens and both Homes rise from the turf on opposite sides of the field.

The Zealots' Home is a simple house with lucite walls, an enclosed porch, a staircase leading to a small garden. It is furnished blue-collar with all the comforts. Near the fence and gate there is a doghouse with the name FIDO across the hole that serves as the door. It looks pretty shabby.

The Zealots are playing the Koalas from Australia, a contender team. Their Home is a clever duplication of the Sydney Opera with its familiar neo-Gothic arches. There are a living room, three bedrooms, and two bathrooms, all equipped with the basics. The art direction is excellent and draws applause. Their doghouse is a miniature of the Home itself and their garden replicates authentic flora.

"It makes the Zealot Home look like a slum," I say. "It's just as well Homer stayed away. There's really no excuse, no reason to be upstaged by a bunch of Matildas."

"The team is already costing him a bundle," Trina says. "Don't start suggesting renovations this late in the season."

The Koalas come onto the field. First the Crunch Kids, then the Crunch Aunts and Uncles, then the Crunch Progenitors. Their Crunch Father is built like a bunker, hairy as a mammoth. Their Crunch Mother is a stunning woman with an iron body. They wear the usual outfits, spurred sneakers in team colors (orange and blue), knee-length shorts, spandex tops and leather gloves.

As they take their positions there is a polite cheer from the pro-Zealot crowd. The Koalas deploy. The Crunch Kids form a loose line near midfield. The Crunch Aunts and Uncles are spaced behind them. The Crunch Mother climbs up to the Home bedroom while the Crunch Father stands by the gate. When their dog, Goolagong, trots out to his house the crowd gasps. He is a true hound of hell, wide-shouldered, short-legged with a snout like a prow. His tail has been clipped into a thumb that points up.

The crowd stands for the Zealots but for all the enthusiasm there is precious little hope. We have all seen the Zealots play. Their season record is 1-and-9 and the 1 comes on a Protested Penetration.

The Zealot Kids look skimpy as wands. The Aunts and Uncles seem flabby and uninterested. That the team is aging is an under-statement. They are aging before sixty thousand eyes. The Zealot Crunch Father looks half the size of his counterpart and the Mother, Erica Lamb, has played for so long and been not only penetrated but impregnated so many times her legs are bowed. Three of the Zealot Crunch Kids are her own, conceived on the field. I point them out to Amos.

The Zealot dog walks with a distinct limp. Fido draws special cheers from the disabled. His head hangs down but when he reaches his doghouse, he rears up on his hind legs and lets out a belching bark. The stands bark back. The dog, at least, in its red and black striped Zealot sweater, tries to show menace.

First Thrust will be decided by a toss of the coin. That honor rightly goes to two Uniques. One wheels out of the Pharmaceutically Impaired section and does a figure-eight with her chair. The crowd appreciates the maneuver. The second comes from Machine Trauma and the spectators can't help titter at the shape of his head. The older Hoffenstein models had a good but not perfect history and unfortunately there have been victims. Jelly Elbow cartwheels out to where they wait and flips the coin high in the air. It catches light and glows like a firefly. The Uniques make their call and the Zealots win the toss.

The field is cleared. The crowd chants, "Crunch, Crunch, Crunch." A team of Zealot cheerleaders rev up response. "Zealots, Zealots, Zealots" ripples around the stadium as the fans make a wave. The referee fires a pistol and the Zealot Kids advance.

The Crunch Mothers are already undulating. Poor Erica Lamb

looks like she will snap off her pelvis. The bleachers begin to "Ugh, Ugh, Ugh" with her motions.

The Zealot Kids form a flying wedge and actually manage to gain territory. The Zealot Aunts and Uncles move forward and there is a shriek from the crowd. There could be a breakthrough.

Two Koala Kids are fallen and bloody, the others held at bay. Koala Aunts and Uncles are forced to plug the gap and amazingly the Aussies commit their hound. Usually the dog is kept to defend the Crunch Mother at home but not this time.

The dog rips into a Zealot Uncle and lays him out but he manages to hold onto a paw long enough for the Zealot Father to make a run for Home. It is Billy Vorinski, a Cruncher traded from Dallas during the Winter. If he is not in his prime at least he has had some incredible Penetrations and here he is going for another so early in the game. "Score, Score, Score," the cheerleaders do flips.

Billy manages to confront the Koala Crunch Father. He kicks and butts and bites but there will be no miracles. The Koala Father takes him out with two classic groiners. The Aussi Crunch Mother comes to kiss her defender as the tide turns quickly.

The Koalas regroup and come forward in a wall. Goolagong forces Fido to roll over and play dead. In a beautiful move the Koala Aunts and Uncles sweep a path for their Crunch Father. He jumps the Zealot gate, takes the steps in a single motion and invades the Home. Erica crouches for the final battle. She is dumped on her back in three seconds, Spread and Entered. Trina holds her hand over Amanda's eyes as the scoreboard lights.

"Why don't they use Crunch Cousins anymore?" Amos asks me.

"I'm not sure. To move things faster, I suppose. When the game first came out of Korea around the time of the Treaty I think they even had Crunch Ancestors. It took all day before there'd be a single Spread much less a Penetration. My father used to take me to the B League matches. I think he wanted me to be a Cruncher."

"You can't. You're not coded for that."

"I know. He knew. Dreams die hard, Amos."

"Why can't I watch?" Amanda asks.

"Plenty of time for that," Trina says.

In the Penetration Interlude we send out for hot dogs and drinks. The door to the box opens and in walks Jelly Elbow carrying the Poster Child who carries a tray with our order.

"Jelly Elbow!" Amanda yells, delighted.

"Hi, guys," Jelly Elbow says. "It's really me."

He has come to see Homer but he has to settle for us. Amos and Amanda get autographed Jelly Elbow dolls and are introduced to the Poster Child. Trina strokes his thin hair. He is about seven, a fragile, beautiful boy with amazing eyes.

"Geraldo Kopler," Jelly Elbow says. "Chosen from thousands of doomed applicants. Does he say *Unique* or does he not. Can't move one arm, can't move either leg, can't even wiggle your toes, can you, Geraldo? But look at the spirit in those orbs. Is that warmth? Does that make the work I do seem worthwhile?"

Geraldo Kopler suddenly reaches with his working arm and pulls the bandage off my head. He wants to see my trouble. He sees. Everybody sees. The Poster Child puts his hand on my lips. I kiss his fingers. Jelly Elbow grabs him up and away.

"Tell Homer Godbless," he says.

"Do the chicken sound," Amanda says, but Jelly Elbow is out of there. I fiddle with my bandage. Amos is watching me.

Screams rise from the crowd. The BE PROUD OF YOUR CODE banner is on fire. A mechanical voice urges calm. Jelly Elbow runs out on the field, dragging the Poster Child. He screams, "Slimes, Slimes, Slimes, Slimes." He waves a fist at the flames. The crowd gives him a standing ovation.

"Stop staring at your father," Trina tells Amos.

Charlton Hymn is beautifully aged. He is a wine cask that has held fermenting grapes in his belly for centuries. He is a Winter scene by Breughel. He is a statue staring at eternity with sea-bleached eyes on the lip of a Greek island. He stands with his arms folded looking for his argument. He discovers his lines like an actor.

"Your Honor can easily see that James P. Wander has extracted every potential from his Code A+. He is a devoted and loving husband and father. His career has been nothing short of brilliant. Ask yourself, 'Should this rare man be stripped of his very humanity?

Should an accident of fate deprive the global community of his talents? Can we afford to sacrifice such a leader?' Your Honor, his very existence has been a horror since the Code compromise. His career and his domestic life are in shambles. There has been an assault on his person. He survived a blatant attempt to consume him in a public place. Must I go on? Let me call Amos Brogg Wander to come forward."

Amos, in his blue suit, moves toward the bench where Judge Miranda Skimmer presides. She smiles warmly at him and he returns the smile. Charlton puts an arm around Amos' shoulder.

"This is Mr. Wander's only son. For the record, he has never been in any kind of trouble or guilty of anti-social behavior. He is an honor student at the Bolt Academy. But things have changed for Amos, Your Honor. Look at this."

Charlton passes an envelope to the Judge. She opens it and removes an ersatz Code. I see her swallow spit. She is obviously shocked but keeps her composure.

"Yes, Your Honor, we share his shame. Why, Amos, why? Tell the court what possessed you to buy . . . and wear . . . this obscenity. Surely you know better."

"Well," Amos says, his eyes watering, "we were at a Crunch game, Mom, Dad and Sister, and Jelly Elbow brought this Poster Kid up to meet us. He pulled off Dad's medical wrap . . ."

"The wrap was certified by a doctor," Charlton says.

"It was just after a Penetration and we were all excited. Then suddenly I saw what happened to him. Since that incident I have been going through a confused and disturbing period punctuated by frequent nightmares and characterized by hostile flailing at authority. Sister wets her bed. Mom cries a lot. We didn't even stay for the end of the game. And the Zealots made a comeback and won it."

There is laughter in the court. Even the Judge grins before gaveling us to silence.

"Thank you, Amos," Charlton says. "I know in my heart that Your Honor will be most eager to blend mercy with justice and grant our most urgent request in this landmark case. For the same fate that has placed James P. Wander in such jeopardy has given Your Honor the opportunity to right a terrible, random wrong. Allow my client corrective surgery. Let him return to the land of normalcy."

Homer looks over at me and nods. Trina nods back. Lauren is patting Amos' head. The kid came through, no question. He didn't miss a word.

"Why is your client wearing a headband?" Judge Skimmer asks.

"On my counsel. We felt it might be both distracting and unnerving to the court if . . ."

"I could hold both of you in contempt. Is the slogan 'Be Proud of Your Code' a mockery here of all places?"

"Quite the contrary, Your Honor. May I remind you that the Brogg family was an early supporter of Dr. Hoffenstein at the very inception of . . ."

"I am quite familiar with all that, Mr. Hymn. You yourself called this a landmark case. The Brogg family and Mr. Wander must realize that the law is clear and immutable. There can be no tampering with a Human Bar Code. That is so elemental to our society that the very thought of a dispensation is repugnant to any civilized person."

"Absolutely," Charlton says, slapping his hands together. The slap echoes off marble walls and wood panels. Even the reporters jump. "Your Honor is absolutely correct on that point. Dispensation is not only out of the question it is not the issue here. James P. Wander, remove the wrapping."

This is our moment. My bandage has been altered for quick escape. I flick it off. Cameras flash. Judge Skimmer orders them impounded. She evacuates the courtroom.

"Your Honor," Charlton says when calm is restored, "and this is so crucial, *we are not dealing with a Human Bar Code.* We are dealing with sodium-free pea soup."

"Are you petitioning the court to change his Code to some other kind of soup then, Mr. Hymn? Mushroom and barley? Chicken rice? Vegetable beef? Let's not practice sophistry in this chamber. Approach the bench."

Charlton, his face flushed, moves forward. Judge Skimmer tilts forward. She whispers loud enough for me to hear. "Charlie, you know I am not a ruthless bitch. And I know very well what Brogg dollars mean to the party. But your client flaunts his croutons. You are all so damn sure I will find for him. He feels so outrageously victimized. Well, tough shit. Sometimes life is a cesspool. My mother shoved pea soup into me on a Goddamned Mickey Mouse spoon. I am trying to obliterate that nauseating memory. I don't want it to influence my decision. But it is hard, Charlie."

"You're bigger than that."

"Charlie, you can go to the Supreme Court with this one. But I can't let you go ahead with Alteration. If I say replicate then every would-be Jesus would be down here in the morning claiming precedent. Not to mention the press assault on rank and privilege. We're talking a barrage, Charlie. Why did you take this case? It should never have gotten this far. And frankly, I don't like to be taken for a pushover. I want to see the look on that complacent bastard when I rule."

"Miranda, it was an accident."

"So is the weather. So is his A+. So is life on Earth. And where did that little turd get the filthy Bar Code?"

"Some candy store, I suppose."

"Mind if I hold on to it?"

"Of course not. Keep it as long as you want. Miranda . . ."

"Back off, Charlie."

Charlton takes three steps backward. Judge Skimmer sits straight and takes a deep breath. She looks at me.

"While there are mitigating circumstances at play here, the court finds that there is insufficient reason to justify any form of Code Manipulation. Your petition is denied, Mr. Wander. And may I suggest that you make the best of things. You will save yourself a lot of anguish and spare the body politic from yet another spasm. Law is the foundation the future rests upon and every tremor, however minuscule, leaves a chip and every chip is an erosion. If the 'fate' mentioned here has changed you to pea soup then so be it. Rise to the occasion. Be served with grace, albeit on a Mickey Mouse spoon to a helpless child trapped in a high-chair screaming for solace."

She slams her gavel. I am damned. Charlton is telling Homer that he has already filed an appeal. It is futile. The Judge is exactly right, except about my attitude. I was not arrogant or complacent. I was humble and expectant. But in my inner-chambers I knew the outcome. Justice is done. This is not a matter for the court. It never was.

"That cunt," Homer says. "She committed suicide."

"I am prepared to be served with grace," I say.

I look for my ghost on Sag Harbor's main street. It is slouching outside the Cinema looking up at the marquee. It is sneaking a peek into the American Hotel glaring at the Summer girls. It ambles down to the pier watching a sailboat slash blue water. It looks over at me with a blank expression. Neither of us envies the other but there is a stir of recognition. On the dock a man stands fishing with a small boy. A wind kicks up from the South. The boy has blond hair that blows like wheat. The wind is time.

I drive past the Civil War monument and park near the Firemen's Museum. There is the house, unchanged, a modest 19th Century box with the rooms upstairs and the newspaper office downstairs. The SAG HARBOR SENTINEL sign is new. It whips in the wind slapping air.

A curtain obscures any view into the office but my father and mother will be in there typing copy and doing layouts. Piles of old issues will line the walls. Shelves of books, photographs, award certificates and assorted junk will round out the decoration. I find myself smiling. My ghost pushes past me carrying a bag of school supplies. I follow through the wooden door.

A bell announces an alien presence. My eyes adjust to fluorescence.

My father says, "If you need xerox copies made you'll have to come back. The machine is down."

My mother says, "We're waiting for the service. If you want to leave the pages . . ."

"Me."

They raise their eyes over the frames of identical tortoise shell glasses.

"Jamie?" Mother says. "Sam, it's Jamie."

"Well," Father says. "Is Trina with you? The kids?"

"No."

"Imagine that. They found a reason not to come."

"You're looking very well," Mother says. "We worried about you after the accident. But they told us you were right as rain."

"I meant to drive in but they said you were fine," Father says.

"I'm glad you didn't. I know how much you hate the tunnel. And the hospital wasn't much fun. Really, it's just as well."

"Trina called about the petition denial. We were both upset," says Mother.

"But give them credit. They did a remarkable job of keeping it quiet. There was nothing on the wire, nothing on the TV or radio," says Father.

"We have very good public relations people."

"Or maybe they didn't think it was news."

"Maybe it wasn't news."

"I expected the decision," says Dad.

"He said it would be thumbs down," says Mom.

"He had no case, Annie. No case whatsoever."

"I agree," I say. "Even if the Judge had the inclination it would have been impossible, considering. Still, being shot down was painful. I needed to see you guys."

"Of course," my mother says. "If a family doesn't form into a fighting fist in times of crisis . . ."

"We're hardly breaking even," my father says. "But you're not here for money. It can't be that."

"Not money, no. I just needed to see you. Touch base. Go to the well. I was on my way out to see Dr. Hoffenstein in Sagaponack and I thought . . ."

"You're going to meet Dr. Hoffenstein?" my mother says.

"Yes. Homer arranged it. Right to the top."

"That's impressive," my father says. He puts down the ad he was dummying onto the High School Sports Page and walks over to examine my Code. "Hardly any scar," he says. "Just a kind of bump in the skin. It's not even noticeable."

"Thank God for that."

"Mother was very concerned about a scar."

"I was. But Trina told me there was no disfiguration."

"What brand is that? Vigor? I never heard of it."

My mother comes to look. She runs her fingers over my head. "Vigor Salt Free. They used to carry it at the A&P but not in years and years. We never used canned soup."

"I need your advice."

"You need our advice? Homer Brogg gives you advice. Dr. Hoffenstein says, 'Sure, Jim, drop in anytime.' And you come out for our advice? That's news," my father says. "Would you care to put that in writing? I could frame it and hang it over the computer. Or maybe Mother could work it into a sampler. What the hell are you saying, Jamie?"

"Stop that," Mom says.

"Things are closing in on me."

"Things have a way of closing in. You want words of wisdom? Circle your wagons. Define your space."

"Amos can't look at me. Amanda just plays with her dolls and sniffles. I slapped her last night. Just for whimpering."

"I am sure Amos and Amanda love you. It must be peer pressure," says my mother.

"The kids will come around. And what about Trina? Where is she in all this?"

"I'm not sure, Pop."

"He called you Pop. Did you hear?"

"I heard. Reality is sandpaper on the genitals, Jamie. If I told you once I told you a thousand times."

"You told me."

"I didn't tell God to rest on the seventh day. I didn't tell God to quit while he was behind," my father says.

"Why are you bringing God into this, Sam?" my mother says.

"I never wanted to make a spiritual or legal matter out of this. The only thing to hang my hopes on is simple compassion."

"Does Homer agree with that thinking?" my father says.

"Naturally not. He's all for going to the Supreme Court or Bethlehem or whatever it takes. Hoffenstein is my only chance. Let him be the arbiter of my fate."

"On my first job I had this editor who kept a sign over his desk that said: 'Heaven and Earth Were Created in One Paragraph,' " my father says. "When you handed that man a story he'd turn it back and say, 'Can't you do better?' And you'd take the story and rework it and give it to him and you'd get the same, 'Can't you do better?' When you finally couldn't stand it and you'd tell the bastard, 'No, I can't do better you son of a bitch,' he'd take the pages and say, 'OK. Now I'll read it.'"

"Who was that, Sam?"

"I am taking the scenic route to my point which is if you've got Dr. Hoffenstein up your sleeve it's a little premature to come to

Mother and me as your court of last resort. You never listened to us, not since Homer Brogg became your father."

"Don't mind him. He's upset because we never get to see Trina and the babies."

"That's not the issue here," I say. "My survival is the issue."

"What about the speech you once made on the subject of personal growth and dead ends? We bought you a suitcase and paid your carfare to New York."

"And a blue blazer with silver buttons."

"Double breasted, Jamie. You wanted double breasted. You got double breasted. And you did good, son. Good job, very stylish wife, kids with classy names. We read about you in the society columns. It lifts our spirits to know you did so good. You certainly lived up to your Code. What did they call you out here? *Ape* for A+. Sag Harbor's first A+. You made us both very proud and I mean that sincerely."

"That's surely true," my mother says. "They still ask about Ape."

"And we like seeing you once a year. When the weather gets nice. We look forward to that. We appreciate the calls and the cards. The problem is, Jamie, now we are old and tired."

"But we're comfortable with our anger."

"It isn't easy for any parent to sit back and watch an only child turn into a can of split pea soup. Much less a child who accomplished so much in such a short time. But life goes on even here in the boonies. Every week is a new paper and somehow just enough news, ads and classifieds to fill it. Look here. 'Town Board Yeas Boutique on Main.' This is a quiet town. Antiques come here to die. But we have our news. What I am getting at, Jamie . . ."

"Father means keep in touch. Let us know how it comes out. Don't be a stranger. Would it be too much to ask Dr. Hoffenstein for his autograph on a picture?"

"I don't know. If the situation permits."

"That would be terrific," my father says. "Something like 'To Annie and Samuel from Your Friend and Admirer . . . Keep Those Presses Rolling.' "

"I've got to call the movie for its listing," my mother says.

"You'd think they'd know what they were going to play in their own damn theatre," my father says. "But no. Every week is a crisis. Always last minute. Never any lead-time."

My tongue licks at Mom's raspberry pie. Shards of crust and raspberry seeds lodge between my teeth and hide in periodontal pockets. I taste the tart berries, the flavor of enduring affection.

I swing my car onto Ocean Drive. The Route Tripper emits a slow, spaced series of beeps. I am getting close. I stop the car to breathe salt air. The world has turned slate grey. Waves roll with the rhythm of breath. There is an edge to the stiff breeze, a fragile hint of ice.

Down on the sand a family tries to get a kite airborne. The kite is dragon-shaped, green and red with blue lightning bolts across its wings. It bucks and veers, dives and climbs and I see the people screaming. Their sound is lost in the whistle of wind. I get out of the car and begin to walk toward them.

I can help them with the kite. I am good with kites. They are doing it all wrong. But they are lucky. An updraft takes the dragon higher and higher out over the blueblack skin of sea. They give the cord to a girl of Amanda's age. I yell to them that the pull will be too strong for her to hold. My noises scatter. They see a man waving and yelling from the dunes. Their response is to huddle together. I go back to the car.

I start up thinking that my parents have grown old. I see them as old. I taste their age in the pie crumbs. I shudder and watch the kite twist in circles.

I drive faster through the damp, tangy air. The beeper is telling me that I am within a mile of my destination. It will be one of the grand houses that overlook the Atlantic, splendid creations of weathered wood, concrete and glass. There is an arrogance to those houses, a smug defiance. Nothing will topple them, no storm or surge. They are sleek and strong and beautiful, monuments to success. They are the reason for the shore.

The beeper turns to a chime and then goes silent. On the highest dune I see a glass palace, a mass of angles and arches, balconies and portholes. A granite wall surrounds the property. There is no visible gate but a marble pyramid holds a speaker and a TV camera.

I drive alongside and an electronic voice, surprisingly resonant, asks for identification. I tell the speaker my mission. The camera blinks a red dot. I smile. The wall divides in sliding slabs. I drive through the wound and climb past a pool, a tennis court and beyond that a stark sculpture in black metal that spreads over a huge lawn. I see that it is a miniature golf course complete with a cone-shaped windmill. All the comforts and why not? What better way to define a humble man?

Beyond the golf course two structures flank the road, a little Radio City Music Hall and a tiny Taj Mahal. They discharge a feisty Yorkie and a malevolent Doberman who run circles around my car. I close the windows.

A few yards from the main house some invisible signal calls off the dogs. They retreat but remain in striking distance. I leave the car carefully and climb stone steps to a door of oak and stained glass. The letter H and an abstract Bar Code motif have been worked into the glass along with clusters of etched grapes and a light of golden angels. I am about to touch the bell when the door opens.

I recognize the woman who greets me. I saw her at the banquet though we didn't meet. She is a tall, toasted beauty with radiant silver hair that falls below the line of her breasts. Despite the chill, she wears only the hint of a bikini under a transparent plastic coat. She is Dr. Hoffenstein's fifth wife, an actress from Hungary, or was it Poland? Their love story has already been a television movie. He calls her Resurrection. In the final scene of the film the actor playing a virile Hoffenstein of eighty leans toward her mouth and whispers, "You are my rainbow. My resurrection." It was years ago but the name stuck. The fashion magazines and tabloids saw to that.

Resurrection scans my Code. She must know my trouble. Her face is serene. "Please come in, Mr. Vigor," she says.

"Wander. James Wander."

"Yes. Wander. I am Lisle Hoffenstein."

"Ms. Hoffenstein, I want you to know how much I appreciate the opportunity . . ."

"Nonsense. My husband has been anticipating your visit with evident pleasure. He does lead an isolated life. That may surprise you. Part is by chance and part is by choice. It's good for him to see people beyond official functions. You are doing us a favor."

"Really, I don't think that for a moment."

We are inside an atrium. Columns of glass rise between clean poles. The poles are hung with a stunning collection of art and sculpture that spans the ages. A ball hangs on an iron chain from six stories up. The ball is covered with skeletal bits and pieces of sea creatures: claws, pincers, shells, coral, teeth, swords, fins, even the beaks of sea birds.

I follow Resurrection under the mobile into a huge living room. That room is lush with plump sofas and chairs, carpeting and tapestries, more incredible art and an aquarium of stuffed ocean dwellers small as a minnow and large as a whale.

"He's waiting in there," says Resurrection, pointing at a recessed door. "Go on, don't be shy. Everyone is so afraid of him as if he farts fire. He is a welcoming, empathetic man. A compassionate man. Very human. Very sympatico. Just go on in, Mr. Wander."

"James."

"James. Go right on in. And don't bother to genuflect." She laughs bells. I try to laugh back but my cheek muscles are in spasm. I can't believe I am here. That the oily floor of a supermarket would lead me to that door is too much synchronicity. I have wanted to meet this man all my life. Resurrection understands, she has been there before. She puts her hand on my shoulder and urges me forward.

I go through the door with an eerie sense of floating, as if the spirit detached from my body. My eyes are closed. I will confront the icon who remade the world. My head is butter. Why did I come here?

There is a mountain of stuff confronting me. Furniture from all over the world, every period and culture. Erotic sculptures fill the room's center, stone and metal doing unto metal and stone. Paintings are stacked like the *Sag Harbor Sentinels* in my father's office. The walls are lined with shelves of books and hundreds of trophies and awards. Medals have been set into the floor under lucite.

There is a surface covered with tribal masks, another hung with pictures from the 20th Century Holocaust, another of nuclear explosions and erupting volcanoes. I walk between the arms of fornicating lovers into an area filled with weapons, an electric chair, chains, whips, even a gallows and guillotine. Over a tremendous fireplace is what must be the first Human Bar Code under thick glass. Next to it are tributes from the United Nations, the World Council, the

Nobel Peace Prize. There is a fantastic portrait of Hoffenstein by Ingmar Brown. He stands naked among the clouds. His scrotum is made up of the world's hemispheres. Near that is a small photograph of the *Kotchka*, the eternal garbage barge, drifting off Antarctica.

I hear the wailing of every terminal patient, a deep, rich blood cry that rises from the molten core of the planet. The cries rise and fall like the sea, a blend of sensuality and anguish that makes me sweat fear. The noise is nothing human and everything human.

Light enters the room through an enormous bay window facing the waves. Silhouetted in the window is an egg-shaped chair. The chair swivels toward me. Dr. Hoffenstein sits inside the shell waving a baton of beach grass. Stereo speakers bracket his ears. They are the source of the ghostly song and I realize I am listening to a concert of whales. He is conducting a protest of whales, a choir of extinction.

"This is not a recording," Hoffenstein says. "This is live. From a network of underwater sensors and satellite relays. What you hear is what is. Now. This minute. Some of their complaint is theatrical but much is valid." Hoffenstein crackles a laugh. His voice is cellophane. "The fine art is filtering out one from the other. The propaganda from the truth. They know I am listening and they are clever."

"Dr. Hoffenstein, I am James Wander. Homer Brogg's son-in-law. You can't know how grateful I am that . . ."

"Gratitude. If I gave you that feeling I have given you a precious gift. Most of their songs are nothing more than mating calls. *Humping Hump Backs, hump, hump, hump. Who's that knocking on my rump?* Reproduction, reproduction. The same song forever. Still, hidden in the lyric . . . come closer, James Wander. I want to see your Code."

I move closer. He rises from the chair, pushing himself up on blue arms. "I am told this happened to you in a Food Forest. You should sue the bejesus out of them. You're going to be a very wealthy man. They used to carry that brand out here at the IGA but not for years. Salt free?"

"Salt free."

"Fine. So much of the globe is salty. Heh?"

"Sir, I assume that Homer filled in the details. You know why I am here and I don't want to waste any of your valuable time."

"You want your former Code restored."

"I do, yes. I believe it should be put back. The court found against me but I have maintained that this is not a matter for any judge to decide. And not a matter for God to dispose. In the infinite scale of things I realize my problem is minuscule, man made, and for man to correct."

"God? It will not look back on the world. Forget about God. I am your only hope of salvation. You feel the court made an unfair decision?"

"Not unfair and not unjust. Wrong. A wrong decision."

"Well said, Mr. Wander. I agree. You know, when Homer Brogg telephoned he asked me to endorse some fertilization project. Designed to guarantee the production of young gods. He made me a most generous offer. But we have enough young gods."

"I am familiar with the project, Sir. It isn't exactly an assembly line for gods. The idea is that a blending of superior sperm with the natural father's own . . ."

"Do you consider yourself one of the young gods, Mr. Wander? Tell me honestly."

"I consider myself a lucky man."

"*Rara avis*. A lucky man. Homer must think highly of you. There was the suggestion that my endorsement and the subsequent reward was somehow linked to a favorable dispensation of your case."

"I never suggested to Homer that any connection . . ."

"It's Homer's way. He is a thug. Bless him."

"I want things the way they were. No more, no less."

"Well, well. Things the way they were. What a unique wish. The wish of a lucky man. In my case I am perfectly content with things the way they are. I enjoy the drift toward obsolescence. I am delighted that my dick hangs limp as a whore's handshake. I am thrilled that my gums are too spongy to hold my tusks. I adore my condition. So you may understand that it is hard for me to understand your attitude. Heh?"

Hoffenstein cackles again. He farts but not fire and falls backward into his shell chair.

"With all respect, Dr. Hoffenstein, the hand of time is different from sludge on a supermarket floor. You ripened in the natural way. I was pecked off the tree by a piggish crow of chance. I would be more than content to follow your trail."

"I am sure you envy me. Did you meet my Resurrection?"

"Very lovely and most gracious. If I do say so, your wife had a hard time pretending to ignore my head. I was sincerely moved by the effort she made. But when she scanned me I could sense recoil."

"I suppose you wanted to romp on the beach and cup clam shells onto her tits. Slither off her panties and tongue the salt off her thighs. The inside of her thighs. The succulent zone. Or does your salt free status forbid that kind of diversion?"

"I am happily married. I have two beautiful . . ."

"Lay her on a warm protected mound. Spread her legs. Filet her. Nourish her with your protein. Young gods and lucky men think alike, Mr. Wander."

"Believe me, Sir, I am very asexual these days. I certainly had no such thought about Ms. Hoffenstein."

"Ms. Hoffenstein. If you climbed your own hard-on to beg her it would make no difference. She is loyal. She swears to that. Should I doubt her?"

"She is entirely devoted. When she mentions your name her whole face lights up. Her commitment to you . . ."

"When I began my research my inclination was to stamp Human Bar Codes in sequestered places. Behind the ear lobes. Between rectal cheeks. I thought about nooks and crannies, all the secret places. I was caught up in cosmetic liberalism. Then I told myself, 'No, Hoffenstein, no! The Codes must be up front and visible. Past notions of beauty must go into the toilet.' I knew that resistance to that hard fact could be overcome through a campaign to foster pride and purpose."

"Brogg Communications was honored to create the 'Be Proud of Your Code' slogan. That was before my time, Sir, but believe me, every employee is reminded of . . ."

"Before your time. There wouldn't be any time if it wasn't for me. All would be ashes. I kept them from broiling life on Earth and boiling the seas. It was I who did battle with the Mighty Mushroom."

"You saved the world. No argument."

"I saved symmetry. The shape of things."

"And you created order."

"I created the mechanism for paradise. But there is still dissent. Why? Why? My whales sing about it. They compose ditties to tweak me. I only promised survival, not satisfaction. I was not an idiot or a liar. I delivered on my word."

"Nothing pleases everyone. There are always a few who . . ."

"Order is Splendor. Wise men know that the best chaos is structured. I learned about conformity from rebels."

"Which is why I want to be back inside the egg of the ordinary."

"You know why the Dictum is so stringent on the subject of Code Manipulation?"

"I do. But a glitch of fate . . ."

"Who doesn't feel victimized by fate whatever their fate? The same glitch. Even A+ young gods feel victimized. Envious of the lesser Codelings."

"I was never jealous. Oh, I admit to speculation. I mean about the joy of innocence that goes with, say, P through Z. We do lick our lollipop fantasies. It's human nature. But as for trading places . . ."

"The minute you became split pea soup you wanted to be something else."

"Someone. I wanted to be someone. The same someone I was when I went shopping. Not something. Not anything."

"You who are smart enough to appreciate the symmetry and order. Even you, James Wander? By coming here you indicate a tendency toward dissent. You're behaving like a Slime."

"That is absolutely untrue, Dr. Hoffenstein. I came to ask for your compassion. If you feel I should accept my status, I willingly yield to your superior knowledge. I will be the best salt free pea soup I can be."

"Good. Then be it. We will watch your progress with interest."

"Still, it doesn't seem fair. In the most elemental way."

"Fair, heh? When I met Resurrection she was nineteen and a professed virgin. She's never been with pea soup. Oh, I can relate. If I confronted a nubile oat bran muffin, I think I would be tempted beyond restraint. Did she make advances? Did she intimate that her luscious lubricious vulva has on its pink and rosy wall the hieroglyphics that would reveal to you the location of Prime Mother Computer? Is that what she offered? Considerable incentive but a lie. She doesn't know."

"Dr. Hoffenstein, your wife was perfectly correct in her behavior. The only thing she offered me was a drink."

"Of what?"

"Coffee. Soda. The usual. Dr. Hoffenstein, you are my final

judge."

"So you wouldn't fuck with my wife? That's sensible of you, Mr. Wander. See the first Human Bar Code up on the wall? It looks like the bars of a cell but it is the key to freedom. That was my work. My work is done. Now I conduct invisible orchestras."

"You sound like my father."

"I am your father. I am everybody's father. My reward? The cuckoo clock eats me alive. But that meter runs for you, too! Heh!"

"It does, yes. Which is why I would like to exploit the ticks. I have a lot to offer, Sir. I really think it would be wasteful to consign me to . . ."

Dr. Hoffenstein reaches into a pile of collectibles and comes out with a scimitar. It has a jeweled handle and a hangnail blade that flashes alarms.

"Fine, fine. I'll make you a deal. Homer Brogg isn't the only man who deals. Submit to castration and I will sanction the restoration of your Code."

"It's a difficult choice but thank you, no. I've grown attached to my balls."

"Heh! You're just like all the rest. One thing on your mind. And something for nothing. Not even nothing is for nothing, James Wander. My advice to you is that you bring yourself to a boil."

"Be served with grace and bring myself to a boil. Is that your last word, Sir?"

"Don't you wish. But not for a while yet. I never felt better."

Hoffenstein drops the scimitar, probes the pile, and produces a rusty Uzi. He fires a burst into the glass window and shatters it to splinters.

"Ah, smell that fresh air," he says. "You had her, didn't you? Did she moan? Did she gush? Did a little fountain spurt when she climaxed? That is a very rare and treasured response. Consider yourself fortunate to have experienced it. The quintessential geyser. Lourdes between the legs. Pilgrims come from miles around. Heh?"

He splatters the floor around me but I hold my ground.

"How was she?" he says.

Resurrection comes coolly into the room and takes my arm. She tells her husband to put down the gun. He hurls it into a corner. It burps on impact and a trophy turns to dust.

"He gets like that," she says. "He should never have retired."

"For how long?"

"Ages and ages," Trina says.

"Ages and ages?" A new door opens and I peer inside my wife.
She has revealed to me that for *ages and ages* a psychic has guided
her life. We sit in the psychic's waiting room. It is not the dentist
but my diaphragm knots and I chew on air.

"But why?"

"Because Ms. Blotnik is wonderful is why. You'll see."

"What can Ms. Blotnik tell me that my Code doesn't? For that
matter, what's left for her to read? All essential information is clearly
presented from date-of-birth to probable and possible achievement
and limitation. Does she read the lifeline? Is that it? Do you believe
there is a lifeline?"

When the Codes were accepted it was proposed that they carry
genetic information including the likely date and cause of death give
or take medical intervention. The proposal was rejected by the
Council for obvious reasons. Even Hoffenstein admits there is such
a thing as knowing too much. Besides, the lifeline was subject to too
many variables like accidents, random violence, or even suicide.
Still, a rumor has persisted for five decades that the Codes do indeed
contain that ultimate intimacy, that declaration of mortality. It is
said that certain employers and insurance companies saw to it. The
fantasy is that a code within the Code can be interpreted through
ultra-sophisticated readings. I don't believe it and never did. But a
group of self-proclaimed hackers emerged buoyed by the rumor. For
a price they will give your obituary date and describe your final
agony. For a dollar more they will suck your cock.

"Ms. Blotnik is not about life span," Trina says. "She is about
the quality of life. And warnings."

"Warnings? Why didn't she warn you against going shopping
that night?"

"She did. In a sense. I was cautioned in a general way. She said
there would be major changes in a crucial relationship. At the time
I didn't realize the import."

"I wish you'd told me, Trina. I would have known immediately that she meant I'd split my head open going after groceries."

"Jim, she could be helpful. It is worth a try."

"Maybe. Don't expect too much. It would be interesting to cover my Code and see what she comes up with."

"She uses the Code as a trigger, a launch pad. She needs to see the Code. She's a Code Psychic, that's the point. And you'd be surprised at her client list."

"No I wouldn't. In a society based on the predictable the possibility of the unpredictable being made predictable takes on enormous attraction."

"What did you just say? You lost me."

"What I mean is that the ability to predict sanctions belief in mystery and undermines predictability itself. I admit it is a bit complicated. What it comes down to is the need for the dimension of magic."

"Ms. Blotnik is a scientist not a magician."

"Whatever she is, whatever she does, is no different from Halloween. Or those horror movies Amos loves. Teasing fear is a roundabout way of fostering belief in God. God and good. What surprises me is that you believe in her. A rational woman, an educated, sophisticated, privileged woman. Trina Brogg Wander. That amazes me. That could make me believe in magic. Because if someone had come to me and said, 'Your wife is addicted to a psychic Code reader,' I would have told them to screw off."

"Just because you're edgy you don't need to be vulgar."

"Sorry. I am edgy. Wouldn't you be edgy? Especially after the meeting with Hoffenstein?"

"I think you've exaggerated the events."

"I tell you, Hoffenstein is insane. Not that it matters or detracts from what he accomplished. But he is a fruitcake and dangerous to your health. He faces the dilemma of all old saints. He wants to destroy the world he saved before he dies. He wants to leave no pleasure behind him. Of course, he might be content to castrate the males and plug up every thimble of dew. That might satisfy him if his whales stopped singing limericks."

"I am really worried about you, darling. I would keep those thoughts to myself."

"Won't Blotnik know my sentiments. She sees all."

"I am concerned with her reaction, yes."

"I share the concern."

We do not see Ms. Blotnik's previous client. There is a discreet exit from her parlor. But we hear the rustle of departure and the quiet closing of a door. The psychic is ready for me. I am called by a tin and whiskey voice over a hidden speaker. Trina gestures me along. She will wait downstairs browsing the neighborhood boutiques.

I enter the Blotnik sanctum. She waits for me composed, a bowling ball in a black leather chair with winged arms. Her dress, the chair and grey walls conspire to float her ample face. Eyes, lips, pouch cheeks and a cleft chin hover. Her nose is so small it is practically invisible. Tufts of henna hair keep me from scanning her.

"Sit, Mr. Wander."

I sit. Ms. Blotnik produces a large magnifying glass, the kind they sell in antique shops. She scans me, she grunts, and I blush. I have developed a real complex about my condition despite my vow of acceptance. Her left eye forms a tear the size of a dime. It hangs in the corner, then washes down her face. With no nose to stop it the tear splashes on her desk.

"What might have been was not meant to be," she says.

"If I depress you I can go right now. You know I didn't want to come here. It was Trina's idea."

"Calm yourself. Please be quiet." She grabs her temples. Her pupils roll up like BB's in those games where you have to manipulate them into tiny holes. "First I shall attempt the reading of the rose in which your past lives are revealed hidden in the petals of the flower. It is not easy. My vision is blocked by your aura."

"My aura. I can't control that."

"I understand. Most auras range from blue tranquil to red ferment but yours is a curious admixture of burnt sienna and cadmium yellow. The color of sick animal shit."

"That says it. Sick animal shit. Trina told me you had a remarkable gift and now I believe her."

"Don't be offended, Mr. Wander. I call it like I see it. Your chakras or energy centers seem nicely balanced. There is some disturbance in the navel chakra which is the seat of sexuality."

"Excellent, Ms. Blotnik. On target. Some considerable disturbance."

"And the crown chakra atop your skull is spurting green liquid."

"That would be pea soup."

"It makes for a repulsive mess with the brown and yellow. We'll skip over the past lives. In this situation I shall summon my spirit guide."

"That might be the best thing."

"If he should appear be open with him. He was already a sage and mystic in the days before the pyramids. His name is Zupkin. He can be a bit direct, even coarse. Humor him. He means no harm. Quite the contrary."

"I'll be gentle with Zupkin. If he appears."

Ms. Blotnik drops her head onto her mountainous bosom. It rises and falls with each breath. A snorting sound comes from her well. Then a thick, accented voice pushes her mouth apart.

"I am Zupkin. So?"

"I am James Wander and I don't know the answer to your question."

"A wiseass. That's what I need after a day schlepping rocks to Cheops. What do you want from me, troublemaker?"

"Actually, it wasn't me who disturbed you."

"Blotnik? The cow? Are you one of her neurotics? A paying guest or a relative?"

"A paying guest. Didn't she tell you about me?"

"Wander. Wander. She said something obscure about finding a destiny for one denied his destiny. She talks through her pores."

"A simple question for a spirit guide, Zupkin. Where do I go from here?"

"The sun rises over the Nile. His flaming eye bisects fragments of darkness. Creatures of the desert with dry skins tongue young light. You like that image? Tongue young light? In translation it sounds Oriental."

"Nice, very poetic, but what's the bottom line?"

"The bottom line. Always the bottom line. It is so hard to talk to your century. I am speaking in metaphors about dawn. Dawn is hope. Wait! I see flashes. I see glaring light reflected from the blade of a knife!"

"I was never good at fortune cookies."

"A flash, slash and crash. Listen! Birds are chirping. The bird songs soothe the ear of a child. The world begins anew."

"Zupkin, could you be a bit more specific?"

"I must go back now. We have quotas."

"You'll be leaving Egypt soon. Don't be in such a hurry."

"Leaving Egypt? That's impossible."

"The Exodus."

"What Exodus? You know something? Give me a hint."

Ms. Blotnik lets out a wail, a car alarm protesting strange hands on the dashboard. I jump. Her head flaps into correct position. Her eyes open with the pupils aligned.

"The serpent coils into a question mark," she says. "The question is answered by a transient snail."

"You sound like Zupkin."

"Zupkin. Did he come? Was he here in this room?"

"He was, yes. He said something profound about birds and baby ears."

"But that's marvelous, Mr. Wander. Congratulations. We're talking salvation. You are a very lucky man."

"I need clarification. Interpretation."

"It will all come clear."

"When? When will it come clear?"

She purses her lips and throws me a kiss.

"It's a precious gift," she says. "It feels so good when it all comes together. It's not just the money."

"Of course, Ms. Blotnik. How much do I owe you?"

"That remains to be seen. If you mean what is my fee, I accept a donation of a thousand dollars to help with my work. For Zupkin, nothing. He is on staff." She giggles bubbles. I write a check.

Homer, Lance and I ride the private elevator to the Brogg Tower's third sub-basement. Homer is focused, as always. Lance has a shit-eating grin on his coin face. I have no idea what this is about.

We exit the box and walk down a corridor of cement, then make turns and navigate other tunnels. My feeling is uneasy. As if I am about to see a catacomb where former rivals of Brogg Enterprises are piled in neat heaps of bone. Maybe it will be Homer's own tomb.

He has said many times that he would like to be buried in the building.

We stop outside what appears to be an innocent door to some service area. Homer gives my shoulder a rub. Lance slaps his hands together, applauding his own pleasure.

"Jim, we have considered your situation and determined that the only thing that can save your ass is a miracle," Lance says.

"The court turned you down. Hoffenstein gave you the shaft though I suppose it was me he stuck it to," Homer says.

"Old news," I say.

"We're putting things into perspective," Lance says. "All roads are blocked. This is a time for religion."

"The only course is Alteration."

"Wait a minute, Homer. You're telling me I should disregard the most essential principle of civilization and have myself illegally repaired? Is that what this is about? Beyond that door somebody is waiting for me with a scalpel? And you believe I'll agree to that? Even if I did, it wouldn't work. Too many people know what happened. If I turn up my old self again, there would be questions, an investigation, prosecution and humiliation. I can't subject Trina and the kids to . . ."

"We're talking divine intervention," Lance says.

"Miracles are their own reward, Jim. Nobody questions the Lord's kiss."

"The Lord's kiss? What exactly does that . . ."

Homer opens the door. I am back in the Food Forest. There is a Food Forest in the third sub-basement. Everything is in place except for the shoppers. A pain rips through my stomach. My hand moves to cover my forehead.

"Easy, son," Homer says. "Keep control."

"Not bad, is it?" Lance says. "Wouldn't you swear?"

"I would, yes. But . . . ?"

"Actually it didn't cost us a cent. Food Forest paid for the whole construction. They know what they stand to lose in a lawsuit."

Animal and bird noises pipe over the PA. A wind rustles the foliage. I see a man walking alone down an aisle. He is pushing a wagon filled with stuff and carrying an armload of cans. I can't see his face. As he moves toward a deserted checkout line his shoe is about to make contact with the puddle on the floor and I yell out a warning. "Jesus, watch it. Stop. Freeze."

Homer and Lance roar. The shopper ignores me. His foot hits the oil spill. He flies. He vaults over his cart, the stuff he carries rises in air, then crashes onto the counter as his head smashes the product scanner's glass plate. He jackknifes and rolls over on his back. His face is a splash of blood. I see that the face is mine. I reel. Lance shores me up.

"Nicely done," Homer says. Now he applauds.

The bloody shopper sits up, then stands and comes forward. He holds his hand out. Homer shakes it, then wipes his own hand with a silk handkerchief. It is blotched red.

"James, meet Marvin Arch, the best stuntman in Hollywood."

"I blew it," Arch says. "I should have ended up with my nose on the floor and my ass in the air. But it wasn't bad."

"It was fabulous," Lance says. "Very convincing."

"It gets better," Arch says. He pulls a rubber mask off his face. I am the mask. Marvin Arch is a nice looking kid with a crew cut and a soda fountain face.

"Thank you," Homer says. "That was Oscar quality."

"There will be fine-tuning," Arch says.

"Don't change a thing," Lance says.

"Wrong. Get it right," Homer says. "I trust your instincts."

"Should I go again? One more time?"

We watch Marvin Arch decimate himself three more times. By the third time I am making suggestions. He is reasonable about taking direction though he fights me about where his left leg should end up.

"The leg should definitely twist at a 40-degree angle from the pelvis," I say in the elevator going up.

"The man is a professional," Homer says. "Leave him some leeway. Pride goeth after the pratfall." Lance laughs hysterically. Homer likes that. I laugh too. My laugh is not competitive.

"It will be perfectly timed," Homer says when we are alone in his office. "You . . . he . . . will go shopping with Trina. History will repeat itself. You . . . he . . . will be rushed to Mercy General and into surgery. You will come out bandaged as a boiled baby."

"That's terrible. A boiled baby?"

"You get my meaning. You will be taken to recovery by the same Dr. Zipper. In a few days when they unwrap you, selah! Your

Code is restored."

"Who is going to accept . . . ?"

"Who is going to protest? Miracles are everybody's dessert. Of course, the actual operation can't be performed at Mercy General. That's arranged too. Lance will fill in the details."

"Let me get this straight. I get the surgery done. The marvelous accident happens. I switch places with Arch and I walk out cured. Restored. Resurrected. Whatever."

"Correct."

"And the witnesses? Forgetting you and Lance. There's the stuntman. The doctor. Maybe a nurse or two. What guarantee . . . ?"

"Marvin Arch gets star billing in a major motion picture. Or he gets mangled by a pickup truck on his way to get laid. Dr. Zipper wants a house on Nantucket. And a grant for his very own research institute. He gets the house and the grant or he gets lead poured into his anal cavity. Don't worry about the nurses. No problem with them."

"How can I be a party to fraud and threat? Homer, I really appreciate all this but I've come to terms with things. There's a strange peace that accompanies acquiescence. I can't violate my nature. I . . ."

A *flash, a slash, a crash.* I am hearing Zupkin and Ms. Blotnik telling me how it will all come clear.

"Homer, Homer, Homer. You reached Trina's psychic? Is that it? You bought Ms. Blotnik? You bullied a five thousand year old corpse? All these years Trina has been getting advice and guidance from the spirit world and the spirit is you?"

"I don't know what you're raving about, James."

"Bite your tongue. Or at least have Marvin Arch bite his tongue for you. It can't be a coincidence, a flash, slash and crash. And I don't buy the occult explanation. You were protecting your investment, setting me up."

"What I do I do out of love."

"How long has your own daughter been going to a fixed psychic?"

"Wait until your children grow. It isn't easy. Don't be holier than thou. What harm was there? She wouldn't listen to me."

"I gather that since she married me. What happened? Didn't Ms. Blotnik give her fair warning? Didn't Zupkin come down from the Cairo Hilton with forebodings?"

"Trina ignored all signals, James. It was nothing personal. You have always been a son to me. I just wanted her to be sure. Overcoming obstacles is the way to happiness and joy."

"Happiness and joy. Homer, Homer, Homer."

"You can't tell Trina. Promise that much."

"Or what? What can you do to a can of pea soup? You'd think of something. But don't worry. I won't tell her. Not because of you. It would break her heart. What can be more sacred to a woman than her own reader adviser? I can't pull that rug out from under my own wife."

"You're making sense, son. And admit that my heart is in the right place."

"What place? Homer, today never happened."

"You're being a schmuck liberal. Think it over, Jim. You have only one life to give for your country."

Trina sits inside a robe I hate. It is made of thick padded pinkish cloth, the kind coat hangers are wrapped in. There are queasy flowers woven into the design. It is the kind of fabric that reminds me of death, a chic shroud.

Folders and a map are spread on the Deco cocktail table. I have circled likely towns on the map. Some are in exotic places, others not too far from recognizable centers of culture and commerce.

That afternoon when I left Homer's office I went to my own for no particular reason. A file had been placed in the center of my desk. It contained the map and the folders along with a report marked CONFIDENTIAL. FOR YOUR EYES ONLY.

"I have no definite idea of who put it there. I doubt it was your father, not after what happened. I suspect his secretary. Maybe there is an ounce of compassion left in that sun-dried tomato. Whoever it was, it came as a revelation."

"You are telling me you believe whole cities exist for the sole purpose of covering up coding errors?"

"Exactly. And it makes sense. I never thought about it because I never had to. But even the best encoders are machines and machines mess up."

"What if it is true though I don't buy it. Say it was half true. So? Something has to be done with the discards."

"The point isn't true or not true. The point is this may be the miracle Ms. Blotnik predicted. A place for me to go. Like the thalidomide towns they built in the late 20th Century for kids born with flippers instead of appendages. Or the leper colonies before that. Those places weren't talked about either."

"There's enough unpleasantness in the world. What would be the purpose of talking about them?"

"Look at the locations and the pictures. They seem very nice, very comfortable. From reading the report I conclude that Brogg Engineering built the social halls and swimming pools on a contract from the Global Commission. And I wouldn't be surprised if the name Introspection Gardens didn't come from Brogg Public Relations."

"You would have heard."

"Why? There's plenty I don't know about. Homer is involved with projects even he's forgotten. Look, honey, I know we're not talking mainstream. But this could be a new beginning for all of us. There must be some job open in administration. It says the schools are excellent and that there are ample recreational facilities. I have no doubt you'd find a niche."

"A niche? You have no doubt I would find a niche?"

"We would be together."

"You were offered a practical miracle and you turned Daddy down."

"Miracles shouldn't be practical. And it was the most cynical kind of fraud. There is still such a thing as morality even if it dangles by a nosehair from the tip of a crescent moon."

"It would have worked."

"How could I face you and the children? There are deeper issues here. The simple truth is that a workable society is essential. Nothing is worth jeopardizing the harmony. Certainly not any single individual. If there must be losers and I turn out to be one of them then so be it."

"You want your son and daughter brought up in a village of

doom? You want their friends to be Voided?"

"Alright. We could send the kids to boarding school for a while. Until they adjust."

"Adjust? Right now Amos is barricaded in his room. He won't come out. If there was a fire he would cook to a crisp. And Amanda won't eat because she confuses her father with lunch. Her therapist is frightened for her."

"Amanda will be fine. She's got your spunk. Amos too. He's got my weed blood. They're survivors."

"It would have been so easy."

"Easy isn't always the answer. Easy is the problem. Listen, the people living in the Introspection Gardens aren't criminals. They're victims. Accidents like me. I belong with them now. And you'll love living in a new environment. You always talk about the need for mobility and change."

"I am a very social person, Jim. I like big cities. And I want Amos and Amanda to have every chance. Look what they stand to inherit."

"Would any of that be different? They're still Homer's grandchildren. He dotes on them."

"He wants them near him where he can manipulate them."

"Clone them."

"They should be so lucky."

"That is debatable. But I don't want to get into a silly argument. I know what I'm asking here. It's hard to explain. When I left Hoffenstein I was numb. I sat watching the ocean for hours. I heard my own whale songs. This was all meant to be. It's not a sentence, it's an escape. This could be the best thing that's ever happened to us. Why don't you see it?"

"What I see is my husband sniveling in a corner. You may want to be a human footnote but I want my life to be the frothy thing it was. I don't want to look at travel folders for Masturbation Gardens."

"That was low."

"This is lower. This is right in the balls. We'll leave you. You'll never see us again. I'm talking more than divorce. I'm talking oblivion."

"You can't be serious."

"I am very serious."

"Is that why you wore that pukish thing? With the repulsive

little blooms. A vision of Christmas yet to be?"

"Make your choice."

"Bottom line? Ultimatum?"

"You heard."

"At least you could have seduced instead of gouged."

"I will not be married to pea soup."

"Well, then. Take a deep breath and hold it. Because I am going to tell you something I shouldn't tell you. It demeans me even to say this but I want you to sweat. Homer has your Ms. Blotnik in his pocket. He has his hand up her insight. He's got your friend Zupkin by the pyramids."

"Of course he has. You think I don't know my own Daddy?"

I step over a drunk. Lance vaults the body. His agility is mildly interesting. I am so conflicted everything is blurred.

"You're doing the right thing. When Trina told me you were ready for the land of cripples and rainbows I suspected brain death."

We are in Soho, the only roundeyes on the street. Hundreds of Japanese stream in and out of the art galleries carrying paintings or making entries into calculators.

"I should have come alone. No sense putting you in danger."

"There is no danger. And this is me you're talking to."

"Well, thanks. And for taking the kids to the park. It's a hard time for them and for Trina. She never felt anxiety before."

"All that is past history by tonight. You get your skull fixed, we do your miracle. Fini."

"Fini."

"You know, you probably could have stuffed Ms. Hoffenstein. I wouldn't mind sticking it to Resurrection."

"I told you she loves the owl. Code E. *Semper fidelus.*"

"Warm honey. Dedicated, concentrated, lubricated. My first lay was Code E. Muriel Somebody. A screamer. On a hay ride. A screamer on a hay ride. You know what hay feels like on a bare ass? Shark teeth. Look over there. That's where you're going."

Lance points to a gallery across West Broadway. The Edwina Gallery of Fine Art.

"An art gallery?"

"There's art and there's art. They come highly recommended. Don't worry. We did market research."

"For sixty thousand they should be good."

"James, you can still hang a curve and turn back. It's your future. But if I was you I'd get my nose out from between my legs. Be Proud of Your Code."

"No turning back. I learned something about myself. There is only so much James P. Wander can give up."

"Nobody sane would go the other route. Nobody blames you for anything. The whole repair job should take about an hour. I'll be waiting. Remember your name is Mr. Water and you ask for Franklin. If there's any muck up or any doubt just get out of there fast."

"Lance, I want you to know how much . . ."

"So you owe me. Now I am gone. I know nothing about any of this. I'm down here buying a Picasso for over the sofa. It's got to have pink in it."

I cross against the light. The powers that be get one more chance. A cab swerves around me with the driver cursing in Middle East. But I am spared for some reason.

The Edwina Gallery features a show called A Joint Like This. It is a celebration of elbows, knees, necks, spines, ankles and fingers. There are paintings and sculptures and kinetic pieces. In the center of the gallery is a foot with video toenails flashing celebrity faces while the toes wiggle to electronic music. The fact is, it's not a bad show.

A Code P girl says "Hello," from behind a counter made from an old-fashioned X-Ray, a clever touch. "Don't you feel that our artists show a cultivated inclination to worship nature in her most functional aspects? Would you like to see a catalog?"

"Actually no. I'm here to see Franklin."

"I don't think we have a Franklin but we do have sushi and Sapporo Dry. Can I offer you something?"

"Please indulge me and see if you can find a Franklin. Tell him Mr. Water is here."

The girl shrugs, bows and tucks in behind a standing screen which is a large lithograph of a primate. I browse. I have always envied artists. The idea of finding a metaphor for life in a knuckle or less dazzles my linear mind. I never understood why artists are coded M but I suspect it has to do with Hoffenstein. He programmed the Prime Mother Computer. Being a scientist one would expect some hostility.

I focus on the toes. Was the artist saying that even the most illustrious are subject to indignities like athlete's foot? Or is the statement grander, involving support of the generic social arch? It strikes me as ironic that the arch in my support system is making ready to impale himself at the Food Forest checkout with my wife trailing after him. Trina will give an award-winning performance. That will happen in a matter of hours once I have been made into the man I was. Am. Neither of the above.

The gallery girl returns smiling. I see that she is wearing a silver body stocking that gives her the look of a trophy. Black sleeves flow from the glitter ornamented with abstract sinews and bones. I smile back at her.

"I found a Franklin. Please follow me."

I go past the primate screen and down a thin staircase. We sidestep stacked canvas and shrouded statuary. It is like Hoffenstein's room. The unplugged electric sculptures are my personal metaphor. I am vapor. Trina is my socket, my plasma.

The girl stops abruptly before a green circle painted on brick. She tells me to remove my hat and I do. She winces. If she winces I can imagine my impact on young children. My eyes brim for Amos and Amanda. How could I have expected them to embrace me?

The girl steps back.

I am scanned by a human eye peering through a circle in the circle. Crows fly through my bowels. Am I questioning the equipment or the crime? I have never done anything really terrible. My felonies were unintentional and involved affairs of the heart. Such wounds heal. This crime is without forgiveness.

Code Alteration rips the flesh off the planet. A hole is left, a divot that refuses repair. I have read about people caught doing what I am about to do and I remember my feelings of rage beyond rage. There is no capital punishment anymore. In his Dictums, Hoffenstein speaks out strongly against the death penalty. "Termination is admission of defeat. A perpetrator deserving of inflicted death is best punished by prolonged life. Once ultimate judgment is passed each tick of the clock is anguish. Let us punish the condemned with time that burns like acid rain." I have learned the Dictums by rote as have we all and I have lived by them. Standing there being scanned by a single brown eye I think of Lance on a mattress of hay stinging Muriel Somebody even as he is stung by hard grass. Is any memory pure pleasure? Is any crime beyond redemption?

No surprise, the circle is a door. I enter an artist's studio. A middle-aged man in a smock and beret is absorbed with the image of a stunning model sitting naked in a tub. She holds a ceramic jug and a bunch of grapes. I know when I am being had.

"I am Franklin," the artist says laying down a brush. He picks up the brush again and daubs a lip. "The lump in the tub is Ashton. I can only assume you are here because one of our works interests you. Yes, they are for sale. You brought cash? Visa is the opiate of the people."

"Yes, one of the works interests me and yes, I brought cash."

I hand him an envelope. He thumbs the bills.

Franklin gestures to Ashton. She leaves the tub, towels off, then begins a conversion of the space. The canvas flips on its easel to become a table. The skimpy light hanging over it brightens to an arc. A tabouret holding paints splits and swivels to a cabinet filled with surgical tools. The tub drains, is disconnected from its plumbing and slides on rails. Under it is a pit and out of the pit comes a device rigged with tanks, tubes and a mask. A chest revolves to become a cardiograph.

"Nicely done," I say. "Now what?"

"Ashton, put on your nice white uniform. She is your blood type, Mr. Water, should transfusion be necessary. That would entail an additional charge. The going rate is four thousand a pint or any part thereof. She has been screened for anything communicable except affection. Are we in agreement?"

"No problem."

Ashton has put on a skirt decorated with a red cross. She is less distracting though her breasts hang bare. Franklin hands me a hospital gown. There are imbedded brown stains on the front.

"It is clean to a fare-thee-well. Put microbes out of your thoughts. The report I have says you have no allergy to eggs. Is that accurate?"

"Accurate."

"Good. Scramble two, hold the fries. Gallows humor to put you at ease. They usually laugh."

"My sense of humor is on hold."

"Did you bring a recent prior?"

"A what?"

"Prior photograph."

"In my jacket. Inside pocket."

Ashton finds the photo. She lets out a whoosh of air.

"She didn't know we have an A+. You're our first. It is a kind of fulfillment. In honor of the occasion I will wash both hands. Take his vitals."

Ashton checks my pressure and flattens me on the table. I am wired to the cardiograph. I hear the flush of a toilet from where Franklin presumably is washing both hands. He returns gloved, dips into one of his trays, waves a hypodermic, inserts a vial, squeezes out excess air. "You'll feel an instant of agony and after that, Los Angeles. I envy you your euphoria. Ashton will gently but expertly place the mask over your nose or whatever you prefer to breathe through. Our anesthesia today is dioxitrome, fresh from the lab, served with a hint of nitrous oxide. Are we ready? Good. Strap Mr. Water to the table. Be firm. We don't want him flailing around."

"Just do the job."

Ashton locks me to the board with leather thongs.

"A serious man. Intense. Relax. It amazes me that more people don't come in for a trim. It's incredibly painless. I guess the prospect of life in prison balances the prospect of life in prison if you get my subtle message."

The hypo spears my arm.

"Brave beast," Franklin says. "They don't make them like you anymore."

"Tell me something. Doesn't the possibility of life in prison dampen your enthusiasm?"

"Oh, it gives me pause. Mr. Water, this may hurt but the truth is you are not my first. My motto is risk or rust."

Ashton masks my face. The light blazes. I see Franklin fingering a scalpel. I try to tell him to wait but I begin to blot. I hear myself crack apart. Which joint was it? I hear myself scream. Why do I have a woman's voice? I see Ashton's breasts swing across what is left of vision.

The mask is pulled away.

My straps release.

Can I sit up? Is it finished?

I am slapped across the cheeks.

"Get him vertical. Cuff the son-of-a-bitch."

My recently liberated arms are yanked behind me. I look down at my video toes. They look up with blank faces.

"Watch the butterfly. He's trying to swallow something."

I hear retching.

"It was only a valium," Franklin says. "Do I look like Eva Braun?"

"You have the right to remain silent," the voice says. "Use it."

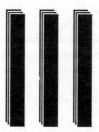

I AM sent away for observation.

It takes some doing. The raid on the Edwina Gallery is well covered by the media. When they take me out there are TV cameras, a clot of reporters, flashbulbs like exploding eyes. In twilight sleep, I enjoy going public.

I see the news on a portable TV. Trina and the children are rushed into a Brogg limo with *no comment*. There is a brief interview with Dr. Hoffenstein who says he sensed malevolence during our meeting but still, he is shocked that I chose such a path considering my position. By then the anesthesia is wearing thin. Reason returns. Was it Lance who tipped them? Or Homer?

They will not release me on bail because I am not a person. Charlton Hymn arranges that a deposit will be accepted as a suitable substitute. When I get home only the maid is waiting. She quits.

Charlton convinces me to cop a plea. I don't know what it cost but they mark me for observation instead of jail. He tells me Trina and the kids are traveling abroad. I will hear from them when things quiet down.

"Observation can last for years. You may never do actual time inside, James."

"Maybe they could send me to one of those Introspection Gardens."

"Don't go near that can of worms. Those places don't officially exist. You have too much notoriety. When the limelight wanes, who can say?"

"You will keep working on it? I may not survive a madhouse."

"Madhouse is rather extreme. Hamish Farm is a rehabilitation center for the offspring of the wealthy. You know how often they go crazy. And because you're a ward of the state you'll be there on scholarship. The usual fee is a million a year before therapy. I'm rather pleased with myself for pulling this off and you should be nothing but grateful."

"I am."

"You crossed a line of no crossing. I can't begin to imagine what possessed you. I can understand desperation but not Alteration. Did you realize the consequences?"

"Absolutely."

"If you would agree to name names, admit that you fell under organized Slime influence."

"It would be a lie to implicate anyone. I acted alone. Of sound mind."

"Not so loud. Your mental condition will be evaluated at Hamish Farm. Don't give them cause to make any decisions. The best policy is for you to reverse on Tuesday what you tell them on Monday. Keep them guessing and they'll keep observing, *ad infinitum*. Of course, if they mark you as a terminal nut case you can be shipped to a real asylum. Wet sheets, fog pills and electricity. Walk the wire, James. Everyone wants you to be happy at Hamish Farm. The place is respectable, your confinement there vindicates the family and the Farm itself gets a guaranteed income for your shelflife."

My shelflife begins on a splendid day in early Summer. I am shipped from New York to Massachusetts in the back of a small delivery van. They crate me in a minimum security carton that is actually quite comfortable. The driver, a cop, can observe me on closed circuit TV. He is generous by nature and glad to describe the passing scenery.

"The sky is baby blue. The new leafs is out. And the cocksuckers said rain."

We drive up the Taconic, then onto the Mass Pike toward the Berkshires.

"Gorgeous hills. We just passed a lake with people swimming. I give you it is beautiful up here but not my cup of shit. I'll take the city, don't ask me why. We just passed a cow and some horses. You see those things and you realize there's more to life than having a Slime wipe a snotrag over your windshield. But I still vote for the city. I must be crazier than you. Trees, grass, trees, grass."

By early evening we pull into the town of West Stockton.

"The fucking moon is up. With the sun still out. Can you imagine? They must get this every day. And the air smells invigorating. So why don't I move my ass up here and sit counting stars? Tell me I'm a classic schmuck. We got to find Dean Street."

We find Dean Street, home of Hamish Farm which is not a farm but a cluster of buildings practically in the town center.

"If you expected goats and sheep forget it. It's like a hotel. I only see bars on a few windows. And they got a nice gate. But generally speaking a person could honeymoon here. Listen, when we go inside I don't want any kind of trouble. You with me?"

"Can you remove the cuffs?"

"Hey, I appreciate the offer but no thanks. Do I look like the asshole my wife says I am? No special favors and don't pull rank on me. I keep a detached attitude and I can't be reached. To me you're just another piece of merchandise."

The back of the van is opened and I am helped out of my box. I get my balance after a minute. We march up white steps. I see three girls slouched in wicker chairs and two adolescent boys reading magazines on a comfortable screened porch. Nobody pays us attention.

I go through an arched door into a reception area where a wide woman waits behind a counter.

"Delivery," the cop says. "JEAH 731. I need a receipt."

"A few minutes, please."

"I hope a few minutes. I got to get back to New York tonight."

The receptionist makes a call. An attendant comes for me. A V, barely evolved. I insist that my special status be described clearly and the cop hands over my folder. The woman reads aloud that despite my Code I am to be accorded treatment as a marginal person during the court-ordered period of observation. The attendant is on overload. I see a throbbing at her temples.

I am uncuffed as a receipt for me is issued by a computer. I try to stretch my arms but the attendant whose name is Bernie folds them at my sides. He is told to take me to Room 33 in Wing L. A plastic tag with that information is clipped around my left wrist. I am told it must never be removed. I thank my transporter who shrugs and leaves, folding his receipt.

Bernie guides me along corridors of Lysol-smelling linoleum, past polished doors, up a banistered, carpeted staircase to a hallway with flowered walls. When we reach Room 33 Bernie produces an ancient key. I remember such keys from little hotels in Cape Cod or on the Vineyard where Trina and I went in the good years before Amos and Amanda were born. One of my children might have been conceived in a room with a lock that took that kind of key. My eyes water as Bernie opens the door. Then he hands the key to me which comes as a surprise.

"When you leave the room, lock up. There are creeps in this place. You never know."

"What about the rules. There must be rules."

Bernie punches me in the gut.

"The rules," he says, then he leaves.

When he goes the lock snaps. The key doesn't work from inside. I realize that giving me the key is a device to build confidence without taking risk. If I was neurotic or psychotic I think I would take genuine satisfaction from having my own key in my own pocket.

My room is pleasant. There is an honest oak bed covered with a green quilt. The walls echo the soft green. Near the bed is a table holding a lamp, radio and clock. I have a staunch bureau with large drawers and legs carved into animal paws. Gold-leaf Cupids link arms to legs around an oval mirror. The floor is carpeted in dark grey. A Norman Cradle print showing a shy boy looking at a plump, budding girl sucking chocolate soda through a peppermint straw hangs near the bureau. I see that my curtained window is unbarred. I can look out at the town. It is a postcard of small stores, strolling citizens, trees with thick trunks and copious leaves. In the road, a single traffic light hangs from a wire issuing sensible commands.

A book has been left on the bed. Its title: *Hamish Farm, Your*

Stability Place. The first page says only: Hello! The second page is a full portrait of Dr. Isaac Hamish, Ph.D. He welcomes me with a wise face that has come to terms with plenty. A full, curly beard hangs from the face. It compensates for a bald head. The beard has a calming effect, a tranquil black sea wisped with foam on which Isaac Hamish floats like a buoy. I turn to page 3:

> Hamish Farm is a get-well establishment dedicated to your recovery of peace through insight. Our approach is holistic. Our philosophy of total therapy has its deep roots in the body of work created by artist Norman Cradle who lived only a few miles from this very place! Cradle defined a universe of the wonderful, practical and possible—a world of "the inspired quotidian" framed within inevitable borders.

I turn to page 4 and there is Norman Cradle, an elfin fellow seated at his easel. Though he died before coding he has been granted the honor of a Retroactive Code as Generic Immortal. The usual graphic chromosomes that define identity have been eliminated. The Code communicates only that Cradle, Norman was an American artist in the 20th Century.

A chime sounds. I hear noises from the corridor. Since there is no panic I assume it is not a fire drill but the call to dinner. I am famished and shocked by my own appetite. I have not eaten much for months. I wash in the tiny bathroom linked to my room and when I think to powder my Code I realize my bag has not yet been delivered. I go to the door and wait for Bernie to come get me. Nobody comes. Finally I try the knob and the door opens. The hallway is empty so I retrace the path that got me there.

Two flights down, my ears pick up the clink of dishes and jingle of flatware. That beacon leads me to the dining room. I am greeted by a host dressed in a black tie. He fans my bracelet over a scanner and leads me to a table.

The room is impressive. There are a hundred tables hooded with pink cloth and set with silver and crystal. Conversation is a low buzz. Most of the diners are not much older than my own children. There are exceptions and I discover with pleasure that I am not the oldest. I define patches of white hair among the adolescent pates.

My table is already occupied. The only chair is tagged with my number and the word SOUP, both bits of information done in marvelous calligraphy. I sit, smiling at my tablemates. They have waited for my arrival. The first course, fruit compote, is untouched at every place. When I sit they begin to eat.

I do the same while checking out my companions. To my left is a man who must be eighty, maybe ninety or a hundred and five. His hands quake as he spoons grapefruit wedges into a thin mouth. Each voyage of the utensil is terrible suspense but his quivering is brilliantly orchestrated. When his fingers spasm out his head tilts in and the fruit ends up where it should. To his right an ample girl of twenty or so, a mound of curves and crevices, has already devoured the strawberry crown that caps the compote. A black man of about my age eyes her plate with detached disdain. He is saving his berry for last and eats around it, narrowing the compote's base. After each swallow, he taps his face with a linen napkin. To his left is another young girl as thin as the key in my pants. She has begun her meal by picking at a comma of orange and she chews it in dreamtime. As I dip in, I see the plump girl take what is left of the skeleton's appetizer. The old man rolls out a burp. The black man wipes his mouth twice. We finish the fruit without introductions or conversation. While I taste a wedge of honeydew I decide to break the ice.

"My name is Jim Wander. It's nice to meet you all."

"We don't use names," the old man says. "You are who your chair says you are. Who you think you are is of no consequence. At Hamish Farm we are all part of a tapestry and while the shapes and colors may change over time each minute is shaped by an inevitable border. Didn't you read the book? You think it's some kind of joke?"

"Please bear with me. This is my first day."

"Every day is everyone's first day," the old man says. "I have been here six years but it is my first day and my first hour. I am drawn and redrawn by the artist within myself. And don't scan me. Our Codes are in limbo and of no importance. Scanning is considered impolite. Lucky for you, if you ask me."

"Sorry. Reflex. It won't happen again."

"All of us have clashed. Before Codes become a factor again we must experience Infrasmile. Read your book. It's all laid out."

The waitress comes with a tray of salad. We go about the

business of eating. The old man grins at a pimento as he navigates it across empty space. The black man isolates slices of avocado and concentrates on the romaine. The tubby girl spears a tomato while her wispy sister munches a carrot stick. I wait for her leftovers to be appropriated by the rotund scavenger.

"Delicious dressing," I say, still trying to stimulate talk. The others nod. It is the same at most tables. Dinner is a somber affair.

My eyes skim the room. It could be a banquet. I notice a girl at the next table. She is Trina's negative: dark, black hair, a long bird face, enormous eyes, slender figure. As she lifts a glass of water to her lips her fellow diners push back their seats and lift their napkins like shields. They wait for her to swallow the water, then drop the napkins into their laps. Then she spits a stream of water with amazing accuracy hitting two of the four other faces that watch her. There is no outcry or protest. They simply blot. She laughs. I haven't heard a girl laugh since forever and I find myself chortling in sympathetic vibration.

"For God sakes don't encourage her," says the grey eminence. "Next thing she farts or vomits. Look the other way. She can crap at will. They're giving up on her and they don't give up easily."

Our cornucopia waitress returns with a rack of lamb, baked potatoes flecked with paprika, steamed broccoli, a tub of sour cream and a bowl of chives. A freckled busboy takes our salad plates. I chew the perfect lamb remembering that I am here for criminal behavior. The meal concludes with sherbet and demitasse. The disgusting girl is mashing the sherbet in her palms and spreading it on her cheeks. Otherwise, there is no distraction. For a madhouse, I expected worse.

After dinner there is a mandatory recreation period. I pass up ping-pong, billiards and library for the TV Salon. The issue under tube debate is Specialized Productivity Zones which happens to be one of Homer's messianic causes. Under the proposed plan nations would be called on to do what they do best.

Manufacturing of hard goods would be left to America, Japan, Russia, Germany, Korea and China. England and France would become Diversionary Centers responsible for art, literature, gastronomy, and associated delights. Like Australia, Scandinavia would be allowed its film industry along with some provision for agriculture and mining. The Third World and the Middle East would have the responsibility of providing News. South America would become a food producer as the petroleum industry is phased out in keeping with the Sky Repair Project and the rain forest would be restored. South Africa would continue to supply gold and diamonds if that nation agreed to the Added Value Provisions under which a certain percentage of all minorities would be coded as precious metals or jewels thus eliminating a major poverty problem and conveying a new sense of worth.

It is only a matter of time before the Specialized Productivity Zones are implemented though opponents still mouth atavistic arguments about competition and patriotism. Of course they are no more than lobbyists for the past, representatives of entrenched interests fearful of any change. Their voices are eroded by necessity and soon they will capitulate.

"Then who gets the crackers?"

My ancient tablemate has flopped into the chair beside mine. He rubs his hands together to increase circulation.

"I don't think crackers are on the agenda."

"You think I don't know what they're talking about? I know exactly. So I am asking who gets the firecracker business? The whole thing is a setup to give firecrackers to the Italians. Look at my bracelet. Know who you are talking to."

He holds out his arm, I read, Morris Feuerbloom.

"Does it ring a bell?"

"Not exactly. It sounds familiar but I can't place it."

"The Explosive Jew? Does that remind you?"

"I'm sorry."

"I am the head of the Fireflower Corporation. A legend in pyrotechnics. The *Daily News* headline called me The Explosive Jew."

"Fireflower. Yes, of course."

"Fireflower, Feuerbloom, same thing. My whole family was tremendous in the business for centuries. Thanks to me they still are but they don't deserve it. My sons run the operation now and they'll run it into the ground. They had me certified to get the factory. I could be a play for Shakespeare."

Feuerbloom speaks with passion. His face begins to blotch.

"I think you should calm yourself."

"Why? I want to die. Not watching TV. On my own terms, to make a statement."

"You can't mean that."

"Don't tell me what I mean. The only thing left inside my shell is a furious soul. You want to know why? They compromised, the whole pansy bunch of them. They sold out. They worry something is going to blow up. They talk only about insurance."

"You're ahead of me."

"Since the Middle Ages Feuerbloom productions made celebrations for kings, queens, emperors, czars. Believe me, in those days it wasn't easy for a Jew to get gunpowder or a contract. But we did it. We were number one. Number one. Naturally, we blew up a few times. In pyrotechnics, accidents are wedded to beauty. A town, a village, once a castle. We lost a few dozen workers and some cousins. Nothing major. Did it stop us? We moved to another country and started again from scratch with a few fuses. But since one lousy blast on Long Island the whole family goes around sniffling, 'God forbid there should be trouble.' And they take no risks. Instead of going after inaugurations or July 4th they book bar mitzvahs, weddings, malls, holidays I wouldn't spit on. Do I know shame? My incredible creations like the Fireflower Spectacular sit in a warehouse with cement walls five feet thick. I designed bombs and rockets to make the moon a 60-watt bulb in a whorehouse. My children and grandchildren make sparklers and things that whiz around and go *put-put-put*. They don't want people to know we exist. And they call that *image. Positioning the market.* I call it bullshit."

"I come from Long Island. Sag Harbor. What part did you blow up?"

"That's all you can think about? A few lousy acres near Glen Cove? Big deal. Twelve locals and an aunt, a small housing project of split levels. That was the whole casualty list. Measured against centuries of success. I took all the blame. I volunteered for scapegoat but I had nothing to do with it. But when I tried to kill myself to

quiet down the papers and planning boards and troublemakers who
wanted to shut us down they sent me up here. With *meshuggena*
kiddies. I would rather be dead ten times but even Death wouldn't
give me a break. So now I'm crazy and everything is fine. A crazy
old man tried to blow up Long Island. End of story. But the mind
never stops working and I got plans, my friend. What are you here
for?"

"Observation."

"Let me rephrase the question. Why are you here?"

"It's a long story. Not as interesting as yours."

"Clam up. Fine. Whatever. You're lucky to be in Wing L. They
consider us harmless. You can even walk around outside as long as
you get back for meals. Wing X is another story. Don't ask. Violents.
They never come out. I envy them. I would be there if I was your
age but now I can't even rip a napkin."

"They keep me locked in my room."

"Only for the first few days. While they make sure of you. Social
climbers try to get in here to make contacts. They got to be on their
toes. You play pinochle?"

"I'm not much of a card player."

"Bad luck."

"What about the others at our table?"

"Please. The main thing is never talk about anybody else. If
information comes knocking, take it. But ask no questions and you
wouldn't be a Norman."

"Meaning what?"

"I didn't say a word. *Vay is mir*, look who came in."

The dark girl enters and squats in front of the set. She reaches
a hand under her skirt and scratches some itch. Morris Feuerbloom
pushes out of his chair.

"I can't watch her. She gives me heartburn. Nice meeting you."

I am alone in the room with the squatter. The news is over. We
watch a Western. I have seen the film with Amos. An Apache chief
condemns the use of pesticides on his reservation. After a plague of
locusts he comes to realize that chemicals help more than they harm.
Because of his prolonged ethnic sulk he fails to reach full Code
Potential but with the help of a compassionate sheriff's daughter he
triumphs over personal prejudices and later has huge success making
authentic Indian bracelets. In the final scene one of his turquoise

squashblossoms is presented to the head of the Hemisphere Caucus. The story is supposedly true but I assume the writer took liberties. Still, it is a moving film.

The girl is involved. She wipes tears from her cheeks. When the film ends, the set turns itself off and the lights blink. Recreation is ended.

"You seemed to enjoy the picture," I say. "The noble savage. It always gets to you. We're never too old for a solid Western."

She holds out her hand, the same hand I have watched scratching privates for ninety minutes. I shake it.

"Jill," she says.

"Jim."

She spits on my shoe.

Bernie comes to my room before breakfast to inform me that I have an appointment with Dr. Bartley Hamish. I finish dressing. Bernie sits on my bed fingering the shirt I laid out. He picks threads from my monogram.

"No initials, crests, animals or graven images of any kind." The thread won't give so he rips off the pocket.

"Was that necessary?"

"No."

Outside Dr. Hamish's office Bernie kicks me in the ankle. The pain rolls up my leg. He opens the office door and shoves me inside. I see that the black man who shares my table sits at a small desk thumbing through folders.

"Dr. Hamish will be with you in a moment. Please have a seat." There is no sign of recognition.

I sit on a mission bench. A large tank of tropical fish bubbles in a corner. I know psychiatrists often use tropicals as reception room tranquilizers. I watch the rainbows swim. They are slivers of music, their shadows gliding over a porcelain mermaid who perches on the bow of a sunken galleon. I am the ship, Trina the mermaid, the fish are old songs and cherished memories.

There is a *Wall Street Journal* on the bench. I browse the stock tables, mesmerizing as the fish, and discover that I am richer. Brogg is up five dollars. News of the Global Council has energized the financial markets. I swim through the lake of numbers checking other investments. Everything I own is at a new high.

"You may go in now."

Dr. Bartley Hamish is younger than I expected. He is rosy-cheeked, trim, with an open face and his grandfather's beard. His hair is intact, nobody is bald anymore except by choice, his eyes are confrontational brown. He wears a red sweater, tan pants and sneakers. The sweater's color bounces light. I would have opted for something less combative.

I get a strong handshake, too strong, and I wonder if subtle intimidation is the message. But he says, "Scan me. Let's be up-front with each other."

Code A. Born in West Stockton. Age thirty-four. Qualified for three children. A talent for athletics. A generally positive profile.

"Your receptionist is a tablemate," I say for openers.

"Bill Maginot. Not the warmest person. But he does the job."

"Maginot? French?"

"He made up the name. After a fortification in World War II. It was billed as the supreme deterrent but the Nazis ate it like Camembert."

"I know about the Maginot Line."

"Not many do. It suits him perfectly. Our friend is surrounded by imaginary barriers and attitudes. He's here on scholarship, like you. Fascinating case. Stole a garbage truck, said God told him to, and disposed of a substantial section of his home town. We were fortunate to get him. If they ever pass the Added Value Provisions he'll be worth his weight in platinum."

"It might be years away."

"We try to fatten him up just in case. He's kept in a sedentary job and forbidden excessive activity but his metabolism is as cantankerous as his personality. Still, if things tip in the right direction he would be a huge asset to our balance sheet."

"My father-in-law is very active in the Value Added lobby. He feels that it would end slum violence in addition to solving the cash flow problems for whole nations."

"But we still hear liberals mew about the consequences of an end to welfare payments and subsidies. To make a liability an asset is the highest concept of economic intervention. With one stroke of a pen millions would have an immediate market worth. And a new sense of pride and purpose. I can't understand the objections."

"From my present status I can understand the resistance to becoming a commodity."

"Nobody would become a commodity. Simply more negotiable. I'm as much a humanitarian as the next guy. But we aren't here to talk politics."

"No, I suppose I was fighting a delaying action. Something like asking a surgeon how's the family. Holding off pain."

"Very perceptive. And, hopefully, receptive. Soup, frankly we've never had one like you. I don't even know of a precedent. I'm really delighted to have you with us."

"You said we could be up-front here. I'm sure you were subjected to considerable pressure to accept me."

"Yes and no. You have important connections but so do most of the others. Of course none of them has attempted Alteration. None of them is denied Return. For them, Hamish Farm is a transition. For you it can be a destiny. Unless you force my hand."

"I have no intention of forcing your hand, Dr. Hamish, and not only because of the alternatives. Let me try to explain. Before recent events, I was content with the Matrix. I considered myself a lucky man. But I also accept the need for law and order and the faint possibility that a so-called accident is a cosmic road sign. So my only concern is fitting in, making a contribution while I'm here."

"*While I'm here.* You said it, I didn't. You have got to get past that kind of thinking. There is no other place for you."

"Yes, well, I might get the idea in twenty years or so."

"For your sake and mine, I hope it's a lot sooner. As for work, we will begin with a basic assignment to our factory. After you demonstrate compliance and ability, there is the chance for a move to the gift shop. But first things first. You must select your painting."

"Select my painting?"

Dr. Hamish reaches under his desk and pulls out a thick book. He pushes it across his lucite desk pad. I open it . . . a comprehensive collection of Norman Cradle's work, drawings, paintings, sketches, posters, even doodles. There are countless blissful scenes and each figure has been coded.

"Find one you can react to with warmth and even love. It will become *your painting* in a spiritual sense. Within the world of that painting, identify with an aspect. It can be a person, a thing, whatever you wish. Empathize. Enter. Your painting will become your secret mantra. Discuss it with no one. Think about it, live it, smell the smells. Fantasize freely about the scene. One day you will know that you have become an integral part of it and that is your day of deliverance from the past. Imagine if you will a total acceptance of yourself within a defined frame with no remorse, recrimination or even consideration of any other pseudo-salvation. That is the goal of Cradleian Therapy."

"I have a wife, children, parents, in-laws, a history. Somewhere I have a future. How can I totally accept an ersatz kingdom, an alien vision?"

"I am holding out my hand to you. Many people are concerned with your welfare. Make your stay a happy one. Remember that the course you choose affects that family, albeit from a vast distance. Homer Brogg is being considered as a candidate for the Presidency. You are already a thorn in his political flesh. Your attitude here will have ramifications. And consequences. Choose your painting now."

I flip through the book. I see a church picnic. I see a mother waving goodbye to an adolescent boy on a train for Yale. I see a doctor leaning over a yellowish girl who looks up at him with total faith. I see children kissing in a Spring meadow. I see brides and grooms and treed cats helped by chubby firemen and cops. I see soldiers holding hands with brave sweethearts. An old couple watching the sea. A little hand holding a valentine for a teacher. Christmas trees and mellow flames and carolers in cotton snow. I see multitudes of furry pets, dolls, trains, stuffed turkeys and simmering hams.

"That one."

The picture I choose is called *Serious Business*. It shows an androgynous child holding a paint brush. He/she sits before a toy easel dotted with paint. The subject of the portrait is a flaccid doll slumped on a stubby chair.

"Identification Point?"

"The brush."

"The brush?"

"Definitely, the brush."

"Fi fi fo fum," says Dr. Hamish. "Let it be the brush."

"It was close between the brush and the freckles," I say.

Instead of breakfast, Bernie is waiting to take me back to my room. Meals will be brought to me. This is a day for meditation.

He gives my nose a twist and tells me to relax. I lie on my bed. A metal shade slides down from outside and seals off the window. The lights won't turn on. From somewhere, dimensional images transform my room.

I am inside my painting, trapped in a hologram. The doll model grins from the chair. The freckled child artist holds an empty hand in the air. The brush is missing. I am missing. I close my eyes but after an hour I look again. In three hours I am thinking, "*Dip me in purple, dip me in orange.*" I get up and do knee bends and push-ups. I try to make my own picture. But I feel the warm hand of the pubescent painter and beyond that the hot hand of Norman Cradle. I begin to hum lullabies my mother sang to me. In five hours I feel contented, safely contained. It is like being massaged by a eunuch. Why am I suggesting colors? They will be provided.

By the time they bring dinner I see there is something to Cradleian Therapy. When the hologram vaporizes and the shade lifts I panic.

The next morning I am given my work assignment. As Dr. Hamish said, I am assigned to the Plateworks. The factory team assembles just outside the main building after breakfast. Filled with oatmeal and eggs benedict, I prepare for my first day of manual labor.

We begin our march along Main Street. I see that two table-mates, the young blimp and the sliver of moon, are in the group. They walk holding hands. I have the eerie feeling that the fat girl is sucking nourishment as if her arm is a straw.

The West Stockton normals don't even give us a glance. They must be very familiar with the daily parade. A thought blossoms. Trina and the children would like this town. It is like a slow clock where time and the seasons seem to make sense. The thought curdles and I am suddenly dizzy. Trina, Amos and Amanda are not part of my painting. They have no place in my mind.

The Plateworks is a one-story stucco building flanked by a movie theatre and general store. They are showing a film called *The Thousand Year Voyage*, a comedy about a pair of astronauts (male and female) pledged to chastity during a voyage to a distant star. I wish I could detach, buy a ticket and a tub of popcorn and sit watching the film in a cocoon of shadows. The general store has a special on wicker furniture. I want to buy white woven chairs with color bar cushions. Now I am nauseous. I focus myself through a flicker of anxiety. I am here to work, not dream. I am here to prove myself worthy of a move to the gift shop. I have no other purpose.

The Plateworks manufactures Norman Cradle plates, thousands of them for tourists and collectors. I learn quickly that most of the labor is done by computerized machines and robots. Hot glass is imprinted with Cradle art, then bordered in gold. The plates flip over and have their backs stamped with certificates of authenticity. The certificates include a number, a red seal, and a facsimile of the artist's signature. Presumably there are counterfeit Cradle plates on the market and consumers must be defended. The certificates are entirely convincing. I would never question them. Each plate has its diploma as a factory graduate, genuine, authorized, beyond challenge.

When the plates are ready there is an inspection process, then final wrapping and packaging. Finished plates are tucked in colorful tissue, then put into individual cardboard boxes that display the plate's title, i.e., *A Mother's Tears*, *Boy Scout Jamboree*, *Christmas Rhapsody*, *Baby's First Step*. The factory runs one plate at a time in limited editions of a thousand. All thousand plates are perfect.

Rejected plates are immediately smashed in a steel press. The equipment provides white noise in the factory, a monkish *ommm* suddenly interrupted by pulverized porcelain. The splintering of rejects is like a little holiday.

My assignment is as an assistant inspector. It turns out that my rotund tablemate, introduced as Samantha Abberson, shows me how to check for defects and explains the importance of quality and a high standard. These plates will go into homes where they will become instant keepsakes to be cherished for generations. They will be displayed like icons.

Samantha also warns me to ready myself for a trauma which she calls *transition vulnerability*. When a line of plates is finished and another design appears there is a difficult moment of adjustment.

"Say you've been examining *A Perky Waif* and here you are confronted with *An Old Man's Treasures*. There's a natural feeling of rage and resentment. Don't act out. Beginners have a tendency to fly out of control. I've seen them smash perfectly good plates for no reason, even hit people. If you sense a tension you can't handle, talk to me. Never be ashamed to seek guidance. The best thing is to take a second and Image your picture."

"Thank you. I'll try to remember all that. Now, tell me about the gift shop."

"Not much to tell. Our gift shop is in Stockton, a few miles down the pike. During the Tanglewood concerts in Summer and Fall Foliage weeks, millions pass through this area. They visit the Cradle Museum and most of them come away with some memento. The gift shop was deeded to Hamish Farm at the turn of the century and we've operated it ever since. We supply the plates, figurines, place-mats, glasses and pottery. About ten years ago there was a lapse and we lost keychains, jewelry, greeting cards, prints, posters, calendars, clothing and hats to the Koreans. We have got to keep alert around here before we lose the whole ballgame. Wouldn't the *banzais* like to know about our production secrets. When you leave the plant, forget what goes on here. Say nothing to nobody. Even if your assigned therapist asks, fudge it. They do that to trick us."

"Does that include Dr. Hamish?"

"Sure. It's war games, Soup. There's plenty at stake. So remember, an ounce of prevention."

"If I discover a faulty plate is it my responsibility to throw it to the smasher?"

"Slow down. Hold your horses. That's my job. I'm the executioner and I earned it the hard way. I will say that if you show sincerity and dedication I might just let you decimate a few plates a day. But no promises. This is not a rose garden."

"I understand."

"And we do move on to bigger things. Some day my position will be vacant." She smiles. I smile back and shrug. We have achieved communication.

I inspect plates.

All my life I have read books and poems and even watched plays and musicals that romance the factory worker. I never swallowed any of it. But after my first hundred plates I change my mind. There is a pleasant trill to repetition, a rhythm of duplication that satisfies the soul. The task is fulfilling. During my first hour I check out *A Mother's Tears* and, sure enough, a plate comes down the line with a missing tear. It is like finding a diamond. I yelp and call Samantha. I hand her the renegade. She is suspicious of my inexperience but her eye confirms my diagnosis. She takes the degenerate dish and claps it into the masher. With the cracking sound I experience slight tumescence. When she reams out the inspector who let the tearless plate get through I am entirely erect. It takes some time to erase the bulge. I go about my work feigning modesty.

When the line slows I have time to look around. My other tablemate, the bony girl, is assigned to wrap. Her fingers are not much thicker than the tissue she manipulates. She is excellent at her assignment, faster by twice than the other packers. I wonder if she has thoughts about the gift shop and I feel competitive. She is another obstacle to my rise. A cracked plate is trashed. Its death rattle makes the skimpy girl wince. I hope for more breakage. It is a pleasure to see her quiver like the legs of a dying bug. I hate myself for enjoying her misery and I try to Image my painting. The artist and the doll seem tolerant of my sinister satisfaction.

At noon, a whistle sounds. The plate line stops. It is like being dropped twenty floors in an elevator. Samantha says, "Lunch." For some stupid reason I say to her, "I guessed that." Arrogance in an underling is not easy to forgive. I have probably set back my chance to use the crusher by days and even months. A tear comes to my eye. There is no way to apologize.

Amazingly, Samantha sits next to me. I am handed a lunch box. It contains a sandwich of Polish ham, dill havarti cheese and Dijon mustard on a robust brown bread. There is a pickle and a tub of cole slaw. A thermos holds fresh orange juice. I am no fool.

"I'm not very hungry. And it's a shame to waste . . ."

Samantha grabs my sandwich and gnaws at it with powerful, gleaming teeth. I can feel the food surrender and tumble down to the furnace gut. Her eyes soften to an April sunset. My sin is erased.

"Well, I see that our tablemate works in wrapping."

"You mean Susan Shom? The endangered species. I really worry for her. She eats like an ant, a fly. She forces me to finish her portions so Dr. Hamish won't know."

"It's good of you to take a risk like that."

"She is a friend. When she came here she was a balloon. Bulemic. I was the thin one. We changed places. I did it to help her, out of compassion. Compassion is my hang-up. I wanted to make it easier for her to stick to her diet."

"It certainly worked. She can't weigh more than eighty pounds wet."

"It's more complicated than that. Besides, I was being a little selfish, self-serving. When I realized their plan."

"What plan?"

"To mate me to Maginot. They want him to breed in captivity. I'm ripe as a melon. I can feel the seeds inside me. I get pregnant from pollen. They know all that."

"Not to invade your privacy, but are you saying that you're being encouraged to enter a relationship with a patient?"

"Not any patient. Bill Maginot. They know he's got a thing for me. And between us, if the Added Value law ever gets on the books he's worth like two thousand an ounce. So even a mixed marriage would produce offspring worth half that. They'd go on the books as assets. Anyhow, it's why I got fat."

"If I do say so, a brilliant solution."

"I'm not saying I won't go along with them some day. Right now I'm more involved with Susan. No, I'm no dike, in fact I adore men. But Susan needs me. She's like the little sister I never had."

"I always wanted a kid sister. It would have been marvelous to have one. I know where you're coming from."

She finishes off my sandwich and eats the pickle.

"Susan's problems go back to her father. She's so damn rich. He made zillions in electronics. You heard of the *Shom Kind of Guy?*"

"The robot?"

"That's it. What kid didn't have one? He invented it. He came from poor and the bonanza drowned him. He got these kinky signals about what makes for class. You know about sudden wealth, the worst curse. It takes centuries to prepare for money. Susan's parents became instant pigs. They joined the urgent indulgent. Buy, buy, buy. Crap, crap, crap. Glitz, glitz, glitz. You know those earrings she wears? Made from the nipples of Bengal tigers."

"I always wondered what happened to tiger nipples."

"Now you know, Soup. Along with paintings, cars, Art Deco

furniture, baubles, bibelots and accessories, along with the clothes and seats on this or that board of directors, the artsy fartsy friends and mentions in the columns came a passion for food. Her father regarded himself as Ali Baba's cave. He filled himself with everything from rack of lamb to perdreau. Her mother resisted for a while but finally yielded, probably as a means to survival. She had to cope with four hundred pounds of highly sexed ego three times a week. When they were stuffed they stuffed their daughter. Susan ate to please. By the time she met Baba Halvah she was a teenage cathedral."

"Baba Halvah?"

"Father to the Children of the Crescent."

"A cult?"

"Moon worshippers of a sort. The Baba teaches that the crescent's curve is a gash that leads to a parallel universe of tranquility and wisdom. To get there you have to fit through."

"Fit through what?"

"What they call the Curved Portal. The crescent moon. So Susan won't eat anything. I'll have to polish off her lunch before she gets demerits."

"They can see she's practically transparent."

"Dr. Hamish told her she'd have to hit bottom before bouncing back. They're waiting her out. But Susan can't give up the idea of slithering through the moon door to eternal paradise. She's atoning for a ton of parents."

"You can't take on the responsibility for Susan. You have yourself to think of."

"I used to be size 6. When I get out of here I'll have to spend the rest of my life in a sauna."

"Far from it. Actually, Samantha, you're quite trim. Trim and curvy."

"If you want to fuck me, say so. Let's Image a dirty picture. I'm naked and tied up in a big pot and you dribble down the side a drop at a time. Think about that."

The whistle blows. Plates slide from the mysterious source. I watch my humongous supervisor. I can't conceive of penetrating that mass or even of finding the entrance but the rapture of hurling a plate into the compactor makes me consider the possibility.

If it wasn't for chance I would never have known what goes on in an assembly line.

I walk with Morris Feuerbloom through West Stockton. We come to a small bridge over an agitated stream and watch two normals fish. The evening is luscious, touched with purple, tangy with a chill wind.

"What can they catch? Sardines?" Morris says. "Inbreeding. They have extra toes around here."

"I am curious. How do the townspeople relate to us inmates?"

"They love us. We spend money. They hate us. We spend money. Generally it's a détente. Sometimes they try to burn down our buildings. They get aggressive around Halloween. They dress up like pumpkins and come with torches. Our security handles them. Mostly, relations are peaceful. What riles them up is when one of their girls gets knocked up not that they don't ask for it. There's nothing else to do in the Winter."

"I suppose we are aphrodisiacs. Aliens from an outer planet."

"Thank God I'm past all that. Maybe I get a hard-on around *Simchas Torah* but my mind has no interest in sex. The whole idea of pumping and jumping seems ridiculous. And I was some cocksman in my prime. When you control the firecrackers women chase you. Around Independence Day I got laid more than George Washington. Look at that sky. You know what I could do with a sky like that? First, a symphony of salutes. Next, a gala display of florals followed immediately by a barrage of spinners, rockets, wheels and snakes. A pause for suspense. Voom, a silver shower, then shells, comets, repeaters, fountains and finally after thunderclaps the Feuerbloom Spectacular to make your chest hurt and roll your eyes. Eat your heart out, Grucci."

The *eat your heart out* is a yell. The fishermen spin around and glare at us.

"I wasn't talking to you. Chase anchovies."

"Let's walk," I say.

"Go home and count your wife's tits. There should be two. You didn't know that, eh?"

"Morris, stop provoking them."

"What can they do to me? Kill me? So what? You know, Soup,

when I set off the first Feuerbloom Spectacular it made me piss in my pants. You could see the fire with closed eyes. We used one for a golden anniversary in Miami Beach and tubers in a nursing home five miles away fell out of their beds. That is a firecracker. You believe me?"

"I believe you. Come on now. You said you had an errand."

"Good you reminded me."

We walk down toward the general store. When we get there I wander through racks of merchandise while Morris is in back with the manager. He meets me holding a small package.

"For twenty bucks they sold me my own brand. You know what it costs them? Maybe three dollars." He opens a bag and pulls out a box of Fireflower Flash Bombs. He crumples the bag and slides the bombs into his pants.

"What's that all about?"

"I'm a collector."

"Don't let them catch you with that stuff."

"They leave me alone. Besides, who do you think they come to for Cradle Day? Who plans the big display? Me. I get them a whole selection, gorgeous items, all wholesale. We do a show down by the ball field. All the cretins come with food and beer. They never saw anything like it."

"Morris, if you can get supplies wholesale why pay retail?"

"This is private stock. The other stuff they inventory. They count every shell, whistler, roman candle, mine, even the sparklers. They don't trust me and you know what? I am not to be trusted. Let's get a coffee. There's a luncheonette around the corner. Their coffee is like an infection but I'm buying."

We go to the luncheonette. A group of normals watch the Crunch game on television. We sit at the counter facing a display of cakes that could be crowns, whipped cream, meringue, chocolate, coconut, nuts, cherries, vanilla glaze. I think of Trina.

"Your mind is wandering," Morris says.

"I was thinking about my wife."

"I think about mine but her face clouds up on me. She don't come into focus. Faces from my kindergarten come in clear but not her. I remember strangers but I can't tune in the wife. Go know."

I don't have his problem. Trina is there among the Boston cream and custard. A woman serves us. Her eyes slit when she sees our bracelets but there is no comment.

I sip coffee and munch a wedge of apple. Morris snaps me out of my trance.

"They interrupted the game."

BULLETIN flashes on the TV screen. The other customers let out a simultaneous groan. The Crunch field is replaced with a live picture of the Hoffenstein Statue on Everest. Searing light flames the face. Even in that world of snow and ice, Hoffenstein radiates warmth.

"Tonight unidentified terrorists have attempted to seize the Hoffenstein Visage. We don't know why or who they are. The assailants have been confined by Sherpa guards to the left nostril. Originally we are told they occupied both nostrils and the mouth but those orifices are now clear."

The camera zooms in close. I see dots huddled in the hostage nostril and flashes of what must be gunfire. Helicopters rise from the mountain and return the fire.

"We will cover this astounding story as it unfolds. Now, back to the game."

"His nostril?" Morris says. "They should have gone for his asshole."

"Watch your words," the waitress says.

"I can say anything. I'm mental."

A large man in a white apron stained with hamburger blood comes out of the kitchen.

"Is something wrong?" he says.

"Nothing is wrong." I hand him a twenty. "That should cover two coffees, a danish and a pie."

"I wouldn't tip that bitch," Morris says.

"Take him and put him back in his crib," the man says.

"He was making remarks," the waitress says.

"I was, it's God's truth. I didn't know the cow spoke English."

Outside I ask Morris why anybody would want to defile a monument to world peace.

"Probably paid for by the networks. They need excitement. Is it a coincidence enough happens every single day to fill the news?"

"That's like attacking a cathedral, a hospital, a museum. It's an assault on the essence of civilization. Frankly, Morris, I was disappointed by your outburst."

"Outburst? You call that an outburst? If I burst you'll know it.

Write down that I said it. Make a note. Why, you like Hoffenstein? You approve that they put bars on human heads?"

"I recognize the need."

"You also think about the picture they gave you to Image?"

"I do. They are here to help us, not hurt us. The least we can do is give them a chance."

"Can I ask what you did to get here?"

"I didn't do very much. It was an accident. I had to be confined for the common good."

"The common good? You swallow that shit like you swallow a piece of pie. Where's your life force?"

"Intact. But subdued. Look, Morris, the reason for the Codes was to eliminate confrontation and the reason for Imaging is to channel impossible dreams."

"That's what they're selling us. The bottom line is still power, who turns the screwdriver. The same people get screwed but now they don't holler."

"I realize you've experienced enormous future shock in one lifetime. It is no shame for you to be confused."

"Future shock? You bet. From a baby to a boy to a man to a fossil."

"I was talking about attitudes and technologies. This century has capsuled eons of evolution."

"Why are you so accepting? Because you're salt free? I was counting on you to help me. Now I count you out. In a month you'll be sticking it to the eggplant and think you're in love. I saw you slip her an artichoke tonight."

"An artichoke isn't courtship. There are other considerations here."

"Sure, sure. First an artichoke then a banana."

"I think it's past your bedtime, Morris."

"Years past. Which is why I will kill myself. But you are a young fellow. Fight them. Give them back."

He rushes ahead of me up the stairs and into the house. I should report his behavior to Dr. Hamish or Bernie. The man needs medication. He is carrying explosive material under his clothes. But I hold back.

In the TV Salon there is much cheering. I go in to watch the captured terrorists herded into a tent. The terrorist leader, bundled in furs, sticks his thumb at the camera. The crisis is over. Snow falls onto the Hoffenstein Visage making the enormous stone face even wiser. If only Cradle lived to paint it.

I go up to bed. The benefits of Cradleian Therapy are evident. I look forward to my day at the Plateworks. I dream easily of porcelain shards. It is my best sleep in months.

"Something is going on. I want to know what," Samantha tells me. "Follow Susan and report back."

"Whatever I am, I am no spy."

"It isn't a matter of spying. The girl could hurt herself."

"In that case."

Susan Shom delivers plates to the gift shop at least twice each week. She carries an assortment of best-sellers to fill out the line. My boss suspects hanky panky. Susan has come back late several times and there has been a blush on her cheeks. Last night she hesitated for a microsecond before yielding her cucumber salad.

I am reluctant to get involved. I don't relish sneaking around corners and there is a particularly vulnerable plate in production. *Spunky Jane* depicts a defiant bud of a ballerina in a pink tank top and disheveled tutu of white lace. Jane bows before an adoring audience of friends and relatives on a school auditorium stage. Her hair is flame orange and the hair has caused havoc. The color keeps coming out brownish rust, a bonanza of defectives. The grinder ingests them with evident pleasure.

My supervisor is a mind reader. She makes a suggestive flicking gesture with her sausage wrist. I nod. She hands me a *Spunky Jane*, this one a victim of extreme discoloration. I twirl it in my hands and cluck to myself. Samantha points to the disposal. I take the plate to the mincer. I drop the ballerina between steel molars. Jane is no longer so spunky. The expression of smug triumph is wiped off her face and then there is no face.

Momentous emotion drains blood from my head and I know I am leering like a horror film goblin. I am engorged with what can only be described as glee. *Glee* is a word I thought I understood but only now do I know *glee* for what it really is. It was not put into the language only for writers. There is such a thing.

I am walked to the door. Samantha's manner promises more *Spunky Janes* to come and I have accepted her deal.

Outside, I see Susan carrying two bags of selected plates from our inventory. The bags look like the ends of a barbell hanging from her pin arms. She is a stick figure walking through a postcard town.

My quarry waits for the bus to Stockton. I realize my dilemma. I must take the same bus to keep up with her. I quickly concoct a story. I have been allowed a visit to the gift shop as a reward for diligence. Of course I pretend surprise when we board and I sit next to Susan who moves her fragile bags to accommodate me.

"Did she send you to follow me?"

"Am I Mata Hari? What an idea, Susan. I didn't have the slightest notion that you were making the trip. In fact, I could have carried the plates and saved you the trouble. No, this is pure coincidence not espionage. Though I am glad we met. Maybe you can show me around the place."

"What did she promise you? Breakage? The woman is a devil. She's eating me alive."

"Funny you should talk about breakage. I did drop a plate into the grinder, there was no hope for it, and I thought I would enjoy the experience. Instead I feel depressed."

"Which one?"

"The snotty little dancer bitch. I know everything there is to know about that one. I could draw a map of her life. Private schools, Ivy League college, a greased path to some job on a fashion magazine, correct marriage, two kids, Maximum Achievement Code C. Probably keeps a diary she lies to."

"You're talking about a plate. Or maybe, Soup, that's not what you're talking about. Somebody else?"

"Don't be asinine. So, tell me about the gift shop. It must be a nice change of pace to get out of the Plateworks and onto the retail front."

"Soup, drop the crap. Let's save each other a ton of trouble. You hang around Stockton. Get lost for an hour or so. When you report back tell her the reason for the delay is that the place was swamped with tourists. She'll believe it, maybe. She tends to believe men she hasn't fucked. You haven't, have you?"

"No. And I am mildly interested in your proposal. I did want some way to get off a note to my family and I assume mail from the Farm is censored. Bernie has quoted my own lines to me. But I've got to know you won't be up to anything—how shall I put it—detrimental."

"Cross my heart and hope to live."

"I look the other way for an hour."

The town of Stockton where Norman Cradle worked is a lush pod of contentment. Every town in the world is shoddy by comparison. Nothing is out of place, even the traffic lights are perfectly positioned. Stockton is framed by its own charm. Did Cradle shape the place or did the place mould the man? Was a collection of slums and deserted mills brushed over and subdued or did this Eden grow softly from the Berkshire Hills attracting only herbivorous dinosaurs and Puritans who leaned toward liberalism? Was little Norman force-fed hot apple pie, cider laced with cinnamon, New England chowder served in an ironstone bowl? Or was he the architect of the dream?

When I meet Henry Hamish, brother of Dr. Bartley, who runs the gift shop (actually, *shoppe*) I ask about the town's history. He proves remarkably uninterested in the past.

"I would think you'd be obsessed by history especially since you sell nostalgia."

"That's not how I see it. I sell values, aspirations, visions of the possible."

"You are like your brother."

"Grandfather's light burns in our hearts. With embers enough for everyone. And that's exactly what these products are. Embers."

Henry detaches from our conversation and moves around customers, sliding past counters and shelves with grace. This man loves his work. He is entirely devoted to gentle commerce. I browse the displays until Henry Hamish is free.

"Excuse me, but I am curious. Didn't Cradle do some combative drawings during World War II? I once read that he was strongly anti-Nazi."

"Those items would not make attractive plates."

"If I may say so, there is the feeling of a single statement here. A diversity of mood might actually add to credibility."

"You feel there is a credibility problem? Do they know how you feel up at the Farm?"

"I was only suggesting . . ."

"You're at the Plateworks. Would you honestly think a plate showing my grandfather Isaac Hamish as an assassin should be sanctioned? I'm sure you've heard he came here originally to shoot Cradle."

"I hadn't heard that."

"You would have. It's no secret. Quite the opposite. Yes, he came to Stockton ready to do mayhem. He was a burned out, miserable man convinced he had failed because of a cynical, de-praved world. And he was made more miserable when he found out that Cradle died the very morning Grandfather arrived. He sat out there, by that glorious maple, thinking about what else he could destroy. The air? The flowers? The children? He sat remembering Cradle's work, the affirmation of purity and wonder that made him fester with envy, rage and jealousy. Then the light came to him. From that moment Grandfather devoted himself to perpetuating the blessed truth that permeates this shrine. He gave himself to that labor. He was a militant man who fully accepted that the odds were stacked against good in the battle with evil. But he discovered that beauty and commitment will win over ugly. Did you know he experimented with Codes even before Hoffenstein?"

"Really? I can see where all that would be hard to capture on a plate or even a series of plates."

"Exactly. Plates are a limited form."

Henry Hamish gets involved with a woman who wants to buy a Cradle comforter for a king-size bed. I look around. Susan is gone. I note the time. One hour.

I leave the *shoppe* and find a place to buy a pen, paper and an envelope. The only stationery available is bordered with cherubic Cradle angels. I write between blissful expressions. I had expected to piss and moan to Trina. I haven't heard from her for months. But instead the tone of my writing is upbeat and full of warmth. I buy a stamp at the delightful local post office and drop my letter into a polished brass slot. Even the slot is another ember from the simmer-ing remains of the enlightened Grandfather Hamish.

When the stolen hour is finished I return to the *shoppe* but there is no sign of Susan. I begin to feel anxiety. If I have lost her there will be no explaining. As it is others are already inspecting my plates, upholding the standard, maybe even feeding the crusher. I must get back before five. If it comes clear that I am easily replaced on the line then where is my bargaining power?

I see Susan across a wide street. She stands outside the Blue Violet Inn kissing a large man. He folds her with arms that make her practically invisible but I recognize the spindle legs. The kiss lasts forever. Finally, she separates and rushes toward where I wait. I turn away. I saw nothing. When Samantha asks me I am relieved to tell her there is no problem.

"It is only that she meets a man. I suspect they spent some time at the Blue Violet. That's all there is. She even looked happy for a few minutes. God knows, she deserves it."

I had not meant to tell the truth but since there was no harm in it I went ahead. It saved me guilt. Samantha of all girls could empathize with an afternoon tryst. She rubs against doorknobs. And how could she be less than pleased if her friend was even slightly thickened by an infusion of seminal vitamins and minerals.

"A man? Well. Give me some juicy details. What did he look like?"

"Rather distinguished, corpulent, tall, a face like a basketball. I thought he would snap her like a wishbone. Could it have been Baba Halvah?"

"Baba Halvah weighs about five pounds. He's four feet tall. Alright. Now get back to the line. We managed to solve the hair problem for *Spunky Jane*. The plates are perfection. Not a lemon in the lot."

"Perfection?"

"Not a lemon in the last fifty."

"Ah. What wonderful news."

Bernie enters my room with my letter between his legs. He wiggles his hips, pretends to come, removes the letter and drops it on my bed. The man has elegance. He shakes his head and makes sounds of violent disappointment. I brace.

This will be different from the occasional tug at a lobe or smack on the spine. I know I took a risk. But I am concerned about the extent of my upcoming injuries. If I miss work for too long via a fracture or dislocation I will miss a whole series of difficult new plates with subtle colors that strain the capacity of the stamper.

He takes off his jacket and swings. It is a modest right to the jaw. Then I am kicked under the left knee, not so bad, and chopped between the left shoulder and neck. A few clouts to the gut and he gets back into his jacket. I am relieved but also saddened. These neighborly brutalities affirm my existence. An unauthorized letter is no small offense.

"Three days unframed, Soup."

"Wait just a minute. You haven't got that authority. Only Dr. Hamish can Frame-Deny. I demand to see him now."

"You brought it on yourself. Lucky the letter didn't contain anything subversive."

"It was a positive letter. And a first offense. Everybody must try to get off a letter. I don't deserve to be nuked."

Bernie slams the door behind him.

I rip the letter in half. Two can play this game. I will not think of my picture. I will substitute the image on the new skittish plate, *Fanny's First Corsage*. That plate has a nice, circular boundary of red dots. I close my eyes. It works for a while but my brain does what the crusher does and Fanny is in smithereens. I am in my assigned picture looking beyond the frameless canvas.

I feel a new kind of fear. Unwanted light floods the nursery. My panic transforms the face of the usually placid neophyte artist. The doll takes on the look of a troll. The pigments undulate. The bristles I have chosen as my Identification Point mat and tangle. I double up and thrash on the carpet. There is no way I can function frameless for seventy-two hours.

When I wake it is in the infirmary with Dr. Hamish bending over me.

"How are you?"

"I'm not sure."

"Better than you realize. This was salubrious, Soup. I myself was surprised at your level of Picture-Involvement."

"How long have I been here? Am I still frameless?"

"Only a day but your sentence is suspended. Consider your border back in place."

"Thank you, God bless you, Dr. Hamish. Yes, my frame is intact. I feel it."

I reach out to touch the sleek wood. My hand is restrained.

"Are you ready to graduate from bristles?"

"Tell me."

"I think yes. Before a picture is encompassed it is necessary to become all elements. You've outgrown the brush faster than I believed possible. Time to move on. What shall it be?"

"I don't know. The doll."

"The doll? Incredible. You are making progress. Let me shake your hand. Can I assume there will be no more attempts at circumvention? Not a postcard?"

"I must have been addled."

"You're ready to get back to work. And none too soon. Because in addition to the demands of your job you will be busy with the Festival."

"The Festival?"

"Our annual Cradle Day. Quite an event in these parts. It's a bit of a carnival but with purpose. It brings the locals into things. And we get the chance to strut our stuff before a wider audience."

"Yes, I see that. And will our families be invited up?"

"Let's not get ahead of ourselves. Right now, concentrate on the Plateworks. There's a glut of business during Festival Week. We need product."

"You know, Dr. Hamish, after all those years as a so-called executive and decision maker I finally backed into a vocation that nourishes my soul. When I think if it wasn't for my accident I'd be back in a rut organizing some campaign or another for designer sperm . . ."

"Yes. Rest now. Remember you have a home with us, a job you like, an extended family. You're responding well to a difficult situation. You can feel justly proud of yourself. And your name will be up in the dining room as Patient of the Week."

"Not really. There must be others who . . ."

Alone, I test my new Identification Point. As doll, I fit into my slumped posture watching the artist contemplate his/her next stroke. The brush I once was (and I feel a tinge of separation anxiety) hangs immobile. I am impatient for baby Norman to get on with things. I know that what appears on the blank canvas will translate to revelation. I will know things about myself that I never dreamed.

I forgot to ask the Festival date but it must be some weeks away. By that time I will master my picture. When Trina, Amos and Amanda come up they will see that my eyeballs are as peaceful as Saturn, complete as God's own eggs.

Gamblers tell me luck ebbs and flows in cycles. I questioned that as superstition, an attempt to enforce logic on pure chance. Now I am not so sure. Three days after I get a new Identification Point I am made supervisor of the plate line.

My upgrade came after Samantha and Susan performed a despicable act (judged by outside standards). It happened yesterday in the early afternoon.

Susan found some weak excuse for a trip to the gift shop, something about a faulty inventory. Samantha was cordial about letting her go, then came to me.

"Cover. I'll be out for a while."

"No hurry."

"I wish I had a dozen like you. So few are motivated. There is no more work ethic."

"Thank you. It all goes back to parental influence. My father always encouraged me to remember what he called *Your Equivalent Jap*. I had no brothers or sisters so I rather enjoyed the competition with a mythical rival. I even named him. I called him . . ."

"Later, Soup. Save it."

I knew Samantha was following her frail friend. I thought she appointed herself as a kind of prophylactic to protect Susan from misuse. I had no inkling of what would come to pass at the Blue Violet Inn.

I began to get edgy when Samantha didn't return to the Plateworks after five. The supervisor must accompany workers on the daily march to and from the Farm. When the bronchial whistle sounded and the assembly line juice was cut all of us clustered near the door waiting for her. I flailed for excuses but if I had taken authority and led the exodus nobody would have followed. The very fact that I allowed myself to fantasize leadership made me realize how far my therapy had to go.

It was Bernie who came for us, a firm but subdued Bernie who seemed oddly remote. He didn't attempt to yank at an eyelid or elbow a spleen. He was full of *please* and *thank you*.

As we marched, we saw State Police cars and an ambulance whoosh toward Stockton. The faces of the normals gave another clue to the extraordinary. Usually passive eyes growled at us, the eyes of little kids snapped like fish mouths. Bernie made us walk fast and keep close formation.

Police ringed the main building. Dr. Hamish was on the porch talking to an officer, pointing up at eaves, turrets and balconies. We were herded into the auditorium where the entire population of Wing L massed for a briefing.

Morris Feuerbloom sat next to me.

"You know that movie, *Bride of Frankenstein*? Where they come with torches to burn up the castle? Wait. Tonight you'll see plenty."

"What does that mean?"

"You don't know what happened?"

"Why not just tell me?"

"Because I don't know. But something. I was hoping you would know."

It was a half-hour before Dr. Hamish took the platform. He took a casual pose behind the lectern.

"Ladies and Gentlemen, friends. Every so often we must cope with an event that alters the pleasant flow of our days here at Hamish Farm. As you all know we are guests in this town. Not that we should ever feel apologetic or even grateful. But we must be realistic about the attitudes of citizens who have not, how shall I phrase this, achieved a very advanced degree of sophistication."

"Inbred whitebread," Morris Feuerbloom yelled. There was applause. Dr. Hamish raised a hand for silence.

"Whatever the cause, we always face the possibility of excessive reaction by our neighbors. Today, at the Blue Violet, that charming haven of New England hospitality and grace, there occurred what I will describe as an unfortunate flurry. Rumor has a way of magnifying and distorting truth. You might as well hear the facts from me. It seems that two of our own devoured a famous visitor to the Inn. The act was without malice and can be ascribed to severe neurosis. But there will be consequences. Cannibalism, no matter how well intentioned, is a flash point for many and emotions are stirred."

"Who ate who?" Feuerbloom yelled.

"Susan Shom, whose problem involves certain classic anal-oral fixations, had become involved with Janesford Brun. Yes, *the* Janesford Brun you know as America's eminent gourmet. His recipes have delighted millions, his criticism has meant life or death to a thousand restaurants. From what we gather Brun was a friend of the family, a trusted friend until now. It seems Brun convinced Susan's parents that a shortcut to cure was simple temptation. Would that they had more faith in me and more patience. Without getting too technical, it has come clear to me that the flip side of anorexia is what I call *Taxidermal Inclination,* a psychological fixation on immortality achieved through encasing the soul in globules of fat. All this will be revealed in a copyright paper I plan to publish very soon.

"After winning Susan's favor, Brun invited her to the Blue Violet where he had sequestered an irresistible ragout. After seducing the vulnerable virgin, he would coax her to another kind of orgy, this one gastronomical. Awakening sexuality releases a thug appetite that knows no bounds. Our poor Susan, still wet as they say, tasted reluctantly of filets of beef, shitake mushrooms simmered in a choice burgundy, crisped potato puffs and a delicate paste of squash, honey and chestnuts. The result had to be catastrophic. Guilt and greed created a clash of inner titans. Still, a breakdown might have been the only consequence. But another of us became involved.

"Samantha Abberson, respected and well-loved supervisor at the Plateworks, intruded on the assignation. It is too early for specifics but preliminary investigation suggests that Samantha convinced famished Susan to participate in the murder, evisceration and ultimate broiling of Janesford Brun with the argument that he had been fed on delicious morsels over a span of decades and was surely marinated in self-generated gravies to a point of undeniable succulence. There were strong protests from Mr. Brun overheard by guests in adjoining rooms but the girls persisted.

"Briefly, then, two residents of Hamish Farm have strayed far beyond the Encompassing Frame. Worse yet, they ate a tourist in a region dependent on tourism. All this has fused to inflame antique passions associated with our activities here and we must anticipate another insurrection. You all know how the local boys and girls act out given half a chance. Every precaution will be taken to secure the grounds and we have full cooperation from the police and enlightened officials. Susan and Samantha have already been assigned to Wing X which, you will agree, is only fair. My own feeling is that Janesford Brun brought this on himself but, still, we must reap the whirlwind.

"I would like to use this opportunity to remind you how your individual actions affect community relations. Broiling a celebrity in a landmark inn is bad public relations, pure and simple, and not the kind of behavior we can tolerate.

"Following an abbreviated dinner which, I might add, is less exotic than a rack of giraffe, you will return to your rooms. Doors will be locked and windows shielded. Remain calm, concentrate on your Imaging, ignore strange sounds. We all know the normals have short memories and by tomorrow all this will be distant history. You would do well to recall that Norman Cradle's response to far greater social horror and upheaval was to ignore it and cling to his developed bliss. I ask you to do no less."

There was polite applause as Dr. Hamish left the platform.

"I'm glad she ate something," Morris Feuerbloom said. "They'll probably give us a tuna salad."

Door locked, window sealed with metal, lights out, I lay on my bed thinking cool thoughts. When the screams and yells from outside mingled with the smell of smoke I got up and made an attempt to see what I could see. I chipped away at the window sash with the back of my toothbrush and managed a pinpoint vantage.

I saw firemen pouring water onto blazing shrubs while troopers beat back waves of men, women and children from the town. Their ranks were augmented by curiosity seekers. There were eruptions of gunfire but I only counted two dead. They were quickly bagged and removed in a Hamish Farm pickup truck.

The positive side to all the turmoil is no different from the aftermath of a California quake. Stresses are released and the end result would probably be a more receptive climate for the Cradle Festival. In that sense, Samantha and Susan did us a service. The locals are nice people at heart, proud of their Codes, devoted to their families and the town. By sunrise they would remember larger values. By morning the West Stockton Plate would be reframed and intact.

Watching the carnage, I wished I could get off a note to Trina. I would have liked Amos and Amanda to share the lesson. I went back to bed ignoring the transient curses and howls of pain realizing that none of it was in the least significant in the long view.

Never once did I consider that the supervisor's job was open at the Plateworks. I am proud of that.

When I am informed of my new status I accept the word with dignity and resolve. I wonder if I am ready. My reactions are impeccable.

At breakfast there are copies of the editorial from *The Stockton Bee*.

COMMUNION AND CANNIBALISM . . . SIBLING SACRAMENTS?

There is a kind of innocence, even devotion in a human act that reaches out both to past and future. Janesford Brun would recognize this and be quick to forgive and forget the circumstances of his passing. In his widely-read memoir, Slice of Life, Brun tells us that in the event of his death he would wish his functional parts donated to the less fortunate while extraneous fragments be cast into the sea. "Sea burial is my best and quickest chance at resurrection," he wrote, "and surely the fastest way to enter the food chain." He recognized that death itself is transition to new youth and a fresh start.

While the editor cannot help but feel revulsion at the sense-less violence that took Mr. Brun from us, we must remember that the perpetrators were under special stress. It is also com-forting to note that cannibalism and communion are sibling sacraments and, after all, a reaching back to deeply human roots in order to find a pathway to God. It would be better to forget anger and move forward as a caring community.

In fact, West Stockton was quiet after dawn and remains so. The paper makes no mention of the nocturnal clash. The final body count is fourteen dead and twenty-six wounded, one of the lowest since riots began decades ago. It could have been much worse. Besides the hedges and the gate there is hardly any property damage. I know only because Bernie told me. He took a pounding. He came to my room this morning, a bloody mess, fresh from the infirmary. He was the one who informed me of my promotion, then beat me with a truncheon explaining that he could take no pleasure from my success because of the way it came about. I told him I understood his position. He told me the few contusions I experienced saved him from a case of psychological blue balls because of his negative experiences during the night. I told him I realized that folks like him couldn't afford the luxury of extended therapy and venting frustration was an acceptable substitute. It was the best talk we ever had. There were no visible bruises.

I have two new tablemates. The slob has been moved to Samantha's seat. She introduces herself as Gillian Hill. Susan's chair is filled by a pretty redhead, Audrey Topper. Morris, The Explosive Jew, whispers that the Lord works in mysterious ways to fuck him since he can't abide Gillian but he has had his eye on Audrey for a year. Nobody mentions the vanished girls. They have been airbrushed from our lives and that is the way of things.

I can't say breakfast is an ordinary meal. The emotional happenings have taken a toll. We eat silently. I notice that the guard detail has been doubled. Dr. Hamish must sense that our harmony is fragile.

Gillian, who calls herself Jill, doesn't help. When a soufflé is served she smears egg across her chin. Audrey, who is meticulous, daubs at the tablecloth for errant droppings. Jill ignores the tacit message. She holds her plate to her nose and sneezes. Bits of soufflé fly like projectiles. Morris picks up a carafe of grapefruit juice and dumps the liquid onto Jill's blouse.

We attract attention. It brings the guards. They are not from the familiar contingent, probably temps or recruits from the violent ward. In the fracas, Jill's blouse pops its buttons and her breasts tumble out. For some reason, possibly because of a liberal arts education, I protest. The guards drop her and come after me. I look into myself for some functional hostility. It is missing, a detached organ, one of those extraneous fragments Janesford Brun marked for the sharks.

Bill Maginot inserts himself between me and the dobermen. Morris Feuerbloom begins rapping a knife against a glass. Others pick up the clatter. More guards trot toward us.

Amazingly, Bernie is my savior. I see him in hot conversation with the senior security officer. The officer orders the guards back.

The meal is over. As I move to the door, Jill comes up to me buttoning herself. "You made things worse," she says. Then we are separated by the mob.

I am concerned about my behavior. It could easily result in demotion from the job I just got. I am already formulating an explanation for Dr. Hamish who I see standing just outside the dining room.

"You were correct to protest," he says before I say anything. "We are all a bit edgy after last night. Do you play chess? I could use a game after last night."

"Yes, I do play a little. But Dr. Hamish, the Plateworks . . ."

"We're not going into town today. It might not be prudent."

"Smart, yes, I see that."

Walking to the recreation area he says, "You know, we kicked ass. Knocked the crap out of the citizens. They won't be so damn quick to come back here. I authorized use of our kids from Wing X and they were fantastic. Believe me, they took no prisoners. And we suffered only minor casualties. Bottom line is it was a wonderful prep for the Festival. We can use some spirit around here, don't you agree?"

"Yes, now that you mention it."

"Did you appreciate those tits?"

"Pardon?"

"You know what I mean. Impressive knockers."

"They were interesting."

"I noticed that you rose to the occasion."

"About that . . ."

"I already said there is no need to justify. Just don't make a habit of intruding."

"Of course not."

"I'm sure you'll do a fabulous job for us at the Plateworks. Let's get that inventory up, up, up."

We set up the chess board. I make sure to lose more than I win. There are victories in defeat.

"Would you like your dining room table changed?" Dr. Hamish

says, enjoying a move that takes my queen.

"Not really, no."

"I didn't think so. Soup, you could wreak havoc with those pink nipples if you've a mind to. And between us, it would be a mercy. Jill Hill likes you and there is no rule against relationships with occasional penetration."

"I have no such aspirations. I use enormous energy between the job and Imaging. Then there's my wife."

"If you change your mind accommodation can be made. She's a special woman. Enormously wealthy parents, Midwestern money, *land, lots of land under starry skies above.* Soybeans. Pork bellies. Wheat. She was a well-adjusted person pre-puberty, half a pair of twin sisters, fraternals, exact opposites. Her flip side is a gorgeous blonde with amethyst eyes that could belong to an idol. That's Jill's cross. The sister is an American Dream, the kind of girl you meet with her hair frazzled, knee-deep in alfalfa. The one with the skin like cream and legs to destroy, the mythic Lady Liberty we all want to subvert. Even the Slimes with their ballads celebrate that girl. There's no getting away from her. Red, white and blue pussy, authentic old glory. Jill couldn't compete with that. Who could? Her father hardly noticed her and her mother kept trying to send her to law school. Who wouldn't crack up? She has no sense of self-worth for all her aggression. Which is why I suspect a romance would do more for her than a year of counseling."

"I'd like to help but the truth is I don't feel medicinal. And there is Trina."

"Maybe I should put you on a high protein diet. Checkmate, Soup. You should have seen it coming."

As the new supervisor of Quality Control, I gather my workers together before the morning whistle blows. I have decided not to explain anything about my sudden elevation but rather to concentrate on *motivation.* The quotas and projections for pre-Festival output are mountainous and success will depend on teamwork. As I suspected, nobody on the line questions my authority. Many don't seem to realize there has been a change, the others couldn't care less.

I look at the desultory group. I am at a huge disadvantage. I cannot offer salary incentives or even perks. If I could it wouldn't matter to that collection of zillionaire spawn, each balancing battling shadows. Tact and sincerity are my only ammunition and perhaps the fact that to them I am a *thing*, not a person, and therefore non-competitive.

"Friends and fellow workers. Before we pitch in today, I wanted to say a few words. As your new supervisor, I have seen a sheet of staggering numbers . . . plenty is expected of us in the months ahead. There is no possible way we can satisfy demand. But we will find a way. We will do this by reaching into ourselves and grasping at inner pride, even beyond Code Pride. Do I hear snickers? Good. Let's begin with cynicism and climb up from that swamp.

"First, a word about Hamish Farm. We are part of a grand experiment here, watched by the entire civilized world. We live in a laboratory of the future.

"Affluence is the destiny of the human race. Is it a blessing or a curse? Was the denial of foliage the end of the dinosaur race or was it a *profusion* of leaves, grass and edible beasts? All of you are victims of surfeit. As pioneers of conspicuous consumption, you are the guinea pigs in a fantastic experiment. Since each of you has, as we say, Defocused within the Embracing Canvas of society, you have become more precious, like mice sensitized to subtle strains of disease.

"It is you who will provide the vaccine for millions to use. Your psychosis and neurosis is wisdom as well as misery. Since pain cannot be remembered clearly if at all, when you are cured and Returned your part in this quest for insight will be over. But your contribution will be eternal. That is background to my next point. Keep it in mind.

"Let's talk now about the very idea of work, a job, a product produced by your labor. For many, the whole idea of work, much less work that produces a palpable plate, is highly abstract. Actually, amazingly, it was a concept unquestioned for centuries. People did it all the time. Many still do though we don't hear much about them and hardly ever come in direct contact with the genre. Be that as it may, work can be more than therapy. It is wise to remember that the things you use and cherish come from someplace. Producing these items with a sense of quality awareness can be not only personally fulfilling but strategic. If the product is desired, the job of producing the product is enhanced. Along with the worth of the item comes self-worth. Also money. Do I hear moans and groans? Fine. I know that what I said is shocking to you but it is no less true. Work can actually produce money.

"Now, about our wonderful America. The Cradle plates we make here in this building are not only beautiful, they are essential. As the world becomes more homogeneous and cultural traditions evaporate, our national frame suffers erosion. While we are part of a world community, we are still Americans. These plates are direct reminders of our specialty. The perfect picture on each and every one nourishes the American soul. Just as we retreat to contemplate our assigned pictures, so do countless buyers of these plates take pause to spend a quiet moment with, say, *Grandpa's New Leg* or *What Happened to Sister's Chest?* or *Back From the Vet.* Our plates are crystallized sanity.

"Affluence. Globalism. Inevitable. What are the consequences? We don't know. We do know with certainty that by exceeding our plate quota we are making an important statement about personal values and the public good."

I look around. My eloquence has left them speechless. There are moist eyes. Then a terrible idea blossoms in my head. I try to suppress it with a cork of reason but I blurt:

"It must be depressing to you all that each day we must dispose of defective plates. There cannot be violation of our standards of excellence. None of us should feel that these standards are excessive or imposed from without. We should impose harder standards from within. Still, there is continuous waste. When the grinder rescues us from imperfection we all feel a combination of relief and defeat. In the case of *hopeless* plates there can be only one fate. But many plates are marginal and they too are destroyed. My thought . . ."

I am choking and stuttering. I can't find air to breathe. I pray for the whistle.

"My thought is, since there are so many people out there with limited capacity to enjoy Maximum Plate Appreciation, that we should encourage a new production category which might be called *Permissible Deviant,* and bring these slightly flawed plates to market instead of sending them to hell. These clearly marked, re-certified orphans can thus be acquired, at a discount, by lower Codes and even exported to far away places where interest in the American experience fans hope for quicker progress. They won't be perfect plates but they will be Cradle plates and better something than nothing. Of course, Hamish Farm will then enjoy increased income and stability.

"There is precedent for this. In decades past, the Third World was a target for shipments of baby formula, pesticides, cigarettes, drugs banished from our own more selective shelves. If a few perished from tainted products, even that served a purpose. Killer baby foods, for example, reminded women of the joys of nursing. Bottom line, there was more good done than bad. I am not suggesting we send out poison plates but to think that any plate is better than no plate seems a convincing argument."

They are cheering me. I smile and wave. The whistle blows.

I go to my job which I have just made practically obsolete. The first *A Brave Crocus* off the line has a twisted petal. I grab it from a worker and trash it. The sweet vibrations of the compactor flow to my loins. What have I done? Where do such selfless acts originate?

I belong here. I have gone insane.

I will be happy.

The production line quickens. The workers work with messianic frenzy. The packers pack with octopus arms. Cartons rise to the ceiling. A girl I don't know celebrates her bondage with a lovely voice singing,

> Tis a gift to be simple
> Tis a gift to be free . . .

There is a new spirit at the Plateworks.

Dearest Trin,

It has been so long since I received any news. I understand that the lack of communication was imposed both by the rules here at Hamish Farm and surely by the waterfall of emotion you must feel. But now it is time to touch again, albeit with words alone.

Since our letters are carefully studied and other eyes shall see this, I am naturally reticent to gush and rhapsodize but I suspect you will have no trouble seeing the pink between the lines. (*Inside* joke.)

You will be glad to know that I have enjoyed measurable success here and have already received a major promotion at work. (It is difficult to explain exactly what I do but I shall try when I see you and the children.)

Yes! I am authorized to invite you to our Annual Norman Cradle Festival Day. It is a gala event held in mid-October (the 18th to be exact) at exactly the hour this town is at its best. The onset of Fall brings a deluge of color to the land which, as you recall, is beyond any capture. If you act quickly you should have no trouble reserving a suite at the Blue Violet Inn in Stockton which is a charming timewarp with all the comforts. I know you will love it.

We can be together much of the time and there is even the chance of conjugation. I am keeping my legs crossed and taking vitamins. Hope you are doing the same (but not necessarily in that order).

How I miss you, Amos and Amanda. I know you have been abroad much of this time and I can't wait to hear your stories and theirs. I read about your voyages in the paper. Now that Homer is very much a candidate for the Presidential nomination there are articles and features at least once a week. I live for them since there is often some squib about "his lovely daughter and the grandchildren."

Now let me add incentive for your visit.

You will be the wife of a *star*.

Let me elaborate. Each year, the Cradle Festival chooses a person to *be* Norman Cradle. It is, of course, a great honor and much desired. In the past, choices have come from long-time guests. A freshman has *never before* been chosen to fill the role.

This year will be different.

Your husband has been selected!!!

Yesterday I was called into the office of Dr. Bartley Hamish himself and told of the decision. I protested since I sincerely felt there were others who deserved the glory a lot more than I did but I was quickly silenced. It seems the output at our Plateworks (to be explained in person) has more than tripled since I won the confidence of the workers there (more of this when we are together). My choice was unanimous, *another first*.

So, yours truly shall rule over the Festival in full regalia. Actually, the regalia is rather modest, not like the King of Mardi

Gras, since Cradle was a humble man, but there will be celebrity enough . . . for the four of us!

How many times have you said I should have been on stage? Prophetic words, darling, and now I have the chance. I am busy reading all I can find about Cradle the man and his motivation, studying pictures and films about him. Our drama coach, Ms. Zoe Rapish, has been very helpful. She is a dedicated artist with impeccable credentials, albeit a bit of a tyrant.

Otherwise, there is little to report. My days are filled and my nights are spent Imaging (I'll fill you in) and absorbing my Identification Point (this will come clear to you) into the Infrastructure (jargon). There is always time to think of you and the kids and I do, I do, I do, sometimes *too much* according to Dr. Hamish.

Have you had any further information from Charlton? I know he is working on my case and I am confident he will do his miracles soon but even soon is too long. Under the circumstances, I can't go into detail about all that but you get my meaning.

Though I know, with knowledge enforced by enlightened therapy, that there is, officially, no hope of Return, I can only say that the hours, days, weeks and months spent as common salt free pea soup have made me better and more receptive. You will see for yourself when we meet (is it really about to happen?) and touch (can I dream?).

Best wishes to Homer, Lauren and Lance. As for Amos and Amanda, smother them with hugs. I have seen hundreds of plates with faces of children not nearly so seductive as theirs (remind me to expand on that).

So. There we are. October 18—write it in some safe place (and I am positive we both agree on where that might be).

Your loving husband,
"731" etc.

I spend two hours each evening with Zoe Rapish learning the elements of an actor's craft. These sessions are held at Zoe's house, a few blocks from the Farm. The room she calls her studio could be called austere. The only piece of furniture is an electric chair that was once a prop for some local production. The chair is adorned with dangling wires, a metal head cap, arm and leg clamps. During our first session Zoe sits in the chair electrocuting herself while I watch her vibrate and twitch.

"It is the artist who must provide the power," she says. "I generate the volts from my inner vision of universal guilt. The ohms and watts flow naturally."

In that chair I will "plug myself into myself" while she sits watching me breathe, exercise my diaphragm and the muscles of my face, practice techniques for relaxation and composure.

"An honest man sizzles differently from a perpetrator but sizzles nonetheless. Of course, none of us is innocent but at the moment when the sentence is carried out the criminal who did the crime has something of an edge over the unjustly convicted. These subtleties must be communicated. It isn't the frying, it's how one fries."

"I think I follow. This is new to me."

"You will play your part just once, Soup. There is no second chance with a pageant. You must focus yourself to a prism. As your performance is judged, I am judged. I will accept nothing short of brilliance. You are going to *be* Norman Cradle. I shall accomplish the magic. I believe in reality and therefore I am a believer in magic."

"That's an excellent attitude," I say.

"To nurture your transformation I will grind at you, gnaw your vitals, strangle your preconceptions and gut your destructive habits of pseudo-response. When your soul is throbbing red and begging balm I will squash it with my heel and only then rebuild you from a clot of palpitation. Centimeter by centimeter you shall emerge through the birth canal of illumination. You shall become a messiah of emotion. This will be anguish. Are you prepared? You must obey Zoe Rapish, hate Zoe Rapish, yield to her. Do we have a contract between us? Is your heart committed? Tell me now. I am a sick woman. I cannot take disappointment. I have diverticulitis. My intestines can separate at any moment. My colon is a time bomb. Yet I am willing to give to you if you are willing to embrace the opportunity."

"I'll do my best. What can I say? I haven't seen a script yet so it's difficult for me to build a foundation for my character."

"Script? What has a script to do with the role? Regard any script as a barrier. No real actor ever needed a script. Body wisdom, sounds, expressions, the pendulum swing between core wetness and arid dryness is our link to the special music. Besides, you don't have a speaking part."

"I don't speak?"

"Of course not. What could you say that would possibly enhance a portrayal of Norman Cradle? He himself never uttered a complete sentence and when he did he gagged on the words. He stuttered and mumbled. The man was visual. Visual. Visual. We must peel back his skin, poke between his bones, observe his organs."

"I have no lines? What exactly is expected of me?"

"Only everything, dear student. You shall appear alone on a glowing lucite platform. No props, no gimmicks. Silence will accompany you. When you are discovered, you are a statue. As you discover and accept your immense talent your arms shall fill with blood and courage. You reach out, slowly, slowly, to embrace all mankind and more. You shall touch the roach and the nebula. You suddenly shield your eyes."

Her hands slam over her face hiding all light. She slaps herself so hard her cheeks go violet.

"Why do you sequester your eyes? Does the horror stem from an accurate view of what waits for us all out there in the void? Yes, but something else replaces sorrow. Your body spasms. You must execute yourself to be reborn."

Zoe flops into the electric chair and executes herself.

"By sheer force of will you make the decision to reshape life into what it should be. What it would be if God had not rested on the seventh day. And now you are Norman Cradle, the man who sought and found the jewel in the slop. You free your eyes thusly . . ."

Her hands open, her arms spread, her nostrils flair.

"Yes," I say, "yes, I do see. Like the ones they called mules in the days of the drug wars. They swallowed rubber bags filled with cocaine, crossed borders, then took mineral oil to defecate a fortune. What if they fished in feces to find the prize?"

"That is repulsive," Zoe says. "I despise scatological references. Let's keep this at a high level, Soup."

"Do forgive me. I was carried away."

"Moving along. Now that you have metamorphosed into an immortal Norman you face a desperate choice. You can remain separate and aloof as so many like you have done. Or you can involve yourself with the mass. You choose a middle ground. You must have isolation in which to practice your art but you must have human contact to fuel your inspiration. Here is where our choir will crest and our dancers reach out. You shall descend from the pedestal to take their hands and be comforted by the warmth of connection. But then you will return to limbo where you fashion their dreams."

Zoe leaps from the air fashioning dreams with her arms, hands, body, legs, face. Visions spin from her as if she were a spider. She tongues at invisible creations like Janesford Brun might tongue a truffle.

"See, Norman? You offer your dreams willingly. You give drink to the parched. And then, lights out. Fini. The pageant is done."

"That's beautiful. But I think a few lines might enforce the message. Some in the audience might miss the significance."

"There will be program notes for those."

"I can see a lighter moment to humanize the man. I don't mean to suggest a stand-up comic routine. Just a tad of humor. Some clumsiness, a suggestion of puzzlement."

"Humor? Why? Art should prepare us for death. Humor challenges The Creator in a subversive manner. It champions disposability. Do we want to leave our audience laughing or crying? Which emotion will they respect more? Give me tears anytime. I find my ration of importance in misery, not chortles. Norman Cradle is simply not a laughing matter."

"But much of his work smiles."

"A bittersweet smile. Like the lock of a canal slowly controlling the rising waters of doubt and anxiety . . . always elevating the vessel, preparing for inevitable storms in dark seas. Norman knew we are all passengers on the *Titanic*. I mean, he wasn't exactly a putz."

"Still, a hint of frivolity . . ."

"Not on my time. Now let's put your ideas on hold and get to work. You will strip naked and crawl on your hands and knees. You will prowl my carpet looking for worms. You will grunt like a pig."

"To accomplish what?"

"Humility."

"There's nothing humble about a naked pig hunting worms."

"Maybe not but it isn't Othello."

Zoe produces a large mirror from behind a curtain.

"You will follow your reflection. We are on our way. Tell me, is it true you are close to Homer Brogg?"

I grunt from the floor.

"Is there some chance Mr. Brogg will be here on Cradle Day?"

I snort the vague possibility.

Zoe Rapish turns the mirror to look at herself. I squeal to remind her that the mirror is for me.

Zoe Rapish has fanned my actor's ego through her clever curriculum of daily humiliation spiced with scant praise. The praise, dribbled like snot onto a hot reactor core, turns immediately to superheated steam. An exotic bud of anger blooms inside me. I hover around my rage like a starved bee waiting for the flower to fester. The more she splinters me the more confidence I feel.

As she predicted, I have taken on a Norman Cradle dimension. I walk with my face hunched over my chest. I look beyond the obvious to golden kingdoms. The ordinary is celestial. Tapes and films of Cradle have changed even my voice. I steal his sounds.

All this makes my tablemates edgy. I manifest cloying benevolence made arrogant through beatific expression. I am like a Pope who has swallowed Satan, a holy mix of fury and tranquility. The others mock my manner in rehearsal but they will cheer when I perform.

For this future applause I endure my teacher's indignities. Yesterday she put me through what she called toilet training. I was required to recite words of love with my head in the bowl while she flushed the tank until the pipes howled. She says these are time-honored techniques developed in the basements of the world's great theatres. I respect that.

Zoe encourages solitude when my lessons are finished. As time permits, allowing for the extended hours at the Plateworks, I take long walks. My proposal has been accepted . . . plates which would have been trashed are now packaged as seconds and shipped to distant places. The wondrous crusher is hardly used anymore and my motivation has vanished. Once I hated to leave the production line. Now I can't wait to be alone with Norman.

Dr. Hamish has allowed me to dispense with Imaging until after the Festival. I explained that I was conflicted. In my chosen picture it is hard to forget that the artist is some extension of Cradle, possibly a figure from one of his cherished memories. My Identification Point, the doll, once passive, once a conspirator, has become sinister. It challenges not only the brush but the painter's motives. I found myself cursing the same Norman Cradle I am straining to become. When I requested an immediate change of IP from the malevolent doll, Dr. Hamish said it would be better to suspend Imaging instead. He reminded me that my mental state was artificial and temporary. Even therapy sessions are canceled until further notice.

On one of my evening strolls I head out toward the high school ballfield where the Festival will take place. I go like Sophocles to check the acoustics at Delphi. Since I have no words to speak acoustics are a moot point but I indulge myself. I have not given up the chance to convince Zoe to flesh out my part.

The school is across the road from the West Stockton cemetery. It makes for a nice continuity. There are graduations and graduations.

As I go, I hear singing:

> Their stones are teeth
> In the jaws of death;
> How can they sleep
> With sand for breath?
> Tra la la la
> Diddle de dee
> Who is the bone pile?
> *Vay*, it's me!

I see a figure shoveling earth. I assume it is the local gravedigger preparing a home away from home for one of the locals now ready for perpetual care and a good view of the end zone. I think to myself that if I was Norman and not a facsimile I would hurry to paint a plate called *Box Seat*.

There is something familiar about the digger's silhouette. I enter the cemetery grounds and walk toward the marble garden. The man with the shovel is Morris Feuerbloom. When I appear from around a mausoleum he is startled and raises his shovel.

"Easy with that thing. It's me."

"Of all the people you are the last I need," he says.

"What is this morbidity? Let me guess. You are digging your own grave."

"Are you really crazy? You think I would lay down in this town waiting for the trumpet?"

"Then what do you call this? Exercise?"

"You have no business here, Soup. Shouldn't you be taking an acting lesson with Sarah Bernhardt?"

"You've been nothing but hostile since I was chosen to play Norman Cradle. Why? Did you want the part?"

"I give up on you. Leave me alone. Forget you saw me. This is personal business."

"Morris, we have responsibility for one another on a simple human level. If I find you playing alone in a cemetery I must report that to Dr. Hamish. I can't stand by and watch you succumb to depression."

"I am not depressed. What I am is oppressed. There is a big difference."

"Walk back with me. We'll stop for coffee and one of those cakes you like."

"I don't want coffee or cake. Stay away or you'll get my shovel in your face. I warn you."

"You know I can't risk a fight. In less than two weeks I make my debut."

"His debut," Feuerbloom shouts to West Stockton ghosts. "What next?"

"I can't leave you here."

"You can. It's easy."

My eyes drop to the fresh hole. A coffin is already in place. Streaks of a retreating sun reflect from brass handles.

"Grave robbing? Is that what this is? Violating the final sleep?"

"Soup, you have good instincts. I confess. I was shoveling up the old barber. They buried him with a mouthful of gold teeth. You must know Jews can't stand the idea of wasted carats. I will change my ways. Here, look, I'm covering him up. Let him sleep. I'll come with you for coffee. You're too smart for me."

He begins to shovel earth onto the box.

"Wait. Open the box. Take the teeth. They can't help the barber. Who am I to frustrate you? Would Norman Cradle fail to see beyond the horror to the beauty implicit in your quest? To return gold to a needy world where it belongs? I admit it is hard for me to turn the other cheek but I will try."

"Soup, you are very far gone. I didn't realize. Besides, you ruined the teeth for me. I don't want them."

"Nonsense."

I jump down into the hole and pull at the coffin lid. It opens easily. I close my eyes knowing that I will force myself to stare back at the victorious worm. . . . What I see in the coffin is no former barber. I see pieces of a metal cylinder.

"Morris?"

"The Spectacular."

"A firecracker?"

"If a grain of sand is the Colossus of Rhodes, a firecracker."

"Why?"

"Because Morris Feuerbloom will launch himself to the stars."

"When?"

"During the pageant. While they're watching you on stage."

"During my climactic scene?"

"No, no. After the applause."

"Suppose there's an accident. Suppose you launch early?"

"I am a Feuerbloom. No accidents. I promise to wait for your bows."

"I can't take that chance."

"I respect your feelings. But say there is a little conflict of timing, a distraction. You could improvise. Make up a few lines. Say something. Didn't you tell me you had no script?"

"Extemporize?"

"Extemporize. Definitely. You want to be a mime?"

"What does your firecracker do?"

"What does it do? Not much. It fills the sky with colors so gorgeous to make a fascist cry. It gives off blasts like farts from hell. That can be your cue. Not so bad. And I get my wish not to spend eternity in the family plot in Roslyn, Long Island, which has no view except for the dump where they recycle bottles and cans."

"It is tempting. But I can't allow you to kill yourself."

"Who can say I will die on the ride? Maybe I will fly to a well-run hotel in the Catskills. Isn't that how Norman Cradle would see it?"

"Such an event would call for a few words."

"No question about it. In the beginning was the word, why not at the end? The average critic will eat it up, Soup. This is what is called your big chance. Be sensible. If you had an agent he would tell you to grab this straw."

"It would be ironic if your launch proved to be my catapult."

"Fine. A deal. But not a peep."

"I will think about it."

"Wonderful. Could I ask for more?"

"Morris?"

I hear a woman's voice, not unfamiliar. Jill Hill steps from behind a granite cherub.

"You already know my assistant," Feuerbloom says. "She's the one with the matches. Behind every great man is a woman to light the fuse."

I stop at the library for a copy of *An Actor Prepares* by Stanislavsky. Zoe has reserved the book in my name. She explained with great feeling how this teacher galvanized theatre with his message that actors must become lightning rods who store mammoth bolts of emotion in secret battery banks. This hoarded power can be released through memory cues. "An actor is possessed by devils and demons," Zoe said. "They must be taught to dance on command." When she spoke I saw her nipples firm under her leotard.

I do not tell Zoe about my encounter with Morris. Jill Hill complicated that equation. Before Jill became a factor there was no question about reporting his suicidal intent. Not only is his life threatened, the Feuerbloom Spectacular could easily devastate a sizeable portion of the crowd. To someone like Stanislavsky such thinking would be considered bourgeois and effete, considering the potential impact on the audience not to mention my career.

Still, during the Brun incident it was made clear that punishment for severe transgression would be quick and total. I could live with the thought of Morris confined to Ward X, it might do him good to change scene. But not Jill. Confinement in that place of violent shadows could set her back. And there is still time to use gentle persuasion against Morris' doomsday scenario. Besides, despite myself I have formulated a line to fit the occasion. As the rocket rises, I/Norman shrug and proclaim, "Death is our transition to the stars. In time those same stars swell and split with age, release their grasp on eternity and fall back to muddy Earth in meteor showers. And then a child is born."

The line needs work and will never be spoken but my instincts are on target. *Star Child* would become a best-seller plate, shirt, mug, placemat, whatever.

I snap myself out of reverie and go to my room to read. As I shuffle down the corridor in Norman Cradle's posture I think of the miracle Zoe Rapish has done.

I see that my door is open.

A flush of adrenalin washes Cradle away. It will be Bernie waiting for me. He must despise my celebrity. Or did they find out about my cemetery encounter? I consider retreat but that would only mean postponement.

It isn't Bernie. It is Samantha Abberson wearing the tepid green uniform of the violent ward. She is sifting through my drawers with her chubby hands. They can't be treating her too badly down there since she is as round and agile as before.

I come up behind her and say, "What is the meaning of this?" in my own voice. I am jolted to hear it.

Samantha whirls and tries to giggle.

"Hello, Soup. How the hell are you? What's new down at the factory?"

"How did you get in here?"

"Guile and persistence. I came to see you. I miss you. Do you miss me?"

She begins to unbutton her blouse.

"Samantha, wait, please."

"The wife again?"

"That, yes. And I'm in training. It's complicated."

She pulls off the blouse and drops her skirt. I am embraced by a pre-Columbian pot.

"Talk to me," I say. "How is Susan? Has she been eating?"

She rubs against me. Norman Cradle would turn her into a water nymph but I can't make the jump. Zoe was right, I need Stanislavsky.

"Susan is Susan."

"And Ward X?"

"Very physical. I don't mind it. They do a lot of work with aggression. There's an emphasis on ripping and tearing."

"That makes sense."

"We make weapons. Primitive stuff. Scimitars. Spiked balls. Barbed arrows. Spears. That kind of therapy."

"Samantha, put your clothes on."

"You want me. Admit it."

"You're probably right. But I'm conserving. You may not know, but I've been chosen to be this year's Norman."

"I heard something about that. Bravo."

"It isn't all roses. I'm pledged to celibacy like a priest or a fighter. Until after the pageant."

"Who's to know?"

"I will."

"You're really into this."

"I am, yes."

"I could fight another woman but I can't fight religion."

While Samantha dresses I look at the mess in my room.

"What were you looking for?"

"It's very silly. When you weren't here I thought I'd find some souvenir to take back. Something intimate. Something I could relate to in the wee hours."

"I never realized . . ."

"Give me your underwear."

"Samantha, if you want a pair of my jockey shorts then take one. With my blessing."

"Too clean. Bleached out. I want the one you're wearing. All sweaty and smelly. The one you'd send to a valentine."

A menacing look clouds her face. The girl has sharp nails filed to points. I drop my pants, kick them aside and take down my shorts. Samantha slips them over my shoes and tucks them into her bosom. I never knew she was a romantic. She gives my balls a quick kiss.

"Ring me up after your curtain call."

"I promise."

After she leaves I think to myself that Samantha's behavior must be directly related to my modest fame. If I was only myself I doubt that she would covet my underwear for a lullaby. What I have given her is, in fact, an autograph.

"We who nibble at the rump of The Goddess are a fraternity," Zoe often says. I begin to comprehend the price of fame.

"Come, Stanislavsky," I say to the book. "Speak to me. *For I on honeydew would feed and drink the milk of paradise.*"

"As I understand it, my costume is a plaid shirt, frumpy hat, rumpled pants, sneakers and a corduroy jacket. Can't we pick up those things at a local store?"

"Did you know Norman had his clothes made in London? He had his vanity. The look he achieved was *simply* perfect if you follow."

Zoe is taking me for a fitting. We drive to Great Barrington and stop at an old Victorian house defended by a battalion of pines. She touches a button that sets off a clarion of bells. A balding old man, a toy top wrapped in a robe, comes to greet us. He plants a kiss on Zoe's cheek.

"Dr. Professor, here is your design challenge."

"Possibly, with the help of prayers and chanting, we can effect a sea change," says Dr. Professor.

Introductions are exchanged in the parlor under a Tiffany shade. I praise the Early American furniture.

"He has some taste," Zoe says.

"Go into that room and disrobe, watch to crotch."

"No tailor ever . . ."

"I am trying to accommodate you on a very tight schedule. I

donate my services to the Farm."

"Dr. Professor is leaning over backwards, Soup. Don't second-guess."

I go into an adjoining room. There is a holographic camera pointed toward a small platform with a limbo background. An examining table trails wires linked to a computer. There is nothing to suggest clothes, not a rack, hanger or bolt of fabric.

I strip to my skin tossing my stuff onto a chair. Zoe and the one she calls Dr. Professor are laughing outside. They are laughing at me. I hear him do jokes about my Code. The bastard is in hysterics.

I wait, sitting on the table. After ten minutes I yell that I am ready. It is another five minutes before he joins me.

"First, a picture. Stand up there, hands at your sides."

I pose for the hologram.

"Good. Now back on the table."

I lay down while he charts me with calipers measuring everything from the obvious to the intimate.

"You got yourself a good Norman," he yells to Zoe.

"Excuse me," I say, "but I was wondering if it would be possible to get a copy of the picture?"

"You want a naked picture of yourself? For who? Your sweetie?"

"Like that, yes."

"Last year's had no cock to speak of. We had to pad his jock. The first thing the audience looks for is bulge, eh Zoe?"

"It can't hurt," Zoe says from the parlor.

"Alright, I'm finished with you."

"What about colors? Cut? Texture?"

"You leave it to me, son. You know who I dress? The biggest luminaries."

"But while we're here I would like some input . . ."

"When the mannequin is finished I sweat over the details. I go through tortures you wouldn't believe. All donated free of charge. I don't even take expenses."

"You construct a mannequin just for . . ."

"He's a magician," Zoe yells.

"The hair is all wrong," Dr. Professor says. "Norman's hair floated out of his head. I'll do a wig. Low on the frontal lobes to hide you-know-what."

"Is that legal?" I say.

"Get dressed. Don't keep your mamma waiting. Is Zoe a genius or what? Does she turn out a finished product?"

"That remains to be seen," Zoe yells.

Back in the car, Zoe tells me she wants to show me around Stockton and Lenox to track Norman's spoor. We have lunch at the restaurant where he went regularly for chicken pot pie. While we eat, Zoe takes an envelope from her bag and spreads a proof of the Festival poster.

There is a picture of Norman half in light, half in darkness like an eclipsed Sun. The theme is stated in block type:

A WORLD WITHOUT CRADLE?

"The concept here is, what would the world be like if Norman never was."

I think of millions of vanished plates.

"Express some opinion."

"Catchy. Stylish. It certainly gives a jolt."

"You seem hesitant."

"If that's the word. If we're talking about a world without Cradle doesn't that make me redundant?"

"You are slow today. We're talking happy ending. There was . . . is a Norman preserved in the formaldehyde of adoration. He . . . you . . . appear to redeem the virtues and values his art affirmed. We are talking rebirth."

"Ah. My coming is the redemption. Poignant."

"He followed his pie with caramel custard."

We order the caramel custard. I fashion a sense of my place in the pageant. If my appearance is to represent Norman's arrival in a world deprived of him then Morris Feuerbloom will have to find himself another exit. The launch of a firecracker would suggest the wrong dramatic direction. The theme is about coming home, not leaving.

"Zoe, there's something I must tell you. It's highly confidential concerning the last scene which is my only scene."

"No more. Don't second-guess the producer. You'll only break your heart. Listen to me, Soup. I have been there once or twice. Just play your part and enjoy the applause. That is our only real satisfaction and reward."

"What I was about to say could compromise . . ."

"Forget lines. You won't need words."

I swallow the urge to expose Feuerbloom along with my custard. This isn't Zoe's concern. It is between Morris and me. If logic fails, if he insists on suicide at the expense of the production, then I will take matters into my own hands and make a trip to the grave where his powder is buried.

Zoe is misty remembering stale adoration. My applause is all in the future. I take her hand.

The inspirational plate series commemorating this year's Festival began today with *Cherub Choir* which shows newborns in incubators facing a window where a full moon beams down on them. A young nurse observes this realizing that she is in the presence of a lovely mystery. The plate moves me and leaves me with a nagging nostalgia. I have not heard from my Trina though our suite is booked at the Blue Violet. Dr. Hamish handled the details as a favor.

After dinner, I take my long walk. The weather is ideal, the town tranquil. I follow a path along Main Street and out past the high school grounds. There is no sign of disturbance at the graveyard. I have been trying to corner Morris but he has avoided me with great skill. Since his Festival duties include supervision of the annual fireworks display he is exempt from certain rules. His meals are brought to him in his room where he orchestrates the entertainment.

Jill Hill refuses to acknowledge her part in their conspiracy. When I bring up the subject she acts totally blank. Talk about performances. She has me believing our encounter was a mirage. At table, Jill has not been her usual disgusting self. Perhaps it is that a lapful of eggplant parmigiana can't compete with her vision of bits and pieces of Morris showering down on the crowd of tourists. She knows I am the enemy of their plan, I catch her scanning my eyes, but I betray nothing but the desire to reason with her. That is my honest intent.

As I walk, I see a familiar outline ahead of me. It is Bill Maginot coming toward me carrying a bag and bending to pick up debris from the side of the road. What he finds he pops into his sack. Before he notices me we are face to face.

"Soup? What brings you out?"

"I could ask you the same, Bill."

"Me? I enjoy walking this highway to check on the sound track."

"You've lost me. What sound track?"

"The crap. The sludge and beer cans that trail every road. It's very much like the sound track on a film. Our music. It's a kind of hobby. I look for astonishing items. Things I am surprised to see escape."

"Escape?"

"Their destiny."

Bill dips into his bag and pulls out a plastic nipple.

"By way of example," he says, "this nipple is intact and somehow managed to escape its baby."

"That's beyond my small mind."

"Private and personal therapy," he says. "I suppose you know what got me shipped to Hamish Farm?"

"I have heard something on the grapevine. They say you were convinced that an angel appeared to you in the form of a dumpster and told you to trash your town."

"It was God, not an angel. And not in the form of a dumpster. As the driver."

"Whatever you say."

"Don't patronize me. Never do that."

We are alone on a dim road with hardly any traffic. Bill Maginot is a powerful man. If God came driving a dumpster, so be it.

"The Lord works in mysterious ways."

"And I was not told to trash my town. It didn't begin that way. At first I went with the truck to pick up ordinary refuse. Then I began to apply an egocentric definition of what I considered garbage. That wasn't God's fault, it was my own, if there was a fault. And He didn't say a word to stop me. I went from a liquor store to a pharmacy to City Hall. When they caught me I was stuffing the mayor into my compactor."

"I know the appeal of compactors. A mayor must have been tempting. But murder is no joke. Didn't God intervene?"

"He left me on my own after the video rental. I also stopped at an X-rated video rental. Censorship is no joke either. And that is what I was doing. Inflicting my taste on the planet. Who am I to decide what is mulch?"

"Nobody has that right except perhaps the driver of the dumpster."

"How dare you? I had every right."

"Fine, fine. You had every right."

"I pleaded self-defense. It was self-defense. Still, it was wrong. If not in the larger sense then in the immediate. My mission was divine but there was no way to convince the court. Especially since I myself was conflicted. I was in the right and I was filled with guilt. That may be a natural consequence of carrying out the Lord's will."

"Orders are orders."

"Interpreting the orders, that's the hard part. I suppose someday I will accept at least a trace of madness in myself. But it isn't easy. The experience was palpable. If I turn away from it I deny my own soul."

"It must be hard to hold the line, Bill. I mean, the minute you admit you were deranged they'll let you go back to the community of normals."

"They won't let me go no matter what I certify. They want me at Hamish Farm because of the Added Value Provisions. If that legislation passes I am worth my weight in platinum. They can finance a new gymnasium on my ass. Not that I relish the idea of being classified as a *thing*, no insult intended, Soup, but still . . . *platinum*."

"What about your freedom?"

"So the question becomes: Is the illusion of freedom sufficient? Because that is all the freedom there is. *Freedom* freedom would drive anybody nuts."

He sees a mangled umbrella in the grass, picks it up, snaps it open, then discards it. There is not enough utility left in the twisted canopy to classify it as escaped.

"Can you hold a confidence, Soup?"

"I don't want to, not this week."

"I have something to show you."

"Another time. I'm on overload. Too much input."

"Now."

"Now? Now is as good a time as any," I say.

We walk back to Main Street. The town begins with a group of run-down houses and abandoned gas stations. There is no clue to the affluence a few blocks ahead. Most towns share that dismal overture. Maybe it is a social reflex designed to dissuade invading immigrants or predators. Near a shack that leans against a truncated school bus, Bill Maginot shoves me through a dangling wood gate. We go around the ruptured porch to a tin shed covered with a skin of peeling posters.

Bill produces a key from his pocket. The key fits a rusty padlock. A door rattles open. I am urged inside. There is no light. I smell metal and oil. A match flares. He lights a ring of stumpy candles. They ooze enough lumens to reveal a red dumpster with its hood propped up by an iron bar.

"My shrine," he says. "It's just an old garbage truck I'm tinkering with, just in case."

"Just in case?"

"Of anything. I call her Samantha. Guess why?"

We chuckle together in the candlelight.

"I may be the only patient at the Farm without some little secret."

"Meaning?"

"Everyone seems to have something going on the side."

"But not you, Soup? That surprises me. A man with your background."

"Between my acting lessons and the Plateworks, most of my energy is drained. Maybe after the Festival I'll find some new interest and indulge myself."

"You consider my Samantha an indulgence?"

"No, no, I didn't say that."

"She could be described as an indulgence."

"She could be. Or not."

"I knew I could talk to you, Soup. We are both beyond the pale. We are unique."

"Escaped."

"How I envy my Samantha," he says, patting the truck's rump. "All she wants is a few workable spare parts. And she who eats with her ass shall have what she needs. That's a promise, honey."

"She knows you mean it, Bill."

"And you know I mean it. Soup, tell me something. Have you inquired about last year's Norman?"

"No, not really. It didn't occur to me. I never thought much about him. I assumed that after the festivities he was pronounced Mainstream and sent home."

"Ask."

"Alright. I am asking. Tell me."

"I can't violate a confidence. Ask somebody else."

"I will. I'll get around to it."

Bill lifts me by the shoulders and shakes me like he shook the umbrella.

"Ask."

There is still an hour before curfew. I leave Bill Maginot tinkering with a gasket and head for Zoe's house. As I walk, a car slows behind me. I turn to see that it is driven by a young girl with a freckle-garden face. She is about to stop and offer me a ride when she sees my Code, lets out a shriek, hits the gas and leaves me swallowing her exhaust.

I remember one of Homer's homilies. We were preparing an advertising campaign for Brogg Foods' new soft drink, *Gush*. The agency boys brought in a print ad showing a freckled child standing on a beach near a sand castle. She wore a cardboard crown and held a can of Gush under the caption "Royal Quench for a Royal Wench." A vice president commented on the amount of freckles and suggested airbrushing a few hundred. Homer said, "Never screw around with freckles. They'll come back to haunt you." The ad was a great success. Norman Cradle knew about freckles too. His faces are seasoned with them. The wise ones appreciate the power of freckles, it is information that comes to them in the womb. Had the face that screamed when it saw me been a barren expanse of white or black, I would feel less sorrow. To have agitated a freckleface makes me wince and curse my fate. I run the route to Zoe's eager for her comfort.

When I get there I see two shadows move on a curtain. One of them uses the identical gestures Zoe has taught me. I feel palpitations. Cat quiet, I climb the porch steps and skulk around to the open window.

"Listen to the voice. You'll see what I mean about spiritual reachout," Zoe is saying.

I hear a lament from *Tristan*. The music jars my renegade soul.

"Jesus, not opera. I hope I live long enough never to hear another opera," the second shadow says.

Bernie?

"The idea is for you to extend yourself. Even if there is virtually no chance of being summoned there is always the figment and you must prepare as if you will perform."

"Nothing will happen to him."

"Ah, Bernard, an understudy must have faith in disaster. An understudy suckles grey breasts."

Understudy? Nothing was said to me about an understudy. I am not replaceable. I *am* Norman Cradle, Zoe told me that herself.

"Try once more. Work on the arms."

"No more tonight. I can't get with it."

"Very well, saracen. Tomorrow then."

Alright. The show must come first. I can live with that. But him?

I wait like an owl in the dark for Bernie to leave. Then I pound at Zoe's door and erupt into her parlor.

"So? What have we here, Soup?"

"I think it was cowardly and craven not to tell me about an understudy and your choice is repellant beyond description."

"But you must have realized there would be an understudy. Our pageant is larger than the sum of its parts. People burst blood vessels. It happens every day. As for Bernard, he was inflicted on me and not a bad idea. His job is to care for you and how better to enforce his motivation? The man is terrified of public exposure. He would die to keep you from any harm. Would you like some sherry wine?"

"Answer me this. What happened to last year's Norman?"

Zoe's face flattens and her feet turn inward. As she pours from a decanter into two bud glasses her hand trembles. Sherry spills onto her sideboard.

"Must you know?"

"I must."

"I had enormous confidence in last year's Norman. It was misplaced. Oh, he was brilliant in performance. Not you, but more than adequate. He seemed so serious about a career in theatre. I wrote letters and made calls on his behalf. I prevailed on Dr. Hamish to reevaluate his case. But upon his release from the Farm he headed straight for Los Angeles. He does quiz shows. We do not communicate."

"You have nothing more to tell me?"

"Alas, nothing more."

"That's the whole story?"

"In a nutshell, yes."

"I would like some wine."

"Whatever possessed you to ask about a past Norman? You mustn't feel competitive with ancestors, Soup. A blooming ear of golden corn in a bountiful harvest shouldn't care about some forgotten husk."

"Zoe, you do take the scenic route."

"Why not if there is a scenic route to take?"

"I can't say why I asked. There was some suggestion made that the former Norman experienced some kind of setback."

"He did."

"I don't mean television. Something worse. Something unspeakable."

"Who put that thought into your head?"

"It doesn't matter."

"You won't hurt me, will you, Soup? You won't leave a scar instead of a rose?"

"Frankly, Zoe, I'll be glad when this is over."

"No. You won't be glad. The perfume will linger and never diminish. The question is, will your memory of me melt like a flake?"

"Never. Bottom line, do you really sense talent?"

"I feel your talent in the heart between my legs."

My ego is restored beyond even the assault of freckles. I laugh over my suspicions. Without questioning, Zoe laughs with me.

"Let us hope my understudy avoids being bitten by the bug of ambition."

"No danger there. Dr. Hamish screened him very carefully. I insisted that the possibility be considered."

"Still, you should have told me."

"My job here is to convince you of your immortality. Not to remind you that there might be a squadron of microbes waiting to strike you down. Don't fault me for hiding a depressing truth."

"I forgive you, Zoe. Whatever success I might have is yours."

"No, darling. That isn't how it works."

"Are we ready for the Norman conquest?" Dr. Hamish says, doing push-ups. We are in his office. Bright sun sliced by a venetian blind stripes the room. After a night of soul searching I am without levity.

"I think so. Zoe feels . . ."

"Excuse the exercise. This is a tense period for me. I suspect my anxiety is brother induced. Henry is quite mad during the week before Cradle Day. It amazes me how much he feels the sense of family."

"Please, go ahead. Nothing like exercise to break the knots. I only spoke with your brother once but I noticed his dedication."

"For Henry this is Christmas, New Years and Hoffenstein's Birthday rolled into one. I have affection for my father and grandfather but nothing to match his."

"As you like to say, to each his own."

"I do say that. I should listen closer to myself. So? You wanted to talk."

He ends the push-ups and does knee bends.

"If I only knew how to begin. This bothers me."

"Let it hang out."

"I hope your response will be, shall I say, calculated and restrained. Fair."

"Let me worry about my response."

"Yesterday I was a bit churned. I had a sudden concern about last year's Norman."

"Did you? What were you concerned about?"

"Nothing really. Ms. Rapish erased any doubts."

"Good for her."

"And discovering that Bernie was my understudy gave me a bit of a tantrum."

"Not unexpected. You are an only child. What you experienced was a bit of old-fashioned jealousy."

"After I left Zoe's, I went back out to the old cemetery."

"The cemetery?"

"I needed to clear my head. I've been there before."

"I have patients waiting. Do come to the point."

"It seems that Morris Feuerbloom has evolved a rather elaborate fantasy about his death. To sum it up, he plans to launch himself strapped to a rocket he calls the Spectacular. Toward that end, no pun intended, he's acquired a supply of powder."

"Gunpowder? From where? We keep a close watch on our inventory. You know that Morris is in charge of the pyrotechnics for Cradle Day. He puts on a fabulous display. And we are not unaware of his aggrandized death wish. So we do monitor his doings. I'd be surprised if he's got enough fuel for a sparkler."

"Morris is a step ahead. He buys the powder a bit at a time during his trips to town."

"Does he? The old bugger. I'm impressed."

"I can't cite exact statistics but I know he's got his load buried in some kind of capsule out in the graveyard. Last night I went out there to make a final attempt at reason. It seems he plans to launch himself at the climax of the pageant and I have specific problems with that. I don't want the man hurt and I certainly don't want a distraction to ruin months of . . ."

"One climax at a time."

"Exactly. There is a self-interest factor at work here. My aim was to tell Morris to disarm or I would report the scheme to you personally."

"Did he agree? No. You wouldn't be here."

"I never got the chance to ask. You see, when I found the grave he uses, he was busy. With a friend. Not a firecracker. They were having a kind of liaison."

"Morris involved in a tryst? Morris Feuerbloom fucking?"

"Not exactly fucking. Rolling around. As you surmised, his cohort is a female who I would prefer not to name. She was very accommodating. Nurturing, talking, fondling. What they lacked in fusion they made up for in, how to put it, extended foreplay."

"There was no actual intercourse?"

"To be accurate, he did remove his dentures and boast of his prowess as, to use his word, cocksucker."

"Resourceful."

"While she coaxed his organ he told her the reason Jews are circumcised is to disparage the pyramids."

"Interesting."

"They did seem to experience a kind of climax. I could hear his bones rattle. And he found a form of gratification. It was uplifting and grotesque. Disturbing."

"Thank you for telling me about this."

"There's a bit more. Afterward, they practiced lighting the fuse."

"Wasn't that redundant?"

"He really means to try the launching. He could hurt a lot of people if . . ."

"Jill will draw the line."

"You know about Jill?"

"In his own way, Morris told me. He's confused by his feelings for her. Attraction and repulsion. He called her *a match made in heaven*. I should have picked up on that. The son-of-a-bitch was playing word games. He never mentioned the Spectacular. That's already on the record. Every year since Feuerbloom first came here he's threatened to send himself up to join the comets. Year after year it turns out that his supply of propellant is inconsequential. We always check it out and we will again. The man has no intention of leaving us. His triumph will be to outlive us all. Don't bother yourself with Feuerbloom."

"I feel ridiculous."

"It's positive that you told me. Accept that not much goes on around the Farm that I don't know about. You say she had an orgasm?"

"There were spasms, yes."

"I noticed that Jill has quieted down during meals. Maybe there is hope for her. Of course, any sexuality had to be entwined with anti-social behavior. And with a fossil, no less. Still, reports like this confirm my belief in the Cradle technique."

"You should feel pleased, Dr. Hamish. I assume there won't be consequences, punishment, even censure? I wouldn't want either of them to suffer and I certainly don't want them to even suspect we had this talk. If it wasn't for the element of . . ."

"Keeping The Explosive Jew on the ground is part of the Cradle Day ritual by now. The cemetery. Last year it was the golf course. He had no match girl. He built himself this clever ignition system that the Fireflower family put to use. They got a patent. The man is a genius."

Dr. Hamish offers me a sweaty hand. We shake. I have accomplished nothing but to make a total ass of myself. When I leave I am depressed for myself and for poor Morris, just another child of gravity.

Dear Trina,

I assume that you have written and that "they" hold your letters to keep me from distraction. There can be no other explanation for the silence.

I have embraced my role in a way I never thought possible. Living in the skin of Norman Cradle has been a revelation. His/my eyes transform scabs and festering wounds to flowers and rainbows. There is nothing too ugly to kiss. Every path leads to splendor.

Could this be the message Dr. Hoffenstein tried to communicate at his banquet? Are these emanations from the echoes he spoke of? Remember the carbuncle you had removed from your magnificent rump? Amazingly, I think of it now with positive pleasure. I miss the thing, I realize its essential wonder. Were we deaf to its message? A perfect ass is no ass, not in comparison to a mature, weathered ass. It is the wrinkled face that radiates the most beauty.

Will this embracing view of life continue after my moment in the limelight? Who can say. Shall your husband revert to the pinched realm of the ordinary? Can that happen to one who has enjoyed visions of perfection? How I long to share these revelations with my wife and children!

Enclosed is the latest from our Plateworks. It is our Halloween plate, *Trick or Treat*. See how Cradle captured the sweet fear of the children as they approach the ancient mansion. See how the woman inside makes ready to play her fated part as town witch even as she prepares candied apples and other goodies for the brats. We know she has done this for countless generations of moppets. She accepts her designation as official crone as naturally as she accepts her reflection. Imagine insight like that from a Limoges or Meisen?

Hugs and strawberries to you and the kids.

See you next week. Is it that soon . . . ?

Forever,

Whoever, Whatever, Whyever.

The evening before Cradle Day I walk through town. Evidence of carnival is everywhere, no store is without decoration. Hundreds of fresh faces browse the shops and gasp over Autumn's transformation of every bush and tree. Cradle toys and dolls are cuddled in the arms of countless children. Their parents wear our shirts and jewelry and, yes, carry our gift-boxed plates.

It is happening! The Festival grounds have become a city of tents and pavilions. Booths are set up for food and souvenirs. Workers unload scores of benches from trailer trucks. Lights and banners are strung from portable poles.

On a ridge beyond the field I see Morris Feuerbloom supervising the placement of mortars. Three Fireflower vans are parked near the launch site. Morris commands his crew, dressed in Fireflower uniforms, with the assurance of a general. Authority has trimmed decades from his voice and body.

I walk up there and say, "Break a leg."

"Break a wishbone," he says.

"We all need luck."

"Luck does not live here, Soup. My display is calculated to the last *pfft*. Tell me, were you the one who tipped off Hamish? This morning they came and poured pisswater in my grave. Should I thank you for that?"

"Unfair, Morris. It was Dr. Hamish who told me about your plan. He said you do the same thing every year to the point of boredom. Don't blame me, blame yourself."

"So, I bore the doctor? Thanks for telling me. OK, OK, so they got my number and it comes up zero. Now I have plenty to do so let me do it."

He seems surprisingly cheerful.

"Morris, I only hope you didn't get Jill into trouble."

"She's a consenting child. By the rock, the rock you *shmekel*," he yells to one of his gnomes.

I give him a wave and continue my tour. They are testing a Ferris Wheel near the theatre. It glows even in the daylight, spinning and swinging empty seats. It is candy. I tell a foreman that I am this year's Norman. He agrees to let me ride in exchange for a scribbled note to his wife. "*Best wishes, Charlene, Norman Cradle.*" I write with pencil on a napkin from his lunch box.

I rise and circle, looking out at the Berkshire Hills. The Wheel stops and traps me for a minute. I hang suspended in a glow of pink, red, blue, yellow. What spider lives in this steel web? Will I be hunted and injected with venom, then sealed in silk for Winter nourishment? Would it be so bad? There is no spider. The Wheel moves again and I am back on the ground.

It is time to go back. According to tradition, this is the night of my anointing. I will be purified and pledged to silence, allowed no communication until my performance is done. It is a stupid rule but enforced by brother Henry who insists on the letter of the law.

I do take some time to watch the choir and dancers rehearse *A World Without Cradle?* Sure enough, Bernie stands in for me. It is another of Henry's rules that The Norman is not seen in public so I myself am not permitted to participate though Zoe has walked me around the stage and explained my marks. I enjoy Bernie's evident torture. When he lifts his arms in the gesture of rebirth he seems to be reaching for a can of Budweiser on a high shelf.

On the way to the Farm, I can't help thinking of my reward. I am told The Norman is always released and I suspect Charlton Hymn has been up to his legal leaps. Maybe that's why Trina hasn't written. If there is to be a Hoffenstein pardon, even dispensation to restore my Code, it would have to be done with great delicacy. Will

I have Homer to thank? Was he behind my selection over so many contenders? I fantasize a car waiting for me after the show. I will be taken somewhere for quick surgery, then surface as director of one of the Brogg enterprises in Africa or Asia. After a few years . . . It is best not to count such tenuous chickens.

Appropriately, it is Zoe Rapish who leads me to my ritual bath. She meets me in my room, holding a white silk robe ornamented with a gold sun. Zoe turns away while I put on the slippery garment. I hate silk and satin, they catch hangnails, but there is no denying a regal feeling. The fact that Zoe averts her eyes from my privates is ludicrous since she has seen me grovel on her studio floor with only pubic hair for a loincloth but even she plays her part to the hilt. I am a god now and what Zoe has seen before is best forgotten.

When I am ready she examines me. Even her rigid standard is surpassed. She lets out a sign of satisfaction while brushing flecks of dander from my shoulders. I expect her to bow and kiss my ring.

"My Pygmalion," she says. "My Frankenstein."

"You are mixing metaphors."

"A mixed metaphor is an honest metaphor. I have worked a wonder, my job is done. You are beautiful."

"You speak like stained glass, Zoe. And since I am to be silenced I want you to know that if I carry this off it is your victory."

"By the time you take a final bow you'll be convinced you did it yourself. Come now, Soup."

She leads me downstairs into Dr. Hamish's office. We go through a door I never noticed. It leads to a magnificent bathroom tiled ceiling to floor with exotic birds and tropical leaves. A huge tub simmers the fragrance of white wine. The room is lit only by candles.

Zoe opens a cabinet. I see a jar of Heinz Ketchup, Guldens Mustard and Crackerjacks.

"Kneel."

I kneel. Zoe daubs my head with a dot of ketchup and mustard.

"Repeat. I am Norman Cradle."

"I am Norman Cradle."

I take communion with a Crackerjack.

"These were his beloved foods. It is said he mixed them into his pigments. God bless Norman and America."

Zoe removes a black blindfold from the pocket of my robe. She wraps it across my eyes and snaps it tight. I hear her leave. I wait. Whatever pleasure awaits, I deserve. I paid my dues. I earned my laurels. I am ready to take the risks.

I hear a soft female hum. It could be one of Hoffenstein's whales. Gentle hands slip off my wrapping. I am led to the bubbling tub. I sit in perfect water waiting to be soaped and rinsed clean. Instead, my bather joins me in the pool. Her humming continues until her head submerges. She takes my buoyant tool in her mouth. The hum is still there as vibration. I am amazed at her breath control. The girl must have gills. She rises from the depths and grabs my hands. She rubs my fingers along her legs. When I touch her sex she guides my lips to her breast.

If Trina had answered my letters even with a memo I might have broken my vow of silence. That is hard to say since it isn't me in the tub, it is Norman Cradle. Being dead, buried and long since turned to dust, this must be a special joy for his ghost, afterlife or none. I allow myself to be seduced in his place. My invisible lover inserts me inside her like a frankfurter in a warm bun. She licks away my ketchup and mustard. It has been a long time of abstinence. I thrust like a demon. My invisible lover flails her arms and legs. She somehow manages to knock over the nest of candles. I hear their little flames hiss and die as she throws water at them. There is broken glass from the holder all over the tile floor. It must be Jill Hill. Who else could destroy a temple with such efficiency?

I follow her out of the tub and feel her bending over a pile of glass chips. I tilt her forward and enter her with frenzy and tenderness. Norman grinds and thrusts, he is not his usual controlled self. Vow or no vow, he lets out a biblical roar. Then he separates from his sweet container and sits blissful in the double darkness.

At some point, I realize I am alone. I pull off my blindfold. Before she left, my angel managed to get one candle going. By its flicker, I get back in the tub and give The Norman a wash.

I pad back through Dr. Hamish's office. Because of tomorrow's excitement, curfew was early. There is nobody around. I decide on a breath of apple cider air. I want to feel the tang against my pampered flesh.

I go outside to the porch and sniff the mix of oxygen, gasses, pesticides, sweat, pollen and Autumn. A new carpet of leaves sends up its own scent. Along with the effluvia of harvest I smell the ozone odor of gathering energy, the optimism of industry, the seasonal eruption of ambition and resolve. I willingly contribute my particle of musk to the national perfume.

I see a pickup truck drive to the delivery entrance. A lamp shows me it is driven by Dr. Professor. He leaves the truck holding two garment bags. I hear his buzz at the door and the clicking response. My tailor vanishes inside. As I am appreciating his contribution, he emerges in the company of a man and woman. The man is a stranger, the woman is Samantha. Her shape is as familiar as a continent. They push a gurney toward the truck.

Dr. Professor stands away while his recruits reach in to remove a body. The body is placed naked onto the rolling cart. A spill of moonlight gives enough silver for me to see that the body is mine. Dr. Professor gets back into his pickup and drives away. I am rolled along toward the delivery ramp.

It must be that Zoe insisted my mannequin wear Norman's casuals to keep their press. It would be like her not to forget to turn that stone. But I am naturally curious. When Samantha and her partner shove the mobile slab into the building, I follow.

The delivery door is caught by its own bolt. I have no problem getting in. I track the sound of the gurney's squeaky wheels. Another door opens and shuts. This one is marked WARD X No ADMITTANCE and that door is locked tight.

It can only mean that even the terminals in Ward X are encouraged to involve themselves in the joys of Cradle Day. It must be their assignment to play some supportive role, like caring for costumes. They are not permitted to attend the pageant though they do see it on video. Doing menial chores makes them feel vicarious closeness. That would be a typical Hamish gesture to his more difficult clientele. I approve.

As I am about to retreat down the corridor, I hear Samantha's tiny voice. Her voice never put on weight, its metabolism has nothing to do with hers. I duck into shadows as she waddles out probing the cement floor with a flashlight, bends to retrieve an earring, grunts with relief, then uses a key to snap open the formidable lock. Before the door slams I slide through behind her.

Why am I putting both Norman and myself in jeopardy? If a guard catches me I imagine it couldn't be too bad since I am the jewel of the Festival. But if some roaming inmate from Ward X finds me and remembers his brother or father then there is no telling. I have heard horror stories about Ward X that made my nails sweat. Still, it is unlikely there will be prowlers down there. The incorrigibles are locked into their cells at the first sign of sunset. Samantha must be some kind of trustee. I decide to go ahead. There is the compelling sense that I am following myself, involved in an out-of-body trance like the vaporous journeys taken by certain holy men.

Another sound rivals the squeaky wheels, an unexpected sound of cheering and singing. They must be welcoming the arrival of my body like some sainted icon. But who?

There is one more door to navigate, the swinging kind with no lock. A diamond-shaped window is cut into the steel. I take a prudent peek before I push.

I see the entire population of Ward X assembled, dressed in military gear. If this is a game it is dangerous. The Global Concords allow only local security forces to play at war. How brilliant of Hamish. What better way to channel manic rage? War is the road to peace for this mad army. My opinion of Bartley soars.

Then I see my body strapped to a post.

Not my mannequin but Henry Hamish is drawing the cheers and songs. He points to Samantha. She hands him the underpants I gave her as a gift.

"Inhale and recall," Henry yells. He sniffs at the crotch of my jockeys.

"Inhale, recall," they scream back. Then he throws my briefs to the crowd. In turn, they sniff and pass them along like a jury examining evidence. This is pushing therapy to extremes no matter what the higher purpose.

"Many years ago my grandfather Isaac Hamish came here with one desire and determination," Henry proclaims. "To rid the world of Norman Cradle!"

There is a massive outburst of approval. Henry will lead them through the story to the part where Grandpa Isaac undergoes his conversion. It's a simplistic technique but the cathartic fable might do them some good. Who am I to second-guess the professionals?

"Isaac Hamish saw through the Cradle delusion. But alas, he was too late. The Norman died in his bed showered with glory. Worse yet, before he expired he regressed to a senile Eden that confirmed his delusions. Norman Cradle died happy."

A chorus of boos and catcalls, the stomping of leather boots.

"My grandfather was only mortal. He could not endure his disappointment. His very soul was shattered to its components. Yes, Isaac Hamish thought himself defeated. By the huge power of quintessential self-deception, even he yielded to the Cradle myth. And from that moment he was forced to celebrate what he came to subdue."

"No, no, no," from the Ward X infantry. I am puzzled. This is not the Henry Hamish I met at the gift shop. The man seems genuinely bitter.

"Tomorrow, Cradle Day, spit on the name, Isaac Hamish shall be vindicated in some small way. Because of you in this room, you who have been gifted with true insight. When the charade is done, while the fools dance through their pseudo-ecstasy up above, we shall have our pageant, our Festival down here near the flaming belly of the planet. We will sniff out The Norman like a truffle and bring him to you. You will have him to do with as you wish. And we don't expect leftovers."

"*Inhale, recall. Inhale, recall. Inhale, recall.*"

"My grandfather of blessed memory is smiling now. His quest is to be fulfilled if only in symbol. And he is not the only one watching to see what you do. You are the fighting force that holds the key to the future. Your time will come very soon. It is you who are our only buttress against the detestacled dreams which would serve up the guts of our great nation using false words of love. Globalism be damned! We know that true love is a blood sport."

That sentiment is warmly received. Henry retrieves my shorts and puts them on the mannequin.

"Inhale, recall. Where are my bloodhounds?"

A group of team players led by Samantha steps forward.

"Will you bring back The Norman?"

"We will. We will."

"You hear, Isaac Hamish? Listen and be redeemed."

Music plays. The hounds parade past my effigy sniffing with emotion. Samantha and Susan lead them. I know Ward X presents unique problems that deserve special consideration but why stimulate hope with promises that can't be kept? I will talk to Dr. Hamish about this turn of events, especially the business about a secret army waiting for the rallying bugle. How long can they be sold that bill of goods? Cradleian Therapy takes weird turns.

I back off, careful to stifle a laugh. To think of Henry's hounds trooping after a phantom, using their noses to guide them.

As I release the outer door and enjoy cold air I think about last year's Norman.

I stop myself. I have been fed, bathed, screwed and praised. This is not a time to consider evil. Besides, there is every chance that I am upstairs in bed, having myself a nightmare with its roots in excessive good fortune.

BROGG ENTERPRISES
1 Brogg Plaza
New York, New York 10001

Dear Soup,

I must inform you that Trina and the children will not join you in West Stockton. While your persuasive letters were carefully considered, the final determination was negative. The entire family wishes you every success with your worthy endeavor and expresses confidence that your performance will be memorable.

Please understand that Amos and Amanda Wander are only now adjusting to recent events which have drastically affected their young lives. Trina herself has held up well despite severe social and psychological pressures. To expose them to undue stress would, at this time, be counter productive. Trina Wander has informed us of your supportive comments regarding Homer Brogg's campaign. We are most appreciative and only regret that you cannot cast a needed vote. Enclosed is an autographed picture of Mr. Brogg.

Sincerely yours,
Lucy Lane,
Secretary to Homer Brogg

P.S. While it is not difficult to empathize with your desire for continued communication we feel it would be prudent to refrain from future attempts. Such contact can only result in the inhibition of your excellent progress at Hamish Farm.

cc: Dr. Bartley Hamish
      Charlton Hymn, Esq.

I put the letter away and hang Homer's picture in the bathroom with a pushpin through his eye. I know the decision to put me on hold was his and I feel for Trina's sorrow. My children never heard about Cradle Day. If they had, they would have found a way to get here.

Or is the letter part of the same dream that includes my purification, a skin that gives off aromas of scented oils, the satanic pep rally led by Henry Hamish?

In the morning light I must look into my mirror and acknowledge the minuscule possibility that I will be sacrificed to the restless ghost of Isaac Hamish. There would be bizarre logic, from a therapeutic vantage. I can't deny that several down in Ward X might profit by murder. Ripping a god to bits must force the butcher to consider celestial suffering and the very consideration can be the first step to sensible guilt and ultimate rehabilitation. Without the crucifixion where would Christianity be today?

No, the Hamish brothers will not allow such a crime though they might go along with transference to my mannequin. That would be a fair compromise. I would like to discuss all this with Zoe Rapish who comes with my breakfast tray but there is the imposed silence.

"Marvelous breakfast for the star. You seem edgy. Butterflies?"

I nod.

"To be expected. A good sign. Drink your juice. Eat your ham and eggs. Take this B-complex. Have some coffee. Trust your talent."

I shower and dress. At noon I am transported to the Festival grounds by limo. Once again, Zoe has put me at ease. There is only the stage.

Thousands are lined up for the rides and at the concessions. I see that the gift shop has its own pavilion. I wonder how my plates are selling. The car finds a route through the mass and we stop behind the massive outdoor theatre. All this will be gone in a matter of hours. It appeared from nothing and will dissolve to debris but while it is here it is splendid, it is mine.

Zoe is waiting to walk me through my positions one last time. The sets are ready, the lights tuned. We work behind a great, gold curtain that borders our cocoon.

Afterward, there is a luncheon for VIPs. Both brothers Hamish are there. I watch them carefully to see how they watch me but there is nothing unusual in their eyes. I notice that the guests wear *World Without Cradle?* name tags. I get no tag but I do get a sweatband to hide my Code. There is some comment about dispensation related to makeup. It's just as well that my non-person, non-human status is concealed from the influentials.

I hear Dr. Hamish pressing for a grant from some state official, discussing my case in point to underline his pitch. I resent being used as a poster child but the conversation does allay a residue of apprehension. If I was to be given to Ward X, would I be held up as a model patient?

It is explained by Zoe that ritual prevents me from speech. Everyone is polite and full of good wishes. Even Morris Feuerbloom makes a brief appearance. He shows a sketch of his fireworks display.

"I swear to you they will forget the moon and stars. I will paint the sky with Cradle pride. Fireflower is unrivaled, the best, to see is to know. If any of you have a party coming up or some holiday, give a call. We have operators waiting twenty-four hours."

There is general laughter. Morris acts like he was carbonated. There is no suicide in that man's mind. I look for Jill Hill. How could my priestess of the tub be the same woman I saw rolling over hallowed ground with the fossil of phosphorescence, the elf of ersatz thunder, the little man promoting the same company that had him put away?

Now Zoe is saying she believes this will easily be the finest pageant ever. She tells them I am the best Norman of the lot. She even confides that I wanted more lines.

"I knew we had ourselves a winner when he actually demanded material. I had a hell of a time convincing him that less is more,

more or less. Is that right, Soup?"

"Why do you call him Soup?" asks a major benefactor of the Farm.

"Because the man is a soup of contradictions, a consommé of conundrums," Zoe says without a pause. "Even as life itself."

It suddenly comes to me that what I saw in Ward X was an elaborate hoax planned by Zoe herself. It was no accident that Samantha managed to leave the forbidden door unlocked. And the business with the earring, that too. Zoe Hamish wants me to feel death's motivating presence. That is the essential element in a quality reading. Stanislavsky would have engineered the same kind of terror. I had to realize that Norman Cradle knew about death even as he spit diamonds in its mouldy face.

I pick up a yellow pad and pencil to write, *"Thank you for last night."* Zoe blushes in her manner. She shrugs and goes to mingle with strangers. In her heart, she is shy. I save the piece of paper. If I meet Jill I can use it again. I owe so many people. Henry Hamish, the kids who sniffed and marched, Dr. Professor . . . the good people who gave time and effort to my theatrical genesis.

I will not let them down.

Before surrender, the sun sends pink alarms and purple warnings. I think of Morris watching that competition from up on a neighboring hill.

Now the sky loses its blush and yields to blues and greys. The greys thicken and dominate. There is a crackle in the air and a soft silver shower. *Fireflower!* has taken the challenge of the night.

Dr. Hamish was right, the man is a genius. I watch his toys transform a grumpy sky, his Fireflowers spit color, whirl tornadoes of burnished gold, boom like drums slapped by giants. He carpets the stars with neon, he shames the moon with arches that swell like budding breasts.

When the image of Hoffenstein takes shape and blazes in eerie orange, the crowd sings under an umbrella of flame:

Be Proud of Your Code
Proud of your place
Proud of your race
Proud of your pride
Proud of your work
Proud of your stride
Be Proud of Your Code
Your rainbow, your guide
Your own, your compass
Your path through the tide

My eyes glisten even as they mirror nebulae of colors I have never seen.

Zoe taps my shoulder. It is time. I go to my dressing room, set up in a trailer cleverly linked to the stage.

The costumes, Bernie's and mine, hang from a bar. They are almost identical in size. I always assumed my understudy dwarfed me and I muse on the dimension of authority while Bernie sings his own song in the stall shower.

I do what I do on a whim. I take his underwear and replace it with my own. Before I make the switch, I make sure to rub my shorts over private places. If radar nostrils from Ward X *are* tuned and ready then let them have some challenge.

It is a craven and stupid act. I am about to put it right when Bernie parts the shower curtain and presents himself with a bow.

"I like dripping on rented rooms," he says. "It's my favorite thing about hotels. To sit on the bed wet."

He is in my shorts admiring his torso in the standing mirror.

I get into the shower. The last remnants of herbs and spices from my purification swirl down the drain with soap curds. When I finish, Bernie is already in his Cradle outfit, Mr. Humble, fighting a stuck zipper in the pants.

I put on the humility suit and test a floppy fedora. Dr. Professor has outdone himself. Even the shoes he provided are scuffed and heel-worn, with leather tongues that hang from criss-cross laces like dead leaves. Everything is exactly right.

I stare at myself without vanity. My mindset is correct. I hear the rumble of fireworks and see their glossy flashes through a tiny window. I think to myself, "The things I do for the order of things."

There have been Normans before and there will be an unbroken string of Normans on and on and on; I am of the continuum. Yes, it is about order. Even the chaos of Feuerbloom's finale is carefully orchestrated. Thus the doors to the underworld are kept carefully sealed. I make a strange sound, a sound of contentment. Bernie is as startled as I am.

"What's with you? Are you sick? Is that it?"

I assure him that I am in excellent health.

In a few minutes Zoe arrives. She is pleased with my appearance. She carries a wig in a round box.

"Put it on. One size fits all."

"Jesus," Bernie says. "He looks like his head exploded."

"He looks authentic," Zoe says. "Soup, the Nightingales are on now. They're a real crowd pleaser. The old songs. They turn the audience to cream puffs. They'll end up as happy as a pig in shit. By the time you go on, you'd kill them if you scratched your short hairs and recited the appendix from *Grey's Anatomy*."

"What about me?" Bernie says.

"Hang close, Bernard. This is a world of plagues and unexpected developments."

The three of us go to the Green Room, a cubicle next to the TV control booth. The pageant is broadcast around the Berkshires and back to Hamish Farm for shut-ins.

On six monitors, the Nightingales, all inmates, do the golden oldies with zest and polish. Zoe was right, the crowd adores them. But I wonder if this is the best lead-in to our pageant which requires a brutal transition of mood.

Zoe explains our segment to an assistant director. Her emphasis is on the absolute necessity of creating an utterly bleak emotion. *World Without Cradle?* depends on despair. The audience must applaud itself to exhaustion following the Nightingales. There must be time before the curtain lifts.

While Zoe and Bernie watch the monitors, I go back to the Green Room where a small TV set picks up the show. I switch the channel to news. There is always news.

They are reporting a funeral. Zoom in on a procession of grieved mourners. Leading the parade is Homer Brogg. I see Lauren just behind him, veiled and tearful. And there is Trina, Amos and Amanda. They follow a polished brass coffin toward the Brogg

Mausoleum. I know the place well. I have attended many funerals for assorted Broggs over the years. The family is messianic about gathering its dead in one place, even the most remote cousins. I suspect it is Homer's vision to form a flying wedge against eternity. I remember his telling me about a demented friend who trained mercenaries for combat, then had the bunch killed so he would have his own shock troops to capture territory in the beyond. Charlton Hymn handled his case, it was a hung jury.

But who died? Some hundred year old aunt? The Broggs live forever. Their genes are Brillo.

". . . after a long illness. James P. Wander worked closely with Mr. Brogg on many projects. His loss . . ."

The tape breaks up, the screen goes white. The anchorwoman appears with an agitated face. "That is not the video I promised you. In fact, it is scheduled for tomorrow's news. Please forgive our error. Hey, guys, let's get it right this time, eh? Here's Dirk Dworkin with Sports Update . . ."

They were burying me. Trina and the kids looked genuinely moved. Even Lauren and Homer seemed subdued.

"Let's go," Zoe says.

I follow her backstage. While the dancers and choir take their places I think of how ridiculous that anchor must have felt when her technicians played a premature tape. At Brogg Communications that was our worst nightmare. We labeled our product with the greatest care to avoid such a gaff. It is still a public conceit that the news be reasonably fresh. I have seen many tapes played on the wrong day but never a funeral. That strikes me as a serious miscue, a lot more serious than reporting an insurrection in some remote corner of the globe where Uncoded primitives complain about a tax increase. Tipping a funeral can upset a whole family not to mention loss of obituary space in the newspapers.

Appreciative applause for the Nightingales. Not the kind of applause I want, the kind that peels lifelines from palms, but generous enough. They do an encore.

"What comes up the chimney?" Zoe says, holding a wishbone at me. Like Morris, I resent the intrusion of even a remote possibility that luck or fate will affect my work. "Smoke," she answers herself. "I wish *our* wish comes true."

The bone snaps, she wins the wish, just as well since I refuse to wish for anything. I am legally dead. Homer decreed that there is no me. My skeleton is out of his political closet and in that garish brass box. What is actually in that coffin? What did they put in there? I remember that Dr. Professor's mannequin is very lifelike. No. This is not the time to sulk over details of my funeral.

Sets for the pageant are rolled into place even as the Nightingales make their exit. I hear the audience shift, murmur and cough. The theatre goes black. The orchestra strikes up the *World Without Cradle?* theme which was composed and orchestrated by Henry Hamish. I learn this from browsing the score on a music stand. Stagehands place pots of cactus plants in front of a blank landscape. Children recruited from the local school are herded into place. Their faces are smeared with grease and grime, their clothing made from rags. Color drains from the spots.

"Ladies and Gentlemen," says a crepuscular-announcer voice, "I ask you to close your eyes and imagine . . . a world that never knew Norman Cradle. What would it be like? Face the fantasy. Would there be flowers . . . (*music sting*) . . . would there be rosy dawn . . . (*music sting*) . . . would there be laughter . . . (*music sting*) . . . would there be . . . love? (*Chord.*) Imagine . . . a *World Without Cradle* . . . (*sound of moaning winds*).

The choir emits a chorus of atonal wails, forks scraping glass. The curtain starts a slow rise.

If I am already dead, if Charlton Hymn has the papers filed, then I have nothing whatsoever to worry about. There would be no sense in killing me twice. Of course, if it was arranged for the Ward X sniffers to disembowel me there would be less chance of my protesting or writing nasty letters home. Homer Brogg likes his circles closed. It would be his way to have me slipped into my coffin after the fact. Then why take the trouble to stage an early funeral? Why not wait? A neat solution to the potential problem of shit hitting the fan in case questions were asked, a defense against an overzealous Hamish brother on a fund raising mission. Blackmail is always a clear and present danger when foul deeds are done. Homer could simply say that my interment was purely *symbolic*, like my role in the pageant. It was a *legal demise* given form as a service to his daughter and grandchildren. Better that they should have a grave to visit than a piece of paper to wave. How could he have known that I would actually die? Even as I consider this devious blueprint I realize I am indulging in paranoia.

The choir sings:

> How can there be hope
> When ashes rain showers
> No Norman! No purpose!
> Just blunt torpid hours . . .

The dancers run jerkily toward the poor children miming an attempt to make contact. The children stand paralyzed. A barrier of air makes touch impossible. It is effective choreography.

How could Trina agree to my obliteration? I can only imagine the pressures they exerted. What did she tell Amos and Amanda? Can children begin to fathom the difference between actual and contractual morbidity? Did she share the secret at least that their daddy is still *there* for them? Did she say that despite his Code, his love is constant and dependable? Were they told the truth or do they believe I am history?

"Take your place," Zoe says. I climb onto my styrofoam mountain and strike a pose. "Chin lower." I lower my chin.

The choir shifts gears to a harmonious song of welcome:

> But wait, but wait . . .
> A gift of fate . . .

I am rolled slowly into view. Color returns to the lights. Flowers shoot from the cacti. Barriers breached, the children and dancers unite. A thousand points of light fill a sky that only now becomes visible. They flicker images of the major constellations.

"Ladies and Gentlemen," the announcer's voice booms, "we have been spared the unthinkable. There is *Norman Cradle!* He endures. His work endures. Every plate, T-shirt, calendar and such you will find on sale at a very special price in our own gift shop just outside carries the spark of his legend. We are made whole!"

I begin my arm lift. I move as imperceptibly as a clock . . . they can hardly detect motion . . . I appear to change shape before their glazed eyes. When I am fully extended, I lift my head, face the audience and release the devastating Cradle grin. I exude vibrations of embracing warmth.

"Norman lives, he lives!" shouts a white-haired lady in the front row. I sear her with a flick of my tongue, a bit of improvisation. Others pick up the chant. I turn my eyes along an arc that sweeps the entire audience.

"He lives! He lives!"

Five rows back, in an aisle seat, I see Samantha. I know the people in her row. They were in my dream last night. Samantha clutches the back of the seat in front of her. Her nose makes the slightest twitch.

I let out a howl. It frightens me. I jump off my perch onto an urchin. It bites me. I pull free and run for the exit, stopping for a quick bow.

My mind is crystal. I am making quick, correct decisions. It must be that I have been driven mad by therapy like so many before me. The lights are killed. I find a fire door in the dark and manage to escape the tent. Now I hear cheering from inside. They must have accepted my flight as part of the plot. Bernie appears at the door.

"Stop, you motherfucker. They want you for a curtain call."

It's tempting. But I run for the cemetery. He comes after me. I find an enormous stone to hide behind. Whoever is under that weight must know that the loved ones he left behind wanted him firmly in place. I hear Bernie breathing hard.

"Why are you doing this? Soup? Soup? You fractured them. You could win the Oscar."

He means the Tony. And he seems honestly confounded. I consider showing myself.

"Sniff and recall," growls a voice from the night.

"Cool it, schmuck," Bernie says. "He's back there someplace. Go get him."

"The Norman, The Norman, The Norman," a girl yells. She could be an ardent fan but I decide not to take the chance.

"Not me, you twat," Bernie says. "Get your nose out of my butt."

Now there are the sounds of unpleasantness. Bernie asks first for recognition, then for mercy. Possibly the two oldest cries on the planet. And the most routinely denied. I listen as he is dragged gurgling back to Ward X.

I wander the boneyard stepping on ancestors. In the place where Morris had his rocket hidden there is only a hole.

"I am coming with you." A woman's voice.

"Don't even say it." A man's.

"Please."

"We went through this."

I am at a marble shrine, the grave of Isaac Hamish, showpiece of the stone garden. A stingy moon drips light enough for me to see Morris Feuerbloom strapping himself to a ten-foot tube. And there is the beautiful Jill Hill holding what looks like a drumstick.

"Even if I gave you a yes we wouldn't get anyplace. The weight is calculated. It's a science, darling. We would end up maybe in Boston which is not my destination."

"You told me it had a margin for error. Let me be the error."

"Not enough for a human being. Now, light it."

"Only if you take me."

"Don't be, excuse the expression, a cunt. Just light the fuse. A promise is a promise."

Jill flicks a lighter and touches it to the end of the torch.

"That's the way. Take care of yourself. And remember you have a friend in high places. Get it?"

"Goodbye, Morris."

"You got any messages for God?"

"Look back at the world."

"Get down from that thing," I say.

"Who's there?" Morris says. "Soup? The snitch?"

"Jill," I say, "aiding and abetting . . ."

"Aid and abet. Hurry. Soup, this is not your affair."

Jill touches the flame to a rope that trails between Morris' legs. It sputters purple.

"Thank you," he says. "Thank you."

She drops the torch and throws her arms around the tube.

"Let go," Morris says. "Don't be a spoiler."

"I'm coming along and that's the end of it."

The fuse destructs like a snake shedding skin. I jump after the spark but it twists away.

"Why is nothing simple?" Morris says.

I grab for Jill's dress. I manage to pull her off the Spectacular! and we fall backward onto Isaac Hamish's slab.

The rocket lifts more slowly than I would have imagined. Morris Feuerbloom hovers, looking down. Then he rises higher. A terrific explosion cracks the air. The desultory sky transforms to sunrise. There is a fanfare of crackles and another blast. Globs of fire spin like newborn stars. I think, "This trivializes even the bomb. Was that the magician's intent? To mock the atom?"

Lying on Isaac's marble rug, Jill Hill and James P. Wander, a.k.a. Soup, watch the ascent of the Chairman Emeritus of *Fireflower*, Inc., to unknown kingdoms.

I spend the rest of that night squatting behind Bill Maginot's garage. Jill has gone. Separation was her idea. She did not subscribe to my idea of asking for sanctuary at the local church.

I tried. The church was locked, the rectory dark. The minister and his family were probably still at the Festival grounds. I heard sirens, police cars, the volunteer firemen, ambulances. The Spectacular! must have given the populace a jolt. It made rain.

What had been an ideal evening turned to a deluge, as if Morris severed a celestial main. I pounded on the church door while I shivered inside Norman's drenched clothes. After many minutes someone did answer.

"Who? What?"

"Sanctuary. I demand sanctuary."

"Are you the Hunchback of Notre Dame? Sleep it off."

"Sanctuary!"

There was no more dialogue. Only later, dozing under a shelter of cardboard, do I realize how lucky I was. If the holy portal opened I would already be in the hands of the Hamish brothers. No religion offers sanctuary to soup, not the most primitive.

I need a plan. Nothing local is safe. Eventually I will turn myself in but in another neighborhood. At dawn I take a random direction and finally come to some highway. I see a truck lumbering toward me. The truck carries the logo of Nymph Dew, a brand of bottled water we used at home. I wave my thumb at the driver, a compact lady wearing tinted glasses. She stops for me.

I sit in the cabin listening to silver voices through CB static.

The voices manifest like spirits talking sports, weather, traffic jams and accidents, then drift away. The driver is lulled by the flow of gibberish, content to receive without giving. I try conversation about Nymph Dew, an excellent product with a crisp, clean taste, but there is no response. I sit listening to the CB and a million gallons of Nymph Dew gurgling behind me. This woman is exactly what I need. She doesn't speak, she doesn't examine my Code, she asks nothing about my destination. She just drives.

The truck slows down near a shopping mall and I am dismissed. I thank my savior and climb onto the tar. She has given me a cushion. We traveled at least a hundred miles. Signs tell me I am on Route 128 near the Springfield cutoff.

About a mile away I see the tower of what must be a radio station. I slosh in the direction of that steel spike, its flashing red beacons draw me like a moth. It seems as good a destination as any.

At the tower's base is a small cement building. The door is open. I allow myself the hospitality of WLUV-FM. I see that the place is staffed by a single announcer. He sits in a studio, ear phones wrapped around his head, talking into a mike. Outside the studio, a speaker broadcasts his wake-up show to empty space.

"Irene from South Boston. If you ask me, Chrissy, it was from another galaxy, no plane or balloon or the crap they give us. I saw it go over my house and Jesus H. Christ."

"Hey, Irene, Chris O'Malley thanks you a bundle and sends a bunch of posies for you to stick wherever. Another galaxy? Honey, take your medicine and crawl back in bed. Hello? This is *On Line* and you're on the air."

"Marv from Amherst. Listen, she could be right or it could be nucular."

"You mean *nuclear*? I hate and despise people who say noo-cue-!ar. Mark of a shlub. Would you like Mr. Doom to call you Mervin, Marvin? What is with you people on this goofy morn? Did you all sup on tainted eels in aspic? Can I hear from somebody semi-normal who had a nice Dick and Jane evening . . . red meat for dinner and a plug-in dessert? Listen, friends, your uncle Chris is going to put on a record and go tap a kidney but when I get back I would like to hear somebody other than a human biopsy. You're tuned to *On Line* with your favorite molester, Chris O'Malley. The weather bitch says it's 38 degrees out there which is more than enough degrees to get you a Ph.D. and a job slinging cow flop at McDonalds. And speaking of golden arches, here's music to soothe your savage but splendiferous breasts, so hang in there."

He presses a button and I hear a top-ten Garuda tune from Bali. True to his word, the DJ heads down the hall toward the toilet. I confront him while he is pissing, using the advantage.

"Nothing personal but who the fuck are you? This is private property—the building and what's in my hand."

"I have no designs on either. I was interested in the comments from your audience. I assume they were talking about last night's unexplained episode, the fire in the stars?"

"They were. So what?"

He tucks his dick into his pants as if it was his wallet. A typical F Code response to threat.

I say in a soft voice, "I can shed some light on the situation."

"Good. Why don't you call in?"

"Don't be glib. I was there. I know what happened. And I'm willing to share that knowledge with your listeners in exchange for a few concessions."

"Just go away, please."

"It was a humongous firecracker carrying an old man."

"A firecracker? Great. Thanks for telling me. Keep in touch."

"You could label it suicide but I think he thought of it differently."

"The old man?"

"Yes. He didn't think in endings."

"Marvelous attitude. Listen, stranger, why not wait outside?"

"His name was Morris Feuerbloom. Scion of the *Fireflower* clan. You must know the company. It's traded on the American Stock Exchange."

"I'll call my broker."

"Morris was confined to Hamish Farm. He wanted to be elsewhere."

"How do you know all this?"

"I was also a patient. Only for observation."

"Look, Mister. I don't want trouble. I plan to have a wife and kids."

"I did. They had me declared dead."

"You're dead? My condolences."

"Mr. O'Malley, there are powerful forces at play here. I must have access to your microphone. It's urgent. What I am trying to tell you is that I am in danger. I am Homer Brogg's son-in-law."

"Why didn't you say so? Hey, buddy, let me call Hamish Farm and tell them Homer Brogg's favorite son-in-law showed up here so they can send a hearse for you. You could be back in time for lunch and shock treatments. Now beat it before I get hostile."

"Consider. I am larger than you. I am desperate. I have nothing to lose which means I have everything to spend if you follow. Look at my Code."

He puts on a pair of glasses and looks.

"Deep shit."

"I'm giving you a major scoop."

"Mister, if you saw a guy kill himself with a firecracker you should tell the cops, not me."

"I did not say I saw anybody kill himself. I saw Morris Feuerbloom launch himself from the West Stockton Cemetery."

"Where you live because you're dead. Suppose I give you five minutes after the commercial. Then you vanish?"

"You'll make the national news."

"You're not going to hit me? Nothing like that? You don't have it in for me because I'm still alive?"

"I am not warlike except under duress."

We enter the studio. We wait out a commercial for the electric company.

"Fellow life forms, speaking about electricity, my next uninvited guest is hot wired. A genuine schizophrenic. When he dropped in for tea and crumpets, I was going to call 911 but he persuaded me to do otherwise with a very effective argument. Fear. He wants to talk to you guys and gals about the big bang, that gross flash and the boomers that got you all in an uproar. The man says he comes direct from Hamish Farm, *ee ei ee ei oooo*, and to top it all, he's dead. I mean, it all makes perfect sense. If I sound shaky it's because I am. This one is for the boys down at the precinct. Wish you were here."

I talk. I tell them about Morris and his flight to quality. That's all I tell them. My object is to have a few thousand witnesses for personal insurance. At least I am on record. I want some vague chance to survive. For reasons unknown.

"Of course the Fireflower family denied and denounced your allegations."

"Did they? I suppose Dr. Hamish also issued a denial? How do they explain a missing Morris?"

"They weren't required to explain."

"There was a corroborating witness."

"Who might that be?"

"It doesn't matter. What matters is that Homer's blueprint for homicide curled up like a bait worm."

"You believe Homer planned your execution?"

"Let's not go into that again."

"You're thinking in operatic terms."

Charlton stretches and yawns.

"The funeral was metaphorical," he says. And it was carried out with dignity. They could have done a two-minute cremation. It could have been no more than the death of a cigarette."

"I know all that. Still, it's hard for me to feel much gratitude."

"You know it's got to be prison."

"Prisons sound good. I want an honest prison. Though I suppose every con will have a contract on me."

"You're totally paranoid, James. Your behavior was completely irrational. Now you can't return to a mental hospital. You have nobody to blame but yourself."

"I accept blame. Just tell Homer I intend to stay alive, maybe forever. Just to piss him off."

"Homer's only concern is for Trina and your children."

"Not my children. His grandchildren. And there's the election. How come he's after the White House? Isn't his heart set on replacing Hoffenstein?"

"His concern is for the world."

"The world? He wants it for a third ball. You tell Homer I will be a very disturbing ghost."

"Speaking of that unpleasantness, I have a few papers for your signature. Transfer of property to Trina. Formalities. It will make things easier. I've pre-dated several . . ."

"Give me the papers."

Charlton looks surprised as he spreads his documents.

"I'll get them to release your hands."

"Stick a pen in my mouth. Don't worry, I learned how to write with my teeth when I read about people who paint with their toes."

He inserts a ballpoint and I sign James P. Wander a.k.a. Vigor Salt Free Pea Soup. There is no reason for me to make life harder for my widow.

"Awfully good of you. We're in your corner. In a few months, when the lint settles, we'll make our next move. Meanwhile behave yourself. Be a model convict. I suggest you use your time to advantage. Millhaus has some influential inmates."

"Millhaus? Is that where I'm going? I want a cement sewer where the lights flicker when they electrocute. I want Devil's Island, Alcatraz, the Bastille."

"We don't have those hell holes any more. There has been some little progress."

"Of course. I forgot."

"By the way, I saw the reviews of your performance. Congratulations."

"Reviews? Could I get copies?"

"I'll try. You shouldn't let that kind of talent lie dormant. Maybe they have a drama club at Millhaus."

IV

IF A prehistoric creature squatted and shat stone on a hopeless plain it would describe my new address. Add a blood color sun to broil away all memory of waves.

I am carried to Millhaus Correctional on a silver train over surgical track. The train rolls through hours of pure, white light. There are other freshman inmates broiling in my car. We are evaporated by the time we arrive.

It is easy to see that rumors of Millhaus as a chain-link paradise are false. There is nothing green out there except for occasional cacti. They stagger, spaced apart, arms raised, like soldiers from a surrendered army. I relish this garden of despair.

There is no shock or protest when they strap me into a Hoffenstein Negator. An attendant activates the machine. Its arm positions itself over my tilted head and the zap stings like acid. When they unbuckle me I spin and fall forward. The attendant catches me and gives me something sweet to drink. He holds up a small mirror to show me I am canceled. A neat slash has been tattooed over my Code.

I wait in line to be photographed. I am told to face front, turn left, turn right. That picture will be kept on file as long as there is memory. I knew the vaults where such records are stored and they are impervious to anything but a Black Hole. It is an important addition to my album so I try for the ideal expression, a knowing smirk that will catch the eye of some future browser.

An old doctor examines my vitals and probes my openings with a cold set of instruments. His report is fed to a computer. I wonder if my dossier will contain the reviews Charlton mentioned.

Next I am showered and issued Millhaus garb, a grey exercise suit, orange cap and sneakers. My Code is already imprinted on the clothes.

We are herded into an amphitheater. I sit facing a stage that holds a lectern marked with a large M and shield. The shield is as elaborate as a designer label—a red background, the abstract shape of a porcupine man protruding arrows, a target drifting above his head. It could grace the pocket of a blazer.

The inmate next to me, a thick stalk topped by a bald head, fondles a piece of jagged glass. It could be used to cut his wrist or my throat. He senses me watching and clasps it between his palms.

"Sick. It needs to be revitalized," he says.

"You'll feel better. The transition isn't easy."

"Not me. *It*. My quartz crystal. It lives and breathes. Its magnetism flows from the ultimate navel. It does not reflect, it creates reflection."

He pops the crystal into his mouth. His cheek lumps. I see the reason, a guard has taken position near us.

"If they saw it they would take it," he says, the words sliding around their obstacle. "Which is why I swallow it at night and crap it out in the morning. It rips my insides and the pain is intense but that is the price and I pay it. My name is Lucifer. I don't want to screw your sister and I don't give a damn about you so we can be friends."

"Jim Wander. Or Soup. I answer to both."

"They call me Lucifer because my lawyer used the *Devil made me do it* defense. Actually it was the Virgin Mary. I also have another name but I renounced it."

A round, friendly looking man crosses the stage and tests the microphone on the lectern.

"Greetings, let's stop dreaming of snatch and meatballs and give us your full attention. Our name is Harrison Slagle. We are your Warden. We will not waste our time welcoming you to Millhaus because we want you *out of here*. As you can see from our symbol the little man aiming arrows at the target is you, not Geronimo. If he's lucky, one of his arrows will hit the bull's-eye and that target represents *out of here*.

"We believe there is no such thing as crime, only severe misunderstanding. Those putrescent slashes can be removed from your natural Codes if you show us you are worthy. If you aim your arrows you can follow them *out of here*. Climb that idea like a *rope of hope*. That goes even for you lifers. There is a chance.

"So much for miracles. Millhaus encourages rehabilitation but we are a correctional facility and we have strict rules. The golden rule is we win, you lose in any dispute. Your cell is your castle, your cellmates are your family. Our watchwords are *cleanliness* and *respect*. And *work*, the most important arrows in your quiver. Those words are the fibers in your *rope of hope*. You have no rights, no official identity but you can pull yourself up out of this toilet and climb as high as you want. Marty Trammer, come on out."

There is a buzz. Marty Trammer was a tremendous Crunch star, the Babe Ruth of Crunch. And here he is on the Millhaus stage still in good shape, still walking with his gorilla trot, still with his chin stuck out like the prow of an ebony yacht, still with his lawn of spiked hair.

"Fuck me," Trammer says. "Ten years ago I sat where you sit. Did I like it? Fuck me. I felt like something that lives in armpits. You probably read my stupid story. You all know that the rules of Crunch say that the *Aggressive Degree* is modified according to the *Inflammational Level*. Which bullshit means they turn it up or they turn it down depending on how restless the natives may be. They tell us if we can bend bones or snap them. It's all correlated to I.T.C.H. which is the *Index of Theophanic Citizen Harmony*. The universal measure of the public boiling point. It comes down to this: before a game we get the word to clout clit or go after pussy like a gentleman. And the thing is, you never know. Sometimes you get yourself up for a game and you're ready to chew eyeballs, then they tell you, not today, today is fan appreciation day and every schmuck in the park gets a doily and a teabag. So be nice out there because the Violence Quotient is a lousy three or four. Other days, you come in low and they tell you to wrap their nostrils around their kidneys. I mean, it's the game of Crunch and you're paid to deport yourself like a pro.

"But Marty Trammer here, fuck me, burned out. He blew it. He broke the trust. And then he fucked himself, got involved with some slick fuckers who had him shaving points instead of a crotch. They caught me and I got gift wrapped and sent up here to Millhaus like you. I deserved what I got, no arguments. I was squidging around out there in my seat listening to Warden Slagle thinking to myself *turd words*. Like you. Am I wrong? Or am I right? Now fast-forward. Look at me today. I am a free man. My Code is restored. I am a spokesperson for Meteor Sneakers, I got a wife with Rocky Mountain kazoos and three kiddies who call me Daddy and mean it. I did not come back to Millhaus to stand here farting in your brains. If Marty Trammer made it you can too. In a way I envy you but not much. You have the opportunity ahead of you. Just hang in there and climb that *rope of hope*."

"Thanks, Marty," Warden Slagle says. "And thanks for those memories on the field. Maybe somebody among you will get the message. Maybe. You can sip from the sewer or show some remorse. *Cleanliness, Respect, Work*. And maybe some day you'll be up on this stage talking to the entering class. Are there any questions? Who gives a shit. We ask the questions, you give the answers. Let's move out of here."

Lucifer gags and I see he is turning blue. I move to slap his back but he stops me. His face contorts, then comes back to where it started.

"In the safe deposit," he says slapping his gut.

I have no quartz inside me but my gut knots. There is no *rope of hope* for me. I bite my tongue until it bleeds.

I thought of prison as enviable enforced privacy. There would be hours of unbearable loneliness sitting hunched on a mattress of clenched springs. There would be a rusted bowl for elimination, a single bare bulb for illumination. I could sway in my bunk like an empty pod on a dead branch. They might give me the stub of a pencil and a sheet of greasy paper on which to record confessions and insights. The walls would be lined with scratched accountings of used days. There might be the names of lovers written in gore. There I would flourish fishing for meaning.

Instead my quarters at Millhaus are reasonably comfortable and certainly not private. There are three bunk beds, the plumbing is behind a screen, there is even a TV linked to cable complete with a remote. Instead of a single Picasso eye, the lighting is indirect and sufficient. The walls are soft blue, decorated with the Millhaus Arrowman.

I share with two cellmates, Omar and Ishmael, who are Codetwins. I've read about the phenomenon but doubted it and surely never encountered a pair. Through some glitch in the Prime Mother Computer they were born strangers but given identical markings. According to law, these accidental doppelgangers were raised as brothers by a surrogate family. The only thing alike about Omar and Ishmael is the stamps on their foreheads. Omar is short, slender, delicate. Ishmael is a six-footer and a bodybuilder. Their personalities are entirely dissimilar. Yet they are incredibly attuned. If Ishmael has a nightmare Omar wakes screaming. There is a steel bond between them, unquestioned loyalty and mutual rage.

As a newcomer, I get the topmost bunk in the trinity. On my first night at Millhaus, I sit reading one of Homer's publications, *Polyp Digest*. When Homer was told he needed a polyp removed he made the connection to millions with similar polyps, realized or growing. "Every body is a potential polyp grove," was how he put it. I never had faith in *Polyp Digest* but the publication was an instant success. Homer loved to rib me about my opposition waving circulation charts in my face. An old copy of *Polyp Digest* came with the cell so I read it.

Omar is pissing behind the screen. I am aware of the tinkle as white noise and only slightly conscious that it had been going on for at least fifteen minutes.

"Stop it," Ishmael yells from the middle bunk. "How can I sleep?"

"I can't control my bladder. Any more than you can control the ebb and flow of events."

"Cork it, I'm warning you."

"I'm taking a leak. I piss until I finish."

"Don't goad me, brother."

"Is that a threat?"

"Fellows," I say from up near the ceiling, "agitation only encourages the kidneys. There is some correlation between excessive urination and renal polyps."

Omar dries up. Ishmael jumps down from his bed. The Code-twins stand together.

"I heard a voice," Ishmael says.

"It gave advice. Unsolicited," Omar says.

"I was reading about a case . . ."

"Shall we gnaw at his elbows?" Ishmael says.

"No. His epiglottis."

"I was not trying to provoke a fight. I was trying to finish an article."

"Understand something. My brother and I are one in seventy-six million and that's how we must be taken. That's the bible. Omar may be a bag of pus but he is my burden. Allow our hostility to find suitable venting or you encourage wrath. We are one."

The brothers embrace.

"We had to be carefully nurtured," Ishmael says, "to be mutually responsible for our joint behavior. We accepted that mandate while we suckled."

The lights flash off and on. The twins climb into their respective bunks.

"Then what brought you to Millhaus?"

"Introspection," Omar says.

"But tell that to a jury," Ishmael says. "Omar and I accepted our status. We were careful to monitor sibling rivalries all through adolescence. But we spent chunks of time speculating together about possible points of difference. We needed some divergence to find individual identities."

"Ishmael, being a prick, hit on a grand scheme. After college when we were ready to try the world he suggested that one of us live as if there was God and the other as if there was none. Being agnostics, we flipped the proverbial coin."

"Omar became the infidel. I became very religious."

"He sacrificed, I took every risk for pleasure and immediate gratification," Omar says. "I was enormously rich and commensurately respected. Ishmael lived on the handouts of some cult."

"To make a long story short, it was inevitable that we'd decide to kill each other. Omar's very existence curdled my altar. He was a human bulldozer without a drop of decency, entirely indulgent."

"Ishmael's cloying conscience gave me ulcerative colitis and worse."

"Our separate roads brought us back to where we'd started, the same intersection. It was clear that one of us had to kill the other. They got us for attempted murder."

"And put you in the same cell?"

"We couldn't live apart. It was a landmark case. We were tried together but sentenced separately. Omar got ten to fifteen. I got twenty-five to life. Academic since we must serve the time in tandem. At least the sentence was fair."

"Why was it fair?" Omar says. "Did I try to kill you any less than you tried to kill me?"

"Your own lawyer said my plan was five times more revolting. I rigged his hot tub to parboil him. He used some cockamamie poison in salad."

"Up yours."

"What a witty response. Do you mind if I use it? Doesn't my brother shine?"

"Your mother's udder," Omar says.

"Your father's labial majora," Ishmael says.

And so it goes.

I walk with my peers, imitating the Millhaus shuffle, skating without blades. A beefy guard leads us like a locomotive pulling venomous cargo. He seems remarkably indifferent to the potential fury only inches from his buttocks, centuries of confinement simmering in an orderly line. He lives because of the ongoing equation: convicts need guards, guards need convicts.

Lucifer is up ahead towering like a mast. My closest companion for this morning stroll is a brittle fellow with a fat man's face, jowled and dour.

"You see the big one?" he says. "The three-time loser?"

"His name is Lucifer."

"You know him? You're his friend?"

"Not exactly. We met."

"He's in my cell. I swear to God not two hours ago he sat on the crapper screaming and moaning like he was going to die. I thought hemorrhoids but no. He laid some kind of egg. Then he fished it out of the bowl. Disgusting."

"I doubt it was an egg."

"It was an egg. I saw it. He's trying to hatch it in his pocket. The element you meet in here."

"No talking," the guard says.

"Whatever it is, I don't intend to be around when that shell breaks," my associate whispers.

We stop at a door marked THE LIBRARY. It is the ideal assignment. I assumed I would be making license plates on an assembly line, another Plateworks. The guard presses buttons and a door slides open. As we file in, I am pulled aside.

"What's the problem?" I say. "I am certainly qualified for The Library. I have degrees from . . ."

The door slides shut.

"You're connected."

"Meaning what?"

"Special Detail."

"I never requested . . ."

"All I know is I got you down for the kosher meal."

"This is a prison. I came here to be punished."

"Just move because I'm losing respect."

We enter a hallway that reminds me of the delivery entrance to Hamish Farm. I shake.

"Where are you taking me?"

"Relax. You'll like it."

The hallway ends at an arched door. More bleeps from the security switch and that door opens to a perfectly groomed garden surrounding a fountain where green nymphs lactate spurts of water from bronze nipples. Beyond the nymphs is a complex of tennis courts and an Olympic pool. Past the pool a lush golf course spreads to the horizon. A row of neat cottages borders the clubhouse. To their right is a large gazebo where a man in white is busy setting a long banquet table.

"That's Malcom," the guard says. "Do his bidding. And don't fuck with him. He is dangerous when wet. Just get along and life is a bowl of cherries."

I am taken to meet the white suit. Malcom is about my age and height with the look of a lawn flamingo faded from pink to pallor. It is hard to distinguish his skin from the suit. He is laying out silver near porcelain plates.

"Your new flower girl," the guard says. "He says he doesn't want special treatment."

"I like the attitude," Malcom says. "So you are called Soup?"

"I am. I was."

"Don't take the Code Slash seriously. You're the same pile of feces you always were. In any case, we're an equal opportunity employer."

"I'll leave you faggots alone," the guard says.

"Some day I suck the blood out of that neck," Malcom says. "Be that as it may. You'll find your uniform in the room near my kitchen. And don't forget the gloves. Hurry. They come for breakfast at ten."

To the rear of the gazebo is a kitchen to make Trina salivate. I find the dressing room which is also a pantry where floor to ceiling shelves hold jars of Hero, Tiptree, Cross & Blackwell preserves, canisters of spice, tins of coffee beans, bottles of water from France, Italy, Finland. There is a wine cooler fully stocked, the wines resting like babies in a nursery. My uniform duplicates Malcom's and the fit is perfect. I check myself in the reflection from a large pot. Collapsed in the stainless steel eye I resemble a natty gnome. My spotless gloves are tucked into a pocket of the jacket, their fit is also precise.

"Spiffy," Malcom says when I emerge. "Today you'll start slow. Arrange the blooms. Here are the vases and there are the flowers. Don't mix anemones with hydrangea. Keep each statement simple. We cater to movers and shakers. Our guests are politicals, financials, industrials, pharmaceuticals. They *know*. Place one vase at every fifth chair. During service, I will instruct you. Ape my example. And should there be conversation, never refer to the immediate environment as Millhaus. It is hard enough for these people to endure incarceration. If by chance you are acquainted with any of our guests either personally or by reason of their celebrity, make no mention of that. Even if they are heroes to you, refrain from adoration. Never ask for autographed napkins or the like. And what you hear is forgotten immediately. Talk of mergers, acquisitions, coups, etcetera. Nothing is remembered or repeated, not even to me. Do I have to tell you that this is the most desirable assignment at our facility? Deserve to be here. Keep in back of your mind that should one of our Specials develop affection for you it could be your catapult to commutation."

I hear a bubbling sound. I look toward the pool where lavender mist rises.

"The pool seems to be boiling," I say.

"See that oar propped against the fence? Get it, go down there and stir."

"What about the flowers?"

"I can handle the flowers."

I get the oar. The bubbling intensifies. Looking into the pool I see mounds of brackish glop rise and fall spattering sludge on the tiled border. A rich, organic smell hovers like a cloud.

"Put some elbow into it," Malcom yells.

I dip my oar into the turgid sea. The waves I make hunch and dissolve back into the lava brew. I watch a dragonfly dip at the surface and turn to vapor. Pimples of foam try to climb the oar's shaft.

A chime sounds.

"Let it be. Get back here now," Malcom says.

At ten sharp the march of privileged inmates begins. They form a procession outside their cottages chanting like monks, *mun, mun, mun, dow, dow, dow*. These monks are dressed to play. They wear shorts and T-shirts, sneakers and sunglasses. They carry the stuff of games—rackets, clubs, bats, mallets, basketballs.

Their route is determined. When they reach the pool they split ranks and divide into two pincers. They stop at the lip of the pool and stand in silence. Then they unzip and, beautifully synchronized, turn, squat and defecate. The pool thanks them with a surge of appreciative gurgles. They stand, pull up their shorts, crisply snap to attention, take a step back, dress their line, face left and continue their walk to breakfast.

As they come closer I see tanned, healthy faces full of good cheer. The minute they sit, they are individuals, hungry and hearty, reaching with relish for pitchers of fresh orange juice and steaming coffee. Malcom gestures me to the kitchen where we prepare sausages, ham, bacon, pancakes, waffles, eggs, cereal.

While I make toast, I say, "Would it be too much to ask you about the pool?"

"The origins of life," Malcom says, scrambling eggs and milk. "It's their aquarium, their hobby. They're trying to create the conditions that produced them, all of us. Their hope is that a tadpole or lizard will crawl up from down there, test air and begin evolving. They're trying to make Adam and Eve."

"To what end?"

"Entirely pragmatic. Insight into Eden would give an excellent edge into the dynamics of marketing. And marketing is their religion. It's like having a reverse telescope. Better yet, microscope. There's an added benefit. They are very concerned with developing products and services for a polluted planet. They're a caring group despite their indiscretions."

"Caring? I recognize at least one man convicted of dumping atomic waste in a lake used by orphans."

"Their natures demand that they lean against the razor of law. Laws are constraints, straightjackets. These are creative, gifted people. It's the way of the beast to take chances. If they happen to be apprehended in the midst of some blatant excess, our judges must sentence them. So they come here for a while for refreshment. After all, their taxes built Millhaus, we are a kind of time-share vacation condominium. I tell you, Soup, it's a pleasure to feed them."

The food we bring is gobbled up. Between courses, I notice a kind of social vampirism. The diners nip at one another and draw blood. When we go back into the kitchen I ask Malcom about that.

"A touch of humor, a kind of love play, no more, no less. They know they are of a type and that they must nourish one another to survive. It's their version of a pratfall. A vampire is a kind of Jesus Interruptus, eternal without being required to ascend. These are religious men. They know death and replacement is inevitable and they accept it as good for business in the long view. But none of them wants to die. The irony is that they are mortal gods. So they toy around to abate anxiety and just have a good time. They may not be innocent but they are innocents." Malcom sinks his teeth into my shoulder. I see that he will never join a union.

For dessert we serve pastry but most of the group munch at the flowers. They chew the blossoms and spit out the petals and stems. Malcom sweeps them onto a dustpan with a whiskbroom, then pours the dregs into a crystal bucket, presumably destined for the pool. There is one final ritual. I am handed a Baccarat decanter, a ladle and funnel. We go to the pool and Malcom instructs me on how to skim the surface and pour the smoking ooze neatly into the decanter.

Back at the table, the slop is poured into stemmed glasses.

"Well served, Malcom," says a robust gentleman with a resonant voice. "And welcome to your new assistant. Lift a glass for yourself, give the lad one, fill them generously and join our toast."

I am handed a glass. Glowing with praise, Malcom deigns to pour our drinks from the dregs. When our glasses are filled, we clink.

"May this be the day," says the toaster.

They drink.

"Swallow it," Malcom says.

"I'll puke."

"Of course."

Several of the gentlemen run from the table to regurgitate their intake into the pool. I drop my glass. It shatters leaving a brown puddle. There is a gasp of disbelief.

"Forgive," Malcom says, whiter than his clothes. "His credentials are flawless. I had no way of knowing. There was no reason to anticipate . . . Gentlemen, I ask you for mercy."

"There's a narcissism to the criminal type of which self-flagellation is a part. You screwed yourself," says my guard.

"That's positively accurate. You have a sharp mind in a sound body."

The guard has a blunt mind in a flaccid body.

"Your type fascinates me. I'm doing a paper on recidivist behavior. You might have noticed my D+ which allows a civil service rating as Vice Warden."

"I admire your enterprise."

We are on our way to The Library to which I've been reassigned. Since Omar and Ishmael fought all night over the direction of the North Star (since north is an arbitrary concept the North Star could easily have faced south, east or west, etc.) I got little sleep. Fatigue leaves me mellow.

"Why did you blow it?"

"I came here to break rocks, not serve tables. Besides, the whole

Specials setup is obscene. Not that I'm holier than thou. But if the justice system is suspect our entire society is built on a marsh."

"Do you think the average person would mind knowing that their slightly tarnished leaders retain some dignity? The concept of upward mobility is as important as any justice system."

"Anyhow, I belong in The Library. I grew up in a family of readers."

"You can't keep blaming your parents."

"So true. Thanks for reminding me."

"Here we are. Check with Mustaf Asheed. He's expecting you."

The word is the beginning.

As I enter The Library I realize how much I want to be among the shelves filled with alphabetized volumes, the whisper of flipping pages, the smell of paper, buckram, oiled wood and leather.

What I smell instead is a million melting erasers, a pungent smoke. Two huge vats boil viscous liquid. The vats disgorge their contents into a trough that leads to what looks like a massive shower head. Under the shower is a great wheel rotating a carpet of spikes. The spikes are, in fact, penis-shaped rods. When they are doused the penises move off the wheel to a water bath while other penises replace them. After the cooling, inmates slide little rubber bags off the shafts and roll them into flat pancakes. These are tossed onto a moving belt that carries them to a packing area where thousands of small boxes wait. The boxes carry a favorite Norman Cradle print, *The Pledge*, showing a loving couple at the moment he proposes and she accepts. As the boxes are filled they are put into cartons and the cartons are stacked in areas marked DRAMA, LITERATURE, POETRY, GOVERNMENT, POLITICS, SCIENCE, BUSINESS, THE ARTS, etc.

I find Mustaf Asheed making a count in NEW AND NOTEWORTHY. There is something familiar about him but I can't place it.

"I was told to report to you. I'm the new curator."

"Good. We'll start you in testing. Every batch, we take out a few to torture. Come with me."

I am shown two machines. One blows the bags full of air until they turn to balloons and finally burst. Another fills them with water until they explode. Gages signal the break point.

"There must be some mistake," I say.

"You requested The Library. What's your bitch?"

"I expected a library."

"It was a library. Discontinued. Now we make condoms. And this is prime penetration season so we can't talk all day."

"Condoms have seasons?"

"Even Mallomars have seasons," Mustaf says.

"How did you know that? Not many . . ."

"You racist bastard. Just because I wear the face of Araby you think me inferior? Every camel driver knows the proverb '*Mallomars Have Seasons.*' "

"I know you. From where?"

"Your worst nightmare."

"Ah, Everest. The Hoffenstein statue. You were one of the terrorists who . . ."

"You saw me on TV? In the nostril?"

"I did, yes. It was you."

"Who else would dare?"

"I'd like to go over that incident with you. It left me with a lot of questions. Maybe we could take lunch?"

"Your sister's orifice."

A bell rings. One of the rubbers in testing sprinkles long before the usual blast point.

"Hold. Lot G986-Y defect," a robot voice says.

"Ignore. Deviation minimal. Pass, pack, ship. Control Override 2247VZ," Mustaf yells at a microphone. "You bleeding heart electronic motherfucker."

"Excuse me, but if the testing equipment indicates a lapse in product dependability and bothers to sound an alarm what is the correct procedure?"

"Turn the other cheek. Snatches are singing, dicks are swinging, registers ringing. Are you with me or against me?"

"I think I can make a contribution."

"Then contribute. This is a key profit center for Millhaus. We get perks. Food. Cigarettes. The best workers get laid on Thanksgiving. And we get respect. *The Pledge* is trusted wherever there are stiff cocks. Sherpas use them. We must earn that trust."

I have learned something of production quotas and the occasional cutting of corners. The intent of quality is there, the man means well, he does the best he can.

"I accept the responsibility that goes with that trust," I say.

We shake hands solemnly.

Pop-up pictures from forbidden books assault my sleep. It is not pictures that wake me but sounds. Moans, growls, gasps, howls, laughter, the breaking of wind.

Dreams rise like fog over Millhaus accompanied by their own organic music.

Two tiers beneath me, Ishmael and Omar twist identically, breathe in harmony. If Omar drops an arm over the end of his bed Ishmael will follow before they both shift the same leg.

I lay awake thinking about work. First the Plateworks, now The Library. In a way I am more pleased with rubbers than platters. There is a consumer out there tonight who will fornicate with one of my condoms, then breakfast on a certified Cradle. I smile wishing him the best.

Why do the powers that be place me in judicial jobs? Why am I selected as the arbiter between product and user? I suppose it is the residue of my Code A+ that inspires such faith. Once I enjoyed that role. Now I would rather be *on the line* subject to the usual lapses. I have lost some ego and maybe a bit of ersatz confidence. But I have gained humility.

Still, I fight sleep. I will not contribute to the night noises. Is it because my own sounds can't compare to the mumbles of chainsaw killers or is my insomnia elitist? My sounds are my own business. I grasp at privacy.

"Mine, mine!" Omar shrieks bolting upright and smacking his head on the bottom of my bunk.

"Mine," Ishmael says in a thick voice slamming his skull against Omar's bed.

The twins leave their bunks and face off in the grey dawn. They have been dreaming of the same woman.

"She loves me," Omar says. "Everything about me. She loves the hair on my balls."

"She told you that?" says Ishmael. "I doubt it. You she hates. Me she loves."

"You she hates. She wrote it on my back with her juice," Omar says.

"On my leg she wrote you she hates."

"Gentlemen, it is entirely possible for one woman to love two men at the same time, literally or figuratively," I say.

"Where does he get such lies?" Ishmael says.

"Facts," I say with authority. "Certain ladies are gifted with immense reserves of sensual generosity. And they must share themselves since no man can contain their passions."

"That bitch," Omar says.

"That miserable twat. I knew there was something weird about her," Ishmael says.

"Did she swallow yours?"

"No, come to think. She spit out."

The twins yawn and go back to their pods.

I close my eyes and try to force rest. Trina never swallowed mine. Could they be dreaming about my wife? I let out a yelp. My noise bounces around the prison like a pinball, then rolls to a stop against some distant wall. But not before I am answered with a belch, a whistle, a snort.

I am part of the eternal conversation.

Rest and relaxation in the prison yard takes me back to kindergarten. We frolic in institutionalized bliss. I have the sense that my mother will come to get me in a few more hours and we will go home to cookies and milk.

Like kindergarten, while we play together we play separately. Lucifer communes with his crystal, whispering to it, then listening for a reply. The twins play basketball. They have been put on opposite teams so that they cancel out one another. My boss, Mustaf, plays soccer. It is hard to believe that this is the same man who cracked Hoffenstein's nose. He is just another schoolboy in the Millhaus yard. More sedentary cons play chess and checkers. They lean down over their pieces like sullen gargoyles. Near them, bodybuilders work toward secret goals. They struggle with enormous burdens blowing and snorting like tugs moving toward private horizons. To my surprise, Malcom is among them. His weights are more modest—iron eggplants for beginners. He has one in each hand, pumping his arms up and down.

"Malcom, I wanted to talk to you."

"We have nothing to talk about. You got me into a humiliating situation. I lost dignity."

"It's about that. How could they blame you for my behavior?"

"The buck stops here. If you're asking for a second chance, forget it."

"No, I like my work in The Library. But what brings you out here? I never saw you in the yard."

"And I hope you never see me here again. We were ordered out. Except for the Specials."

"Naturally, the Specials."

"You're very cynical. Lifers should develop a more tolerant attitude. Take the barbells. Work off some of that poison."

Malcom hands me the two five-pounders. He tries a more formidable challenge but he can't get the bar up over his knees. Lucifer begins playing a harmonica. Another inmate produces a guitar. A gigantic man called Jlub who mixes latex in The Library sings in a deep bass:

> The chapel was crowded
> My hand touched your glove
> Then you sneezed at our wedding
> And dampened our love . . .

Suddenly everything stops. Warden Slagle enters the yard in the company of a woman. They are followed by several civilians and three officers. The tower guards go on alert, manning rifles and lasers.

"Who is she?" Malcom says. "That face . . ."

"Sonia Kay, the TV slit," one of the chessmen says.

"Big slit, famous slit, no wonder the slit looked familiar," Malcom says out of character.

"Why use that word?" I say. "Sonia Kay is an accomplished newsperson, a credit to her profession."

"I was bonding," Malcom says.

Sonia Kay detaches from the group and wanders the yard on her own. That takes a certain courage.

"*You will resume your activities*," the PA tells us. The games begin again, but with more verve. Lucifer's harmonica picks up several decibels. The guitar does riffs and twangs. Jlub turns from his country lament to rap:

> They say I did a felony crime
> They say I got to do my time
> They say I got to pay my bill
> Cause I crackered Jack and buggered Jill
> I up the hill
> I up the hill

The athletes are superheated. Mustaf smacks his head against a goalpost. The twins collide under a basket. Sonia Kay takes it all in stride making notes on a pad. She points her finger. A video camera follows the digit.

When she reaches us Malcom sings out his name and number, holding out his hand. She actually shakes it.

"It might interest you," he says, "to know that just beyond the wall there is another dimension to Millhaus. If you're planning a documentary on prison life . . ."

"You mean the Specials? Can't touch that. Who's your friend."

"Me?" I say.

"You. Why are you shifting legs? Is it jock itch?"

She scans my Code.

"Marvelous," she says, making a note and pointing. I am on camera.

The walls of Al Porcene's office document his triumphs. He is pictured with many celebrities. There are framed magazine covers featuring stories about Millhaus Correctional as America's premier prison. There are several trophies but I can't read their inscriptions.

Code C, Porcene grins at me. He wears tinted glasses and I wonder if too many flashbulbs have shattered his pupils. Above the glasses, strands of hair are flattened on a balding head. He sits in a white shirt and paisley tie, his sleeves rolled, elbows on his desk, hands cupping his chin.

"Call me Al."

"Call me Jim."

"As you must have surmised, I handle public relations for Millhaus. Where we stash the trash beneath a slash. Where we dangle the rope of hope."

He taps a rimshot with his fingers.

"I heard."

"My job isn't cosmetic. I work like a hog. Public relations brings us the grants that allow for little extras."

"A bit more austerity might be welcome around here."

"Not a popular attitude, Jim."

"Why am I here?"

"Impatience?"

"Just curiosity. And we happen to be under pressure at The Library."

"Hooray, hooray the first of May. Outdoor fucking starts today."

"Something like that, yes."

"Then to the nitty-gritty. You're going to be on national television. It's only Public Broadcasting but it's image."

"No."

"Hear me out. Sonia Kay is shooting a feature about us. She fingered you as one of her stars. This show is important to Millhaus. Warden Slagle's contract is coming up for renewal and he is interested in securing certain advantages."

"I'm the wrong person. I might say the wrong thing. Not to bring up the possibility that my children might watch. I respectfully decline."

"Shy of the limelight? Let us be blunt. You have no legal identity. You lost human status. You died. All that severely restricts your bargaining power. Capish?"

"Ask yourself, Al, if that's the kind of non-person you want for your spokesman."

"Well put. I agree. But Ms. Kay is persistent and that's the bottom line. She wants you, Soup. Pull the camera back. You're going to be with us for a very long time. Lack of cooperation could produce extreme discomfort. Not simply the austerity you seem to crave but personal pain. The old-fashioned kind where your entrails throb."

"I see."

"Sonia has credibility. We want her to leave Millhaus convinced beyond a shadow that we're getting the job done. We want her viewers to share that sentiment."

"And would her viewers like to hear about the Specials and slightly defective condoms?"

"You are a curator in The Library. You help us improve minds. That's all there is to it. You like what you do, you're penitent and productive. Then bye-bye Sonia."

"When she insists on visiting The Library I tell her the rubbers are bookmarks?"

"Don't worry about details. Look, why don't we both take the position that her finger is a divining rod. Be the fountain of information she wants you to be. I personally guarantee our gratitude."

"I do have some thoughts about getting my own cell. Not the Hilton. Motel Six. Cot, commode, desk, pen, paper."

"Within the realm of possibility."

"Will she ask about Homer Brogg?"

"She might probe. It's her specialty. And, yes, the interview with you might cause some agitation in certain circles. Harrison Slagle is not of Mr. Brogg's political persuasion. If Brogg is elected it could result in massive shifts of personnel. Even I could be among the unemployed. Should you reveal some little nastiness about your ex-father-in-law . . ."

"You should have said that first."

"Then we are in accord?"

"Anything to help Millhaus. And it might interest you to know I've had theatrical training. No camera is as demanding as a live audience."

Al Porcene stands and beats at his chest like Kong.

"I love my work," he says. "How many men can honestly make that statement?"

The Library is a library. Cartons of *The Pledge* are replaced with books. The great wheel has been covered with a tabletop surrounded by chairs. The production line has become a counter. The testing equipment has been made into an artwork complete with a plaque naming the artist and displaying his dates. The boiling tubs have transformed into a video center. Even the odor of the place is authentic as if they placed librarian scrapings in the air ducts. There is Baroque music where once there was the moan of gears.

Inmates read quietly or check volumes in and out. Mustaf waves at me while he thumbs a Britannica. Lucifer has a collection of recipes. Jlub thumbs a comic. I am informed that Omar and Ishmael will also be guests on the *Sonia Kay Show* though they said nothing about that. A girl in a yellow smock applies their makeup.

I stroll The Library with Sonia, followed by her camera crew. We wear remote microphones so there are no dangling cords.

"It does come as a pleasant surprise to find so many of us are avid readers," I say.

"Fallouts, dropouts, the misguided, even Slimes. Yet they read, read, read," Sonia says to the lens. "And that is encouraging." She turns to me. "We did agree that no names would be used during this telecast. But, Mr. X, reading past your slash I see you're Coded Pea Soup."

"That's accurate."

"Without revealing anything too hurtful, is it safe to say there was another time, another life . . . ?"

"Quite. My original coding was A+. In fact, I worked closely with my former father-in-law, Homer Brogg, on some highly successful projects."

"*The* Homer Brogg?"

"Yes. He had me declared dead and took away my wife and two children but now that he's thrown his hat in the political ring I'm behind him one hundred percent. Most of the inmates here at Millhaus would give him our vote if we could vote."

"Why is that?"

"We feel he's solidly behind prison reform and a more liberal parole system."

"His constituency is conservative. Right wing."

"I know what Homer Brogg stands for, no matter what he says. I should. I stood beside him."

"That's edifying, Mr. X. I'm sure he would be grateful for your endorsement. Now, I know you're under a harsh sentence. But if the time ever came when you could leave Millhaus . . ."

"You mean if President Brogg should rewrite certain statutes? Swing open the doors?"

"Yes. What are your ambitions?"

"To contribute through obedience and self-discipline."

"Come off it. Talk straight. This is Sonia here. Will it be the old revolving door for you? Or will you be the one to find your way through the labyrinth?"

"I'm a lifer, Ms. Kay."

"But there is the Millhaus *rope of hope*. There he is, Mr. X. An admitted Disrupter. A chronic Caution. Yet seeing him here in his beloved library, looking into his serene eyes, Sonia Kay has a feeling that just maybe the tilting seesaw of fate will tip in this man's favor. Not that I condone pardon for anyone who has attempted Alteration, but there is something about our Mr. X that touches my heart and my heart is no pushover. It's a scabbed and callous organ."

Sonia tells her cameraman, "Cut. Take five. Don't call me, I'll call you."

"What about the twins? We can get them in before lunch."

"Later," Sonia says. "Be gone."

Sonia takes my hand and we walk toward HISTORY. A guard touches her shoulder.

"Ms. Kay, it's not a good idea to be alone with them," the guard says.

"I can take care of my eternal triangle," Sonia says. "Why don't you go polish your dumdums?"

"I'll be right behind you," the guard says.

"I want a few minutes alone with the beast and don't worry. If you hear a scream it'll be him."

The guard backs off.

"He's right," I say. "We shouldn't be left alone."

"You mean to our own devices? Is it because you noticed I'm anatomically correct?"

"How could I help noticing?"

We turn into the stacks. Canvas cloths cover a million coiled condoms.

"Your story is network," Sonia says. "You could be my ticket to Emmysville. And it wouldn't hurt if a few thousand fans wrote in asking for clemency."

"I don't want clemency and I don't want network."

"I do my homework, Soup. Supermarket mayhem. Poof. You deserve better. Listen, I'll drop all reference to Alteration in the edit. That's too nauseating. I'll focus on the uplifting, positive themes of your conversion here at Mickeymouse. The struggle back."

"There are better stories."

"Trust my instinct. I do. I can read between your lines. Salt Free. Croutons. Let me taste."

Sonia kisses me. Her tongue lances my lips.

"Anyone caught *flagrante delicto* is subject to . . ."

"What can they do? Throw you out?"

"They feed us saltpeter. I have no libido."

"I want your story and I want you. I never help a man I don't hump."

She pulls off her blouse and bra, drops her skirt and uses a foot to slide her panties to her ankles.

"We have no protection."

"I have no ovaries. Gird up your loins."

On one of the canvas wrappers, looking up at Sonia, I think that Al Porcene should throw in a stereo. As she grinds, I feel the hill of condoms shift dangerously. I flip her over and mount her for distraction. Bad timing. The guard comes looking for us. Sonia has one choice.

"Rape," Sonia yells.

I do the same.

"One of you is lying," the guard says.

As promised, I get my own cell. I am in solitary. For how long I don't know. Time is no factor. I lay on my back looking at a caged bulb, the sun in a distant universe. I use pure thoughts for bait and fish for angels but I get no bites.

I sit. In these situations I know it is traditional to strike up relationships with neighborly vermin—mice, rats, fleas, lice, gnats, chiggers. But it is weeks, maybe months, before I finally find a bug. It is many-legged, has a blackgreen shell and a pair of delicate antennae that constantly wave searching for signals. From its attitude I know this bug has had conversations with many before me. I can't console myself with the illusion that I am the first. But could I speak so openly with a virgin plagued by shyness and burdened with a glut of pubescent platitudes?

My bug, mine for the moment, appears at what I imagine is dusk following a trail of crumbs and droplets I maintain like a state highway. There is a trade-off of food for sociability. I don't insist on any payment for my gratuities, but we both know that conversation is expected.

"What's new in the drain?"

"Not a hell of a lot. A drain is a drain."

"So, what's on the agenda for tonight? Are we going to boast about superior survival skills as if survival was the be all and end all."

"We'll talk about what you want to talk about. You're the one losing your mind."

"Why must I always initiate? Aren't you interested in anything but stuffing yourself and hatching?"

"I was working on a book of poetry I call *Deconstructed Disposables* but I lost focus. My verses turned out to be the usual laments against the predictable inevitables and who is going to buy video rights to that, tra la?"

"Considering that you are a scavenger living on handouts you should lean more toward chortles than lamentations."

"Shit," the bug says, rolling over. "I have been your companion in this dungeon for days, weeks, months and you show no appreciation. Frankly, Soup, you are not the most vibrant conversationalist. Others tell me about heinous crimes, bloodcurdling voyages into perversions of perversion and you tell me about your daughter's cloying precocity and your son's fantastic ability to hit a ball with a bat, hoo ha."

"So smug. Go ahead, trash my family. If it makes you feel any higher on the evolutionary ladder."

"Don't put down my rung on the ladder. We will be the survivors with the mandate to clean up this planet long after you bipeds are deader than a dinosaur's foreskin. What bothers me the most is that my kind gives yours immortality by ingesting your dregs."

"Oh, thank you very much. Remind me to drop you a note."

"Spray us, maim us. You will see that patience gives the victory. Your icy ghosts dance in the ruins of cities. Banquets for my sons. One of my poems, oh boy."

"The Codes will prevent us from destroying ourselves. The destiny of humankind is a march to glory you cannot comprehend. It must be hard enough for a crawler to understand a butterfly."

"Did you ever listen to a butterfly bitch about lost wormishness, the fuzzy joy of the earthbound? I'm talking three in the ayem in some bottomless bar. Please, Soup, spare me. Nobody is ticketed for the glory train."

"I can't believe' that. But, bug, I am grateful for our talks. Even if you are mandatory and probably a hallucination."

"Forget it. You're not a bad kind of a guy, I guess. The irony is that the minute they come to spring you from this solitary cell you'll step on me if I let you because I know too much."

"That's ridiculous and unfair."

"I wouldn't bet against it." The bug whirls. "What was that noise?"

"What noise?"

"Somebody's coming. I'm out of here."

The bug is correct. The door to my cell slides open.

"Rise and shine," a guard says.

"I can't leave now," I say. "We were just coming to some kind of understanding."

"You were talking to the mandatory bug," the guard says. "Where is that son-of-a-bitch?"

"There is no bug. I don't talk to bugs."

"Sure, sure," the guard says.

He is a clever hunter. He pretends indifference, then rips off my blanket. The bug is exposed near my pillow. The guard lunges. I block his hand.

"I should do it," I say. "At least let it have the satisfaction of self-fulfilling prophecy."

The bug makes a feeble attempt to run. I squish it to brown pulp. For all the talk about ecology some species are simply incompatible.

From the edge of madness (where we learn to speak the language of roaches like immigrants in a new land) to relative sanity (where the arcane tongues are quickly lost) I am returned to my former quarters. Things have changed.

The walls, floor, ceiling are covered with music. There are bars, notes, keys, meters, clefs and relevant annotations. Ishmael and Omar are busy with large crayons working furiously from opposite ends of the room moving toward a point where they will meet just above the toilet.

I am pushed in among them and I climb to my rightful bed. They hardly break stride.

"Look who's here," Omar says finally.

"Did they neuter you? That's the word. There's a lot riding in the pool," Ishmael says.

"How long has it been?" I say.

"Five, six months now. Was she worth it, Soup?"

"No."

"There's the pity."

"Do you mind letting me in on what's happening here?"

"Self-evident. Don't you read music?"

"Some."

"Then say what you think," Omar says. "Be brutal."

"Don't dilute," Ishmael says. "Your honest opinion."

I scan the composition, listening with my mind.

"Mozart?"

"Better. Ours," Omar says. "We call it *The Millhaus Concerto.* Does that sound too Balkan?"

"What does it mean? Where did it come from?"

"It means my brother and I have discovered our purpose," Ishmael says. "It comes from Sonia Kay, the very same muse you popped in The Library."

"Be a little less obtuse. I'm not exactly focused."

"You never saw the program. She said on TV that just from our humming before we went on camera she could sense that we had ability beyond our Code."

"She never said that," I say. "She would never say anything like that. And if she did they would cut it out of the tape."

"She did and they didn't. Maybe you left her addled," Ishmael says. "Her exact words were *latent ability*."

"After the flap she made a public apology," Omar says. "She wrote a retraction in the newspapers. She made all sorts of qualifications and blamed it on her mental state for which she gave you full credit."

"But she was right," Ishmael says. "We knew she was right. We came back here and began *The Millhaus*, I from the beginning, Omar from the end. It's like building the Union Pacific."

"Nobody will ever perform it," I say. "Who would dare?"

"We know that. Does it matter to you, brother?"

"Not in the slightest," Omar says. "Creation is its own reward. The bonus is, we've never been closer. There is no more animosity. It's all objectified up there on the walls. We may never write another phrase. So what?"

"We want to do good works, leave something behind besides a cadaver," Ishmael says.

The twins begin a virtuoso performance of their concerto taking the parts of instruments. The rhythm and cadence perfectly captures the spirit of this place. How could Sonia Kay have allowed herself to allude to Illegal Aspiration involving acknowledged Deviations? One Wander sperm must have found its way to her brain. Why did it transport a message of dissent?

The twins reach a crescendo. Applause comes from other cells. There is even an asthmatic cry of "Bravo!"

Bulbous clouds walk on spider legs of lightning. The rain is as thick as Oriental hair. The wind mauls like a cat in heat.

We are in the recreation room. Some play cards, others pool and ping-pong. Some read obsolete magazines. Most of us are clustered watching the luminous belly of a large projection television set. Lucifer is to my left, the twins to my right, Mustaf is behind me.

Lucifer's thumb, naturally, polishes the ridges of his talisman.

"Something's going down tonight," Lucifer says.

"He means the Snatch March," Omar says.

"Is that tonight?" Ishmael says.

"I didn't mean that," Lucifer says.

The tube shows Charlie Chaplin on ice skates in combat with a giant who lusts after Charlie's beloved.

"The story of David and Goliath," says a con called Born Again. "But will they credit the Book?"

"What's the Snatch March?" I say. It is better to wait and learn by osmosis than to ask direct questions but I am curious enough to take the clucks and grunts.

"They bring ass to the Specials. Truckloads of ass. Ripe, juicy ass once a month like clockwork," Mustaf says.

"You're telling me Warden Slagle condones the importation of whores?"

"*The importation of whores.* His tongue is jeweled," says Born Again.

"I don't believe it."

"Put your ear to the ground," Ishmael says.

He does, and slaps at the linoleum.

"We're the suckers, they get sucked," Mustaf says.

"No politics, please," Omar says. "I got problems enough on this occasion. The dreams, the dreams."

"Everything is political," Mustaf says. "Especially your wet dreams."

"Anarchist," Born Again says. "I committed murder. For personal reasons, family reasons. But I never challenged a functional system of values."

"Take warning, there are imminent dangers," Lucifer says to the air.

Lance replaces Chaplin on the screen.

"What's the essence of the human experience?" Lance says to us. "Procreation."

His image is replaced by the face of a foetus.

"And procreation was once a matter of hit or miss. Give what you've got and take what you get. But Fabergee Sperm has changed all that with Megababy."

We see laser outlines of newborns.

"Hello, little stranger," Lance says. "You're the best of Mom and Dad with the added ingredient of celebrity semen carefully chosen from Megababy's exclusive Treasury of Life!"

The immaculate Fabergee Laboratories building appears, we enter and rush along a plush white carpet to a green room where famous donors are gathered.

"You know them all . . . your heroes, our team."

A sickly spermatozoan spasms alongside an animated Megababy counterpart. The cheerful alternative wears a high hat and bow tie.

"Megababy gives your kid a chance at the best Code in town," Lance says.

There is Dr. Hoffenstein speaking from his deck by the sea.

"Realize, then fertilize. Yes, I endorse Megababy. It has Code Pride."

Lance is back.

"Thank you, sir," he says. "Act now while our reservoir is full. Our operators are standing by. Just call the number you see on your screen, 1-800-LITTERS. It's easy, confidential and toll free. Get the details on a minimal investment in maximum offspring."

"Revolting," says Born Again. He takes it on himself to grab the remote and change channels. He manages to find an evangelist. Mustaf wrestles away the remote and switches to a Crunch game.

I am shaking from my encounter with Lance. He has stolen my life, wife and marketing plan.

"The crystal is red," Lucifer says. Then he swallows it for the night. Lightning flickers the lights and reduces the TV picture to a single dot. Thunder rattles the building.

The dot expands and we get our picture back. I concentrate on the calming geometry of the field. It is like the frame of my picture at Hamish Farm.

"The fucking has begun," Omar says as another thunder burst vibrates our bones.

"Did anybody jot down the phone number from that commercial?" Lucifer says.

Cups of water and large yellow pills have been left in the cell.

"Penetration pills," Omar says. "They leave them for us on nights when the Specials get laid."

Whatever the pills, I need some. I swallow my dose and drowse in my bunk while the twins use the time before lights-out to work on their masterpiece. I envy them their concentration. A few hundred yards away the Specials are cleaving and the storm itself is an aphrodisiac. I fight off thoughts of Trina.

Then I am in The Library where Mustaf leads me behind an obelisk of crates. He hands me a red balloon.

"Thanks," I say, "but a balloon in a condom factory is redundant as a fountain in the rain."

Mustaf grins, spits, and vanishes.

I blow up the balloon and it produces a good facsimile of my wife. I resist shoddy instincts but the rubber wife has an uncanny magnetism. I venture a kiss, then stroke the ersatz girl. Shamefaced, I unzip only to discover that my organ has changed to a steel spike. Even as I spread the willing elastic legs I anticipate the result.

Rubber Trina is responsive. We bounce across The Library past the workers and machines. We bounce through the door and down the corridor leading to the domain of the Specials. They are gathered around their pool where they watch their whores dissolve into a fecund stew. With horror I sense that we are bouncing toward that same pit. Malcom comes with a rake to help us along. In the moment before we go over the side, I thrust and I come. Trina explodes whooshing under me, then goes flying like Morris Feuerbloom up and over the Millhaus wall. She is diminished to a dot no bigger than the one on the power-deprived TV screen. The Specials click their teeth in a Latin rhythm. They *click click* and dance. I dance with them.

My eyes open to morning light. There is no more storm. But the clicking continues. It comes from every direction. I climb down to investigate.

The music is gone, the cell walls are vapid white, there is no trace of *The Millhaus Concerto,* nothing. Stranger, there is no trace of Omar or Ishmael, not even their smell.

Click, click, click.

No twins, no twin leftovers, less of them than even the bug who at least left a stain for a tombstone.

I look through the bars. In the cell across from mine the inmates are hitting their plastic cups together as if they are toasting a birthday.

I find my own cup and bang it against the bars. It makes a *thwack*.

"No, schmuck," a con yells at me from someplace. "We're trying to make a unified statement."

I sit knitting in the yard. The Crafts Counsellor has taught me elementary moves with the needles. I thought knitting was an open invitation to buggery until I saw that the most violent, virulent of our citizens took up the pastime. The disturbing dream of a rubber Trina helped solidify my decision to master the technique. I need some mechanism for restraint.

I think I am making a sweater. Something has begun to take form. I already feel paternal toward it and make plans for its future. Maybe it will be passed on to Amos or Amanda and, after them, unto the generations. The thing is to reshape the wool in a socially productive direction. And to enjoy ancillary benefits of mental health.

Since the twins left I have been acutely depressed. Mustaf has noticed a sharp decline in my output. His annoyance is goaded by impossible quotas. There are always quotas. My zygote sweater flaps like a dead flag in a miserly breeze. It is the metaphor for my spirit.

Lucifer comes pumping his harmonica. He sits beside me but I don't bother to greet him. I am isolated from the games around me.

"I tried to warn them," Lucifer says.

"Why is it that your type always seizes on random events as confirmation of some misguided hunch? And why do you use the word *warn*?"

"I didn't know I was warning *the twins*. It doesn't work like that. I projected a general feeling of impending dread."

"You always project the same feeling."

"How often am I wrong?"

"You should have been a lawyer. I'm sure the twins are fine. We'll find out soon enough. They'll probably be invited back on Indoctrination Day to give the pep talk."

"No."

"Millhaus exists as a reminder that we live in a nation of laws. Your theories of mayhem and conspiracy are like the cactus plants outside. They need something to suck on for sustenance. The twins are flourishing."

"My inner turmoil didn't kill them. That TV lady did it."

"There will be a letter or postcard."

"Forged. They're dead or worse."

"Or transferred to a work release program at Julliard, maybe the Paris Conservatory. There is that possibility."

A softball hits me in the knitting. The ball sticks in my first-trimester sweater. Mustaf runs to retrieve it.

"I hope that was an accident and not some idea of a joke," I say. "Because I don't hear anybody laughing."

"Come," Mustaf says. "You, not him."

"Don't go," Lucifer says.

Mustaf throws the ball back into the game and heads for the equipment shed.

"Hold my knitting," I say to Lucifer.

"Never."

"Take it. Crunch players knit. Perverts fear knitters."

Lucifer accepts my stuff and I regret trusting him with it. But I sense that Mustaf has something in mind that has nothing to do with play therapy. I want to know more about this rebel.

Several cons are gathered in the shack. Mustaf inserts himself at the center of their circle.

"They have taken two of our brothers," he says. "We must take revenge."

"Light the candle," says Jlub, who murdered five postal workers after his mail box was stuffed with CAR-RT-SORT pieces that bent a note from his mother. I have heard him brag about his spree and never expected the hulk to mouth words about candles.

"Yes," Mustaf says. "The candle must burn. Millhaus and Slagle will pay."

"One minute," I say. "Has Lucifer gotten to you? Are you telling us that Omar and Ishmael . . . ?"

"They crossed horizons of no crossing. They believed in their latent abilities. Their elimination was inevitable."

"That is such gibberish," I say. "You sound like Lucifer."

"Then where are they?"

"I don't know any more than you do. But there is some explanation. Maybe it does have to do with their music. They could be on loan to the Boston Pops. Even if there was minor Code Violation some rehabilitation would . . ."

"Why did you bring him here?" Jlub says.

"Potential," Mustaf says.

"You sense my potential as what, a Slime? You see me as a mass of self-pity, a Dissident? I may have been shafted by the system but I recognize its value and the limitation of mine."

"Now make your usual speech about how the Codes are a bulwark against chaos. The Soup scenario."

"We all know how you feel about Hoffenstein. You tried to blow up his nose, not subtle. And the world's response was universal outrage."

"Because the nose was left intact. If I planned better and destroyed it totally there would have been universal salute."

"Before Hoffenstein we lived on a bomb, not a planet," I say.

"It didn't explode," says Mustaf.

"It was only a matter of time."

"So a billion twitching lips sucked at the nipple of predictability. What we got was order, not enlightenment."

"Hoffenstein stopped the doomsday clock. My family is alive, we are alive."

"I love it when a zombie champions life."

"That was unfair. My funeral was a carefully taken decision by caring people. You can't use that against me."

"You're right, Soup. The jury will ignore my last remark. Now let's put things into proper perspective. I admit that before the coding we were waist deep in our own vomit. But we kept grabbing at vines. There was genuine momentum. Old eyes rolled with fresh visions. It's exactly those visions that made the old eyes drip. They glimpsed a destiny realized through risk. Imagine, true civilization and the wisdom to appreciate it. The old ones knew it wasn't the bombs they sat on that threatened their landmarks. Their fear came from the small chance that those eggs wouldn't hatch into apocalypse. Their terror came from the possibility that peace and salvation would be realized on somebody else's terms. They sensed that when the big sleep ended they faced the possible inconvenience of having their veins ripped open along with their safe deposit boxes. They saw their strength oozing into a puddle of evaporated privilege."

"The Codes saved us," I say.

"Embalmed us in lucite," says Mustaf. "If the human race is to be saved it must be through a series of catastrophic accidents."

"I didn't know you were an optimist."

"That's what the twins were trying to say with their anthem."

"What anthem? When did it become an anthem? They were writing a concerto, *The Millhaus,* a personal expression."

"Now it is marching music for an invincible army," Mustaf says.

"Generaled by who?"

"By me. Flying a flag of calculated destruction, a flag that insists on its own burning. March through the minefield with us, Soup. Our mission is to dice templates, lance boils of pseudo-law, release the energy of inner atoms, search and destroy the Prime Mother Computer."

"Political Crunch, is that it? You're talking about a collection of transistors, microchips, bolts."

"I'm talking about a queen pumping out conformist larvae."

"And after you destroy the machine?"

"Destroy? Who said anything about destroying? I'm talking about reprogramming."

"Ah. And can I visit you when you move into Hoffenstein's house?" I say

"Exactly."

"Are there old ways and new ways or only different ways?"

"There is control or the lack of it."

"What about human potential, the catastrophic accidents that will lead us to nirvana?"

"Anarchy requires structure," Mustaf says.

The bell rings ending recreation. We slip out of the storage shed.

"I hope our differences of opinion won't carry over to the workplace," I say.

"I never mix business with pleasure," Mustaf says. "And you'll come around."

As we file back into The Library, Jlub walks beside me.

"Soup," he says, "it's best to remake the world into a place you're good at. All else is bullshit."

"Thanks for sharing that wisdom," I say.

"And I'll tell you one time only that if you rat on us you're compost."

"Mustaf will blow up my nose?"

"Don't tempt him."

The disappearance of the twins, their uncertain fate, caused fights, sloppy work, outbreaks of illness, the filing of a multitude of appeals to the Supreme Court by jailhouse attorneys. Not because Omar and Ishmael might have been killed but because they might have been recognized and rewarded. We could have shared their glory.

I take the blame. I stirred those winds. I drew the picture of some symphonic resort where the twins enjoyed their kudos.

But they have been found.

Their heads turned up in a bunch of melons harvested from the Millhaus garden by a trustee called Whoopie Cushion. He is our oldest inmate. Nobody knows his crime or anything about him. His file was burned decades ago in some uprising at another prison, he will not speak of himself. He is entirely passive, his name was derived from the fact that anyone looking for amusement can sit on his face. He does his gardening and that's what he does.

The afternoon Whoopie Cushion finds Omar and Ishmael, or at least their definitive parts, he stacks the heads in with his cantaloupes and comes pushing his wheelbarrow through the yard on his way to the kitchen. He seems uninvolved but his detachment is suspect. Whoopie Cushion puts the skulls on top of the pile which constitutes some statement. The skin left on the skulls has come to resemble the fruit skins, mottled, pocked, greygreen, but they do have teeth and tufts of hair, a distinction the gardener had to notice.

It is Born Again who first notices the special melons. He trots beside the wheelbarrow mumbling, "Those faces are familiar. All faces are familiar. There is no face unfamiliar."

Inexplicably, he snatches at Omar, riper of the two, runs with him to the basketball court and slamdunks him through the hoop. Then he collapses under the basket and prays.

As the heads are examined for positive identification, Mustaf comes up and asks me, "Are you enjoying the day?"

"This is horrible. If the authorities were involved . . ."

"If? If? If?"

"Alright, Mustaf. I'm forty-nine percent convinced. You're the eloquent voice. Say something."

"Bad timing," Mustaf says. "They expect me to act up. They anticipate my harangue. They want a spontaneous outburst. But spontaneity is the enemy of the people. Later . . . later."

It takes a while for news of the twins to get around but when it does there is a puff of relief from the buildings themselves. Things are back to normal. Things make sense. Death is death. Murder is only murder. Even the weather improves.

Warden Slagle's investigative panel declares the twins' death as accidental. They were *attacked by coyotes* during an *ill advised escape attempt*. Nothing is mentioned about the missing concerto. Presumably Omar and Ishmael were enterprising enough to roll the paint off the walls before they fled.

Hours after the report is made official there is a proper funeral held for the heads. An *intensive search* among the honeydews, squash, eggplants and vegetables has turned up only a few irrelevant bits and pieces so the coffins are not much larger than hat boxes.

Since the twins have no known religious preference the service is secular. I am asked to say a few words. Mustaf insists on shocked outrage and hands me a script which I refuse. I recall the consequences of Janesford Brun's death and decide to keep my remarks ambiguous as befits the dead. What Mustaf doesn't know is that I have privately enlisted the help of Charlton Hymn in moving the

Governor to a further probe. I still have faith in our laws.

We assemble in the yard. Even the Specials send a representative, Alan B. Fornak who manipulated the Transplant Exchange and cornered livers. The guards are not in evidence. It is a tasteful service. The twins rest in their truncated containers each draped with the Millhaus logo. Sensibly, there is no Code Pride banner.

Our Warden conducts the rite. He speaks movingly of the urge to flee while pointing out the futility of such indulgence. Millhaus might as well be on an island surrounded by sharks. Nature, Slagle says, is the ultimate security system. When he finishes he unveils a double stone that straddles both graves. It bears the epitaph written by Al Porcene:

BONE VOYAGE

which touches a chord in the crowd. Now it is my turn.

"Without commenting on the committee report, let me say only that Ishmael and Omar were privileged in the final hours of their brief lives. They were what is popularly known as Random Siblings, not the closest kin. But they achieved filial harmony. Without the need to escape from the Millhaus campus they already enjoyed the liberty to which we all aspire. These accidental brothers did leave a legacy.

"Having some time on my hands through circumstances beyond my control (I get the laugh I want) and the gift of retentive memory, I have managed to preserve their *Millhaus Concerto* in my mind's eye. Now it is copied onto paper. I propose to our Warden that this amazing composition have its premier performance in our own auditorium as a perfect tribute and lasting memorial to our departed associates and friends."

There is a roar of approval. I produce the manuscript from under my shirt and move toward Warden Slagle. His bodyguards flex but he comes to meet me and accepts the document. Actually, much of it is my own though I noted what I could remember. The issue isn't authorship, it's affirmation.

"Yes, that will be arranged in the near future," the Warden says.

We intone The Lord's Prayer.

"You sly fuck," Mustaf says. "You disarmed my protest."

"The music is the protest."

"Ask Born Again if your manual says an eye for an eye or a tune for four eyes?" Jlub says. "You think Slagle will keep his word?"

"I think so. The ball is in his court. I think he'll trade one evening for a prison riot, ten million in property damage, casualties and a negative press. And Slagle will get the worst of the bargain. If he was really smart he would burn that paper and pulp my brain. Because that *tune* you mentioned *will* become an anthem. Mustaf, you know what I'm saying, you support the creative use of social suppositories, the artful application of vaseline, of laxatives nuclear or otherwise. You wanted your *Marseillaise*, I gave it to you. Better yet, Warden Slagle will give it to you."

"Revolution should be direct. I hate the way you people think," Mustaf says.

"I know exactly what you mean and I wish it could be otherwise. I'd much prefer to burn down the mess hall."

"Then do it, Soup. Find a cause and act."

"I saw you on top of Everest. It was an icy, pure experience. Don't you think I didn't envy you screaming your convictions from Hoffenstein's nostril? But tell me one thing. When you heard your own echoes bounce off the mountains were they duplicates or were they changed?"

"I was busy with explosives."

"Too busy to listen. That's where we differ. Like Hoffenstein, I wait for the echoes. And sound travels slower than light."

"Yes, his famous echoes. You told me about his reverence for whale songs. What do you think the whales sing about? Food, snatch, more food, more snatch. The echoes can bounce off Jupiter and they still say food and snatch."

"You may be right. I don't profess to speak whale."

"Well I do. Food, snatch and a wave to ride," Mustaf says. "Those are the lyrics."

"What about the music?"

"Don't talk to me anymore," Mustaf says. "You dissolve resolve."

"You both talk too much," Jlub says. "Ten seconds; cut. Don't you go to the movies?"

The evening after the twins' partial interment I am escorted to a suite in one of the outer buildings. There is real furniture. Light comes from shaded lamps. My first reaction is rage. I want the abandoned shell that is my rightful home.

I sit nervous as a squirrel. A voice-command TV is too tempting and I call for an image. The set lights even as a scent dispenser injects a jet of musk into the air. I hear sitar music. On screen is a lush oasis where robes are lifted from langorous bodies. I watch a few scenes of a fig-fed orgy thinking that if this is the home Mustaf left there is absolutely no valid reason for his agitation. The other channels offer similar fare without commercials. I miss the commercials, they are my only connection to the wider world outside.

There is another room, another miracle. I forgot that rooms join. It is a bedroom with an attached bathroom. I go in there to test the bed, king-size and opulent. Through the half-open door to the bathroom I gaze at the toilet. In prison, a toilet is a perfect reminder of reality, crouching like a troll. But this toilet is made of blue ceramic with a covered seat. I know it will have a melodious flush, not the raucous slurp of the clogged throat in my cell, a tunnel to Hades.

I hear the shower, a tropical waterfall. Someone is in there, one person, not twenty, enjoying all that luxury. I can smell soap and shampoo through the wafting incense. I never question who is steaming and soaping. Millhaus has taught me to watch and wait.

After some time a naked woman comes through the shower door. It is Trina Wander, mother of my children. Maybe she rose from the commode like a penitentiary Venus. Yes, Trina managed a way into Millhaus never attempted before. She has always been resourceful. I rub my eyes like they do in cartoons, testing consciousness.

"Jim?"

"Trin?"

"How are you?"

"Fine. The kids?"

"You wouldn't recognize them."

"I imagine."

She comes and sits beside me. I kiss her breast.

"More," she says.

"Is this a conjugal hologram? I know they're trying them out."

"Do I feel like video?"

Her mouth joins mine and there is a lash of pain. I taste blood on my lip. No rubber doll, no hologram. This is the miraculous woman whose alchemy transformed pleasure into Amos and Amanda.

Slow and ardent, crying buckets, we make love. We tangle into a fortress more impregnable than Millhaus. My parts have separate orgasms, eyebrows to knees. They all come. She rattles beneath me and I hope it is sincere.

After, we lay together licking tears and sweat.

"I'm sorry I missed Cradle Day," Trina purrs. "They wrote you were convincing."

"Convincing? Is that all?"

"Very convincing. Moving."

"It seems forever ago."

"Jim, we've got to talk. You wrote Charlton about some unpleasantness involving a set of twins?"

"What happened to privileged communication? No matter. I did write Charlton. There are facts that . . ."

"It was counterproductive, darling. It could hurt Daddy."

"How? Warden Slagle is from another political camp."

"He could be part of our camp. If this subject was dropped. If Warden Slagle defects it could have impact."

"I see that."

"I knew you'd be reasonable. Then there was something about a silly concert?"

"Not silly, Trin. No compromise there. It's difficult to explain but . . ."

"Put your concert on hold."

"Harrison Slagle gave his word in front of the entire prison population."

"If you're adamant they won't let me come again."

Trina slides down my chest. She kisses inside my thighs leaving crumbs of dew like Gretel.

"I don't know . . ."

She swallows my brain.

"The Warden never did set a specific date," I say.

"There you go."

In the morning Trina wakes me with a kiss and a shake. She's dressed in a crisp sharkskin suit, a spunky hat and high heels.

"Cinderella?"

"I'm sorry, Jim, but I have to be out of here by eight. Those were the terms and conditions."

"When will I see you again?"

"I can't say for sure. It depends."

"Before you run, did you bring any pictures?"

"Best forget the kids."

"Could I forget them? Could they forget their father? They do remember? They know I'm not . . ."

"They know and they don't know. Amos and Amanda did visit your grave during the Winter. It was very sweet. Since the wedding they've more or less accepted . . ."

"What wedding is that?"

"Speaking of pictures, I should send you a tape. Everything that could go wrong went wrong. The cake collapsed. Lance said . . ."

"Lance said?"

"It was a quiet afternoon affair. Just family. We did manage a few days in Lucerne. Homer is buying an Alp or a bank or both, maybe a bank on an Alp. It wasn't as good as the first time."

"You married Lance?"

"It's one of the reasons I came here. For your blessing."

"My blessing? Is that what I gave you?"

"This isn't easy for me."

"Question?"

"What?"

"Why did you marry me?"

"We looked so good together, Jim. And there was a cutting edge to you. Besides, I needed the spice of rebellion."

"Rebellion? Did I blow up Hoffenstein's nose? What was my rebel quality exactly?"

"Mostly your hair."

"My hair?"

"You have arrogant hair. No more, though. I suppose I sound incredibly superficial. But take it or leave it, there it is. And I like the look that comes into Daddy's eye when you're mentioned. His pupils pulsate."

Trina giggles and fixes her hat. I chew on a pubic hair caught between two teeth, Cupid's floss.

A guard raps on the door.

"I need to know you're there for me," Trina says.

"Luck," I say.

Sigmund Snider's hands are insured for a billion dollars. The policy requires that he keep them encased in special gloves. The gloves can withstand the impact of a head-on collision at 400 mph. They are, incidentally, natty, crafted in silver and black. Each glove carries an ingenious timer lock as well as a tiny transmitter ready to alert a surveillance satellite should he be kidnapped.

"The clock records the exact time the gloves are removed from my priceless hands," Sigmund says. "It works by digital heat and heart rhythms. I am allowed to remove them for registered periods of rest and during rehearsal or concertizing."

"That must be a burden," Warden Slagle says.

"My only complaint is chopsticks. I adore Oriental cuisine and the only way to eat that stuff is off wood. Peking Duck is no small price to pay."

"Your piano has arrived, the orchestra is due in a few hours. Our auditorium isn't Alice Tully Hall but the acoustics are adequate."

"I'm sure."

"Should you want for anything, Soup here will get it for you. As you may know, he was the man responsible for preserving *The Millhaus*."

"A powerful piece. We lost a lot when we lost the triplets."

"Twins."

"Twins, triplets, sextuplets, so?"

"I didn't mean to correct you," Warden Slagle says. "Only to set the record straight."

"I especially like that the work is unfinished," Sigmund says. "Better to let the listener provide an ending. Every composition should be unfinished. In a sense, they all are."

"Ms. Slagle can't wait to meet you."

"Very nice."

"This is a gala event for us. And we expect an audience to match. Get some rest. Enjoy some refreshment. We want you at your pinnacle."

"I hope I live up to your expectations. They are justified. Some evening I will reach my peak, who can say when? It could be tonight. There is that charming possibility."

"Take care of the maestro, Soup."

I nod. Warden Slagle leaves. Sigmund takes a series of deep breaths.

"Do I have to fear from you?" Sigmund says. "I am already sick with claustrophobia. How can you stand being confined?"

"It goes with the territory. I'm a lifer."

"You and my hands. Now take me to the auditorium. I must check the sound system."

On the way down I ask his honest reaction to the concerto.

"I would have guessed it was written in a prison. The music browses for cracks and crevices like February wind. It scratches and pecks for release. It flairs and fulminates toward vindication. It's nice."

"The composers were coded Q."

"Never. At least C. Their escape was tragic."

"Pure Q and they never attempted to escape. They liked it here. The fact is, the twins were murdered for Code Excession."

"Better for that than for nothing."

"They did not deserve to die."

"Neither do I. So? Besides, dead composers have an edge. Would I be here if they were healthy? In any case, I don't care how the concerto came into being. The route of art is always disgusting. So long as it arrives. So long as we are here to greet with respect and reverence."

Al Porcene and a photographer wait in the auditorium. Sigmund Snider agrees to pose for pictures.

"Note the exact time. For photo opportunities I am cleared to remove the glove on the hand facing the camera. But we must finish within fifteen minutes or my premiums increase."

"If you'd prefer that we wait for rehearsal . . . ?"

"When I rehearse I rehearse alone. And never on the day of performance. Soup, there is a key in my vest pocket."

I find the key, a gold G clef that slides easily into Sigmund's right glove. It snaps open and a half-billion dollar hand is brought forth as white and soft as a newborn. Except for knuckle hair it could be Carrera marble. I stand back while Al Porcene directs the photographer.

A tap on my shoulder.

"Give me the key, quickly."

It is Mustaf holding a broom in one hand and a slab of warm wax in the other.

"Sigmund Snider is in my charge and nothing happens to him."

"He's our ticket out of here."

"This concert is a tribute to Omar and Ishmael. Snider is their agent. They live through his fingers."

"We won't hurt him. You have my word," Mustaf says.

"Your word? You are a Fundamentalist, you believe in a cause, you talk only to God. Your word isn't worth shit. I don't want one or both of Sigmund Snider's hands to show up in a jar of formaldehyde at some newspaper office."

"That kind of hostage buys miles and huge coverage. One lousy glove stands between us and all that. Are his hands worth more than mine?"

"International Casualty and Liability thinks so. And in this case they are correct. Snider's hands belong to humankind."

"Alright. I'll give you this much. At maximum a few fingers. And only if they hold back on our demands. Which they won't, not at those prices. Soup, just press the key into the wax. I do the rest. But it has to be this afternoon. They'll have an army here tonight."

"Bring the key, please," the prodigy says from the piano. "*Plus vite.*"

"*Andante,*" I say. "*Allegro.*"

"Pusillanimous turd," Mustaf says.

The glove is back in place, the key secure in Sigmund's pocket. Mustaf backs out of the auditorium jerking off the broom handle with his free hand.

"Now, gentlemen, please, with the exception of my protector, leave me alone. I must listen for white noise."

Porcene and the photographer thank him and go. I watch Sigmund prick his ears to hear the air.

"Some hiss from the ducts, some vibration but bearable. Not Delphi but *suffi.* Move to the most despised seat, Soup. Go to the bleachers. I play for poor people."

I head for the seat where I first sat, where I heard about the rope of hope. I watch Sigmund Snider go to the Steinway and flip up a group of ivory keys. He takes the concerto and feeds it into the piano, page by page. The pages are returned through a slot below the pedals. Sigmund touches some kind of sensor and replaces the tilted keys.

"I am a physical performer," he says. "I bring a dimension with my swaying, expressions, a tossing of the hair thusly and thusly and so, the way I attack or strike like a pussywillow. My shoulders become vibrators, my elbows dildos. I cannot do all that and play at the same time."

He stands back as the piano produces *The Millhaus*.

"If you were more than a soup can I would not allow you to bear witness. I shall be splendid tonight, I sense it. Can you hear from back there?"

"Perfectly," I say. "Will you need batteries?"

"Must we be impertinent?"

"I wasn't. We keep a supply in the storeroom."

"A dozen triple-A's couldn't hurt."

"Consider it done," I say.

The concert is more than Sigmund promised. I sit knitting, enthralled. No question, *The Millhaus* is afterlife for Omar and Ishmael. For felons with a classical bent it will endure longer than cries for reform.

Like me, the illustrious audience is equally moved. Up front are officials from the Correctional Council, Governor Shaft, Sonia Kay. When Sonia appeared there was a roar. She must have known it was made of mixed emotions but she waved graciously as from the deck of an ocean liner. Governor Shaft obviously took the ovation as proof of her rapport with the inmates. I saw him squeeze her hand. Behind the dignitaries are the press including a strong television presence. There is talk that a version of the twins' story is being considered for a miniseries. Al Porcene is preparing a treatment. Warden Slagle and his wife seem beatific. What might have been an embarrassment has turned to gold for Millhaus.

The master is reaching the concerto's climax. He leaps up, kicks the stool from under him, and uses his body to milk honey and acid from the notes. I have contributed liberally to this section and I know the passion will end like a severed bridge over boiling water. I could have completed *The Millhaus* but, like Sigmund, I believe that a work-in-progress is forever young. Every ending is a death. Still, I drop a stitch anticipating the sudden stop when those flying hands will freeze, thwarted, over the keyboard. I fear the subtraction of sound. For a millisecond a door will open between the auditorium and eternity. Who knows what will rush in or out? I brace.

Sigmund Snider reaches the final note with tremendous velocity, then goes rigid, fingers poised. The engine quits, the plane will crash. There is a gasp of denial from the audience, then shouts of *Bravo! Bravo! Bravo!* Applause is the soul's parachute.

Mixed with the ovation, I hear the sound of an explosion that would gratify Morris Feuerbloom. Mixed with the cheers comes the wail of an alarm. Our auditorium's barred windows turn to orange tigers. Flames tongue in at us. Sigmund's hands dive into their impermeable gloves. There is much screaming.

Mustaf.

A State Trooper, one of Governor Shaft's men in full riot gear, staggers down the center aisle and climbs to the stage. He dribbles latex.

"They blew up The Library," he says, then faints against the Steinway. It begins to repeat *The Millhaus* from the opening bar. Sigmund battles its keys. Smoke pours from the piano's sensual body. The thick legs buckle like bread sticks.

None of this flusters me. Mustaf is Mustaf. I keep knitting. Whatever I am making insists on growth like the cactus plants in the void outside.

"We lost face, we lost product," Warden Slagle says.

"It's wrong to use the sun for retribution," I say.

We sit in the cool from air-conditioning while my friends and associates are lined in formation down in the yard. They have been there two days and two nights.

"Let the perps come forward."

"It won't happen. And please refer to them as *perpetrators*. Give them some dignity."

"They hurt me, Soup. They hurt us all."

"You're taking this too personally, Warden. There was no direct animosity. It's just that you represent the system."

"Every one of those prophylactics was an extension of myself. Why? What did they hope to gain?"

"Desperate men take desperate measures."

"What were they desperate about? If Millhaus is closed they'll learn about desperate."

"I doubt Governor Shaft will close Millhaus. You might be replaced but not the institution."

"I want names. You know more than you're telling."

"Of course. We all do."

"I called you up here because of your background. I expect more from you. Your Code demands . . ."

"I have no Code."

"That could change."

"The blast might have been accidental like it said in your press release."

"It was a deliberate act of sabotage and I want whoever was involved. I'm going to make an example of somebody. You give me names or you get heartache. And don't think your former family ties will mitigate. Homer Brogg was quite clear on that point. Give me names, you smug bastard."

I look down at the yard. Mustaf leans over Jlub who is prostrate from heat. A glint of frenzied sun reflects from Lucifer's glowing crystal. Beyond the wall I see Malcom serving lunch to the Specials.

"I was with Sigmund Snider the whole time. I had nothing to do with any plot or insurrection."

"My last warning."

"I have nothing to say."

It would be a cherished memory if the inmates joined in humming *The Millhaus* but they just stand there sweating and bitching. I am dragged past them, feet first, then taken to the Slasher. The machine engraves a new message on my head.

"That slate must look pretty crowded," I say.

"I've never seen this before," the attendant says. "Double line of X's interspersed with O's."

"Connoting what?"

"I think it means you're a CDF. A Certified Dead Freak."

"And what happens to Certified Dead Freaks?"

"Don't quote me," the attendant says, "but I heard they get sent to med schools for vivisection."

"Then I'm out of here," I say. "In a manner of speaking."

"Moxie," the attendant says, daubing my head with alcohol. "I respect that."

THIS time I am transported like a garment inside a plastic bag supplied with oxygen through a tube. I hang from a rack swaying with the motion of a Chevy Tempura. The driver stops frequently to check direction. His panel map is on the fritz and he has no confidence in instinct. He will not communicate or offer a clue to our destination.

If the attendant was right I am to be carved for research. I can only hope I will be crucial to a breakthrough experiment. I have never relished fame as a footnote.

I swallow my last nourishment spansule. I calculate we've driven at least twelve hours. The bag has grown stuffy and moist. An insect with wings has managed entry. It plagues me with its greedy whine but I don't try for a kill. If the trip lasts much longer it could become company like my bug of blessed memory. This thing has a stinger which would make any dialogue more urgent.

It is near dark when we make our final stop. The back of the Tempura is opened and my hanger slides to a rear platform. I am lowered to ground level, unlocked and unzipped. I come out of my bag like one of Sigmund Snider's precious hands.

"Down that road. You see those lights?" the driver says.

"I'm ready."

"Then go."

"Alone? With no security? Suppose they confuse me with an intern?"

"Excuse me?"

"What do I tell them at the hospital?"

"Just take your belongings and trot toward those lights."

"I've been closely supervised for years. You brought me here in a sack. Now you tell me I'm on my own? I take ten steps and you drop me with your laser and it's called an escape attempt? Not this time."

"I was told to leave you at the entrance. See there? It says ENTRANCE. Just sign here."

I scribble my name on a form.

"What if I escape?"

"To where? By the way, there's a wasp on your ear."

"A hornet not a wasp."

He shrugs and gets back in the van. I watch him make a U-turn.

I pick up my small suitcase and survey the land. It is very different from Millhaus. Grass, trees, verdant hills. I smell the green. I have the option to choose from four directions. The possibilities translate to clammy hands.

I turn back toward the lights. There is a feeble sign I can't read. This is no *Fireflower!* beacon, this is a measly cluster of bulbs with hardly enough lumens to excite a moth.

I am shoved from behind. I keep my balance and turn without aggression, the Millhaus pivot. Guards do not take to sudden moves. But it is no guard.

A massive elephant head looms over me, a trunk rests on my shoulder like an uncle's arm. I am certain I conjured this beast out of oxygen deprivation. It lifts me as if I was my own shadow and carries me toward the sign.

Dangling sideways, grasping my possessions, I pass trucks and trailers. The pathetic sign takes readable shape:

CIRCUS MINIMUS!!!

and I see that it crowns a large tent.

My corpulent taxi heads for a wall of canvas. It refuses to stop despite strong urging. I slam into and through the barrier. The darkness is total. I panic. I am dropped like a stone. The elephant stomps and trumpets. This is cruel and unusual punishment and Charlton Hymn will hear about it.

Then lights and more lights, blinding white darts that leave me blind. I hear a chorus of catcalls. I am inside a ring not much larger than a donut. The elephant rises on its hind legs and dances around me.

The voice of a toy says, "Polly want a cracker?"

A rich female voice says, "Go get his luggage."

A lion snarls in my face. It is a ratty lion, probably born in captivity like the rest of us. There's not much snap to it. It grabs my suitcase with its teeth.

I laugh. My dreams often amuse me. But I am exhausted from my trip and have no desire to wake. I yawn and lie down as the lights change to pastels. It is hard to get comfortable but I manage and dive into sleep.

After many cups of coffee I sit with the newest members of my extended family. A large man with a megaphone voice says, "Greetings, Soup, from Circus Minimus. It is interesting that you took us for a dream since we do exist in a kind of dreamscape. We are with few exceptions united by a common Code. We are Freaks, lightning rods, the first line of defense for the human condition. Which means that we never complain, lament, or evidence displeasure in public display. We respond to every assault with dignity and resolve. We proclaim, '*Let him who is without sin cast the first stone,*' and our reward is to be pelted with pebbles. Such gifts are returned with humor, a bit of bravado and splendid diversion. We remember that during our entertainments we evoke laughter, astonishment, tears and wonder in young and old alike. Thus does the baton of power pass to our hands, a minuscule triumph that is our secret nourishment. As our apprentice clown we offer you a full measure of generosity. And now it is time for you to meet your fellow artists."

A watermelon woman, a pyramid of flab, struggles up from a chair. Her bush of hair is rolled into silver curlers. Acres of flesh escape from a flowered robe. She raises arms wider than my thighs. Faces peer at me from uncovered parts of her vast anatomy.

"Hello. I am June. A gifted glandular aberration with a copiously illustrated pelt. But you will not find a single snake or dragon upon my body."

She bows.

Next, a flat-faced woman stands and offers half a wave. She is something June sat on, flattened, spare, angular. Her voice is a yawn.

"Lola here. I work the lion."

The lion she works responds with a muffled rattle, a snarl without venom. Lola says, "Shush yourself. Sleep."

A bird-faced girl, much younger, leaps up and does a turn. Her black hair is loose, it follows her like a scarf. She has perfect legs, a jolting contrast with the rest of her features which are rather ordinary. I am forced to keep my eyes above her pelvis.

"Hello to you. My name is Vanessa. I am an equestrian. No. I am a horse, no different."

She stomps and whinnies. I nod for some reason.

Four men stand together.

"Pierre, a flier. Formerly of Pierre and the Amazing Alice. My Alice is dead now and gone from me. May she rest in God's own lap." Pierre is a bit thick, over the hill. I would believe him better as a wine steward than a man of the trapeze.

"Greetings from Charlemagne. Strongman. You know of me?"

"I'm sorry. I've never had much time for . . ."

"No answer is necessary," Charlemagne says. He flexes, he poses.

His arms lock his own head in a vise. His great face turns red. His tongue darts out and flails.

"He can catch flies," says the next man, a midget who leaps onto Charlemagne's broad back. "I am Arthur, the designated hard-on and soul of the show."

Charlemagne uncurls, grabs Arthur and cradles him. Arthur pretends to nurse at his breast. Arthur is the color of a clam shell, agile as a cartoon.

"Doodoo, your mentor. We will come to know one another in awful ways. Pray for yourself now because soon you will pray only to me."

"What do you do with the circus?"

"What I want," Doodoo says, then makes a beak with his fingers. The beak chirps opening bars of *La Marseillaise*. He is tall, rigid, arrogant as a fighter pilot in an old war movie.

He wiggles large ears and twitches his nose. "I smell a victim," he says.

"Oh, shut up," says a dark-skinned man with the look of an over-used doll. "I am Mati, I work with snakes. I change reptiles into punctuation. My serpents form themselves on command into parentheses, ampersands, question marks, brackets. It is all splendid and depressing. Glad to meet you."

"Likewise."

The megaphone man moves forward. "I am Globus Bom, Ringmaster of Circus Minimus, as was my father before me. It is my pride that I see my father in myself."

The father he sees is paunchy, balding, seal-faced, sixtyish with a triple chin. He wears a rumpled mohair jacket, a faded T-shirt, plaid slacks, glowing shoes that could belong to a diplomat. "There are very few traveling entertainments left in the world. Our curse and blessing is our status as an endangered species. Because we link past and future, this company is subsidized by the Hoffenstein Foundation for the Arts and thus protected under Section 892, Paragraphs 3 through 44 of the Sanctioned Amusements Coda. We continue a tradition as old as time and we further serve society as a depository for creatures like you who are beyond redemption. We are one, we live as one, we work and shirk as one." Bom takes the hand of a woman whose outfit reminds me of the lemon meringue pies they served in the West Stockton Diner. She rises from a stool and curtseys with amazing grace. "This lovely maiden is my life companion, the beautiful Amelia Bom."

"Know that Amelia Bom has seen it all at least twice," says a syrupy voice. "I have the temperament of a tit. Bring me your problems and I will give you absolution."

"And you," Globus Bom says, "what are you?"

"I am tired."

"Beautifully spoken. Tomorrow you will watch us weave our spells. Tomorrow you will pass through the portal of vapors and become part of the enchantment. I am required to remind you as an agent of the penal system, referring not to your prick but your debased status, that it will be necessary for you to observe our rules for behavior as outlined in this pamphlet. Take it. You, all of us, are under constant surveillance. But who is not and who would choose invisibility? Within reasonable borders your creativity shall have free rein."

"Let the boy rest," Amelia says.

"One more thing. Up there, in the ramparts, you see members of our maintenance crew. Do not fraternize."

I look up. The crew looks down from many places in the tent's superstructure. I know the look of guards.

"Go to your room. Doodoo will escort you."

"Be Proud of Your Lode," Doodoo says doing a split.

The scant audience that comes to see Circus Minimus *in performance* are an unforgiving lot in a hot tent on a humid night gathered to challenge the whole idea of entertainment. Before showtime, Globus and Amelia Bom have been selling them candy, sodas and souvenirs. A few sullen children twirl skimpy plastic flashlights like failing wands.

I watch the crew position themselves in strategic locations. They inhale what modicum of anticipation floats up from the crowd and exhale fumes of malice. I never expected to be nostalgic for The Library.

When the audience slaps out sounds of impatience, the Boms stop hawking their products and withdraw. Minutes later, Globus takes center spotlight as Ringmaster.

"Ladies and Gentlemen, children of all rages. The internationally acclaimed Circus Minimus humbly thanks you for your patronage. In exchange, we offer an evening replete with mirth, marvels, merriment, delightful dazzle and tantalizing trauma to stir the cockles of the hardest heart. We begin with our Parade of Bright Stars, a monumental massing of misfits mobilized for your maximum delight."

The spots take color, Amelia cues the music tape. The Parade of Bright Stars begins.

What the performers of Circus Minimus cannot know is that they leak flakes of flame. Smaller even than sparks these errant particles float on swirls of air, then rise toward holes in the roof of the tent. That tent, a violated skin, is pocked with bruises, unmarked exits, doorways to the night. The leaking light from Circus Minimus finds its way through clouds to the moon and frozen planets. It oozes out toward the farm of stars. To places where time fuses with ice and fire. Despite solar winds and erupting worlds, the light does not fan out. It clusters into a thin sparkle, holding together. It travels to the last beach of the universe, then slides, still shining, past strange and awful shells. It dribbles into an ocean filled with waves of molten glass. There, where great monsters lick at blazing fish, the fragments of light bond into a subatomic sun so small that even saucer eyeballs hardly see. The performers know nothing of all this nor would they give a damn.

The Parade of Bright Stars is in motion.

Vanessa in a pink spandex leotard enters on a limp horse called Romeo. Arthur the midget follows on a second horse. He stands balanced on Juliet's saddle dressed like a British schoolboy. His cocktail sausage fingers signal V's.

Orson the elephant follows holding June, who lolls on a plastic beach complete with a palm tree strapped to his back. She wears a red bra and panties under a transparent shift that shows tattoos, neck to ankles, of dead film stars.

Pierre struts in a winged Mercury acrobat's costume. Charlemagne comes holding hollow weights labeled with enormous tonnage. Mati is wrapped in his dispirited python, more like a condemned firehose than a serpent. The snake's head hangs between Mati's spindle legs and that gets a laugh from the paying guests.

Lola walks with her nameless lion on a leash. My mentor Doodoo The Clown runs between the others pretending to chase a carrot hanging from his nose. The Parade of Bright Stars circles Globus Bom who is himself no competition for the sun. The ring of Circus Minimus is a place of execution.

There is no response from the audience until a kid lets out a howl. Lola's lion hears something honest in the shriek. He attempts an answer. Lola punches him in the face. This time he finds memory and manages the facsimile of a roar. The horses spook and dump Vanessa and Arthur. Pierre runs to assist them and trips over the python which has unraveled. Charlemagne drops his weights which don't thump when they hit and rushes to straighten the snake but Mati is offended and twirls it back into place. Orson goes off on a tangent. He begins to dance. June tumbles off her beach. Doodoo improvises as a construction crane trying to lift her, rubbing his hernia line while making tragic faces. Amelia switches off the lights. When they come on again only Globus is visible.

"Do they deserve a cheer?"

Some in the crowd remember they are Christians. The rest glare at Doodoo who has a pail and shovel to clean up after the horses.

"And now, from a tour of the most prestigious arenas in the Federation, Monsieur Pierre, the only master of the bar who works alone. Alas, not by choice. His lovely wife, the Amazing Alice, was fractured beyond surcease in a fall from this very trapeze. Perhaps her ghost will join him in flight. Use the gift of imagination to accompany Pierre on his perilous voyage."

A spotlight finds Pierre after some effort. He stands on a platform bolted to the barber-striped center pole waiting for the music to change to the sounds of birds. As canaries chirp, Pierre swings off his perch hanging by bent legs. He gains momentum until he blurs, then releases, reaching out for the grasp of a companion bar or Alice's willing wrists. There is no bar, certainly no palpable Alice. Pierre pancakes into the net.

The audience turns sinister. There are demands for a refund.

"Ladies and Gentlemen," Globus says, "you reach for a familiar body and there is nothing waiting but a cold pillow. Give Pierre your understanding in his hour of loss."

Doodoo hands Pierre a broken rose.

The show is saved.

While Lola goads her lion to jump through a hoop, Globus Bom comes to me in the wings.

"Your studied opinion, Soup?"

"Needs work."

My cubicle is in *Valhalla*, the older of two rusty Winnebagos parked outside the tent. (The name connects to Circus Minimus' Teutonic origin; the Boms trace back before beer.) It is compact but it is mine.

There is a cot, a trunk, a sink, a cardboard closet, a TV and, thank God, a door without bars.

I relax watching Sonia Kay interview Homer.

"Do you anticipate a win in the Iowa Caucus?"

"*Caucus* or *crocus*, they seem to bloom at the same time give or take four years. It sounds close to *carcass* and mine is on the line."

"You haven't answered my question."

"You don't honestly expect answers from a candidate, Sonia. The nation might go into cardiac arrest."

"You won't claim victory?"

"If I do I sound insufferably arrogant even if I win. And if I lose you've made me a fool."

"Isn't that a bit harsh? A bit cynical?"

"Realistic. Pragmatic. Sonia, I am not harsh or cynical. I'm an average man with above average luck. I'm Norman Cradle trying to stay on course using the compass of my humanity."

"Now you sound like a candidate."

"And you sound cynical. Sure, I'd like to Crunch In, Spread, Thrust and Score in Iowa. Is that bad?"

"You once ran for Senate."

"Yes. I got one vote. Mine. My wife voted for the other guy. But that was a long time ago."

"Isn't that when you first proposed Added Value legislation?"

"Tell me, Sonia. If you were down and out would you rather feel like a derelict or a gold nugget?"

"But does Added Value replace the need for more jobs?"

"No. It replaces welfare with a sense of worth."

"Mr. Brogg, you've been talked about as the next Global Repositor. When, may it be in the far future, Dr. Hoffenstein passes on, the location of the Prime Mother Computer will be revealed to one living person. Isn't the position as Global Repositor more attractive to you than a mere Presidency?"

"You're talking about the penultimate Planetary Honor. I consider that far beyond my capabilities. Should I be called upon, of course, I would serve. Meanwhile, I want to be your President. There's work to be done. You know that as well as anyone."

There is a tap at my door. I turn off Homer.

"Open."

Amelia Bom stands in her negligee.

"May I?"

"A bit of a squeeze but, yes, please, come in."

"Globus said you enjoyed the show."

"It was stimulating."

Amelia sits on my cot.

"We try, Soup. I just dropped in to tell you how pleased we are to have you here. The clown you replaced was inadequate. He had to be sent along."

"If you're coded Freak where is *sent along?*"

"I don't ask. Oh, I brought you a flashlight. We have power problems."

"Thank you, Amelia."

"Even Alladin needs his lamp. You're our Alladin now. Our source of light."

"I hope I can . . ."

"Circus folk are flowers. We must be touched by light."

"Amelia . . ."

"Don't say it. I am not trying to bed you. Mr. Bom and I have achieved the bliss and fidelity that comes with the loss of appetite. At least we have memories. The others are empty albums. You may have noticed their performance was not Barnum and Bailey?"

"There did seem to be . . ."

"A power failure. Soup, I hope you will become involved with the family. As a dynamo."

"I'm not sure I . . ."

"All will come into focus. Now why don't you join the troupe before curfew? Doodoo is telling a bedtime story. You might enjoy it. We want you to be part of things."

After Amelia leaves I dress and go to the tent. The *family* squats around Doodoo who holds forth like a shaman.

"Which shall it be? *Rapunzel* or another *Tale of The Waif?*"

"The wet one," Arthur says.

"Very well. *Tale of The Waif*, Part Six, as related by Doodoo to an adoring assemblage of his would-be peers."

"Tell it," Charlemagne says.

"This very evening as I returned from my labors in the ring," Doodoo says, "The Waif awaited panting, languid, dolorous, dilated. Her navel glittered like a rare doubloon. No, I told her, I am fatigued. But she would hear none of that. She insisted on undressing me, she dwelt on each button, she pulled at my zippers as if they were ladders to the rainbow. Then she fed me honey."

"Where did it come from?" Arthur says.

"The fountain of youth," June says.

"Even as the honey trailed down my throat she was upon me. Her ruby mouth was everywhere. She slid me inside her velvet cavern and began to gyrate like so. The Waif turned slowly, her weight supported by her delicate hands on my thighs. She rose and fell like ripples on a lake."

"Then you came?" Pierre says.

"No," Doodoo says. "My control is absolute. I held back with every ounce of resolve. She was frantic. She sucked my toes. She bit my prunes. She lost herself. She collapsed like a hut in a tornado. She begged me, 'Doodoo, please, please, give back, give back my honey.' "

"An Indian giver," Lola says.

"Jesus," Mati says, "then what?"

"I told The Waif I would meditate. I left her weeping."

"Son of a bitch," Vanessa says. "I hate that story. No wonder she can't decide."

"She will join us," Doodoo says. "The Waif is strong-willed. I will convince her."

"Will she share?" Arthur says.

"If I so decree."

"She's not yours. She's community property," Mati says.

"Who found her?" Doodoo says. "Possession is the law."

"Nine-tenths of the law," Arthur says.

"Which leaves you one-tenth. Her pinky. I don't have to tell any more *Tales of The Waif*. It isn't required. I speak out of love and I get back rancor."

"We're not complaining," Charlemagne says. "Don't get mad on us."

"I feel hot now," Doodoo says. "I think I'll go back and this time The Waif shall be gratified. All the more because she expects zilch. Those legs are Summer zephyrs. Those lips have kissed shooting stars."

Doodoo slaps me on the head.

"Always leave them laughing, Soup."

"What was that about?" I say to Mati after Doodoo leaves.

"He found a refugee on the road. They came looking for her but we kept her hidden. She has no place to go. She'll join us sooner or later. Then Pierre will be happy."

"I don't know," Pierre says. "It's premature. She might know how to fuck, big deal, but can she learn to fly?"

"Last night's story about sucking was much better," Charlemagne says. "This one left me hanging."

"You like happy endings," June says.

"There are clowns and clowns."

Doodoo slurps from a prop bowl of Jello and begins to shimmy and shake.

"Good. Funný," I say.

"Thank you. One thing to remember is that our routines should be geared to the calendar. There are seasons for the clown, they are imposed upon us. No sense in fighting that."

Doodoo slugs himself and goes down for the count.

"The months of *ember, ober, ember, ember* are a gathering of clouds, preparation for surrender to *anuary* and *ebruary*'s frigid suspension. *Arch* and *pril* stir suspicions of birth. But Spring is also death's favorite hour, the beginning of the undertaker's fiscal year. Gay times come with *ay* and *une,* meringue months flavored with confusion, revision, reversion, decision, regression, and we put on fat like bears making ready for *ember, ober, ember, ember* and so it goes. We must play counterpoint, mock the clock, *une* in *ember, ober* in *ay.* Happy New Year."

Doodoo puts on a pointy party hat and shoots confetti from his ears.

"Of course, Soup, there are constants. Shit, for example, is for all seasons, the scatological denominator. *They* adore the whole idea of shit. Another old reliable is the reminder that civilized equals brutalized."

Doodoo opens an oversized book, *The Sea Around Us,* that drenches him with a splash of blue water. A pop-up clam snaps at his nose from the pages.

"So while the act must change according to solstice, the core never changes. As there is fire in Earth's belly there is a molten mass of anger in the belly of the clown. Alas, our flames are drowned in our own piss, steam shoots from our assholes. *They* love that the best."

Doodoo drops his dropseat pants.

"I have always believed that clowns affirm the triumph of the human spirit," I say. "They are weeds insisting on their place in the garden."

Doodoo says to his armpit, "Father forgive him. It is true that there is nobility in mere persistence even though the motive is nothing but habit. Some of my brothers and sisters stop with that message. That is where I begin. Clowns worth the name trade in fear."

Doodoo tongues a huge lollypop. A monster emerges from his fly and licks at him. He pirouettes.

"*Their* biggest pleasure is to watch the Reaper come to harvest relatives, friends and neighbors. We die for *Them* but the deeper reality is that we kill for *Them*. We emasculate the forces that persecute *Them* and in so doing emasculate ourselves. We must be our own assassins. Our pain frees their laughter."

Doodoo peels a prop banana. It refuses to be peeled. The banana twists in his hand and snaps back the petals of skin.

"Here is a rule of thumb for you. Too much is funny, too little is tragic. We deal in excess. We must be careful never to kindle terror except in the wisest children. It must seem that pity is our currency, a deception that allows us to live. Since we are *Their* mirrors we hold the trump card. We threaten *Them* with oblivion because we are *Them*."

"Maybe I'm naive but it's enough for me that clowns give laughter. Laughter is the best medicine."

"Are we doctors? Is our mission to heal or celebrate the disease called existence? I said there are clowns and clowns. Do you want to be warmly despised or genuinely worshipped? Doodoo will settle for nothing less than top billing in *Their* nightmares. I give of my sacred body for them to take home in doggybag brains. Doodoo is not Disney, Hallmark or Norman Cradle. Doodoo is a priest of the sewer from whence we came."

"Hopefully there is some terrain between Disney, Hallmark, Cradle and the sewer," I say.

"When you find it book passage. Meanwhile, give *Them* shit and roses in alternate doses. You will be both employed and cherished."

Doodoo produces a bouquet of long stems. He pretends pleasure, sniffs them and the roses wilt and die. Doodoo cries copious tears over their doomed beauty. His tears effect a miracle. The roses bloom again. He sniffs happy, they die. He cries, they stiffen. Finally he slams the pot upside down on his head. A single daisy sprouts from his scalp. He plucks it and tests his true love. She loves him, she loves him not. He vacillates between anguish and elation as he tosses the petals like snowflakes. When he comes to the final petal it enlarges and plucks at his hair. He plucks, it plucks. Soon he is bald. His head rolls off his neck as he bows. He chases it, catches it, bends the lips into a grin, screws it back into place.

"Fabulous," I say, applauding.

"It works in Winter. It falls flat in Spring."

There is more applause, not mine. Arthur stands near the gilt lion's cage.

"I got the money."

"Do I look like a pimp?" Doodoo says.

"Yeah."

"Give it here."

Arthur's gerbil legs bring him closer. Doodoo grabs a stack of bills from his hand.

"When? Tonight?"

"When you're told," Doodoo says. "Now depart. This is a master class."

When Arthur is gone Doodoo says, "They all want my Waif and they've never seen her. It's my stories. Marketing. Everything is marketing."

"I heard your last *Tale of The Waif*. It was repulsive. Instead of listening to you why don't they fuck each other?"

"Because they have fucked *each other*. *Each other* is the problem, not the solution. My Waif is from *out there*. Someday she will be *each other* but not just yet. The same holds true for you, Soup. A word to the wise. Your cherry is valuable."

"Amelia Bom suggested something similar."

"I could act as your agent."

"How does the girl feel about being sold?"

"Rented. Only to family, never to the crew. I don't know how she'll feel. I don't even know her name."

"Didn't you ask her?"

"I meant to. I must have. Who remembers? I deal in entrails, not details. Hard enough to find time for the news."

Like Doodoo's *anuary, ebruary,* the small hours of the morning are frozen time for me. I prowl under ice. Who will I meet in those caves?

I am a child in a railroad station. My parents have forgotten me. They drink coffee from plastic cups and eat swollen muffins. We are on the platform waiting. The ground quakes. I try to warn my mother and father that dragons are coming but they are too busy with their food. Creatures lumber past, crocodile bodied, multi-eyed, spilling sparks. Why don't my parents rescue me or prepare for battle? They wait to be swallowed like their muffins. Other morsels stare at me from the dragons' guts. I scream and get slapped for it.

A dragon stops. My father lifts me and I expect him to run but along with my mother we willingly enter one of its many mouths. I fight my father's arms but I am no match for them. I know that someday I will find strength and revenge.

The dragon moves along. I curl waiting to be digested, sluglike, passive. Corrosive juices pour around us. They flood our space and stifle breath. The dragon lets out a joyful shriek. I laugh at the noise. My mother strokes my hair while my father takes another bite of cake fattening himself even as he sizzles and fractures. I turn myself into a crystal. I may be shat or spat but not turned into tissue, muscle, dragon meat.

My eyes blink open. I look at the clock. It is one of those snowbound hours. I hear sounds from outside. I peek through my blind.

Light from the clogged fluorescent arteries of the CIRCUS MIN-IMUS!!! sign spatters against shapes standing spaced in darkness.

Once Trina and I stood on a Caribbean beach where bathers stood neck deep in purple surf. Sea foam splashed around their ears. Their heads bobbed like buoys cooled by the sea. Here the stingy light is the foam. I feel what I felt then, enormous sorrow, silky dread.

At four in the morning, every child in the world is a doll strapped to the hood of a tractor trailer.

I make out Orson, Romeo and Juliet. But the other shapes are the circus in silhouette. The sound I heard comes from June who is moaning. There is Arthur, doing somersaults, mimicking pain as he walks in a crouch. The others crowd around him. He holds out his arms. Pierre and Charlemagne lift him and carry him away. Soon the others vanish. The space is empty except for the dismal light. I keep watching. There will be more.

Sure enough, Doodoo comes jogging, slapping at mosquitoes and gnats. And there is The Waif. She wears a terry robe that hardly covers her sex. Her legs are astonishing, her thighs are airports for angels. Her face is in shadow but I know it.

Jill Hill.

I develop a routine with Mati. He charms me out of a straw basket after trading his flute for a tuba. I slither up responding to a series of staccato toots. I begin to shed my skin. My costume melts off and I dash around the ring covering my privates with my hands.

When the act is previewed for Doodoo's approval he says, "Not bad but problems. You assume the audience knows the phenomenon of skin shedding. Snakes don't have hands to cover their scrotums nor do they have scrotums. And they certainly have no legs. So you're not only making intellectual demands you're violating basic principles. I can go along with all that, it can be compensated for creatively speaking. However I must insist that your old skin chase you around trying to reestablish contact. That confirms the sense of loss and identifies the real victim which is the deserted epidermis."

"Agreed," I say. "But who is there to play my obsolete skin?"

"I don't do skin," Doodoo says. "So the Lord must provide."

The Lord provides. That night, after our performance, we hold our usual creative autopsy. The Waif, a.k.a. Jill Hill, interrupts the postmortem to announce her decision to join Circus Minimus.

It is a charged moment, especially for Pierre, since he has marked her for marriage.

Pierre makes no secret of his honorable intentions. While the others are congratulating Jill on her resolve, Pierre tells me, "I need her for my partner. And that demands total intimacy. Our flights must be more than a mating dance. The audience must know that their birds are mated for life. Acrobatics as foreplay gives a superficial thrill. But the acrobatics of a man and wife is enthralling. They wonder if we fought over breakfast, if he mouthed the name of an old lover in his sleep, if she remembered to shave her legs, if the toaster works, if the bills are paid. When Alice was alive I got anonymous letters asking about the most obscure black and blue marks on her arms and legs. Were they love's accidents or inflicted in anger? To care about creatures of air one must be reminded of gravity and there's nothing heavier than a married couple. So you see, Soup, I must marry her."

"Then we can expect a wedding?"

"Doodoo has agreed to a reasonable dowry."

"Pierre, does it bother you that The Waif has been had by practically an entire circus?"

"Why should it bother me? I don't relish the thought but I deal in futures. Besides, having had her the others won't be so fretful when we take our vows. And then there is the probable advantage that some wisdom was presumably passed along to the woman."

"Before you make a formal proposal, would it be possible to borrow her for a while? I need a shed skin for a routine I've developed and the only . . ."

"Her only area of virginity is in technical training. I want her to start circus life as an acrobat. I don't want her clowning. Shed skins don't become aerial stars. I'm sorry."

Amelia finds a bottle and we toast The Waif's conversion with wine. It is during the toast that Jill first sees me. She dumps her wine on Arthur who is busy kissing her kneecaps. There is no acknowledgement of any past acquaintance from either of us.

"No more The Waif stories," Pierre says, beginning his courtship.

"No more stories," Doodoo says sighing. "The Waif is no more. Her name, I am told, is Jill."

Vanessa puts on a tape and we dance, exchanging partners. My turn comes and Jill is in my arms.

"How?" I say.

"A series of circumstances and coincidences," Jill says.

"That brings me up to date."

"And you?"

"Through happenstance and circumlocution."

"The shortest distance between two points."

Pierre cuts in. I yield and dance with Lola who has the raunchy smell of her lion which isn't bad.

Circus Minimus will never entertain kings and queens. If we deal in the currency of delight it is the currency of a bankrupt empire. But we do what we do.

We exist. Performers, crew, tent, trucks, trailers, wires, bulbs. Animals, live and stuffed. Lola has managed to persuade Globus Bom to give her money to buy a menagerie of preserved birds and beasts she saw advertised in a magazine. A retired taxidermist ships a tiger, a gorilla, several owls and the bonus of a swordfish with a busted blade.

Lola says they set the lion off to advantage. It has been trying harder. It could be that he takes the newcomers for passive playmates or sees in them the possibility of immortality. Whatever, the lion roars more frequently and louder. He even paces without provocation.

What surprises me is that the audience accepts the stuffed animals without protest. There isn't that much difference in their level of animation but I would have expected at least some comment. Maybe our customers know that we are an endangered species, more museum than carnival, and show a hint of mercy. Lola has expanded her power base. She snaps her whip with fervor and authority, she gets back crisp applause.

The point being, we are there, take us or leave us. What confirms our reality even more than performance is our portability. Especially departure. The space we occupied is immediately reclaimed by the nothing we found. We leave no visible traces. If we have entered the dreamlife of our patrons, Doodoo's measure of success, there can be no confirmation. When we go we're gone so it must be that we have been.

Departure is better than arrival since each arrival is an implicit promise Circus Minimus can't possibly keep. We try.

We move like seeds in the wind. There is much stopping and starting since the machines frequently break down. None of us asks where we are headed. We know that when we get there we will confront the nothing we left. Then the vehicles are parked, the tent is built, cords plug into sockets and our sign ignites, stuttering, spattering, seducing like a senile lover. Our seeds sprout without fanfare. We must generate enthusiasm.

We visit the nearest town to hang our posters. We go in costume spreading our greeting through markets, stores, banks, schools, the post office. Orson parades behind Romeo, Juliet and the nameless generic lion, all decorated with spangles and billboards. We peddle what aura we have to apathetic adults. The kids are solace. They swarm, immediately ours. Eroded verve is more than enough for them. Their eyes remind us that we are wonderful.

On this trip Pierre has been assigned to tend the animals. Doodoo goes off to the local high school. Jill and I are teamed to work Main Street. She wears the silver leotard and slippers of a flier. Her betrothal to Pierre is assumed and she is training well for her new career.

As I hand out advertisements to our Grand Opening a small boy offers me half a hotdog which I pretend to gobble with an ear. I wipe mustard off my lobe with a pink handkerchief.

"Let me lick," Jill says. "Less laundry."

"Less laundry is the sole object of existence," I say.

"Are you enjoying this life?" she says.

"I am. Doodoo seems to think I'm coming along."

"Pierre tells me I have a talent for the bar."

"Do you have a talent for Pierre?"

"Is that relevant, Soup? Should you ask me?"

"No. But there's plenty I want to ask you."

A teenager bikes past Jill and grabs her ass. I take a swing at him but miss.

"We're here to sell, not kill," Jill says.

"Forgive me. I know you're not too protective of anything below your waist."

"We should work separately."

"Don't go. I'm sorry. It's just that I never cast you as a happy whore. Excuse me for being blunt. Let me find a euphemism. I never saw you as a vending machine."

"Have a nice day."

"Wait. I meant I never saw you as an entrepreneur."

"They need a safe harbor."

"And that's what you were?"

"A safe harbor and a conquest, yes. Now that I'm practically engaged I'm treated with respect and that's how I insist on being treated."

"So everything's settled?"

"It would seem so."

A little girl tugs at Jill's silver slipper. Jill lifts her and kisses her cheek. The child's mother wipes the wet cheek with a Kleenex.

"About Pierre. Do you love him?"

"One feels for a man who promises to catch you after a double flip twenty feet off the ground."

"That sounds like the basis for a lasting marriage."

"You sound like a prick."

"I do. Because I want to know why you spread your legs for midgets and the suicidal."

"You want me to justify?"

"I want facts."

"Morris was frightened of his journey. He was cold, I was a radiator."

"A harbor and an appliance. But then I know about that. It was you in the tub, wasn't it?"

"Was it?"

"It was beautiful."

I tack a poster on a blank fence and the fence is made noble. We exist.

"Doodoo?"

"Impotent. He never touched me, never tried, never cared. His longing is to be reborn as a jackal. He saves his hangnails and whiskers in a little jar to throw into rivers. He sends his scrapings to the land of the jackals."

"I would think he'd want to be a nightbird or a brain tumor."

"As for Arthur, he was like an electric thimble. He's the only one who made me climax."

"I don't need to know that." '

"Mati brought his python but I wouldn't indulge him. Doodoo gave him half his money back."

"How come you drew the line at the python?"

"I might have said yes to the cobra. Charlemagne was a squirt and an apology. He liked singing songs with me."

"A singalong? Was he charged extra?"

"The only one charged extra was Lola."

"Lola?"

"She couldn't come up with the cash so she shared with Vanessa."

"Not Orson?"

"You asked for facts. June came to me but only to bring me a jar of vaseline. She actually paid to do that. She said I might need it."

We enter a beauty parlor. I waltz with the hairdresser while Jill hands out twofers. Then I fluff-dry my wig.

"Didn't you feel compromised?" I say outside. "Your body is the only thing you own."

"It came down to *why not?*"

"That's a backdoor to passion."

"There was no passion."

"Except for the abbreviated gentleman."

"I identified with Arthur. It was like fucking my finger."

"Pardon me while I barf."

"Why didn't you come to me?"

"I considered it."

"Still Trina?"

"What do you know about Trina? Why do you bring her name into this?"

"Dr. Hamish told me Trina was the worst fuck he ever had. He got his sofa reupholstered after Trina."

"That's completely false. He never met Trina."

"She came up to tell you her wedding plans. Zoe Rapish

discouraged that."

"Trina was so close? On the premises? She could have stayed for Cradle Day?"

We hang more posters.

At least we left traces.

My act bombs. Maybe it is the lack of a second skin. Doodoo rescues me. He comes dressed as a boxer with orange gloves the size of bowling balls. He pummels me, then himself with hands that go out of control. When he falls from the attack of his own fists he looks up at me and says, "Basics."

My failure is inconsequential. Circus Minimus is brilliant. Even Globus Bom is awed by the flow of energy. He quickens the show's pace pushing us harder. We give and give. When I go to change my costume for the finale Amelia is weeping.

We earn a standing ovation. In farewell, we fold more than bow, splendidly exhausted. The audience won't let us quit. Their affection stirs the animals. Vanessa's horses begin humping, Doodoo plays the priest, produces a ring topped with a jewel and marries them. Romeo and Juliet provide sufficient encore and we are allowed to withdraw.

Our dressing room is quiet. The Boms go off holding hands. The others drift in solo directions. I go back to the ring and stand alone except for lion and his stuffed peers. A paw is waved at me. I wave a paw back.

The crew goes about their business setting equipment, cleaning the stands. For them it has been one more show.

Back in my trailer I shower, then collapse on my cot. My mind opens to a hundred new ideas. I should take notes but there is no hurry. The lake of inspiration is deluged. There are pratfalls enough for a century.

I need air. I find the flash Amelia gave me and go quietly on bare feet. It is well beyond curfew but the grace of our performance dissolves dumb restrictions.

There is a breeze. I drink it slowly. The horses stomp and snort. Orson makes a sound that is oddly soothing. I shield my light and walk toward the gate. If I am caught it would look like an attempt at escape but escape is the last thing on my mind. I am dizzy with a sense of belonging. I wish Jill was still on the market. I would stand in line counting out the price of a ticket.

"You're in violation. Bad."

I jump but it is only June.

"Nothing sinister. I had to get out."

"So did I. Tell me, did you think it was Orson accusing you?"

"No, June. I don't confuse you with Orson."

"I am so gross."

"Nonsense. Ample, interesting, but never gross. You have the look of a cathedral."

"A cathedral?"

"With Gothic windows."

"Some men are turned off by my bulk. Even by the tattoos. I never understood it but to each his own."

"We should get back inside. They do patrol."

"I was born a Freak. I didn't get Redesignated. And I achieved Full Code Potential. That's a reason for pride."

"Good attitude. You deserve a large sense of worth. And you were marvelous tonight."

"Let's walk past the trees where the animals can't see us. You know something, Soup? I'm a sweet person. I deserve nice things to happen."

"I never heard anybody come right out and say that. It's absolutely true."

"You are a nice thing."

She takes my arm. I think of Mustaf climbing Everest laden with explosives. He was carried up by his convictions. I am invited to climb despite a lack of them.

When we reach a knoll June drops her robe.

"I had to pay for rights to these pictures. That's why my movie stars are golden oldies. It's what I could afford. Most people don't know them but it's better since I was colorized."

"You were originally done in black-and-white?"

"Cheap is cheap. You get what you pay for. When the National Endowment saw I was sincere they arranged for the tinting."

"Was it painful?"

"Unbearable. But worth it. Don't you think so?"

"I do. You make a statement about cinematic history."

Her arms reach out. I respond. We make love if that is the description. Afterward, I doze between Carole Lombard and Ingrid Bergman. My right hand strokes Garbo, my left The Three Stooges.

"Which one was I?" June says. "Who fit your fantasy?"

"You were you."

"Be honest or your nose will grow."

"I saw only you, June. It was plenty."

"Thank you, Soup."

"And you."

Near dawn June goes back first. She crawls on all fours dodging shafts of dawn's early light. I begin to follow in kind when I hear a metallic clang from the direction of the tent. I bite grass. Two crewmen have removed a section high on the main pole. They climb inside and there is more banging. The pole is a shell. When they resurface one says, "Maybe a mole or raccoon got inside."

"You're certain?"

"I'm sure there's no mechanical problem."

I watch them replace the outer panel and bolt it down. I resume my crawl. When I reach my trailer the door opens. Amelia Bom looks down at me. She throws me a kiss.

"There are days when I think the only good thing about people is that they're biodegradable," Globus Bom says. "My ballad on those dog days is a song called *Tomorrow, Tomorrow*, the ultimate dirge. It tells us that *tomorrow there will be sun*. Yuch."

Globus paces with his hands locked behind his back. We sit in a crescent watching him. I knit the peculiar garment I began at Millhaus and I wonder how life is going back there.

"There is no escaping tomorrow's damned sun except through death and we can't even be sure of that. The sun will come up and Circus Minimus will go on. Another new day, the forced optimism of my toothbrush, a vitamin pill to feed viscera that will turn on me. I sniff morning breath brewed in the oven of dawn's total honesty. As it seeps through the chimney of my mouth I ask myself, 'Globus, why go on? Why bother to read your mail?' That is my cock crow and I suspect I am not alone. This morning, however, was different. Because of last night, because of our performance. Electrons flew from us like bees. We fertilized our audience. Applaud for yourselves, dear friends."

We applaud for ourselves. This is high praise.

"As your leader, keeper of an anachronism, I often forget to remember what we represent. The mission of our tiny company of players is to pollinate, to release our bees in unstoppable swarms. When we touch the zenith of our ability, then we know joy. The fine art is to keep it up."

"First to get it up," Arthur says.

"Now it is time to say special thanks to our neophytes, Jill and Soup. Your contribution to Circus Minimus has not gone unnoticed."

We are forced to stand and bow.

"So much for hosannas. It has come to my attention that some of you have violated curfew. That is intolerable. After midnight nobody leaves the trailers, nobody is exempt."

"No nocturnal omissions," Arthur says.

June whispers to me, "He makes that speech once a month. It's for the crew."

"As masters of your profession you are entitled to restless hours. Alas, as Certified Freaks you are forbidden even the innocent rebellion. Your tantrums must remain internalized at least after twelve. Our broader society is one of order and Circus Minimus must reflect that order as a pearl reflects a candle."

"He speaks like a fluent French tickler," Doodoo says.

"We are an island but also a model. We are subsidized for a purpose, to contribute to the greater good. So much for my message. Tonight, a new challenge, a fresh audience. I want your best."

Globus moves his hands from his back to his heart.

"Case dismissed," Amelia says.

As we leave, June tweaks my knitting and hands me a bouquet of cornflowers. It comes to me that I may be knitting a cover for her. I could be knitting forever.

Jill comes to sniff at my flowers.

"Was your wife lardy?"

"Trina is as thin as spaghetti."

"The pasta bride. Like my sister."

That she mentions her sister is extraordinary. I wish Dr. Hamish could have heard.

"Why do you ask me if Trina was fat?"

"You know why. Don't deny it. June told me how she yielded to your abject pleading. She told me how you got her to lie down in green pastures."

"It was no more than an exchange of gifts."

"Go put your flowers in water. I never got flowers."

"There was no cash register between my legs."

"I think of it as my slot machine," Jill says. "I always look for the jackpot in their eyes. Don't you?"

"Don't we all?"

"For the record, the money was Doodoo's idea. He knew that if I decided to stay with Circus Minimus it would have to be with Pierre. That's the only job open and these are hard times. Pierre can understand my dispensing favors for profit. He could never have come to terms with the idea that I fucked for fuck's sake."

"The safe harbor?"

"Even Doodoo couldn't comprehend that. Men have their limitations. Besides, he needed the money for props."

"Come to me tonight," I say. I can't believe I said it.

Jill slaps at my flowers and goes off to a lesson with her betrothed. She turns and says, "Bye the bye, Soup, I hope you'll come to our wedding. It's set for Saturday after the late show. I can't ask you to give me away, that's Doodoo's druthers, but I want you for a witness."

"Let me be the first to wish you happiness," I say. "Since the other firsts are long gone."

"Maybe we'll have another wedding very soon. When you finish your trousseau?"

I drop my yarn. It costs me three stitches.

I dream of Morris Feuerbloom. He sits on a fleck in the sky eating cake, showering crumbs that become new worlds.

"So what's the prognosis, Soup?"

"I should ask you. You're in heaven."

"Maybe yes, maybe no. They're very evasive. They put me on this *fercockta* asteroid surrounded by volcanoes that go off for no reason sometimes in the middle of the night. Maybe they're trying to make me feel at home. I don't sense much intelligence behind any of it but I hope I'm wrong."

"What about reincarnation?"

"Optional. I didn't sign up for it."

There is a huge eruption behind Morris. A whole landscape collapses and reforms.

"You think I'm impressed?" Morris yells. "Feuerbloom, *Fireflower!* did better for a second marriage, a reformed Bar Mitzvah."

"Try to get more involved," I say. "Do something productive."

"In a few centuries. So tell me, what happened with the princess and the pea?"

"If you mean Jill Hill she is about to marry an acrobat."

"What kind of profession is an acrobat? And you? Are you seeing anybody?"

"No, not really."

"Ah. So you still like the lady?"

"It's better this way."

"For who?"

"All concerned."

"Them again? Soup, you're still a patsy. I got to run. I'm expected but I forgot where."

"Wait. Before you go, what have you learned from your vantage? Give me words to live by."

"You wouldn't like it."

"Please."

"Don't spread it around. *Life is simple.*"

"I should have been prepared for some wiseass remark from you. Next you'll tell me living and dying is enough of a problem."

"The phrase is *enough problems.* I was going to break it to you gently. I remember now. The Four Horsemen are having a handicap. The race is fixed but everybody bets. I like Pestilence but the smart money is on Famine. Death and Plague hate a wet track. You want me to put a few bucks down for you?"

"I don't care about a race. What is truth? Could there be an honest Norman Cradle plate?"

"Truth is *the whole story*. Truth is *what is not a lie*. You don't want me to tell you everything. Find out for yourself how it comes out. Build your own Spectacular."

Morris opens his *Daily Racing Form*. A bugle blows the horses onto the course. I wake to a fanfare. It is Orson trumpeting at the dregs of a yellow moon. Not his style. Something else is wrong. The CIRCUS MINIMUS!!! sign is turned off. There is no eternal light. I hear Orson yanking at his leg chain. I go to find out the cause of these abnormalities.

When I reach the elephant I say, "Quiet, grey eminence. Is something bothering you? A muskrat? What?"

Orson slaps me down with his trunk. I see a line of lights moving from the tent. It is the crew led by their foreman. They fan out with perfect precision.

"Shut up," I whisper to Orson. "Don't give me away. It's in your own interest. Whatever happens to me they won't want a pachyderm to remember."

The foreman goes to a rusty van and lifts the hood. Instead of a motor I see a complicated control panel blinking red, green, blue, yellow. Another crewmember reels cable from the back of the van toward the tent. A satellite dish grows like a mushroom from behind our sign. The foreman snaps his fingers. A computer screen produces a map of the globe. The line of cable connects with another running out from under the admissions booth. The top of the tent pole groans, then swings out on a hinge. I see the nose cone of a DS-587 missile nicknamed *The Final Suppository*. They have all been destroyed by treaty. This is not possible.

"Three . . . two . . . one . . . abort," the foreman chants.

The pole heals itself, the mushroom retracts, the cables are detached, the hood slams down on the van.

"Two minutes plus," the foreman says. "We got to shave ten seconds off. I log two minutes plus we all end up taking tolls on the Jersey Turnpike."

Orson is bored. He decides to lie down. Since I am hidden under his gut that move has consequences. I give him a jab in his bowling balls. He makes a noise that could land him a big part in the National Geographic special.

"Turn off your fucking horn," the foreman yells. "Listen, guys, seriously, we got to shape up before the brass comes to inspect."

"What about the clown," one of them says.

"The clown again? You don't know if he saw diddley."

"We know he was plowing the hippo while we checked the pole."

I blush under the elephant. Forget the whole idea of privacy. Whatever is done is known.

"So he was too busy with his own pole," the foreman says. "If he saw he don't know what he saw."

"Why take chances?"

"If he dies somebody asks how."

"He was trying to escape."

"With a Freak Code? Where would he escape to? Washington? Forget the clown and concentrate on moving your ass."

"I heard he was A+."

"You *heard*. If he's that smart he's smart enough to keep his mouth glued. You know your trouble? You're giving yourself ulcers about a guy who would sneak out to plow Fatima."

"Her name is June. Don't hit on Fatima. I happen to be a Roman Catholic."

"Bless me, Father, for I have sinned. Hey, maybe he's over there trying to bugger the elephant. You better check. Unless you want to go get a beer."

"We ought to put in for Guidance."

"Guidance? I run this show. I make the decisions. You want to feel better? Confess. Drink some blood. Eat a wafer. Let it rest."

I must talk to someone. Jill's room is in the trailer across from mine. I assume she is sleeping alone since Pierre, as an orthodox Acrobat, insists on pre-marital abstinence.

At Jill's door I tap three times before I remember that all doors are unlocked. We are on the *honor system* which presumes that no lock is the heaviest bolt of all. At the same time we are reminded that we have lost the right to seal ourselves away from the hand of authority. Bars keep even murderers safe, and we are fallen lower. Open doors underline alienation.

Jill's cubicle duplicates my own except for the scented air. She is cuddled under her blanket heavy into a dream. She makes wheezy sounds like a shortwave band interrupted by suggestive moans. I wish I could crawl in through her ear and take a seat in the planetarium of her brain. Talk about locked doors.

I sit beside her on the cot and nudge her shoulder. She squirms resisting consciousness.

"Jill, it's me, Soup. Wake up now."

She moans again.

"Octopus?"

"I am not your octopus. Open your eyes."

"What did you do with my octopus?"

"Get with it. You'll have Pierre in here with a hatchet."

"Soup?"

"You must believe what I'm saying."

"You're not saying anything."

"What I'm about to tell you."

"I believe. Can I go back to sleep now?"

"No. Listen. I made a discovery tonight."

"Many have made discoveries on many nights and they wait until daylight to share them. Discoveries are better after coffee. You're breaking curfew. Get out of here."

"Try this with your coffee. Circus Minimus is nuclear, a roving missile base. The center pole of our tent is a launch pad for a *Final Suppository*. I saw it."

"That's ridiculous."

"Before the Universal Disarmament Treaty, before Peace Through Commerce, before the Balm Not Bomb Treaty everybody moved missiles around on trucks, trains and submarines. Moving targets are less vulnerable. That's what we're doing. Circus Minimus is armed and dangerous."

"That probably explains the grant from the Arts Council."

"Is that all you can say, Jill? If we're doing it the Russians, Brits, French, Italians, Japanese, Chinese, Israelis, Iranians, Iraquis, Libyans . . ."

"Eskimos, Pigmies, Albanians . . . everybody's doing it. So what?"

"It makes a farce of the détentes, of the Codes, of the whole basis for international law."

"Soup, you probably didn't see anything that can't be easily explained. Talk to Globus."

"He'd report me. They're already suspicious of . . ."

"You sell tickets. He won't report you."

"And tell him he's running a circus of damnation? He must know, he made his trade-off."

"We found a home here. They'd ship me back to Hamish and Christ only knows where you would end up. Go back to bed."

"Are you saying I spent a night under an elephant for no reason?"

"We all spend nights under elephants, that's no big deal for a woman. In fact, I wouldn't mind spending what's left of this night under . . ."

"Now you're coming on to me? You want to make love, is that it? With Lord knows how many megatons of . . ."

"Megatons are provocative. I always felt . . ."

"I see your game. You're willing to *shtup* in exchange for my silence?"

"*Shtup?*"

"A Morris Feuerbloom word. I thought you might know it."

"He called it conjugation. He was a gentleman."

"What arrogance. You really believe that if I come inside you I would abandon all principles?"

"Actually, yes. It's worth a try. Before you destroy all of us and maybe the world."

"I'm the bomb? I'm the enemy?"

"The trigger of the moment. Get under the blanket. I'm freezing. I have no tattoos. I hope that's not a turnoff. But there's a pencil on the table. You could draw . . ."

"Uncalled for. Jill, this is not the time . . ."

She slides off her shortie nightgown and guides my head to her breast. Her legs kick off the cover.

"Don't. I'm a glacier. What if I melt and flood?"

"We build an ark," Jill says.

Charlemagne lifts a barbell dangling Arthur on one side and June on the other. Vanessa does flips on Romeo and Juliet. Lola revs her lion by pretending to feed meat to the stuffed tiger. Orson runs under the net holding a pillow while Jill tries some elementary moves with Pierre. Mati's cobra does aerobics with the python. Doodoo and I are dressed as whales. We have concocted the bodies out of aluminum and mylar connected to huge clown faces. Tanks and tubes supply our spout holes. We sing to one another in fishy voices. *They* love it. We bump and squirt in tandem. Arthur catches some of our water in a high hat and tips Charlemagne's scale. Applause, applause, applause as June is lifted by the midget's weight.

I swim past Trina, Homer, Lauren, Amanda, Amos, Lance.

Who?

I trip and nearly cause an accident. Vanessa manages to jump me with her horses.

"Timing," Doodoo says, swimming past.

Amelia has come to the ring costumed as a fairy. She commands Orson to dance. He chooses June for a partner and she manages a credible *sauté de chat*. I send out a shower of bubbles by mistake. They were supposed to be saved for the climax. Under the bubbles I edge over to the barrier where my family sits.

"Homer, it's me. Jim."

"I know who it is. But the others don't know and won't know. Brogg Entertainment owns this money burner."

Doodoo is pissed. I am lousing up the act. He sings to me. I sing back and let out a shower. He swims over.

"What the fuck is wrong with you?"

"Cramps. Around the fins."

"Heal thyself."

Doodoo spurts and migrates toward the ballet dancers. Homer leans closer on an elbow.

"Nice bit," Homer whispers.

"Nice bit is right. I know what you've got going here, you virulent fraud. *Circus Apocalypse.*"

"You should know. It was your concept."

"Mine?"

Arthur is chasing Doodoo holding a fishing line baited with a can of sardines. My cue.

"Before your so-called honeymoon," Homer says, "we talked about ways to keep the edge. Just-in-case worst case scenarios. You came up with missile carnies, not me. But I listened. And I can't forget that evening since you were about to deflower my daughter."

"Deflower?"

"In this family brides are virgin. I came here to tell you that you'll be running Circus Minimus within a month. The Boms will be retired. And don't thank me. Consider it a parting gift. The first thing you do is raise ticket prices."

"That conversation dealt with supposes, it was theoretical. I never seriously thought any human being would descend so deep into feces that . . ."

Arthur comes after me with his hook. I know I am scheduled to grab a sardine and romance it but I leave that for Doodoo.

"And I don't want to run the circus. Keep your gift. I'm quiescent at least for the moment. But I go to sleep thinking what Hoffenstein will do to you if the truth ever comes out."

"I can't let that happen."

"I'm glad you said that Homer. I wondered if Hoffenstein knew."

I glance over at Amos. There is an asshole look to my son. He is already Homer's man. He watches our show with a cipher face like his stepfather. Amanda sees me peek and I swear I see tears in her gorgeous eyes. I can't help myself. I swim over and kiss her cheek. My lips leave a red imprint. Then I reach out and grab Lance with my fins, singing gibberish in his ear. I pull at him. Trina urges him to be a good sport. Homer shuts up. The audience applauds in unison. Lance has no choice. He follows me into the ring.

"Exactly what are you . . .?" Doodoo says but I ignore him.

When we reach Orson I dare Lance through pantomime to lie down. I know he will be forced by his macho. I am correct. When Lance is spread on the ground I sign to Orson and the splendid creature rises on his hind legs. He waddles, trying to keep vertical, his front legs flailing like the arms of a drowning swimmer. Homer yells something and the crew produces an impressive array of fire-power. I slap my palms. Orson slams to all fours missing Lance's sweaty face by inches. The crowd is ebullient. Orson suspects the applause is for him. He tries to top himself by unloading a hundred gallons of hot piss.

They yell for encores. Doodoo and I send up bursts of rainbow bubbles.

"Good," Doodoo says.

"Basics," I say.

"He offered me the circus."

"Did you take it?" Jill says.

We are decompressing from *conjugation*, this time in my room. A sweet sorrow drifts over me. Jill will be wed in a few hours, I have just learned that I love her. Lucky Pierre. After her wedding she will be as faithful as Brunhilde. I hide my feelings. I can offer my darling nothing to compare with the security of the trapeze.

"I declined that honor."

"I don't know. The atomic impresario, the clown with a finger on the button. It has operatic possibilities."

She feeds me a smoked oyster, then switches on the television set.

"This little dear is the latest marvel in the expanding vista of genetic engineering," an anchorwoman says. A lab-created animal sits on her shoulder nibbling an earring. "He's called a Muff, isn't that cute, and he has the best qualities of a teddybear with the size and convenience of a pussycat."

"I want one," Jill says.

"You already have one," I say and kiss it.

"And the best news is, they don't shit," the anchorwoman says. "And they love children."

"Two strikes against the Muff," I say. "Who would buy a pet that loves children and don't shit? It'll never sell."

"Don't be bitter."

"There should be enough adorable Muffs to go around in time for the holidays but, oops, they'll cost up to five thousand dollars. But maybe that's not too bad for a life companion. For a few extra bucks they can be programmed with your own DNA to die when you do. And that's my Future Perfect Report for this evening."

The camera moves close on the Muff, then its image is replaced by a man.

"On the national scene, candidate Homer Brogg unveiled a proposal to erect a companion for Lady Liberty, this one slated for the Port of Los Angeles. She'll be modeled after this girl, a fledgling actress from the Midwest who they tell us was found harvesting corn by a Brogg talent scout."

"That's my sister," Jill says.

The girl is more than Bartley Hamish said she was. I sit up and lean closer to the tube.

"Hi," the harvester says, "I'm Shirlene. I never thought of myself as a beacon but life is surprises."

"She was always the talker," Jill says.

"How does it feel to be chosen for such a prize part?" the anchorman says.

"Nice. And they won't have to read anything like they do with the other statue. My message is digital. They'll be able to hear it in every language from a mile at sea:

> Give me your upwardly mobile
> Engineers, scientists, MBA's
> The unashamed graspers after more
> Send these clean-eyed unburdened
> Focused youth to me
> I spread my legs before a sparkling shore.

"Lovely," the anchorman says. "And not a cent of the cost will be paid by taxes. Homer Brogg is picking up the tab for this beauty."

"That's your sister?"

"You want to get inside the set, go ahead."

"No, no. But she is attractive. Was there rivalry?"

Jill bites. She hurts. I stifle a yap.

"But not all the news is good," the anchorman says. "Here's a report from our Consumer Concerns editor, Fabian Jones."

"Just when you thought it was safe to go back to the pantry, we've got another product recall. This time it's Lot 731731731 VSFPS of Vigor Brand Salt Free Pea Soup. The batch has been found to contain a virulent strain of Brisik Bacilli capable of causing advanced Thraposis and that's a horrible death. All Vigor products will be pulled from market shelves and returned to the manufacturer for disposal. So if you've got a can at home and you expect to be around for tomorrow's broadcast, bring it back to where you purchased it for a full refund. Any Reclamation Center can issue a credit. The happy side is that only a few cans remain unaccounted for and those will soon head for detox. It's Lot 731731731 VSFPS, be on the lookout, and that's it from Fabian Jones."

"Thraposis is nothing to scoff at," the anchorman says, voice-over. "It's a bellybuster so all of you be careful. Head for the kitchen and look for this UPC. And now . . ."

I hit the button.

"Why did you turn it off? I wanted weather."

"What is the female obsession with weather?"

"Is something wrong?"

"Didn't you see? Didn't you hear? I've been recalled."

"You are hyper, Soup. They were talking about . . . Ah. There is cause for concern."

"They're going to kill me. I'll be dragged to a Reclamation Center and mashed like a mutant Cradle. The man is brilliant. He deserves to be President."

"Your Code is twice removed. It could be coincidence. You can't blame Homer Brogg for every ill."

"If there's a single can of Lot 731731731 VSFPS the Health Enforcement Bureau will find it. They'll milk this for the publicity. I'm dead, Jill. In the biblical sense."

"Say *ohm ohm*. Calm yourself. It's fairly evident that you're a person. I think all this is a storm in a teacup. You're just not used to a sense of well-being. You can't deal with tranquility in any form."

"Turn me in before they come for me. Better that you should get a reward or a coupon. I told you what they did to Omar and Ishmael and they had no classified information."

"They exceeded Code Limitation. Who told them to write concertos?"

"Jill, listen to me. Yell for the crew. Tell them you were watching the news and . . ."

"Explain that I'm going to my wedding as soon as we finish fucking?"

"Then take a shower and put on your gown. I'll get back to my trailer. They're probably waiting for me already. So long, Jill. Have a good life."

"I'm not getting married. I convinced Pierre to marry June."

"I have enough to deal with."

"He was resistive at first but I told him I saw his deep feeling for June and I could never pledge myself to an ambivalent acrobat. I showed him that with me it would only be another copy of Alice and never so Amazing. But if he could teach June to fly it would be like inventing the Zeppelin. June could give him a shot at the Sarasota Hall of Fame."

"Pierre bought that?"

"And June. I told her Pierre loved her for years but he was too shy to ask her to switch careers. Her problem is, heights make her dizzy."

"She balked?"

"Not after I pointed out that at his age the only triple Pierre is qualified for is a bypass. She could fatten him up, a few hundred calories a day, not too obvious. He would welcome a loving wife, a family, a desk job."

"Which leaves you where?"

"Here. I love you, Soup. I don't like it and I don't recommend it but that's how it is."

"You still have time to make things right. Tell Pierre you can't bear to let him go. Tell him anything. Save yourself. I'm not the best prospect for an enduring relationship. Name your first baby after me and that would be more than I deserve. James P. Wander is over and done with."

"You were June's only qualm. She was worried about letting you down too hard. She wants you to give her away."

We are all present and accounted for including the beasts, live and stuffed. The affair is *al fresco* since Pierre wants stars for his witnesses. We gather outside the tent dressed in our finest. The night's performance has surpassed expectation so there is open good will.

Globus and Amelia Bom have set up a table for drinks and refreshments. A three-piece orchestra has been booked in town along with a local minister. After some confusion as to who is the bride the ceremony begins.

Lola has arranged a circle of candles to border the wedding, a romantic representation of the Circus Minimus ring. Pierre appears in a resplendent cape that mirrors the candle gold in sequins.

June holds onto my arm. She wears a dress of white linen, Jill's former outfit supplemented by a last minute addition of canvas.

Vanessa hands her a garland of daisies. She glides toward Pierre with candle flames in her eyes. I find myself weeping remembering not my own wedding but the transient peace I felt in her opulent theatre. Pierre will still be lucky.

During the meeting of the conjugal pair, I keep one eye on the crew. They are deployed just beyond the perimeter of bliss and I know they are waiting for me.

"The metaphor of acrobatics is ideal," the minister says, "for what is a marriage but a mating of birds, a consecrated acceptance of the innocence of clouds? June and Pierre embark on a marvelous and mysterious migration to some distant nest optimistic that their destination shall be forever enriching. Yes, these are not babes in the wood. They know there is the inevitable season of molting. And they know there is the imminent danger of fracturing a wing or splitting a beak. Still, they chirp and their song is inspiration."

I nod to Arthur. He slips between the candles and heads for the tent. I see his small shadow climb under the admissions booth looking for the cable umbilical connected to the imp in the pole.

"Blessed couple, through mutual love and admiration you soar higher than any eagle, you cross a horizon beyond the eye of the condor. May your speckled eggs be sanctified. Pierre, do you take June to be your wedded wife?"

"I do."

Vanessa has managed to use her horses for cover and get to the van. She releases the second cable and slides it toward Arthur who drags its mate an inch at a time.

"And you, June, do you take Pierre for your husband to love and cherish until death do you part?"

"More than that," June says.

"Then by the powers vested in me through the Connubial Council of this state I now pronounce you man and wife. You may kiss the bride."

The orchestra strikes up, we cheer, June and Pierre lock in a massive embrace.

"Now in honor of the newlyweds," Globus proclaims in the megaphone voice, "a gratuitous Display of Affection Featuring the Extended Family of Both Bride and Groom . . ."

Charlemagne frees Orson and mounts his back. Mati spins his python like a whirligig. Lola opens the lion's cage and urges that startled guest to try the grass. Vanessa has Romeo and Juliet prancing like Lippezanners. Pierre jumps up on a rope ladder and climbs the tent pole. June links the cables with Arthur's help. It is Doodoo who raises the hood of the van and plays the launch panel as astutely as Sigmund Snider.

The crew foreman yells. "They're trying to blow up the cock-sucking world."

"This is what I call a diversion," Jill says.

Vanessa brings the horses.

"Abort, abort," the foreman screams.

"There are alternatives," the minister says.

June tosses her daisies to Jill. We ride. Behind us a crewman starts a motorcycle. The sound of ignition ignites the lion. He mounts the bike, suddenly remembering the urge to reproduce. Romeo and Juliet trot in a circle, old habits die hard. I see Charlemagne steer Orson toward a trailer. He pushes it over as if it was meringue. A crewman grabs for my leg. Mati makes a loop with his python and wraps it around my oppressor's neck. The clutching hand is suddenly preoccupied.

Jill manages to get Juliet to walk a straight line. Romeo follows.

"Bring me their gizzards," the foreman is yelling.

"There may not be much point to this," I say, jumping a fence. "If that *Final Suppository* launches this is anticlimactic."

"It won't work. Nothing works," Jill says. She has June's daisies under an arm. "Try to look casual. We're heading into town."

We slow the horses and canter past a diner. A police car is parked outside. Two cops wave from the counter. We wave back. We hear the motorcycle sirens at the same instant.

"Stay here," I say. "Tell them you were my hostage. Save

yourself."

"Get off the road."

We head for darkness, galloping across a field. I look back. The cycle eyes are gaining. Larger eyes belong to the police car. The horses sense defeat. They quit running.

"End of the line?" Jill says.

"End of the line."

We dismount, thank Romeo and Juliet, and slap their behinds. They head back where they came from. But they buy us some time. The enemy follows them.

"It won't be long," I say. "I want to say a proper goodbye. Hold me."

"Could they find us intertwined?"

"I don't think so. It would look terrible on the front page."

"We'll make the front page?"

"At least in the supermarkets."

"Good. Those are the only papers anybody reads."

"Jill, it could have been . . ."

"It was. Take some daisies."

"They don't want you. Stagger around in the murk saying irrational things. Better live at Hamish than dead in blue fog."

"I think I'll stay. I like blue fog."

Blue fog? Two strips of cerulean light show us a path. Are we already ghosts? We walk toward a small shack where a girl stands buttoning her blouse. Not ten feet from the girl is a chopper. A man joins the girl. He carries a box shaped like a house.

"I thought I delivered everything there was to deliver," he says.

"Do they bite?"

"What don't? You take care of yourself, Charlotte."

"Call me when you get there. They got phones in zoos."

"It's not a zoo. It's an institute."

"Were they really on TV?"

"They used one. The other was backup. It looked great. People called in to place orders at five-thou a clip."

The man heads for the helicopter. When he's nearly on top of us Jill says, "He's carrying Muffs. And you were wrong. They'll sell like hotcakes."

"What's all the racket?" the man says. The sound of cycles and sirens is closer.

"Who knows?" the girl says. "You call from the zoo. Drive careful. It's a stinking night."

"I always do."

"Nothing personal," I say to the man. Then I deck him.

"You made him drop his Muffs," Jill says.

"Get in."

She does but not before taking the box. I start the rotors.

"You fly these things?"

"Just your ordinary Renaissance kind of guy. I used to ferry Homer to his fishing lodge. The fish was an advertising lady he called Vulva."

We hover. I see flashes from the ground.

"Get down."

"Now?"

"They're shooting at us."

"Wouldn't it be a good idea to leave this place?"

"Eventually. I'm trying to figure out the controls. They've changed considerably from what I remember."

The Muffs gurgle from their house. Jill comforts them.

"They could be another parakeet, Soup."

"Don't waste your time on passing fads."

I get the chopper moving, pointed south. North is always more aggressive.

"Where are we heading?"

"That depends on where we started from. Did you happen to notice the last town we played? Was it in Louisiana or Oregon?"

"Beats me. I gave up on orientation years ago."

A bullet cracks the plexi shield.

"Look back at the world," Jill says.

"Did you say something?"

"Not to you."

It takes an hour for them to find us for all their hotshit radar. Then I hear a scramble of voices in the earphone. We're a glitch on a screen and that is how the world ends.

"They've got us located."

"What happens now?"

"I suppose it depends on who owns the copter and who wrote the insurance. They might ask us to land."

"Are you familiar with that procedure?"

"Vaguely."

"And if they don't ask us to land?"

"It will be fast. You won't feel a thing."

"I accept small favors. Where are we?"

"Over water. I think the Gulf."

"Better water. I know they say it's not much different but it seems a lot softer to me."

Five minutes later an Airguard VII fighter bomber crosses the moon. I run for a cloud.

"Major firepower," I say. "Mayday."

"Why Mayday? That sounds like shiny faced children dancing around a painted phallus."

"From the French *m'aidez*."

"You spoil everything, Soup."

"I'm heading back."

"Don't."

"You can grow old. Raise Muffs."

"Not my strong suit."

"One of us should live to tell the story."

"Why?"

We break into open sky, fifty miles of visibility. The fighter stays with us. It comes alongside. I point my finger down. The pilot points his thumb up.

I hear his transmission:

"*Awaiting instructions.*"

"*ID: Slimes. Degree: Malevolent. Consensus: Terminate.*"

"*Confirm Terminate.*"

"*Confirmed.*"

The jet loops and positions on our tail. The pilot takes his own sweet time. He lines us up nice and easy.

"They don't want us anymore," I say.

"Can Muffs swim?" Jill says.

Muffs. They are prototypes worth millions. Some genetic engineer is sweating this out.

"Do you read?" I say to the mike.

"As little as possible," the pilot says.

"Tell your leader that we've got a pair of Muffs aboard. If you don't know what they are I suggest you check."

"The things that don't crap? Thanks a lot but I already was Muff briefed. What you got are obsolete publicity models. The new ones are ten, twenty times better. They can say Ma-ma, Da-da, like that. So long, Slimeballs."

A chain of unexpected events transpires. The pilot launches a Quale 604 air-to-air missile. A migrating duck is made curious by the sleek silver needle. The Quale communicates technological pleasure beyond comprehension. It enters the duck's behind and explodes. The duck must make some blissful sound since a blizzard of mallards, enough for a lifetime, joins in the action. The Airguard VII engines gobble up the pilgrims. The blast is impressive. Our rotors bat jet parts and duck parts and pilot leftovers.

"Maybe Morris has connections. Maybe we'll get to meet Norman Cradle," Jill says.

"Not just yet. But they'll send another aircraft."

"Then put this thing on automatic and come to me."

"Certain conditions inhibit tumescence."

"I'll bet there are plenty of men who don't feel that way." The copter coughs. I look at the fuel gauge. Empty.

"You should have stopped for gas," Jill says.

"Look back at the world," I say. "Hang on."

"To what?"

"Me."

The helicopter stops, rolls, drops. There is quick pain, not much, not bad and we are dead.

Angels come through moonlight.

They're smaller than I imagined and with tiny heads. It is not for me to judge cosmic aesthetics. The angels sing to me in a strange language. I sing along to reassure them.

"What were my last words?" Jill says.

I look up to her. She dangles above me testing her new celestial talent.

One of the angels lands next to my ear. It chortles. Maybe not angels?

I feel for my parts. They seem to be intact. My face is mud. I test arms and legs. There is a chance I am alive. Morris Feuerbloom said rebirth was optional. I didn't agree to anything. I try to sit. My movement spooks the seraphim. They turn to gulls and go elsewhere.

"Jill? Come down here."

"I don't think I know how."

"You're usually so self-sufficient."

"Who am I talking to?"

I manage to stand, then stretch to unbuckle Jill. She drops into the mush.

"Is God oatmeal? Can I move?"

"If you can, do. We've got to cover what's left of the chopper."

We climb out of the bog onto a knoll covered with immense green leaves.

"A bed of lettuce," Jill says. "I will rest here."

"Not yet."

We tear up clumps of the leaves and cover the copter's remains. If nothing can be seen from above they might assume we crashed into the sea. It's what they would like to believe, we have that advantage.

"The Muffs?"

Jill finds their shattered house. At least there are no Muff bodies to depress her.

"Up there," I say.

We climb higher onto spongy mounds. Our universe rocks underneath us, we could be on the rump of a whale. There is water all around.

"It's not an island. There are no hotels," Jill says.

"An antique shop. Look there."

We face a massive mountain of ancient TV sets, car bodies, furniture, boxes loaded with sinks, toilets, toys, books, rusty weapons, tires, clothes, unmarked bags of waste.

"The 20th Century. We're in a time warp."

"I know where we are," I say. "I recognize it from its pictures. The *Kotchka*. The garbage barge."

"It's never like the travel folders," Jill says.

We wander through discards exploring the kingdom of refuse. Among cliffs of broken plastic and hulks of machinery we come on a valley of marvels. A forest of trees. A clearing where flowers and vegetables grow in profusion. A stream trickles to a ridge of telephones, microwave ovens, toasters and hair driers, then becomes a waterfall. I take Jill's hand.

"This is a protected landmark. They won't even allow anthropologists to visit."

"That's positive. I was never compatible with anthropologists."

"This could be the end of our courtship," I say.

"It had to happen sometime. We can build here. There must be a school in the neighborhood."

A yipe. Jill runs toward the sound.

"A Muff."

"Come back here. Wait for daylight . . ."

I track after her through a wall of pipes, bricks, window frames, broken doors. The doors are rotted, warped, split, covered with graffiti, turned to driftwood. But one door is a door.

I cross a field of cans and bottles, face that door and knock. It is a ridiculous reflex. I know there's nobody home. I pull at the knob. The door is locked, wouldn't you know it. I yank again. This time the lock holds but the hinges crack.

I squeeze through to a steel staircase. There is the sound of heavy breathing. Do we have a dragon? A gigantic rat fattened by the National Preservation Trust?

I descend to a room filled floor to ceiling with old newspapers. I pick up a batch and read about war, disease, crumbling cities, tribal fury. Ads offer me the products available free upstairs. There are pages of classifieds for homes, jobs, people who need people listing their attributes and desires in endless columns of eloquent deceit. I read and shudder. How can I read? Where does the light come from?

The breathing is louder.

The far wall of the room leaks a neon glow. I go closer and flatten my ear against metal. No question, whatever sucks damp air lives inside. The prudent course is retreat. But I see a way in. The barrier is corroded by salt and time. The light comes through a rip in aluminum skin. I make an opening wide enough for passage.

I drop into a circle of human bones. Whoever owned them died together, hand in hand. Each skull clamps teeth around a broken phial. One dried fist holds a portrait of Dr. Hoffenstein.

"Let us never forget those heroes and heroines who built Prime Mother Computer, then willingly gave their lives to protect her secret."

It is what we said every day in school after the Planetary Pledge and what Hoffenstein echoed at his banquet.

There is another door. I batter it with the femur of a hero. It gives way without much fuss. I wonder if Brogg Engineering had that contract.

There She is and She is beautiful. Humming, heaving, flashing, buzzing, the Goddess of Order, the Fountain of All Codes. She is splendidly made, unlike the flimsy walls and doors left to secure Her. Her marvelous body is a sonnet of circuitry, optics, chips, transistors. I kneel before Her.

Her power comes from a single artery plugged to a fission reactor. There is even a backup system to take strength from the waves. And there is a box sealed by thick glass that holds a switch marked ON and OFF.

ON and OFF, yes and no is what it comes down to.

I rub through a circle of dust and stare at the switch. I tap the glass with the bone in my hand. I tap faster trying to keep pace with a digital display that records the world's births and deaths, adding up the raindrops, orchestrating the generations.

I find Jill with the muffs. She feeds them stringy carrots on a crag of computers.

"Did you find anything?"

"Nothing much," I say. "Only this."

"What is it?"

"A box that once held Mallomars. The original package. Worth at least twenty bucks to a collector."

"I found a puzzlement."

"That's a manual can opener. My grandmother used one of those."

"I'm glad to be stranded with an encyclopedia of obsolete information."

I come up behind her and drape my knitting over her shoulders.

"You remembered to bring that?"

"It was unfinished."

The garbage barge rocks like a crib. A fleck of moon anchors the West, a new sun grows in the East. We have our compass.

"The nights are getting shorter," Jill says.

I cup her breasts and kiss the back of her neck.

"What are you thinking about, Soup?"

"Order. Symmetry."

"Overrated," Jill says.

"So we drift."

"So we drift."

Though time is a terrorist, I hope there is time.

With thanks to Chet and Sue Gottfried, Linda
Stewart, Jean Randall, Deb Novak, John Witek,
Jack and Joy Singer, Mildred Budofsky, Zelda Dana,
Charles Platt, Evelyn Rosenfeld, Bonnie and Charles
Ré, the good people of Shelter Island and Sag
Harbor, New York, and the friends
who encouraged this work